Mary Elizabeth Ames

Praise for
H'ILGRAITH

"In this second work, Mary Elizabeth Ames has written a novel that is compelling, intellectually engaging and timely in content and scientific challenges. While reading the novel, one can see the characters in a science fiction movie confronting brutality while struggling with life-and-death ethical issues and familial loyalties. What is compelling about the work is that the story gently urges the reader to consider the science of genetics in very small doses at the end of the chapters, thus educating while entertaining the reader."

—Catharine A Kopac PhD, DMin, GNP-BC
Adjunct Associate Professor, George Washington University, Consultant and Ethicist

"This is an adventure tale that both entertains and offers short, clear lessons about genetics. The author has created a cast of memorable characters who can transform into a variety of non-human animals to problem-solve as they explore their changing world. Beautiful illustrations supplement the story of interactions among humans, dragons, foxes, owls, badgers, and other critters. Themes addressed include the importance of loyalty to family and friends and a willingness to adapt to changing circumstances in an interconnected world."

—S. A. Jarecki, PhD
Former RN Faculty

"The adventures are fun to read, intriguing, and fast paced. . . . Genetics come alive in this exciting adventure story."

—Tacey Battley

"With her new science fiction book, *H'Ilgraith*, Mary Elizabeth Ames continues to break the mold when it comes to conveying complex science within compelling fiction. Ames fleshes out a character she introduced in *Homo transformans: The Origin and Nature of the Species,* which offers a different point of view into her futuristic saga about genetic disruption and experimentation. This is a morality tale about interdependence. Monsters don't make themselves and heroes don't operate in a vacuum. Capabilities that aid survival in one setting are handicaps in another. The same plants that heal can also kill. Whether read purely for the story or together with Ames' well-placed scientific annotations and references, *H'Ilgraith* offers new insights into relating effectively with one another in an increasingly diverse world.

—Cheryl Romanek
Former Managing Editor for Creative Services at J.D. Edwards

"*H'Ilgraith*—to this reader—brings to mind two other series of novels, Harry Potter (by J. K. Rowling) and the Earth's Children book series by Jean M. Auel). It is a fascinating blend of fantasy, science fiction, romance, intellectual engagement, exercise of will power, brutal fighting, ethical sensibilities, and familial loyalties. There is heavy use of science research: footnoted, referenced, glossary, and bibliography. Life-and-death ethical issues abound between competing groups and species, especially highlighting the deliberate interdependence of all life forms. The profound flow of action alternating with science will keep the reader engaged and inspired."

—Rev. Dr. Jerrold L. Foltz, Pastor
United Church of Christ

"I finished the book and just loved it! . . . I can't wait for another book. . . . These books would be a great movie!"
—Michelle Mayer, MSN, ANP

H'Ilgraith

by Mary Elizabeth Ames

© Copyright 2020 Mary Elizabeth Ames

ISBN 978-1-64663-000-4

This is a work of fiction. The characters are both actual and fictitious. With the exception of verified historical events and persons, all incidents, descriptions, dialogue and opinions expressed are the products of the author's imagination and are not to be construed as real.

REVIEW COPY: This is an advanced printing subject to corrections and revisions.

Published by

◄ köehlerbooks™

3705 Shore Drive
Virginia Beach, VA 23455
800–435–4811
www.koehlerbooks.com

H'ILGRAITH

Mary Elizabeth Ames

VIRGINIA BEACH
CAPE CHARLES

TABLE OF CONTENTS

PREFACE

In the story *Homo transformans: The Origin and Nature of the Species,* a gamma-ray burst from a supernova left a devastated civilization in its wake. It also altered the deoxyribonucleic acid (DNA) of some *Homo sapiens (H. sapiens),* giving them the ability to metamorphose. Several generations later, scientists found these people could transform reliably into another species of animal and could pass that trait on to their children. The scientists, therefore, declared them a new species of human, *Homo transformans (H. transformans).*

The ability of *H. transformans* to become another animal, especially an apex predator, transformed human society. Society shifted from a post-apocalyptic state to embattled camps trying to find the genes that supported transformation. The Cassius Foundation, a morally corrupt faction, and its key competitor, the Biogenics Corporation, were the primary rivals in an arms race. The Cassius Foundation was intent on dominating all of society. It did not hesitate to use genetic engineering to exploit the capabilities of *H. transformans* and create violent hybrids to terrorize anyone opposing it. Biogenics vied with Cassius primarily to avoid being overrun by it. It relied heavily on breeding programs based on pedigrees to counter the Foundation's aggression.

Neither the Cassius Foundation nor the Biogenics Corporation hesitated to capture and use *H. transformans* in their research. Females were especially at risk. As *H. transformans,* both males and females would have a transforming X chromosome (X^T). Females, however, could have two of them ($2X^T$) and possess far greater capability.

1

Both *H. transformans* and *H. sapiens* were caught in the middle. The two species could not be distinguished when *H. transformans* was in human form. Thus, both species of human were at risk of being captured by bounty hunters who would sell them to the highest bidder. For purposes of self-preservation, *H. transformans* began to cluster together and form a society of their own. The House of H'Aleth was the first of three communities to succor both *H. transformans* and *H. sapiens* from this persecution. The House of Erwina and the House of Gregor followed later. H'Ilgraith's story augments the history of *H. transformans* as detailed in *Homo transformans: The Origin and Nature of the Species*.

This (imaginary) metamorphosis in humans is predicated on the science of genetics. Gamma radiation can penetrate down to the cellular level and alter the genes that govern structure and function. The author weaves gene functions and the complexity of genetic engineering into the story of H'Ilgraith. *Homo transformans: The Origin and Nature of the Species* further describes how genes work and provides additional explanations.

Please be advised that any reference to metamorphosis in humans, fire-breathing dragons, and genetically engineered human and animal hybrids is pure fantasy. The author has attempted to make the content regarding the genetics of *H. sapiens* scientifically accurate as of the time this book was written. The reader is encouraged to consult the Genetics Home Reference website (*https://ghr.nlm.nih.gov*) for additional information about genetics.

For those who are skeptical that Earth could be struck and devastated by a gamma-ray burst, be advised that it would not be the first time, and it may not be the last (Hambaryan & Neuhäuser, 2013; Melott *et al.*, 2004; Melott & Thomas, 2011; Thomas & Goracke, 2016). Wolf-Rayet (WR) stars are massive and prone to collapse. When they do so, they explode into a supernova and release long, stellar gamma-ray bursts that can stream through the galaxy (Crowther, 2008; Tuthill *et al.*, 2008). Wolf-Rayet 104 is a blue star located about 8,000 light-years from Earth, well within striking distance of the star should it become a supernova.

Part I
A Restless Spirit

CHAPTER 1
A PLEASANT OUTING

A Lesson in Arithmetic

Agroup of adults and children, all *H. transformans* from the House of H'Aleth, were on a field trip into H'Aleth's grassland. It was a beautiful day—sunny and warm, with a few scattered fair-weather clouds. The outing was billed as a picnic with games for youngsters who were four to five years of age. Yet there was a hidden agenda behind this excursion.

The purpose of the outing was to allow the children to practice what they had learned. They had been taught their numbers, how to count, how to add and subtract, and how to identify different grains by their leaves, seeds, and stalks. So the adults had prepared balls made from wheat, oat, or rye plants. As the children watched, the adults threw the balls into the grass in different directions. The children were given wicker baskets and tasked to find the balls and bring them back. Afterward, the materials of each ball would be repurposed for other uses.

"Find as many of the balls as you can," one adult directed. "When you bring them back, tell us how many you found, the type of grain used to make each ball, and which parts of the plant were used. Correct answers will be rewarded." There was no penalty for misidentification; however, those who were correct would receive a sweet treat—usually berries, grapes, or similar delights.

When away from a village, children needed to be protected. Hence, four scouts, all skilled archers, were on duty to provide surveillance and security and to help find any wayward children. They set a wide perimeter around the area to form a defense and keep children from wandering too far afield. Although each scout could transform, their arrows could fly much faster than an animal could run. H'Assandra, Mistress of the House of H'Aleth, had changed into a golden eagle to keep watch overhead. As a female with two transforming chromosomes ($2X^T$), she could transform across mammalian and avian classes. As a raptor, she could see small prey more than two miles away. If a predator appeared, she would strafe it at a diving speed of 150 miles per hour to mark its location. Her formidable talons could inflict serious injury.

H'Assandra also conscripted her cousin H'Ilgraith [hil-*grāy*-ĭth] to patrol the area from the ground. H'Ilgraith was less than enthusiastic. Although she loved to be away from the confines of the village, babysitting was nowhere on her list of favorite pastimes. As a general rule, she was ill-disposed toward tending children.

"We should not be asking our elders to perform these tasks," H'Assandra insisted. "As a lynx, you can move undetected through the grass, and you can disable and even kill an attacker."

Resigned to her fate, H'Ilgraith accepted the assignment.

The rest of the group consisted of parents, children twelve years of age or older, and other adult relatives to watch and supervise the youngsters. The outing also provided the older children with experience taking care of young children on field trips and preparing a picnic. Even so, they would enjoy it as well.

A Sudden Turn

The youngsters went about their task of finding balls. There were twenty of them for five children. H'Assandra, perched in a nearby tree, flew aloft when the adults threw out the balls. As if they were prey, she could see exactly where each had landed. The children also watched where they went and had already located several of them. Some children could be seen studying the balls. Others were scurrying around in the grass, looking for more.

Suddenly, three high-pitched peals came from above. Everyone looked up at the warning call and saw the golden eagle bank sharply toward a copse of trees in the distance. The eagle dived and then swooped upward, indicating the location of the danger. A scout, standing perpendicular to the eagle's flight path, spotted something racing through the grass. It was headed straight toward the picnic area. He quickly drew and aimed an arrow, tracking the movement so his fellow archers could see both the direction and speed of whatever entity was moving toward them. The eagle continued to dive at it, marking its progress and harassing it, trying to distract it or at least slow it down.

Abruptly, the adults called the children to return immediately. "Come back now," one shouted. "Run," yelled another. "Drop your balls and leave your baskets behind," called a third. Although they did not yet know the nature of the danger and hated to scare the children, the eagle's behavior indicated the threat was deadly.

Most of the children were already running back. One of the archers left his position to pick up a child who had fallen in the grass. When he delivered the child to another adult, he realized that he was directly in the path of whatever was coming. He quickly turned to mount his defense there.

Every adult in the group and most children over eleven years old could transform into an alternate species. They had the ability to do so, but not the time, and the others were too young. So the parents and other adults each picked up a youngster and began running away, beckoning the older children to follow.

The four archers and remaining adults braced for the onslaught. All adults carried a weapon of some kind, most often a knife, bow and quiver of arrows, or hatchet. Depending upon the assailant, these weapons might be quite sufficient or woefully inadequate.

Suddenly, a deformed creature reared up in the grass and leaped into the air (illustration 1). Its effort to snatch the eagle as she dived at him proved futile. H'Assandra was very experienced and had anticipated such an attempt. She halted her dive as the creature reared up, averting its strike—just barely. In trying to strike the eagle, the creature revealed itself to the defenders.

Illustration 1: A Sudden Onset

When upright, the creature appeared to be a huge, human-animal hybrid (hybrid humanoid) with badly distorted features—likely a genetically modified *H. transformans* forced into a transformation he could not reverse. When it dropped back down on all four extremities, it no longer looked humanoid. It lunged forward with its forelegs and vaulted with its back legs. This accounted for its rapid, if ungainly, rate of movement. Despite the eagle's best efforts to distract the creature, it wasted no more time on her. It focused on the group of people directly in its sight, thundering toward the defenders like a drunken battering ram. As it drew closer, they could hear a mix of snarls, growls, and snorts, and they could see it drooling profusely. The creature appeared deranged, for it seemed to throw all caution to the wind.

Given its behavior and unprovoked attack, the defenders knew that there would be no reasoning with this humanoid. They also knew their weapons would be inadequate against it unless an archer's arrow struck the beast in an eye and reached its brain. With the creature's uneven gait, even a skilled archer might miss so small a target. Even if an arrow did reach its mark, there was no guarantee the blow would stop the humanoid immediately, though such a strike would prove lethal in the end.

Nevertheless, the archers made ready their bows with arrows. "When the creature is in range, aim for its head, neck, and shoulders," said the lead bowman. "Try to cripple its forward motion. Then we might stand a chance."

Unbeknownst to the creature, another member of the group had crept up at an angle to intercept its path. Crouched in the grass, a lynx waited. Just as the creature's head came into view, H'Ilgraith launched her attack. The lynx was no match for the creature's power. Yet, she easily outmatched it in agility. She had noted it had neither horns nor tusks to gore an opponent, nor did she see any canines. It was not without armaments. The four-inch claws on its massive forepaws were impressive, although straight and blunted. The lynx's claws were just as long, curved, and sharp. Given her plan of attack, her claws and canines would hinder the beast and give her people time to escape, even if she did not.

The nearest archer suddenly shouted, "Hold your fire." He had seen the lynx leap onto the head and shoulders of the beast as it passed in front of her. As her claws and canines sank into eyes and nostrils, the creature voiced a high-pitched scream and swiped at the cat with a front paw. In doing so, it lost its balance and fell on the opposite side, taking the lynx with it. The cat barely had enough time to jump aside to prevent being pinned under the creature.

The humanoid struggled to regain its footing. Its heavy torso impeded its ability to get up quickly. At this moment, the scouts saw their chance. They raced ahead to get as close as possible to the beast. As they drew near, the creature finally stood upright to strike down its attackers. In doing so, it became an easy target for the skilled archers, who ended its life.

A Near Miss

The eagle called out a series of piping sounds, signaling the all-clear. Those fleeing the picnic areas stopped and turned to view the scene from a distance. With a sense of relief, the adults reassured the children that all was well. With youngsters present, they did not go back to the picnic site.

"We will still have a picnic when we return to the estate," said one of the adults. "You will still need to report how many balls you found and which kinds of material were used to make them." The lessons would continue and provide the children with a sense that things were back to normal.

After some of the adults took time to transform, a red deer, horse, and black bear gave the small children a ride—much to their delight. Two powerful gray mountain wolves escorted the group on its return to the village. Should another attack occur, there was both speed and muscle to address it.

Meanwhile, the adults who had stayed behind to defend the troupe were trying to figure out how they were going to transport the creature's carcass back to the village's estate for examination. "It must weigh at least five hundred pounds," opined one scout.

"Can anyone here transform into an elephant?" asked another jokingly. Alas, no; however, one scout could change into a brown bear, and another could become a moose. While those two stepped aside to transform, the others packed up the picnic. A large square cloth intended to seat everyone was quite sufficient to shroud the beast. Two makeshift rope harnesses were placed around the shoulders of the moose and bear to haul the carcass back to the estate.

In the meantime, the lynx had disappeared into the grass, heading toward the copse of trees. H'Assandra had no difficulty spotting her and followed in the air. Once H'Ilgraith reached the trees, she found a secluded place to settle. She gingerly turned one way and then another until she could find a position that would let her lie down. The beast's large head and paw had battered her, and she had hit the ground hard when she jumped away. Although she was not seriously hurt, all she wanted to do was rest until the ache in her ribs subsided.

H'Assandra landed nearby. She had picked up both of their robes in her talons when she followed H'Ilgraith. She used her beak to cover the lynx with one of them. Eventually, H'Ilgraith drifted off into unconsciousness as H'Assandra ascended onto a tree branch to keep watch.

When H'Ilgraith awoke, she had resumed human form. She donned her robe for the return trip to the estate. H'Assandra had already done so.

Although it was after dusk, the deepening shade posed no impediment to travel. Both women had excellent nocturnal vision. H'Assandra and H'Ilgraith could transform into multiple mammalian and avian species. Even in human form, the genes of their alternate species enhanced many of their physical characteristics, including their senses.

Supplemental Notes and Citations
Genes and Chromosomes

Genes are the basic building blocks of structure and function in an organism and the means of passing characteristics to an offspring (heredity) (Brooker, 2009e). They consist of deoxyribonucleic acid (DNA) and are grouped in sequences across multiple strands of DNA. Each DNA strand is wound up in a tight package called a chromosome.

In humans, chromosomes come in twenty-three pairs of matching (or almost matching) strands of DNA for a total complement of forty-six chromosomes. The father's sperm and the mother's ovum each have only

23 chromosomes, one half of the full complement. When the two merge, the fertilized egg will have a total of forty-six chromosomes, with each parent providing one strand of each pair.

Body Size

In mammals, including humans, the range in body size (set point) is usually limited by genes (Andrade *et al.*, 2017; Kemper *et al.*, 2012). A multitude of genes with their signaling pathways regulates the range of growth by affecting growth rate and duration (Andrade *et al.*, 2017; Gokhale & Shingleton, 2015). Even given genetic limitations, body size may be highly variable in the same individual. For most people, the range of growth depends on both internal (e.g., hormonal) and external (e.g., environmental) factors (Singh *et al.*, 2017). Body size can be modified genetically. The size of a mouse increased significantly when it was given the gene for human growth hormone (Brooker, 2009a).

Nocturnal Vision

The tapetum lucidum is a layer of cells that lies beneath light-sensitive cells in the eyes of species that live under low-light conditions (Alina *et al.*, 2008; Ollivier *et al.*, 2004; Schwab *et al.*, 2002). It reflects light through the eye to heighten visual acuity. It is an adaptation to a dim-light environment and is found primarily in nocturnal species. *Homo sapiens* and most other primates do not have a tapetum lucidum.

CHAPTER 2
H'ILGRAITH

A ll those who lived in H'Aleth and the surrounding territories were living in a dangerous time. The Biogenics Corporation and the Cassius Foundation were competing for dominance. Both vied for resources. Each tried to breed or engineer powerful *H. transformans* to sustain and expand its position.

Many years before, after a close encounter with bounty hunters, Ruth and Edvar H'Aleth had fled with their extended family and friends to a remote and uninhabited territory. As *H. transformans,* they established a community—the House of H'Aleth—to shelter and succor other *H. transformans* and any *H. sapiens* persecuted for supporting them. As more and more people joined them, their territory expanded and became known as H'Aleth.

Born into the House of H'Aleth, H'Ilgraith was a granddaughter of Ruth, the first mistress of her House (pedigree 1). Thus, H'Ilgraith was a third-generation descendant of Ruth via the maternal line. All female descendants of Ruth were designated sisters and schooled to serve as mistress of the House of H'Aleth, should that duty fall to them. All male offspring who were direct descendants of Ruth received the same education and training to serve as master of the House should that fate befall them.

H'Ilgraith was no exception. Her cohort included her sister H'Umara and her brother Edrian [ĕd-rē-ăn]; her first cousins H'Elvinia, H'Assandra, and Edward; and herself for a total of six. Ruth and her husband, Edvar, were still living at the time and served as role models for their grandchildren.

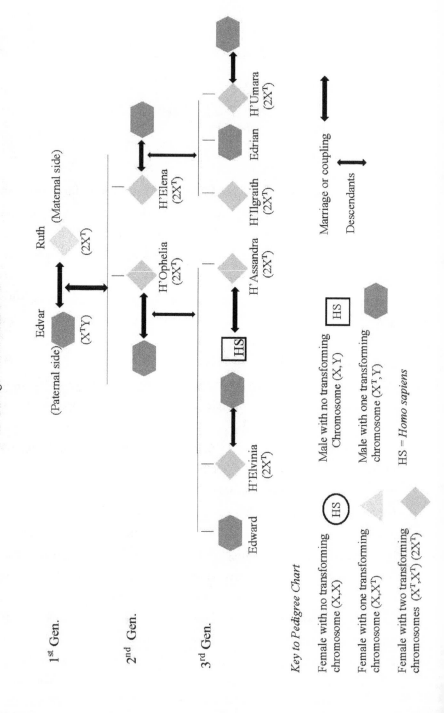

Ped. 1. Descendants of the House of H'Aleth
First through Third Generations

1st Gen.

2nd Gen.

3rd Gen.

(Paternal side)   (Maternal side)

Edvar   Ruth

Edvar
(XᵀY)

Ruth
(2Xᵀ)

H'Ophelia
(2Xᵀ)

H'Elena
(2Xᵀ)

H'Elvinia
(2Xᵀ)

Edward

H'Assandra
(2Xᵀ)

HS

H'Ilgraith
(2Xᵀ)

Edrian
(2Xᵀ)

H'Umara
(2Xᵀ)

Marriage or coupling

Descendants

Key to Pedigree Chart

Female with no transforming
chromosome (X,X)

Female with one transforming
chromosome (X,Xᵀ)

Female with two transforming
chromosomes (Xᵀ,Xᵀ) (2Xᵀ)

HS

Male with no transforming
Chromosome (X,Y)

Male with one transforming
chromosome (Xᵀ,Y)

HS = *Homo sapiens*

HS

Coming of Age

When H'Ilgraith was a youngster, she was content to learn as much as possible about the world around her. Initially, that world encompassed the grounds of her home, a large estate adjacent to H'Aleth's largest village. There were many diverse environs for her to explore. She could wander about at will as long as she remained alert to her surroundings (appendix A).

In school, H'Ilgraith was a bright learner. Consequently, she quickly tired of sitting in a classroom and became restless. On field trips, her world expanded to nearby villages, forests, and grasslands—with adult supervision. This she found annoying. She was often obliged to stay with a group of other students, which limited her freedom to roam and investigate places she found intriguing. So from time to time, she would slip away—much to the annoyance of her teachers and proctors.

When H'Ilgraith turned eleven years old, she came of age. She had developed the ability to transform. She focused on learning which species' genes she possessed (genotype), the capabilities they offered her (phenotype), and the opportunities they presented to her. She also paid careful attention to the risks associated with transformation.

H'Ilgraith first mastered transforming into a gray fox. This transformation was easier due to the genetic similarity (homology) between human and canine species. She could put the fox's abilities to use immediately. It could blend in almost anywhere, squeeze through narrow spaces, and could see, smell, and hear far better than any human. Although it was not very powerful, it was the perfect escape artist.

A Fateful Encounter

One afternoon, H'Ilgraith and five other children took a field trip. As all of them were eleven to twelve years of age, a scout and two adults accompanied them. The children had transformed into their alternate species to experience their surroundings from the animal's perspective. H'Ilgraith became the gray fox. She was already quite proficient at doing so and knew the fox's capabilities.

The exercise of viewing the terrain, sniffing the air, and prowling through vegetation soon bored H'Ilgraith. So she slipped away from her companions and guardians to investigate a small cluster of cottonwoods not too far away. She wondered what she might find there.

H'Ilgraith trotted through the grass toward the trees. Unbeknownst to her, a golden eagle, aloft about a mile away, spotted her. As a young fox, H'Ilgraith weighed about eight pounds—too heavy for an eagle to carry off, yet not too big for a meal on the ground.

The scout spotted the eagle soaring overhead and pointed it out to the children. Given the presence of an apex predator in the area, the adults instructed the children to resume human form. As humans, they would no longer be a prey species. The adults kept a sharp eye on the eagle until the children were human again.

Suddenly, the eagle went into a steep dive. "The eagle has seen a prey animal and is diving to acquire it," explained the scout. Everyone watched as the eagle banked and dove toward the trees, landing at their border. They watched as the bird made repeated attempts to snag its prey. Finally, they lost sight of it among the trees.

The scout asked the children, "What do you know about eagles?"

"Their wingspan is six to seven feet," answered one.

"They can fly over 10,000 feet high," offered another.

"They can reach flight speeds of nearly 150 miles per hour," said a third.

One by one, five children recited a fact he or she knew about eagles. The sixth did not.

H'Ilgraith was missing.

The scout and another adult immediately raced toward the trees. They had a sickening feeling that the eagle was after a fox.

It was. H'Ilgraith was desperately dodging the eagle's attacks. The fox was slender, nimble, and quick. The eagle was also quick and had a sharp hooked beak and powerful talons. Both were engaged in a deadly contest of thrust, dodge, and parry. Suddenly the fox slipped on wet leaves and fell into a shallow bog. The terrified fox struggled to get up as the eagle made its final assault. Its meal was at hand when the bird abruptly aborted its attack and became airborne. It had heard shouts and the trample of footsteps. Humans were nearing.

When the two adults found H'Ilgraith, she was wet, muddy, and scared to death. That did not win her any sympathy. The scout hauled her out of the bog by the scruff of her neck, then toted her back thusly to the rest of the group. One of the adults wrapped her in a robe and took her to the nearest village, where she was cleaned up. Still a fox, she was picked up again and taken back to the estate, where she was deposited in front of her mother.

"Your child will not be allowed to go on another field trip until she has learned to follow direction," the depositor announced, leaving H'Ilgraith to face her mother.

"Sit," H'Elena commanded. She had been told of the incident.

The young fox obeyed.

H'Elena studied her child for a moment. "You must learn restraint," she admonished. "Even now, you have duties and responsibilities to this House and all the people it encompasses. You cannot just run off whenever you feel like it. The loss of two adults, even for a few minutes, exposed your companions to greater risk." H'Elena paused for a moment and then declared, "You will resume human form. Until you learn to be responsible, you will not be allowed to transform again or leave the estate."

A contrite and remorseful H'Ilgraith complied. Her brush with death had taught her a valuable lesson, one her companions had learned as well.

Supplemental Notes and Citations
Genotype and Phenotype

Genotype refers to an individual's overall genetic composition, whether or not it appears (is expressed) as an observable characteristic (phenotype) (Jorde, 2010). Genes provide the basic instructions for developing the body's structure and function. (See coding and noncoding genes below.)

Phenotype refers to an individual's observable manifestations as determined by his or her genotype and the interaction between the genes and the environment (e.g., nutrition) (Jorde, 2010).

Coding and Noncoding Genes

Coding genes provide the instructions for building the physical composition and form of a component of the body (e.g., a protein) and for using these components to build a structure (e.g., an organ, an arm).

Noncoding genes influence the function of other genes, including the coding genes by regulating their activity (their expression) without necessarily altering the gene itself (Kanherkar, 2014). Thus, noncoding genes can affect how—or even if—coding genes are expressed. Regulatory genes comprise the vast majority of genes in the genome.

Genetic Homology

Genes that can be traced back to a common ancestral gene are homologous (Brooker, 2009c). Most of these genes and their gene sequences code for beneficial characteristics, including survival. Hence, they are conserved and reused by many species. Even though evolution may have modified them, homologous genes still share the same ancestry. For example, Hox genes, which regulate development from embryo to adult, are found in all animals regardless of class (Brooker, 2009c, Lappin *et al.*, 2006). The Pax6 gene, which is integral to the development of the eye, is shared by a variety of species across several classes, including insects (fruit fly), amphibians (frogs), and mammals (mice, humans) (Brooker, 2009c).

Humans also share some genetic homology with other classes of animals, including birds (Gardner *et al.*, 2015; Lescat *et al.*, 2018) and even fish (Lescat *et al.*, 2018). The closer the relationship, however, the greater the degree of homology. Thus, homology is much higher within the same class (Van de Pol *et al.*, 2017). For example, the gene sequences for hemoglobin in humans and horses, both of which are mammals, are almost identical (Brooker, 2009c).

CHAPTER 3
Far Afield

After demonstrating compliance with all that was required of her, H'Ilgraith regained her good standing. She was allowed to transform and began to explore the characteristics and capabilities of her other alternate species. Next came the badger and the lynx.

Branching Out

Bother! H'Ilgraith thought. *Of what use to me can a badger possibly be? It is stocky, slow, and it waddles.* She bemoaned the whole notion of becoming a badger.

"Where did those genes come from?" she demanded to know.

Her mother, H'Elena, declined to indulge her child with the answer. "You will simply have to pay attention in your biology classes," she replied.

Fortunately, H'Ilgraith enjoyed the classes on plant and animal biology and attended closely to those lessons. During her studies, she learned that one could inherit a gene and even pass it on to offspring without ever experiencing its effects (gene expression).

Transforming into a badger and a lynx proved to be more of a challenge. Genetically, their species were further removed from humans than that of the fox. But they were still mammals. It just took longer to transform into those two animals. H'Ilgraith was pleased to have the genes of the lynx and breathed a sigh of relief. *Finally, a major predator,* she thought. She would learn later that even apex predators have their limitations.

The great horned owl was by far the most challenging transformation. This was an entirely different class of animal. There was much less homology between humans and birds than among humans and other mammals. Even so, all four evolved from a common ancestor with features that continued down both lines. Thus, both mammals and birds used some of the same genes that made both classes of animal successful (conservation of genes). As a direct descendant of Ruth, H'Ilgraith had inherited the capability of transforming across classes. She, too, could become a raptor.

An Abiding Interest

When H'Ilgraith was sixteen years of age, she became an adult in the eyes of H'Aleth's community, albeit a young adult. Most children of this age had completed their education and training and were expected to assume adult responsibilities. Most had selected the occupation they wished to pursue.

H'Ilgraith displayed an abiding interest in substances that had healing or other useful properties when properly prepared. She decided to specialize in the healing arts, which included the preparation of nutritional and medicinal potions (appendix G). In this manner, she could aid in the protection and care of her family in peace or war. She would provide her potions to people in H'Aleth's villages and show the villagers how to prepare nutritional ones. So she studied plants under the guidance of Floberius [flō-*ber*-ē-us], a botanist who had immigrated to H'Aleth. His knowledge and experience as a botanist was a gold mine. She continued to confer with him whenever she found an unfamiliar plant. Every once in a while, she would find one new to Floberius. Once she began to explore the medicinal properties of plants, he suggested she study at Gregor.

So she traveled to the House of Gregor, where she studied human physiology, human metamorphosis, and the effects of different agents on both humans and animals. She also learned which part of a medicinal plant contained the compound desired. Then she learned how to milk, filter, distill, or otherwise extract and purify the compound. Finally, she learned how to prepare salves, elixirs, essential oils, aromatics, and other potions. Through these lessons, she began to recognize a wide range of complaints and illnesses and how to treat them. At the same time, she acquired an additional skill that would prove quite useful—midwifery.

When H'Ilgraith returned, she enlisted Floberius's aid once again. He helped her established herb, vegetable, and wild fruit gardens adjacent to her cottage at the estate. H'Ilgraith selected species that were nutritional and had medicinal value. Once the plants matured, she found it much easier to prepare her soups and medicinal potions. Most of the ingredients she used were within a few steps of her cottage. Her extensive gardens served one other purpose. They buffered her home from other residences, especially the manor house.

H'Ilgraith knew the locations of the nut-bearing trees within H'Aleth and many within Cassius territory. Tree nuts were rich in nutrients, including high-quality vegetable protein, vitamins, and minerals. Thus, they were an important food source for the villagers. H'Aleth's territory supported walnut, pecan, and oak trees, which provided an ample supply of nuts in season. Since she was obliged to travel long distances to forage for nuts, she usually collected them on her travels to and from H'Aleth's villages.

H'Ilgraith's foraging and gardens benefited many H'Aletheans [hā-lĕth-ē-ăns] and nearly every immigrant. Many of the people who needed assistance were too ill to travel to the estate. So she took her ingredients and essential oils to villages and settlements throughout H'Aleth. She treated the villagers' symptoms and tended to minor illnesses and injuries. For those who needed care she could not provide, she made arrangements for them to travel to the estate.

As a sister of the House of H'Aleth, she also had additional duties associated with her station. Unfortunately, she found many of these boring and stifling. A restless spirit, she enjoyed being outside, traveling to the villages, and searching far and wide for the plants and minerals she needed for her potions.

Far Afield

Plants provided most of the substances used in medicinal potions. Scouting afforded H'Ilgraith opportunities to spend several days away from the estate searching for the plants, seeds, nuts, and other vegetation she used. Most were available somewhere in H'Aleth's territory. Some were not. Her search for plants and minerals often took her into lands claimed by the Biogenics Corporation and the Cassius Foundation. In those regions, she relied heavily on her alternate species—even the badger—to forage deep into their territories without being detected.

As a badger, she would excavate a deep den where most native predators could not reach her. The badger's aggressiveness was well known, and its sharp claws and powerful bite would deter any predator. On a more practical note, she could dig up a large plant by its roots in a minute.

As a lynx, her agility allowed her to scamper over rocky terrain without impediment. The lynx was also a strong if unwilling swimmer and could climb trees. Although a relatively small predator, it can bring down prey much larger than itself. This characteristic afforded H'Ilgraith additional security.

As a gray fox, her size and shape were just right for slipping in and out of small, narrow spaces and for staying under cover. There, she could seek out roots, hide from predators, and conduct surveillance. The gray fox could climb trees and swim, too. All three of H'Ilgraith's alternate species had sharp nocturnal vision, which allowed her to travel and forage at night.

When transformed into a great horned owl, she had the power of silent flight and the powerful curved talons of a raptor. Her tufted ears and large eyes gave her exquisite hearing and sight, especially at night. This and her ability to rotate her head 270 degrees meant there was little movement she could not detect.

As a child, H'Ilgraith had regretted not having the genes of a wolf (for its power) or hawk (for its flight speed). As a young adult, however, she learned the advantages of her species and found them most useful, especially in Biogenics and Cassius territories. When she first entered a region she wanted to explore, she prepared multiple dens in which she could shelter and transform. Native predators were not the only threat. Humans and hybrids were just as deadly, especially in Cassius territory.

Supplemental Notes and Citations
Gene Expression

Genes come in pairs, yet only one of the two genes in the pair will be used (expressed). Several factors affect which gene is active and, therefore, operational. One could be turned off either temporarily or permanently, inactivated by regulatory genes, or suppressed by a dominant gene. For example, genes that code for products used by one tissue may be turned off in another that does not use that gene product.

Transposable elements (transposons) are another means of altering gene expression. These DNA sequences can alter their location within the genome, thereby modifying the activity of genes affected by the change (Elbarbary *et al.*, 2016; Medstrand *et al.* 2005; Nakayashiki, 2011).

Conservation of Genes

The sauropod line (birds and reptiles) diverged from the synapsid line (mammals) about 320 million years ago (appendix B, table) (Goffinet, 2017). All of them evolved from ancestors whose embryos developed within the shelter of an amniotic sac (amniotes) (Suh et al., 2014, 2015). They also all developed as tetrapod vertebrates (four extremities, including wings). Hence, all three share many ancestral genes, conserved across the sauropod and synapsid lines (Tatebe & Shiozaki, 2017; Pérez-Pérez et al., 2017). The Hox genes direct the development of the musculoskeletal system. They appear in all vertebrates and can be traced back to the development of animals with organized tissues (eukaryotes) approximately 700 million years ago (Erwin, 1993; Hueber & Lohmann, 2008).

CHAPTER 4
INTO THE FRAY

H'Ilgraith's search for medicinal plants frequently took her into the northeastern and southwestern mountains. To gather the plant species she desired, she often had to scale steep and treacherous terrain. So she would transform into either a sure-footed lynx or a great horned owl to reach her treasures.

At higher altitudes, her search took her near the remote aeries of dragons. From time to time, they would glimpse each other and keep watch. Neither would approach the other. The red dragons of the southwest knew a prairie lynx could be found in the mountain foothills, yet rarely ranged at high altitudes. The gray dragons of the northern mountains knew that a great horned owl could be seen in the woodlands of the northeast; however, it did not range above the tree line.

Hence, both species of dragons recognized that an *H. transformans* had entered their realm. Although lynx, owls, and almost any other native species could be prey for dragons, dragons avoided contact with humans. Humans were their only known predators.

The Lure of Riches

Red dragons could infrequently be seen flying over the southwestern mountain range. Their aeries were very high and remote, out of sight. Occasionally, they would descend into the foothills to hunt for prey. The people of H'Aleth were especially cautious around them. For a while, they worried the red dragons would view humans as a prey species along with other mammals. Yet the dragons left the H'Aletheans unscathed, so the H'Aletheans reciprocated.

While searching for medicinal plants in the southwestern mountains, H'Ilgraith (as a lynx) heard humans shouting in the ridges just above the foothills. Staying under cover of boulders and ledges, H'Ilgraith stealthily threaded her way toward the uproar. When she reached the scene, several bounty hunters were attacking a young red dragon. The dragon was an adolescent male, perhaps two to three years old. He had the brightly colored scales on his back and head, two nubs atop his head where horns would eventually develop, and a mouth not yet old enough to make fire. The youngster had strayed too low into the foothills and into the hunters' sights. He had been struck by multiple arrows and was flailing under a heavy net. The hunters were closing in for the kill.

H'Ilgraith was furious. This was a shameless act with no other thought than the profit that such a trophy would bring. With no adult red dragon at hand to defend the juvenile, she quickly maneuvered behind the hunters. Once in position, she attacked from the rear, quickly disabling the first and second hunter before the rest of the group realized they were under attack.

Two more hunters turned to battle the lynx, but they were at a disadvantage. In such close quarters, they could not use their bows and arrows lest they risk striking one of their own. They did not carry spears, and they didn't dare get close enough to use their knives. Their only net had been cast over the dragon.

Meanwhile, the youngster had ceased to struggle and no longer moved. Confident of their prize, more hunters joined the battle with the lynx. Now H'Ilgraith was in trouble.

It finally occurred to one of the hunters to wonder why the cat had attacked them. Wild animals usually avoid all contact with humans. He suddenly shouted a warning to his comrades. "This lynx may be rabid," he warned them. With that announcement, the hunters abruptly broke off their attack while keeping the lynx surrounded and at bay. Her posture did not go unnoted. Nothing kept a rabid animal at bay.

"On the other hand," said the same hunter, "this could be an *H. transformans,* perhaps one of the H'Aletheans who live somewhere in this region. If so, this lynx would be a female *H. transformans*. She would have two transforming X chromosomes and be even more valuable than the dragon. We should bring back both the lynx and the dragon."

His comrades appeared less than enthusiastic about this proposal. "We would be rich beyond measure," he added, tantalizing them.

"Are you crazy?" offered another hunter. "How do we capture that lynx alive when it could be rabid?"

"Simple," said the first hunter. "Take the net off the dragon and throw it over the lynx. It is more than large enough to wind around the cat two or three times and still leave enough length to avoid any contact with it."

"Simple, my ...." muttered the second hunter. Still, the lure of riches easily won over his remaining comrades.

A Looming Shadow

The hunters now turned their attention to capturing the lynx. Since they thought the young dragon was dead, the archers kept their remaining arrows aimed at the cat. The rest of the hunters gingerly approached the dragon. When the youngster did not stir, they started removing the net.

H'Ilgraith thought she had come too late to save the young dragon and turned her attention to saving herself. She suspected at least some of the hunters feared she could be rabid and dared not approach her. She also noted the archers keeping her contained were distracted. Their attention was drawn to their comrades as the latter began to remove the net from the dragon. She stood very still and waited. Once all the hunters became transfixed on the dragon, she would make her move.

Barely a moment had passed when H'Ilgraith saw a shadow appear overhead. She recognized its shape immediately. She crouched down just as a gale struck the area. Even low to the ground, she was bowled over by the wind shear. The hunters were sent flying through the air. An adult male red dragon had strafed the scene (illustration 2).

The adult had been searching for the wayward adolescent when he had heard the youngster's cries. With his keen eyesight, the adult readily located him, along with the hunters surrounding him and the lynx in their midst. He bade the youngster be quiet and not move, as if he were dead or

Illustration 2: A Dragon's Wrath

dying. The hunters could not hear the young dragon's cries nor the adult's response because of the low frequencies at which dragons communicate. Hence, they were unaware that an adult dragon was drawing near.

The adult's first pass cleared away the hunters that had surrounded the lynx. These he promptly torched. H'Ilgraith quickly regained her footing and darted behind a large boulder that shielded her from the flames. The dragon turned on the few remaining hunters who were fleeing in a panic. He could not unleash his fire upon them without risking harm to the youngster. So he dispatched them with claws, canines, and a whip of his tail.

Ignoring the lynx, the adult turned his attention immediately to the young dragon. H'Ilgraith wondered if the adult recognized her species. Then she saw that the ensnared youngster was struggling against the net. *He must be in terrible pain,* she surmised. Abruptly, she leaped high into the rocks in a desperate gamble to save the young dragon.

Metamorphosis

The lynx's move did not go unnoticed. The dragon watched as H'Ilgraith ducked behind another large boulder above the young dragon. She peered around it at the adult. The dragon looked back at her. When he made no move to accost her, H'Ilgraith was certain he knew her species. The people of H'Aleth had long protected red dragons from hunters and poachers. Nevertheless, H'Aletheans had maintained a discreet distance from them over the years. This could not be said of other humans, who hunted dragons for their decorative scales, their horns, and their eggs.

H'Ilgraith was taking a great risk as she left the shelter of the rock to lie down directly in front of the adult. Even so, she was determined to help the youngster if she could. Moments later, a chrysalis enveloped the lynx (box 1) as she slipped into unconsciousness. Inside the chrysalis, fur was shed as hair follicles transformed into feather follicles, and feathers developed. Forelegs morphed into wings as back legs became a bird's legs, and claws turned into talons. The head, eyes, and ears of the lynx became the head, eyes, and ear tufts of an owl. Before long, a great horned owl awoke and emerged from the chrysalis (box 2).

The owl flew down to the ground in front of the adult dragon. She began using her beak to tear apart the netting, which bound the youngster. As she tore through the ropes, the net started to fall away. She used both beak and talons to pull the broken edges apart and peel them away from the arrows.

What do I do about the arrows and the wounds they inflicted? H'Ilgraith asked herself. *How do I treat these in a dragon?* Then she decided she would treat his wounds as she would any other wounded mammal, even though dragons are of an ancient order (appendix B). So once again, the owl turned and faced the adult directly. She gave two distinct hoots and then flew off.

Box 1: Formation of an
H. transformans Chrysalis

To form a chrysalis, dead skin cells from the top ten to fifteen layers of the skin's surface (epidermis) are mobilized to coalesce on the surface. Sweat (eccrine) glands provide moisture, and small glands (sebaceous glands) around hair follicles add a waxy substance (sebum) to mold the skin layers together into a flexible shroud. Scent (apocrine) glands provide an oily substance to lubricate the innermost layer of the shroud so that it does not adhere to the body. Since the constituents of the shroud are readily available, it could form within a few minutes. It would be flexible enough to expand and accommodate the movements of the body within it. Once the metamorphosis is complete, the shroud can be stripped away by its inhabitant or left to disintegrate and slough off (ecdysis).

The shroud is not an essential feature of metamorphosis in humans. Although it provides a protective cover, this step can be skipped in an urgent transformation.

Box 2: Metamorphosis in H. transformans

Several hormones were involved in the process of metamorphosis. The thyroid hormone and growth hormone were essential for growth and development. They triggered the action of growth factors, which directed the reconstruction and reshaping of anatomic structures. Since many structures were homologous among different species, there was no need to dissolve and completely remake every one when an *H. transformans* transformed into his or her alternate species.

Corticosteroid hormones mitigated the inflammatory responses to the changes, stabilized cell membranes, and increased production of glucose to meet the demands for energy. The neurotransmitters (e.g., gamma-aminobutyric acid) and hormones (e.g., endorphins) that induced sleep, depressed consciousness, and suppressed pain were released into the brain and spinal cord in large amounts. This resulted in profound sedation, unconsciousness, and amnesia. Once metamorphosis was complete, these substances subsided, and the individual awoke as if he or she had been asleep.

The time to complete metamorphosis depended largely upon the degree of genetic homology between the *H. transformans* and his or her alternate species and how often the transformation occurred. A well-practiced transformation could take place within minutes in an emergency; however, this was not recommended. The risk of incomplete, irreversible, and fatal transformations increased as the time allotted for transformation decreased.

H'Ilgraith returned to the site of her original transformation to pick up her robe. Inside its pockets were the leaves, stems, flowers, and roots of various plants she had retrieved. Then she flew back, carrying the robe with her. She landed not far from the two dragons. The adult, who was keeping his offspring still, watched the owl as she worked her way into her robe and subsequently transformed into her native species, an *H. transformans*.

Ministrations

H'Ilgraith selected aloe vera from the plants she had collected and showed it to the adult. When he did not reject it, H'Ilgraith began to milk the juice from the plant directly into the juvenile's wounds.

Having been surrounded by the hunters with their bows drawn, H'Ilgraith knew what type of arrow had been used to attack the youngster. They comprised a wooden shaft with a smooth, tapered arrowhead made of stone. Although they could inflict considerable pain and were disabling, they were not deadly unless a strong bowman's arrow reached a vital organ. Given the juvenile's sustained ability to struggle, H'Ilgraith determined that his wounds were not life-threatening. Eventually, the arrows could be pulled straight out if the bleeding could be controlled.

As H'Ilgraith ministered to the youngster, two more dragons appeared. These were young adults the adult male had summoned. Carefully, the two slighter dragons tried to position themselves against each side of the youngster and under his wings. In this manner, they would be able to assist the youngster to his feet. One of them could not get close enough. An arrow protruding from the youngster's side prevented it.

Once again, H'Ilgraith reached into her pocket. She pulled out leaves of the yarrow plant and presented them to the adult dragon. Then she pointed to the arrow, mimed pulling it out, and pointed the leaves toward the youngster. For a moment, the adult considered the implications. Then he moved to position himself against the youngster to keep him still, grasped the arrow in his mouth, and pulled it out. Fortunately, the juice of the aloe had already begun its work to soothe the tissues damaged by the arrow.

The wound began to bleed profusely. H'Ilgraith rushed to embed crushed yarrow leaves into the wound and apply pressure on it. Then she waited, bracing the wound to see if the yarrow would stem the bleeding. After several minutes had elapsed, she eased up the pressure and watched for fresh bleeding. Dark red blood oozed from the wound; however, there was no frank bright red bleeding. The yarrow had done its work.

To the youngster's dismay, they had to repeat this procedure for each of the other four wounds the hunters had inflicted on him. Fortunately, three of them were quite superficial—the result of poor marksmanship and lax bowmen. The aloe was sufficient to treat these wounds. The fourth was somewhat problematic because it struck the youngster's back leg, which he needed to lift off. Still, a small amount of yarrow controlled the bleeding.

An Invitation

With the youngster's condition stable, H'Ilgraith knew it was time for the dragons to depart, as should she. Before leaving, the adult turned to her. With his head, he motioned in the direction of his aery. He repeated the motion one more time. It was an invitation to come to it.

H'Ilgraith could hardly believe it. With a nod and a slight bow, H'Ilgraith acknowledged the dragon's offer. Then the adult motioned for H'Ilgraith to take shelter.

The two young adults were ready to depart with the youngster between them. Normally, red dragons have no difficulty becoming airborne. Their relatively lighter frames permit liftoff from a standing position. The young dragon, however, would need help. The two young adult dragons positioned themselves beside him and would power his flight back to their aery. The adult provided an assist in the form of another gale that boosted their takeoff and helped them lift the youngster. Once in flight, the adult took the lead, allowing the threesome to fly in his wake.

H'Ilgraith was thrilled. It had been a long time since she had felt so excited. She decided to seize this extraordinary opportunity to visit red dragons in their mountain retreat. To her knowledge, it was unprecedented. *I could see and learn so much about them,* she thought. *Herbs and other plants will have to wait.* She needed to collect more aloe and yarrow anyway.

Supplemental Notes and Citations
Metamorphosis

Metamorphosis is the radical change of an organism into an altogether different shape, form, and function. Amphibians and insects are the two classes of animals that can undergo metamorphosis as part of their normal development.

For example, a butterfly caterpillar progresses through four stages to become a butterfly: egg, larva, pupa, and adult. A chrysalis comes into being when the caterpillar (the larval stage) sheds (molts) its outer coat (exoskeleton) for the last time and enters the pupa stage. During the pupal stage, the body of the caterpillar breaks down, and the adult butterfly takes form.

Different genes regulate hormones in insect larval and pupal stages (Belles & Santos, 2014; Minakuchi *et al.*, 2009; Urena *et al.*, 2014). When the influence of larval genes subsides, the insect enters the pupal stage, which marks the onset of metamorphosis (Hiruma & Kaneko, 2013). The formation of the pupa depends on several genes (transcription factors), (Belles & Santos, 2014; Urena *et al.*, 2014). At least one of these genes (Manduca broad Z4) has been conserved for over 260 million years (Bayer *et al.*, 2003).

Morphogenesis

Unlike metamorphosis, morphogenesis usually refers to gradual changes in structure, form, and function as an organism grows and develops into its final adult form. Many hormones and an almost endless array of growth factors are involved in morphogenesis. Thyroxin and growth hormone are the predominant hormones of growth and development, aided by androgens, estrogens, the parathyroid hormone, and others (Matfin, 2009; McCance, 2010; Mukherjee *et al.*, 2016). Thyroxin and growth hormone activate the genes that produce growth factors, especially insulin-like growth factors (IGF). These factors are essential for normal growth and development in many types of tissue (Rotwein, 2017a, 2017b). They stimulate protein synthesis, growth of bone and cartilage, growth and function of organs, and an increase in muscle size. There is a high degree of conservation in mammals for IGF genes (Mukherjee *et al.*, 2016).

The Hox genes are another large family of genes (transcription factors) that direct the development of body shape (Casaca et al., 2014; Hueber & Lohmann, 2008; Mallo et al., 2010; Soshnikova, 2014). During the development of an embryo, Hox genes regulate where and when structures are formed by activating and suppressing other genes involved in tissue development (Hueber & Lohmann, 2008; Pineault & Wellik, 2014.).Among vertebrate animals, including humans, development occurs along an anterior-posterior axis and encompasses the formation of the spinal column and the extremities. Some Hox genes remain active in adulthood and have a role in the repair and remodeling of bone (Rux & Wellik, 2017).

Functions of Skin

Skin provides a protective layer over the body. It is considered the largest organ in the body (Nicol & Huether, 2010; Simandle, 2009). It prevents the body's loss of excess water and provides for the secretion of sweat (via eccrine glands) and oils (via sebaceous and apocrine glands). Its outermost layer (the epidermis) consists of several layers of dead keratin skin cells. Keratin is a fibrous protein that keeps the dead skin cells attached to each other. The skin also houses hair follicles, which can grow and replace hair throughout life (Shimomura & Christiano, 2010). Mammalian hair follicles are comparable in structure and function (i.e., analogous) to feather follicles (Oh, et al., 2015).

Inhibitory Neurotransmitters

Neurotransmitters are widely distributed throughout the central nervous system (brain and spinal cord). Gamma-aminobutyric acid (GABA) is the primary inhibitory neurotransmitter, and its receptors lie throughout the central nervous system (Huether, 2010; Nutt, 2006). There are two types of GABA receptors: those that respond within milliseconds, and those that are long-acting (Nutt, 2006; Sigel & Steinmann, 2012). The release of a large amount of GABA can lead to excessive sedation, loss of balance, and loss of memory (Nutt, 2006).

CHAPTER 5
IN THE REALM OF THE RED DRAGON

H'Ilgraith promptly began her search for a site in the foothills to store the remaining plants she had retrieved earlier. After finding a suitable location, she transformed once again into a great horned owl and began her ascent into the southwestern mountain range. As she went well above the tree line, gusts began to make flight hazardous. She was carrying her robe in her talons, and the wind was whipping it, pulling her with it. So she found a place to stow her robe and transformed into a lynx.

A Southwestern Lynx

As a lynx, H'Ilgraith had ranged in the lower levels of the northwestern and southwestern mountains up to about 2,500 feet. As she passed 5,000 feet, the winds began to impede her progress. At 7,000 feet, she was struggling. Although some species of mountain lynx can range up to 18,000 feet, she was not one of them. The altitude, colder temperatures, and wind chill left her shivering, seeking cover, and wishing she still had her robe.

H'Ilgraith knew she was nearing dragon territory, if not already in it. She found a ledge that extended away from the face of the mountain. There she yowled, hoping that the dragon from the foothills would hear it and respond to it. The lynx's cry echoed and reached the ears of many mountain species, including the red dragons.

Much to her dismay, H'Ilgraith soon found several dragons converging on her location. Some were fully grown adults, while others were young adults. The adult she had encountered earlier was not among them.

To appear neither aggressive nor predatory, she sat down and mentally crossed her fingers. Most of the younger dragons kept their distance, while two adults approached and tried to encircle her on the ledge. This made H'Ilgraith very nervous, and she began retreating. There was no time to transform back into an owl. Even if there had been, shrouding herself in a chrysalis would leave her defenseless. There was no point in retreating into a crevice or searching for a temporary den. Dragon fire would readily reach any place she tried to hide.

She continued to back away to avoid a confrontation when she sensed a presence. A third adult had come up behind her. She was trapped. Then her sensitive hearing discerned a low pitched rumble from the third dragon. Shivering with cold and scared to death, H'Ilgraith turned to face this dragon. She was relieved to see he was the same one whose offspring she had tended earlier.

The dragon stood quietly before her and waited. H'Ilgraith glanced back over her shoulder and saw that the other two adults did the same. The younger dragons had moved forward, as if curious to see what would happen next. H'Ilgraith heard the rumble again. *Is he trying to communicate with me?* she wondered.

Using his tail to support himself, the adult leaned back and reached out one foreleg toward the lynx. Its talon-like claws were fully extended, yet the dragon did not attempt to grasp the lynx. He simply waited.

H'Ilgraith got the message. They were not treating her as either prey or predator. She had a ride the rest of the way to the aery. Still, if she accepted the offer, she would be taking a great risk. The other dragons might not be so accommodating. Worse yet, they might decide she would make a nice snack—if not for themselves, then for their chicks. Then there was the minor problem of how to get back down again. Despite all these reservations, H'Ilgraith could not resist the temptation to enter the realm of the red dragons. So she stepped into the outstretched talon.

The dragon carefully grasped the lynx and lifted off with ease. As a lynx, H'Ilgraith only weighed about twenty-two pounds. The male would hardly notice her added weight. As he flew away, the other dragons immediately took flight and followed.

Into the Dragon's Den

The flight took only a few minutes. An adult red dragon can achieve a flight speed of 160–220 miles per hour. So carrying the lynx in his talon, the red dragon ascended rapidly, banking right and left to avoid mountain crags until he reached a large crevice. He dived into it and flew into a large opening on one side. It was the entrance to a large channel leading to a cave deep in the mountainside.

The dragon alighted on the floor and began walking deeper into the cavern. To H'Ilgraith, it appeared dark and foreboding. Even her sharp nocturnal vision would see little of her surroundings in the darkness. Not long thereafter, the dragon turned a corner, and H'Ilgraith saw light reflected on the cavern's walls. She could smell a fire burning, and the temperature in the cavern became warmer as they drew nearer. The warmth was a significant improvement for the southwestern lynx, assuming she wouldn't become the main entrée on the dragon's menu.

Finally, the two of them rounded another corner, which opened into a small antechamber. There, H'Ilgraith saw the young dragon she had treated. He nestled against his mother, who was lying beside him. Clearly, the mother was the adult male's mate, and this was their chick. As the dragon released her from his talon, the dragoness nodded to the lynx.

H'Ilgraith sat down before the dragoness. *She is not surprised to see me,* H'Ilgraith thought, *nor does she feel threatened by my presence.* H'Ilgraith knew all too well that she would have been roasted in an instant if the dragoness thought her chick was in danger. Despite his brush with death, the youngster appeared to be resting comfortably and in no distress.

As H'Ilgraith looked around the chamber, she noted it was heated by a large boulder glowing a deep ruby red. She also saw three young juveniles poking their heads into the space and staring at the new arrival. *Siblings or curious onlookers?* she wondered. Having a live lynx in their midst was quite a novelty.

When H'Ilgraith turned her attention back to the dragoness and her chick, she heard a low-pitched rumble coming from the dragoness. H'Ilgraith was struck by what she heard. It sounded like *thank you*—at least, that was how her mind interpreted the sound.

Is it possible that they understand and can speak the common language? H'Ilgraith wondered. As a lynx, she could not test this notion. She did not want to transform back into human form without warm clothing to don. Despite the heat radiating from the boulder, it was still cool, and her coat was keeping her warm. So H'Ilgraith offered a soft mew in return to acknowledge that she had heard the dragoness's vocalization.

To test her interpretation of the red dragons' ability to communicate with signs and sounds, H'Ilgraith tilted her head toward the youngster and then looked at the mother. She did this twice. The dragoness then tilted her head toward him in return. H'Ilgraith opted to interpret this motion as permission to approach him. Under the dragoness's watchful eye, H'Ilgraith slowly approached the chick—keeping one eye on the dragoness—until she was about six feet away. She looked carefully at the wounds she could see and sniffed for the scent of fresh blood and foul odor. She found none. H'Ilgraith gave another soft mew to the mother and returned to her former place.

Home Again

H'Ilgraith was satisfied that the young dragon was safely at home and likely would recover fully. She turned to the adult male and mewed softly again with a nod toward the way they had entered. She was signaling that it was time for her to leave. The dragon led the lynx back to the edge of the cavern and flew her down to the foothills. After setting her down, he promptly returned to the mountains.

In her short stay with the red dragons, H'Ilgraith had learned a great deal about them. They were social animals who lived in communities and had strong communal bonds. Both parents cared for their offspring. They were intelligent. The juveniles had demonstrated curiosity, and the adults had accurately interpreted the behaviors she exhibited, both as a great horned owl and as a lynx. She strongly suspected that they communicated among themselves with sounds outside a human's range of hearing. *But do they have language as we know it?* she wondered. It was a tantalizing notion.

Supplemental Notes and Citations
Language

Language is the ability to communicate using words and syntax. Humans consider this ability to be uniquely human (Mozzi *et al.*, 2016; Staes *et al.*, 2017). Other animals—especially other mammals, songbirds, and parrots—demonstrate a vocal means of communication by imitating the sounds they hear (mimicry) (Mozzi *et al.*, 2016; Webb & Zhang, 2004). Among other mammalian species, whales, dolphins, elephants, and bats exhibit the ability to alter verbal communication and learn new vocalizations (vocal learning) (Mozzi *et al.*, 2016; Staes *et al.*, 2017).

The FOXP2 gene is required for the development of speech and language in humans (Mozzi *et al.*, 2016; Staes *et al.*, 2017). The gene codes for a protein (a transcription factor) that regulates the function of other genes. It is highly conserved and shared by many vertebrate species, including fish and reptiles. In humans, however, there are two alterations in the genetic code for FOXP2, which changes the amino acid composition of the protein. This change is unique to humans and, therefore, associated with the human capacity for language (Staes *et al.*, 2017; Webb & Zhang, 2004). Mutations in the human FOXP2 gene have been linked to speech and language disorders, learning disabilities, speech disorders, and dyslexia (Graham & Fisher, 2015; Mozzi *et al.*, 2016; Staes *et al.*, 2017; Webb & Zhang, 2004). Although the FOXP2 gene is essential for the development of language, no single gene fully accounts for this capability (Fisher, 2017). Many other factors influence the process.

CHAPTER 6
On Dangerous Ground

Prudent Precautions

The H'Aletheans had established a warning system whereby scouts in their transformed species could alert humans and native animals that a stranger had entered the region. This was not uncommon. Such strangers could be traders and merchants seeking new products, bounty hunters and trophy hunters searching for their prizes, explorers and wanderers, or refugees fleeing oppression, poverty, and bounty hunters.

A scout could watch most strangers from a discreet distance. Once they spotted one, a scout would use the calls native to their alternate species to alert others. The scout would follow the newcomers to determine their intentions. From watching their behavior and listening to their conversations, the scouts would quickly learn the newcomers' plans. Many people carried weapons for protection in unknown territory. As long as visitors acted peacefully and posed no threat, they were left alone. Refugees were welcomed graciously but with caution until security could determine that they were truly refugees and not spies or hunters in disguise.

Bounty hunters were another matter. The people of H'Aleth discovered that other humans were hunting animals, including dragons, for the profit they could bring. So the H'Aletheans extended their surveillance into the prairie and foothills, essentially incorporating that territory into their homeland. Scouts who could transform into apex predators would track hunters, regardless of who or what they were hunting. If a hunter began stalking a particular species, the scout would sound an alarm that would alert any species—the howl of a wolf, the scream of a lynx, the roar of a bear, the screech of an eagle or owl. These calls could be heard for miles by most native species. Of course, this would alert the hunters as well. The scout could then become their target. So he or she had to be able to fade away quickly into the grass or the forest.

Last but not least, scouts also patrolled H'Aleth's borders, especially the northern and northeastern border close to Cassius territory. The greatest danger lay along those borders. Skirmishes between Biogenics and Cassius were frequent in the contested regions they both claimed. These regions were not far from H'Aleth's northern border. Furthermore, bounty hunters were active in these areas. They would have pushed into H'Aleth territory were it not for the skill and perseverance of H'Aleth's scouts.

Over the Borders

On occasion, H'Aleth's scouts would slip into Biogenics and Cassius territory to follow an intruder, identify a threat near H'Aleth's border, or gather intelligence about their neighbors' intentions. H'Ilgraith often forayed into both territories to conduct surveillance. Her aims were twofold: detect signs that either Biogenics or Cassius or both might be mobilizing their forces and learn as much as possible about the two adversaries. Each one had armed outposts surrounding and guarding their territories and ready to engage in battle. Both had villages scattered throughout their lands.

In observing activities in either territory, H'Ilgraith would transform into a great horned owl. Hidden in the boughs of a tree, she could watch without drawing any attention to herself. In most instances, she had to observe daytime activities from a distance. There were few if any trees in the villages and none in or close to an outpost. This posed no impediment to her outdoor observations. Owls have excellent daylight vision. Observation of indoor activities awaited nightfall, when an owl's sight was most acute. Then her silent flight would take her to a building or other structure where she could watch and listen from the eaves, rafters, or other secluded places without being detected.

After several incursions into Biogenics territory, H'Ilgraith had learned that, in the absence of conflict, Biogenics villages held little of interest. They were not unlike those commonly encountered in H'Aleth and other regions. Most of their structures were made of wood or stone and of modest size. Most villages supported some business or industry. All of the inhabitants appeared to be *H. sapiens*. If any of their people were *H. transformans*, they were careful not to reveal it.

The Biogenics research and development headquarters was about midway between its northern and southern borders. It lay just east of the River Della, which flowed along the western border of Biogenics territory. H'Ilgraith had yet to venture that far. One day, she promised herself.

Biogenics outposts, on the other hand, were much closer and provided strategic information. There, H'Ilgraith could observe how an outpost was structured and what armaments it had. Her reconnaissance revealed how well equipped their soldiers were and how skilled they were in using their weapons. Late at night, she could listen to soldiers' idle chatter about plans for defense or offense against the Cassius Foundation.

A Silent Witness

Late one night, H'Ilgraith, as an owl, was conducting surveillance in the contested area along the southern border of Biogenics. She spotted an outpost in the distance. She glided silently into a copse of trees not far from it and perched, motionless, on a branch. It was built like a Biogenics outpost, yet it appeared deserted. There was no idle chatter emanating from this outpost, no light, and no movement on its grounds. All of the other Biogenics outposts she had observed had had guards on duty day and night. *Curious that Biogenics would leave a post unguarded in this region,* thought H'Ilgraith. *Perhaps this one has been abandoned for some reason.*

The owl heard subtle sounds of movement east of the outpost. She immediately zeroed in on the location of the sounds and detected a group of humans crawling on their bellies. They were armed and inching their way toward the outpost. It looked like a raiding party, probably in the employ of Rex Cassius, who controlled the Cassius Foundation. If so, taking control of an abandoned outpost would be a boon for Rex. It would extend his reach without having to build an outpost of his own. Perhaps some strategic or tactical information would be left behind to give his forces an advantage.

As the raiding party breached the outer perimeter of the outpost, a hail of arrows rained down upon their position. It was indeed a Biogenics outpost. Its forces were prepared for the assault and had set a trap of their own. At first, H'Ilgraith stayed to observe the battle tactics both sides used. She would report this information to Weston, H'Aleth's chief of security. Before long, however, arrows were flying everywhere—including at her. Time to go, she decided. She flew well beyond the range of the archers and settled down to wait.

In the meantime, the battle had changed from an air assault to hand-to-hand combat. Both forces had loosed all their arrows. During the air assault, both the Biogenics and Cassius troops who were *H. transformans* had changed into powerful, aggressive alternate species that continued the battle. The fight was fierce and bloody.

Well after the sounds of fighting had subsided, the owl returned to the scene of the battle. The chatter coming from the outpost made the winner of the contest clear: Biogenics had prevailed.

Cat and Mouse

Surveillance in Cassius territory was an altogether different matter. Trespassing in a Cassius village was extremely dangerous for any creature—human or otherwise. These villages were both heartbreaking and intriguing. Conditions were bleak. The impoverished inhabitants, primarily hybrid humanoids, eked out an existence by foraging, growing a few vegetables and herbs, and hunting. They kept no farm animals. Any animal they encountered was killed for food, hide, fur, feathers, and any bones that could be fashioned into a tool or used as a weapon.

By contrast, most of the genetically engineered animal hybrids were designed to be very violent and would attack anyone or anything within reach. If an animal hybrid broke free of its chain or out of its cage, it would attack the villagers.

When approaching these villages, H'Ilgraith exercised extreme caution and stealth, even as an owl. If seen, she could be killed on sight—and not because she was a spy. The villagers would see her as either food or a threat. So whenever she approached a village in Cassius territory, she expected to be in a cat and mouse situation in which she was the mouse. This was a peculiar position for a great horned owl, which typically preyed on mice and other rodents. Yet H'Ilgraith might not be the only one at hazard. If she had to defend herself, she could inflict serious injury on a villager. The villagers' plight was already dire. She had no desire to add trauma to their misery.

The risks became quite evident one night when H'Ilgraith, as a gray fox, left the safety of a tree to get closer to a Cassius village. She could not fly over it without being detected. There was no canopy to cover her flight, and the moon was bright under clear skies. As a gray fox, she could slip through the underbrush without being seen. Unfortunately, she could still be heard.

Suddenly, H'Ilgraith heard the sound of another animal's movement. Alerted, she stopped abruptly and made no further sound. Silence. The other animal had also stopped moving. *Predator or prey?* she wondered. A shifting breeze carried the scent of an unnatural weasel. H'Ilgraith recognized the odor of a hybrid and realized she was its prey.

A mustecanis [mŭst-ĕ-cān-ĭs] was stalking her. A mix of weasel and red fox, this animal hybrid was quiet, cunning, and genetically engineered to be much larger than a fox. H'Ilgraith was in grave danger. She would not prevail against this creature in a fight. Without knowing its exact position, she could not try to outrun it. Ascending a tree would not help. Some species of weasel could climb trees, too. One thing was certain. The hybrid could not fly.

The genes of a great horned owl gave H'Ilgraith a critical advantage. The mustecanis had raised a paw to take a step forward and, in doing so, betrayed its location. H'Ilgraith bolted for the trees with the mustecanis in hot pursuit. The more powerful hybrid was gaining on her, certain of a fresh meal, when it flushed an owl from the brush. The surprised mustecanis promptly reacted with a leap into the air. Its attempt to snare the bird failed. When the hybrid tried to pick up the fox's trail, it was gone. The mustecanis had encountered a powerful *H. transformans* who had successfully forced a transformation from a mammalian species directly into an avian species.

A Quandary

Despite the dangers, H'Ilgraith took the risks and sought out these villages. An abundance of malformed beings populated them. Many of the animal hybrids' and humanoids' features were quite bizarre. Based on their physiognomy, H'Ilgraith suspected the humanoids were *H. transformans* who had been genetically altered and subsequently forced into a transformation that they could not reverse.

Such genetic experiments were not designed to treat a disorder (gene therapy) or benefit the subject in any way. Most of the humanoid inhabitants were crippled with painful deformities, making them too disabled to fight in the Cassius army or serve as storeroom guards. So they were forced into hard labor. These beings were not inherently monsters. The fault for what they had become lay not in themselves but in the ones who had made them. They were and remained humans, genetically altered against their will by the Cassius Foundation. Rex wanted humanoids that would be more powerful and could be used as beasts of burden, guards, and ferocious fighters (appendix J).

H'Ilgraith found herself in a quandary. She was intrigued by the range of the villagers' deformities and wanted to learn as much as possible about them, including the mechanisms that caused them. At the same time, she wanted to provide some relief to the inhabitants, most of whom were poorly nourished, sick, and impaired. She knew she could not help them directly without being discovered, so she devised other means.

Oak trees were plentiful everywhere. As H'Ilgraith traveled, she would scoop up acorns in a pouch she carried with her. Later, she would scatter them along with a few hazelnuts not far from where she knew the villagers foraged. Sometimes, as a badger, she would dig up edible roots and leave them on the forest floor where villagers could find them. Mixed among the roots, she would scatter a few edible herbs. The villagers would be sharing all of these food items with any wildlife that found it first. Sometimes this was a blessing in disguise. If the villagers spotted a squirrel or other animals eating the food, they might have a source of meat as well.

Supplemental Notes and Citations
Genetic Engineering and Gene Therapy

Genetic engineering is an artificial means of modifying and manipulating genes to achieve a goal. The desired outcome is a change in the structure or function of a gene, which, in turn, alters the structure and function of the tissue(s) it affects. In *H. sapiens*, the change is intended to benefit an individual who is missing an essential gene or has a gene that does not function properly (i.e., gene therapy).

There are four broad categories of gene therapy: 1) replacing a faulty gene in single-gene (monogenic) disease, 2) inserting a missing gene, 3) altering gene expression by targeting a regulatory gene, and 4) using enzymes (nucleases) to edit a gene to correct its function. (Haas *et al.*, 2017; Kim, 2016; Prakash *et al.*, 2016; Wang & Gao, 2014; Wood *et al.*, 2007).

CHAPTER 7
A Narrow Escape

A Delicate Sense of Smell

One of H'Ilgraith's incursions into Cassius territory proved most enlightening.

A badger's relatively poor eyesight is offset by its excellent hearing and exquisite sense of smell. While foraging as a badger a bit farther afield than usual, H'Ilgraith caught a foul scent in the air. She recognized it immediately as rotting flesh. She suspended her search for plant species and followed the odor to its source. It wasn't long before she came to the edge of a rocky ledge. At its base about one hundred feet below, she saw an enormous mound of dead flesh. *There must be hundreds of carcasses there,* she surmised. They looked as if they had been dumped or dropped.

The stench was so bad the badger had to back away. *Where is a dragon when you need one?* she thought. A brief blast of dragon fire would eliminate the mound and its odor in a matter of seconds. So she turned to find a way down to it, preferably via a route that would take her upwind of it. Even after she found such a path, the stench remained repulsive.

When H'Ilgraith reached the base of the escarpment, she was much closer to the mound and could see individual forms within it. Nearly all were deformed or contorted in some manner and with some degree of decomposition. Yet she could still distinguish the features of humans and a wide range of animals. Most of the humanoid corpses appeared to be *H. transformans* that were corrupted, displaying a mix of two or more mammalian alternate species. Most of the animal corpses were hybrids, also predominantly mammalian species—boars, bears, wolves, and several other apex predators. Some of these creatures she recognized from spying on Cassius villages. She also discerned a few hybrid humanoids and several animal hybrids with scales, wings, feathers, and other reptilian and avian features.

A Perilous Decision

H'Ilgraith faced a dilemma. *Shall I turn back and report what I have seen?* she wondered, *or should I try to find the source of these creatures?* She had come a long way to turn back without learning their origin. This information could be crucial, especially for the defense of H'Aleth. Yet if she were caught or killed, then no word at all would reach her people.

H'Ilgraith spotted wagon tracks leading away from the mound. Having come this far, she decided to rely on her alternate species and follow the tracks to see where they led. She might discover who or what had been dumping all these dead bodies and the origin of the creatures she had found.

H'Ilgraith was still in a forested region. So she transformed into a great horned owl to begin her surveillance of the area. First, she flew to the top of the tree canopy to gain an overview of the territory. She saw the Cassius River off to her left. The wagon tracks followed the river. Under cover of the canopy, she flew north following the river and the tracks. As she traveled, she took brief flights above the canopy to make a mental map of the region, including the smaller rivers coursing through it. As she flew closer to the river, she found it curious that she had not seen any native wildlife, especially eagles along the river. Upon taking a closer look at the river itself, she saw no fish running. *This might explain why there were no eagles. But where are the fish?* she wondered.

From a perch high in the treetops, farther off to the northwest, H'Ilgraith saw the trees give way to a large expanse of open land. The area was too far away for her to see what lay beyond the tree line. After carefully surveying the sky for any potential aerial predators, she flew along the river just inside the trees on its bank. From that point, she headed northwest, continuing to follow the river, mapping the territory as she went. As she traveled, she grew more and more cautious. She saw an increasing number of deformed creatures. *These must be hybrids made by the Cassius Foundation,* she thought, *at least those that survived.*

As she drew near to the edge of the forest's boundary, she stopped cold. An enormous fortress loomed in the distance. She spotted the wagon tracks in the open terrain. They headed toward the fortress, then curved to go around the right side of it before disappearing from view.

The fortress was nearly a mile away from the forest's edge. Nevertheless, from her perch near the top of a tree, she could see the outer wall clearly. It had watchtowers, iron gates, and guards patrolling the top of the wall. Unfortunately, she could see little inside it except for the giant stone building that towered above it. *What is that?* she wondered.

Watchful Waiting

Having come this far, H'Ilgraith considered her options. Except for short grass, there was no vegetation of any kind between the forest's edge and the fortress nor between the fortress and the river. Hence, she could not approach the structure in daylight as any of her alternate species. She would be spotted and immediately targeted by guards at the watchtowers and patrols along the ramparts. Even at night, the landscape would be clearly visible under a clear sky and bright moon. She would be unable to approach the fortress unless the skies were completely overcast or the moon was dark. Even then, torches could be lit in the towers and on the ramparts to cast light near the walls. So for the moment, all she could report was the location of the fortress, the landscape surrounding it, its walls, and the enormous stone edifice inside it.

H'Ilgraith wanted to screech—literally. Yet she dared not vent her frustration. Even though she had seen no other native animals—not even small rodents or birds—other unnatural creatures roamed through the forest. *Native wildlife is avoiding the area, as should I,* she noted ruefully.

A Den of Iniquity

As a child, H'Ilgraith had tended to be impatient and impulsive. Once she could transform, she learned a great deal during her time spent as her alternate species. Predators must be patient. They must wait and watch, often for long periods, before launching an attack. Although owls are aerial predators, they tend to hunt from a perch where they wait for prey to appear. So H'Ilgraith bided her time. *Someone or something may enter or leave the fortress,* she thought. *I may learn something just from who comes and goes—and what they bring with them.* In choosing this course of action, she still needed to be careful. Even if there were no eagles to prey on owls, humans carried bows and arrows.

Rewarding H'Ilgraith's patience, a wagon exited from the right side of the fortress. It was retracing the tracks H'Ilgraith had followed leading to it. An ursoxinoid [er-sŏx-in-oid] drove the cart, and a bovicervid [bŏv-ĭ-cerv-ĭd] pulled it. Both were hybrid humanoids. The wagon carried some kind of cargo that, at first, H'Ilgraith could not see. The wagon's trajectory and the size of its driver blocked her view. As it wound its way toward the forest, though, the owl caught sight of the cargo. It was full of bodies and carcasses like those she had seen at the base of the escarpment. The sight sickened her.

So that is where those creatures were born—or made—and where they died, H'Ilgraith noted. Most likely, the dead and the dying were carted far away to avoid any connection between them and the fortress. Her sense of pity for these poor creatures was joined quickly by anger at the injustice inflicted upon them by the Cassius Foundation.

A Malevolent Industry

Indeed, the fortress was the seat of the Foundation's operations. There, the genetic engineers tested methods for inserting the genes of one or more species into the genome of another species. They teased out the desired genes by excising the section of DNA where they were located and making a copy of them. For animal hybrids, a geneticist would insert those genes into the fertilized egg of an animal, incubate it, and watch to see what developed.

For humanoid hybrids, the engineers would insert the desired genes into a virus and then infect an *H. transformans* with the virus. After a time, the engineers would force a transformation to see what creature might emerge. Most of these experiments proved instructive to the engineers and fatal to the subject. Either the foreign genes interfered with a critical biologic function, or the *H. transformans* lacked the genetic capability to support the transformation.

On rare occasions, something useful emerged from human and animal experimentation. The hybrid survived with features that Rex Cassius found desirable. Those with the potential to terrorize were transported to a village or settlement for a test run. The gamekeepers would release them and observe people's reaction and the effectiveness of the hybrid's attack. Rex lost many gamekeepers this way. In releasing these hybrids, the gamekeepers often came under attack themselves.

Nonviolent hybrid humanoids or those incapable of effective attacks went to villages within Cassius territory. They became forced laborers under grueling conditions. These were the humanoids H'Ilgraith found in Cassius villages and the ones whose suffering she tried to relieve at least a little bit.

An Aerial Attack

H'Ilgraith had been so focused on the fortress and the wagon, she was unaware that she had been spotted. A harpyacalgryph [hăr-pē-ă-căl-grĭf] (illustration 3), a hybrid aerial predator that had been released by the Cassius Foundation, had flown into the forest and settled in the canopy before H'Ilgraith arrived. Silent and motionless, it watched the arrival of the owl and noted where the bird had landed. As long as the harpyacalgryph remained still, the sharp-eyed owl would not see it. So it also watched and waited. An unwary owl would provide a fine snack for a hungry harpy.

The harpyacalgryph's base genome was the harpy eagle, one of the largest eagles and an apex predator. The Foundation's genetic engineers had modified the harpy's genetic code by adding the genes of a vulture to increase its wingspan. Yet in making the harpy's wings larger, the engineers had impeded its ability to fly through a dense forest canopy. In addition, they selected the genes of a caracal cat's canines to augment the raptor's native armaments—a sharp beak and powerful talons. In doing so, the engineers inadvertently gave the harpy the genes of the caracal cat's long, tufted, and tapered ears. They caught air, increasing friction and further hindering the creature's flight.

By:

Illustration 3: Harpyacalgryph

A native harpy could weigh up to twenty pounds, so it was considerably larger than a great horned owl. In open space, the owl would stand no chance against the eagle. Within a dense canopy, it might.

With the owl's attention focused on the wagon, the harpyacalgryph lifted off and dived toward the owl. The fluttering of its larger wing feathers betrayed it. Alerted by the sound, the owl spotted the hybrid raptor plunging toward her.

H'Ilgraith knew immediately that her life was at stake. She abruptly took flight to dodge the attack. The harpyacalgryph banked to follow her. After several rounds of point and counterpoint—diving and banking and darting through the trees—H'Ilgraith realized the conditions under which the harpy gained on her or lagged. Sharp turns and narrow spaces hindered the larger bird. It lacked the maneuverability of the owl. If H'Ilgraith could reach denser foliage in the trees, she could fly into a narrow lane where the harpy could not follow.

Suddenly, a long snake struck out from a tree branch (illustration 4), snaring the harpy in its powerful coils. Unbeknownst to either bird, another predator, a moresistrurus [mōr-ā-sĭs-trū-rŭs)], had been watching the two of them dodging through the canopy where it lay in wait. It, too, was a hybrid—a tree python genetically engineered to have the fangs and venom of a viper. The Cassius Foundation had spliced the genes of an arboreal pit viper into the base genome of a green tree python. It was an ambush predator that could lurk in a tree, hidden by the foliage, to strike its unsuspecting prey.

The entire incident had left H'Ilgraith shaken. She had let down her guard and been nearly killed. The harpyacalgryph had almost caught her. The snake could just as easily have snared her and not the harpy. Time to go home, she decided. She had had enough excitement for one day—and the day was not over yet. Still, she had gathered a wealth of information to report, including two previously unknown animal hybrids.

Illustration 4: Moresistrurus

Part II
Destiny

CHAPTER 8
CALYPSO

While observing one of the Cassius villages, H'Ilgraith witnessed a humanoid having a series of seizures. They continued, one after another, until they finally ceased several minutes later. Although H'Ilgraith understood what was happening, there was nothing she could do. She knew that many seizures were transient. Once they stopped, the victim would recover. Yet after this humanoid became still, he never moved again. His body lay where it had fallen while other villagers stepped over it or walked around it. Village guards, who were humanoids themselves, finally dragged the body away. H'Ilgraith was shocked when she saw them throw it into a cage of animal hybrids, which promptly began feeding on it.

Later, H'Ilgraith reconciled the incident with the living conditions in a Cassius village. The humanoid was dead and past any more suffering. His body had simply been reclassified as a food source for others. Nevertheless, H'Ilgraith was dismayed by the callous disregard that other villagers had shown the fallen humanoid.

A Fragile Species

Ever since H'Ilgraith witnessed the seizure, she wanted to find *Calypso bulbosa,* more commonly known as the fairy slipper plant. Its roots purportedly would treat nervous disorders. H'Ilgraith wondered if it would treat seizures. She decided to bring the plant back to H'Aleth and grow it for its medicinal properties. First, she had to find it. Floberius described the plant to her and where it grew.

Floberius warned H'Ilgraith. "The calypso plant grows in cool, moist soils in forests close to mountains. It is a fragile orchid, easily damaged when disturbed. I'm not sure we have the right climate or soil to grow the plant here. More importantly, it depends on fungi in the soil where it grows. This is the primary reason why it fails when people try to transplant it. If you cut the flowers, the plant often dies," he added.

This could be an academic exercise, H'Ilgraith thought. "How much soil should I dig up around the plant to preserve it?" she asked.

"Its roots are fairly shallow and very delicate," Floberius answered. "I would suggest a root ball of at least six inches." He thought for a minute and then added, *"Calypso* needs bumblebees to pollinate it. The flower has a sweet scent that draws the bees to it. Since we have bumblebees, it might flourish if it can survive here."

A Sashay into Enemy Territory

H'Ilgraith thanked Floberius for his assistance and then began planning her search for calypso. The plant's only known source was deep in Cassius territory. So one day, outfitted with a knife and several robes in a satchel, H'Ilgraith transformed into an owl. She flew across the River Aguila and headed north following the river on its eastern shore (map 1). She slipped into Cassius territory just below the juncture of the River Pices with the River Feroxaper (known as the Aguila by H'Aletheans).

Once in Cassius territory, H'Ilgraith transformed into a gray fox. She tucked her robe in her satchel and carried it in her mouth as if it were prey. She traveled mostly from dusk to dawn. Since gray foxes can climb trees, during the day, she would scramble into a nearby tree with dense branches and heavy foliage. There, she could nestle high in the tree and rest.

H'Ilgraith continued to follow the Feroxaper along its eastern shore until she reached the confluence of the rivers Cassius and Taurus. There, she paused. As a fox, she could not swim across those waters. She would be swept away. The headwaters of the Taurus and the Cassius rivers were formed in the northern and eastern mountains, respectively. Their gradients led to rapid flow rates that resulted in violent turbulence where they merged.

Map 1: The Territories

KEY

☒ MAJOR ESTABLISHMENT
⬆ SMALL VILLAGE
▲ OUTPOST
HQ HEADQUARTERS
R&D RESEARCH AND
     DEVELOPMENT
M&S MARKETING AND
     SALES

Once again, H'Ilgraith climbed into a nearby tree, carrying her satchel. She transformed into an owl and waited until dusk. Once it was dark, she flew across the confluence. Even at night, she had to be careful to make her satchel look like prey. Although some animals could be trained to serve as couriers, owls were not among them. Anyone seeing an owl carrying a pouch or satchel would assume the animal was an *H. transformans* until proven otherwise—after it was shot down.

Once beyond the confluence, H'Ilgraith resumed her search for the calypso plant as a gray fox. In this form, she was well adapted to forested and mountainous terrains. Her keen vision and sensitive nose could seek out the pinkish-lavender flower and sweet scent of calypso.

H'Ilgraith had been traveling for several days. Periodically, she would transform into a badger and excavate a deep den where she could retreat to rest or seek safety. She would stow one of her robes in the den with some tubers and acorns for food. Eventually, she reached the montane zone, where the calypso plant was rumored to grow. A small cluster on the forest floor rewarded her search. *Finally*, she thought and transformed into a badger again.

The calypso plants grew too close together to dig them up individually. So H'Ilgraith excavated a substantial root ball around a cluster of the plants. It was larger and heavier than she had anticipated. Still, she could nudge it into her satchel with her muscular snout. Then she realized she would have to carry the plants back as a lynx.

H'Ilgraith's last den was not far. So she hid her satchel under dense cover close to an oak tree and scent-marked its location. She returned to her den and transformed into a lynx. Then she returned to the tree and scrambled up it to await nightfall. She would retrieve her satchel in darkness and begin her journey back to H'Aleth.

H'Ilgraith was quite pleased with herself. She had found the plants she wanted, and they were in good condition. Her search for them had given her a respite from the confines of the estate. And, last but not least, her journey had been relatively uneventful. *Perfect,* she thought.

She would not think so for long.

Supplemental Notes and Citations
Seizures

Seizure is a broad, umbrella term that describes a group of disorders characterized by abnormal discharges of electrical activity in the brain (Boss, 2010). These abnormal impulses not only interrupt brain function at the site of the disturbance, but they also may spread throughout the brain. Where these discharges occur in the brain—locally or globally—determines the outward manifestations, if any, of the abnormal activity.

There are two broad categories of seizures: epileptic and secondary. At one time, there was no known cause for epileptic (idiopathic) seizures. Secondary (nonepileptic) seizures are linked to a specific cause (e.g., injury, including traumatic brain injury; tumor; drugs; fever; infection; etc.). If the cause can be corrected, then the seizures will cease.

Genetic Epilepsy

Epileptic seizures have been linked to a variety of genetic disorders associated with gene mutations. More recently, research has identified genes directly associated with epilepsy (Brunklaus *et al.*, 2014; Nissenkorm *et al.*, 2015; Steinline, 2008; Tarquinio *et al.*, 2017). Mutations in the SCN1A gene cause approximately 80% of one type of genetic epilepsy (Dravet syndrome) (Jiang *et al.*, 2018; Lopez-Santiago & Issom, 2019; Medical Letter, 2018).

Genetic epilepsy also includes inherited forms of epilepsy (Helbig *et al.*, 2016; Hirose *et al.*, 2013; Myers & Mefford, 2015; Schutte *et al.*, 2016; Steinlein, 2008; Zhou *et al.*, 2018). Many inheritable epilepsy disorders are associated with gene mutations that alter neurotransmission in the brain. (Symonds *et al.*, 2017). Genetic testing is available for some epilepsy syndromes known to be associated with genetic mutations (Helbig & Lowenstein, 2013; Hirose *et al.*, 2013; Poduri, 2017; Zerem *et al.*, 2016).

CHAPTER 9
UNEXPECTED ENCOUNTERS

H'Ilgraith would have to wait several hours before nightfall. Late in the afternoon, she became restless and decided to leave early. Jumping down from the tree, she snatched up her satchel and began her journey back to H'Aleth. A short while later, she spotted a gray mountain wolf. The wolf also saw her. Wolves prey on lynx.

A Lone Wolf

Fortunately, wolves cannot climb trees. H'Ilgraith promptly dropped her satchel and bolted up a nearby oak. At the same time, the wolf launched after her. Once the wolf reached the base of the tree, the two were at a stalemate. For H'Ilgraith, it was a waiting game. She watched the wolf from her place on a large limb. *How long will the wolf keep watch?* she wondered. *Will its pack join it?* She was safe from wolves as long as she stayed in the tree; however, wolves were patient. She could be stuck there for a long time unless another prey species came along.

The wolf, a large male, weighed close to 150 pounds. H'Ilgraith noted that he had not called any other pack members. He might be a lone wolf. Lone or not, she knew it was highly unlikely that a twenty-two-pound cat would intimidate her adversary. Nevertheless, she did her best, hissing and growling at the wolf.

He was unimpressed.

I wonder what would happen if I scent-marked him? she asked herself. She did not get a chance to test this idea.

The wolf turned his attention to the satchel, while still keeping a watchful eye on the lynx. H'Ilgraith watched him as he sniffed the satchel thoroughly. Then he looked up at her and sat down. He showed no sign of aggression. H'Ilgraith knew that the wolf would have encountered many scents on her satchel—lynx, badger, owl, fox, calypso, and human. It suddenly occurred to her that he may not be a native wolf.

H'Ilgraith was alarmed at the prospect that the wolf could be an *H. transformans*. If so, he might be in the service of the Cassius Foundation. She realized she could not wait for him to make the next move. She had to escape as quickly as possible.

She could not outrun him on the ground and would never reach one of her dens in time. There were no nearby outcroppings where her agility on uneven surfaces would give her the advantage. She would have to fly out. So she ascended higher in the oak toward a cluster of branches that were thick with foliage. There, she settled down out of sight until she transformed once again into a great horned owl.

When H'Ilgraith peeked out from among the leaves, the wolf was still waiting patiently below, looking up into the tree. She had hoped he would give up when she disappeared. Alas, he had not been fooled. This only bolstered her suspicion that he was an *H. transformans*. Before taking flight, she surveyed the area for terrestrial and aerial predators. Her keen eyesight spotted a crouched figure slowly and carefully closing in on the wolf.

The figure was a theracapracanis [*thĕr*-ah-căp-rah-*căn*-ĭs], a large, catlike creature with the body of a leopard (illustration 5). It had two spiked horns angled forward to gore its opponent and exaggerated canines to rend flesh. H'Ilgraith had never seen such a creature and had no doubt Cassius geneticists had crafted it.

When the creature's shoulders hunched down, as if to launch an attack, H'Ilgraith instinctively shrieked a warning. This drew the attention of both the wolf and the theracapracanis. The latter recognized it had been spotted and immediately launched its attack on the still-unsuspecting wolf. At first, the wolf thought the owl was screaming at him. When she abruptly took flight, he ducked as the bird flew past him. When he turned to follow her, he saw the hybrid heading straight for him. He reacted immediately and countered with an attack of his own. With the element

Illustration 5: Theracapracanis

By:

of surprise lost, the theracapracanis had no chance to ambush the wolf. Upon facing combat with a more powerful predator, it turned away and fled, the wolf pursuing it. The wolf was gaining on it until it leaped into a tree and climbed high into the branches.

For a moment, the wolf watched the hybrid from a discreet distance. He did not want to be ambushed again should the creature decide to leap on top of him. It possessed a significant array of armaments that could well prove lethal. When it retreated further into the tree, the wolf darted back to the place where he had encountered the lynx that had become an owl. As expected, neither species was anywhere to be seen. He doubted he would see either one again. In all likelihood, the owl had used the encounter with the hybrid as a diversion and had flown away.

Watchful Waiting

Perhaps not, the wolf thought. The satchel was still where the lynx first dropped it. *I wonder whether she will return for it.* There was no doubt in his mind that the owl was a female *H. transformans* and a powerful one. So he found a nearby place under cover, where he could settle down to watch and wait. He knew his wait might be a long one. Both the lynx and the owl were nocturnal. If the satchel's owner returned, it would likely be at night. He was right.

During the wolf's wait, many forest denizens passed by the satchel. Most were small mammals—mainly rodents. A fox sniffed at it briefly and then moved on. A trio of mule deer approached the area before catching his scent and bolting away. The wolf also remained alert to the possibility that the hybrid theracapracanis might return. It was the middle of the night when he spotted the outline of a low, stocky body waddling cautiously toward the satchel. Its greenish-yellow eyes betrayed its approach. The wolf recognized its shape, scent, and eyes. Although he could overpower the animal, he wanted to see what it would do. So the wolf remained still, expecting the badger to examine the satchel briefly and then move on. Not so.

After approaching the satchel gingerly, the badger suddenly grasped the satchel in its mouth, then turned and ran away with it. The wolf vaulted from his position to head off the badger. He easily overtook it and leaped over it. He landed a few feet ahead of the badger and turned around to confront it. Other than barring the badger's way, the wolf made no aggressive moves. For a moment, the two of them were at a stalemate—again.

H'Ilgraith mentally kicked herself for going back to get the calypso. Yet she had not expected either a native wolf or an *H. transformans* to wait so long for her return. Now she was stuck. She could not outrun him. She could not dig a den without turning her back on him. If she tried to transform, she would be completely vulnerable, even at her level of ability. So she was not going to fly away.

H'Ilgraith realized something else. The wolf was still alone. Had he been an agent of Cassius, he would have been joined by a host of other agents, searching far and wide for her.

H'Ilgraith decided to take a chance with this wolf. A den that housed a robe was not far away. Carrying the satchel in her mouth, the badger took a few steps at an angle that would take her around the wolf's position. Then she stopped and looked at him. The wolf had not moved. Then she took a few more steps, shifting to a place around the side of the wolf, and stopped again to watch him. At that point, the wolf turned to match her heading. When she took a few more steps, he did the same, keeping abreast of her. After a few more practices in the same vein, both began the trip back to her den. They encountered no adversaries or other threats along the way.

A Gallant Wolf

When the two of them reached her den, H'Ilgraith backed into it. She deliberately left the satchel sitting at its entrance. In this manner, she signaled that she was not running away. The satchel also would serve to alert her. If it suddenly disappeared, she would know that something was amiss.

Like all of H'Ilgraith's dens, it was somewhat larger than a native badger's den. A slender human could crawl into or out of it. Yet it was not large enough for a major predator. If the wolf suddenly decided to assault her in her den, he would have to dig into it headfirst.

The wolf knew better than to attack a badger in its den. So he waited outside. *What animal will emerge next?* he wondered. So far, he had seen a lynx, a great horned owl, and a badger. He had smelled gray fox on the satchel as well as human scent.

For her part, H'Ilgraith had to decide whether it was better to remain as a badger, which had powerful jaws and claws but lacked speed, or become a lynx, enabling her to run much faster and climb trees. Having come this far, she did not want to transform into an owl and fly away without her prize. *This wolf has not been aggressive and has not made any contact calls. What does he want?* she wondered. *Who is he?*

Proper introductions would have to wait. H'Ilgraith needed to recover after transforming from badger to lynx to owl and back to a badger again. Multiple transformations from one alternate species into another had left her drained. So she settled down in her den for a brief rest. Her transformation back into a lynx could wait a little while. As a lynx, she was better equipped for both offense and defense, and she could keep pace with the wolf. *I have no doubt he will still be waiting outside*, she thought as she slipped into unconsciousness.

When nothing emerged from the den's entrance after quite some time, the wolf decided to investigate. As soon as he sniffed it, he detected a human scent. He also heard the sound of quiet breathing with no sounds of any other movement. *She is an H. transformans,* he recognized. His suspicions confirmed, he put his back to the entrance and began his watch.

When H'Ilgraith awoke, she saw something blocking the entrance to her den. It was the wolf with his back to her. *He's guarding the den*, H'Ilgraith realized, much to her surprise. Another surprise awaited her when she realized to her chagrin that she had transformed back into a human—not a lynx. She quickly reached for her robe.

The wolf heard H'Ilgraith stir. He got up and stretched, relaxed, and strolled away from the den without looking back. *A gallant wolf,* H'Ilgraith decided.

H'Ilgraith packed her robe in her satchel. It would not do to remain in human form. As a human, she had brought only a small knife and lacked the offensive weapons available to her alternate species. When she emerged from her den, she was a lynx again. She carried the satchel in her mouth, an indication that she was not being aggressive, and began walking toward home.

Now where is she going? the wolf wondered. He decided to tag along.

CHAPTER 10
A TACIT TRUCE

H'Ilgraith headed home. A day had already passed with the plants out of the ground, and she was anxious to transplant them before their roots dried out. She had already identified a place in the woods near the estate where they might thrive.

Keeping Pace

Since the wolf seemed determined to tag along, H'Ilgraith quickened her pace to a leisurely trot. The wolf promptly did the same. A few moments later, H'Ilgraith broke into a lope. Undaunted, the wolf kept pace. Unfortunately, this pace was jostling the plants too much. H'Ilgraith was obliged to slow down. So she stopped and sat.

The surprised wolf ran past her a few paces before turning around to face the lynx. Then he, too, sat down. At this point, H'Ilgraith was fairly certain the wolf was not a threat to her. Yet he could still be a threat to her people. *Perhaps he is an agent of Cassius or Biogenics after all and is only following me to find out where I live. Then he would notify his master where to find us.* H'Ilgraith knew that she must find out the wolf's intentions before going any farther.

H'Ilgraith started to walk away, looking back at the wolf so he would follow her. She sought out another of the many dens she had excavated. When she reached it, she ducked inside it. A badger is about as hefty as a lynx, if somewhat shorter. So a lynx could slip into a badger's den, if necessary. Once again, the wolf could not follow.

H'Ilgraith settled inside the den and transformed back into a badger while the wolf sat outside and waited. When the head of a badger popped out, the wolf thought it prudent to back away a few steps. When the rest of the badger emerged, she began enlarging the den and the entrance to it—extensively.

H'Ilgraith was thoroughly annoyed. This wolf was costing her precious time and a great deal of extra effort. As she remodeled the den and the entrance to it, dirt flew everywhere with considerable force. H'Ilgraith paid no attention to where it landed. *If it smacks the wolf, he can get out of the way,* she growled to herself. He promptly did so.

When she finished, H'Ilgraith issued an invitation. The wolf accepted it and entered the den. *Now what?* he wondered. He watched as the badger pawed a robe from its stash and tossed it toward him. Then she plucked another robe from her satchel and climbed into it. She lay down and curled up inside it.

The wolf understood. The badger was going to transform again. *Into what? Perhaps she will resume human form,* he thought. *We need to talk.* When he saw a chrysalis begin to form around the badger's body, he decided to transform as well. *I'm taking a big risk,* he thought as he drifted into unconsciousness.

Introductions

When the man awoke a short time later, a woman was still sleeping beside him. *She must be exhausted,* he thought. Like most robes for *H. transformans,* their robes contained ample material to shelter a transformation. A badger's den, however, is not so accommodating. The man tried to stretch out as much as he could in such cramped quarters. His stirring roused H'Ilgraith.

"My name is Jak," he said, "short for Jakovic" [*jak*-ō-vĭc].

H'Ilgraith came right to the point. "Why are you following me?"

"A pleasure to meet you, too," Jak replied. "First of all, this is my territory," he claimed.

Typical wolf, thought H'Ilgraith.

"I know it well," Jak continued, "including most of the wildlife that lives here, the villages where humans live, and the human travelers who frequently pass through it. You are not one of them, and I want to know what you are doing in my territory.

"Second, native lynx and badgers do not carry satchels. An *H. transformans* serving as a courier might. That was my initial suspicion, and I wanted to find out who you served and what message or documents you carried. When I smelled plants instead of parchment or paper in the satchel, I became curious." Jak then asked bluntly, "What is your name, and where are you from?"

H'Ilgraith considered Jak for a moment. Had he been a bounty hunter or an agent of Cassius or Biogenics, she would have been captured or killed long before now. Still, she remained unsure of him and did not offer her name or her origin. "I am a healer. The plant I carry is rumored to have healing properties," she replied.

"That is not what I asked," Jak remarked firmly. *Stubborn badger,* he thought. He was no more certain of H'Ilgraith than she was of him.

Then H'Ilgraith said, "I have no wish to intrude further on your territory. I will leave you in peace if you will do the same for me."

Jak considered H'Ilgraith's proposal. With a silent sigh, he said, "You can leave whenever you are ready. You should know that the Cassius Foundation claims this territory—and everyone and everything in it. Their bounty hunters are always on the prowl. They won't hesitate to ensnare a lone human female in the hopes she is an *H. transformans.*" Then he added, "I will escort you as far as my territory extends. Since predators and prey cannot be seen fraternizing, we should remain as humans while traveling together."

"Thank you," H'Ilgraith replied. She accepted Jak's offer with reservation. She had no way of knowing whether his offensive capabilities as a human were a match for her skills and training. She would have to remain wary and alert. *He carries no weapons,* she noted.

"As humans, we are still vulnerable to attack by other humans, hybrids, and even some native animals," H'Ilgraith remarked. "I recommend we carry some form of weaponry. I have a knife and can fashion a bow and quiver and make arrows."

"As can I," Jak said.

Partners

So both travelers began to gather the materials they would use. The forest provided the resources they needed. Small, flexible limbs of a maple would do for a bow. Slender, stiff branches of an oak would become arrow shafts. Pliable, tensile roots became bowstrings. Small granite chips with sharp edges served as arrowheads. Broad hosta leaves were intertwined to form a quiver.

Finding material for the arrows' fletching proved more problematic. Both of them began to search for a bird's nest. They found several; however, only scattered bits of down and degraded contour feathers remained. Finally, H'Ilgraith spotted a crow's nest high in the branches of a tall oak. Crow feathers are flexible, yet they will hold their shape. They could be trimmed and used for fletching.

Weary or not, H'Ilgraith would have to transform into an owl again to reach the nest. To her surprise, Jak said, "I'll get them."

Jak scampered up a neighboring tree with low-lying branches. When he reached a point where branches of both trees overlapped, he jumped to the tall oak and continued his climb. He reached the nest without difficulty and found several suitable contour feathers. On the way back, he didn't bother transferring to the other tree. He scooted partway down the oak's trunk, then jumped the rest of the way, landing on both feet.

He is certainly adept at climbing trees, thought H'Ilgraith.

Using her knife, H'Ilgraith fashioned a bow and arrow shafts. Jak trimmed and smoothed roots into several bow strings. The roots would not withstand the strain placed upon them for long; hence, he needed to fashion as many bowstrings as arrows.

Both worked in silence as they focused on the task at hand. A few hours later, their partnership had resulted in two bows and a half dozen arrows. Of necessity, their newly forged weapons were small; nevertheless, they would be effective at close range.

H'Ilgraith began to wonder who Jak was. She, too, had become curious. . .

CHAPTER 11
IMMANIS

Given the possibility of encountering bounty hunters, both Jak and H'Ilgraith needed to be careful. They left as few traces of their passing as possible and stayed alert. Fortunately, both enjoyed enhanced visual acuity and hearing, courtesy of their respective alternate species. Not long after they began their trek, both stopped abruptly and stood perfectly still.

An Alliance

Hearing the sound of distant footfalls, Jak recognized the timpani of hunters' boots as they struck the ground. Villagers always walked softly. "Hunters," Jak whispered. "Four of them, headed our way." There was no time to transform. "Can you climb trees?"

"Of course," H'Ilgraith replied firmly.

"Then we should get into the canopy as quickly as possible," replied Jak. He pointed to a suitable tree nearby and motioned for H'Ilgraith to begin climbing it. While she went up into the tree, Jack retraced their steps for several yards and scattered any evidence of their passing. Afterward, he joined H'Ilgraith in the foliage of the tree. There, they waited, motionless and silent, as four armed men came into view. The men passed by, unaware they had been detected.

Jak and H'Ilgraith remained in the tree for several minutes after the hunters' footsteps had faded. Then Jak said abruptly, "I have to go. An encampment of villagers, all *H. transformans,* is just a few miles away," he explained. "I have to warn them that hunters are heading toward them. Once I transform, I can reach them in a few minutes. Wait here in the tree. I will come back for you."

"I will do nothing of the sort countered H'Ilgraith emphatically. "I, too, will transform and follow you in the air. As an owl, I can keep the hunters in sight and track their progress. If they detect you or the villagers, I will call out a warning. If they move away from you or the villagers, I will sound a soft hoot."

Once the two of them had transformed, Jak jumped out of the tree. H'Ilgraith followed quickly in flight. For the moment, they had forged an alliance against a common enemy. Jak raced toward the village while H'Ilgraith followed in the air, looking for any hunters along Jak's path. When Jak arrived at the camp, most of the residents recognized him. When he growled and stamped his feet, then started to head away from the camp, they understood. They had just enough time to gather a few belongings and flee through the woods. A short time later, smoke could be seen rising from what had once been their camp.

A Restless Mountain

H'Ilgraith followed Jak as he trotted to a dense area heavy with undergrowth. It sheltered them as both transformed into humans again.

"We need to leave this area. Those hunters will be back with reinforcements," said Jak. "I suggest we head toward the mountains. Crossing over one of the higher passes will reduce the likelihood of encountering hunters. Several passes are difficult to cross and see little human traffic." Jak thought for a moment and then added a warning. "We will need to be careful. The mountain is restless. We can expect rockslides." A canyon was created long ago by a slip fault, which had continued to shift. Over time, many earthquakes had created a deep subsidence in the earth—the canyon pass.

Given their new route, they transformed again: Jak became a wolf and H'Ilgraith a lynx. Both species would have greater speed and agility, superior visual acuity and hearing, and more power. In doing so, however, both sacrificed the protection of a bow and quiver of arrows. Nevertheless, the satchel H'Ilgraith carried still held a steel knife hidden among their robes and the calypso plants.

While traveling along a ravine, both H'Ilgraith and Jak felt earth tremors. Jak knew these mountains well. Although this was not an uncommon occurrence, these tremors were stronger than usual. So the two picked up their pace as they kept a sharp eye on the nearby slopes. It would be best to get through the canyon as expeditiously as possible. Both of them became alarmed when they saw a large boulder shift and several rocks spill down the slopes.

Fearful of an impending earthquake, the wolf and lynx raced through the ravine. They had to get out of the canyon. At the very least, it seemed as though a major rock slide was inevitable, and there was no way to predict when or where it might occur. Since they had reached the point of no return, they had to continue through the canyon.

Before long, they heard low-pitched, deep rumblings echoing through the canyon. They also noticed that the wind had increased substantially, punctuated by short gale-like gusts that ruffled their coats and buffeted their ears. It felt like an impending storm, yet the sky was clear. There were only a few fair-weather clouds. As the rumblings became louder, more stones fell, and more boulders shifted.

A Duel of Titans

As they rounded a westward bend of the canyon, both H'Ilgraith and Jak skidded to a stop. The canyon's western entrance lay straight ahead of them. So did the cause of the rumblings, tremors, and wind gusts. Two adult male great gray dragons were battling each other—biting, clawing, lashing with their tails, and using the walls of the canyon to launch at each other (illustration 6).

Their assaults were ferocious, and their open wounds were evident. This was more than a test of strength or a fight for dominance. These two dragons were engaged in mortal combat. Yet there was no fire. H'Ilgraith realized later that, if the two dragons had fought each other with fire, they would have incinerated each other.

H'Ilgraith spotted what she thought might be the reason for the fight and nudged Jak. Close by lay the body of a young female gray dragoness. Gray dragons do not kill members of their own clan. H'Ilgraith suspected that one of the two embattled adults was the villain—a rival from another clan who had killed the dragoness. *Immanis*, she thought. *A monstrous beast.*

Illustration 6: A Duel of Titans

H'Ilgraith and Jak could see the canyon walls sloping away at the entrance, yet they could not reach them. They could not go forward, they could not go back, and they could not climb up the unstable canyon slopes. They were trapped between the crumbling walls of the ravine with the two behemoths waging war upon each other. All they could do was watch out for falling debris and keep their distance from the dragons.

The fight ended abruptly as one combatant struck a crippling blow to the head of his adversary and broke its neck. The stricken dragon crashed to the ground and did not rise again. The victor watched and waited for a moment, then raised his head, mouth open wide, in what appeared to be a triumphant roar. Yet the two travelers only heard a deep rumble. Suddenly, the vibrations from the dragon's throat loosed several stones, and multiple rocks crashed down from the canyon walls.

As if to put a finishing touch to his victory, the dragon climbed the walls of the canyon, exciting even more rocks to fall. He reached a massive boulder, which sat above his dead opponent. He worked it loose, and it fell to the canyon floor. The resounding crash not only crushed the slain dragon but also triggered a rock slide. H'Ilgraith and Jak scrambled to avoid being struck by flying debris.

The surviving dragon then lifted off and settled beside the dead dragoness. As he did so, he spotted the wolf and the lynx. He looked directly at them for a moment and then turned away. He picked up the young dragoness in his mouth, as carefully as he could, and flew away.

Finally, H'Ilgraith and Jak could continue their journey—over a canyon floor littered with rocks, boulders, and other debris. *Great*, thought Jak. Then the surefooted lynx plotted a course through the clutter, which the wolf could traverse without too much difficulty. Once again, their partnership served them well.

When they were past the debris field, Jak decided it was time for some fun. Looking at H'Ilgraith, he raised one paw and cocked his head toward the end of the canyon. The lynx poised herself for a run, and then both of them bolted for the end of the canyon. The wolf won the race, of course.

A Leap of Faith

After their frightening passage through the canyon, Jak and H'Ilgraith sought out a place to rest awhile. They spotted a tangled clump of brush barely large enough for both of them to scratch their way inside it and lie down. It provided just enough cover to hide their presence and just enough room for a lynx and a wolf to wedge themselves inside it. It would not do for anyone to see the two of them lying together. Once again, the wolf turned his back to the lynx. There, they stayed until dusk when both emerged to resume their trek.

H'Ilgraith set out at a brisk pace matched by Jak. They continued at that pace until shortly after daybreak, when the wolf stopped and stood alone. This time it was the lynx's turn to be surprised. H'Ilgraith stopped and turned to look back at Jak. When she motioned for him to follow her, he did not move. After a minute, he turned around and began to walk away. H'Ilgraith realized they had reached—and probably breached—the boundary of his territory. She yowled at him and ran back to sit down in front of Jak, blocking him for a change.

Now what? Jak wondered.

I must be out of my mind, thought H'Ilgraith. Yet she had found Jak companionable and had grown accustomed to his presence. She walked up to him and motioned for him to continue traveling with her.

The wolf looked at the lynx for a moment. *I must be out of my mind,* Jak thought, as he turned to resume their journey. Both of them were taking a leap of faith to stay together.

CHAPTER 12
Fellow Travelers

By now, both Jak and H'Ilgraith were hungry and thirsty. They hastened to reach the denser forest below the canyon where they would find better cover. Shortly thereafter, they heard and smelled a freshwater mountain stream nearby and headed straight for it.

Fishing Lessons

The stream was fairly wide and not very deep at its shoreline. Its bank, lined with a narrow strip of sand, became rocky as it reached the water's edge. Fresh water flowed briskly downstream, and trout could be seen swimming with the current.

After sating their thirst, both Jak and H'Ilgraith decided that fish was on the menu. As a wolf, Jak was not averse to getting his feet wet. So he stepped into the cold water and began trying to nab a fish in his mouth. After several unsuccessful attempts, he moved to a different spot and tried again.

H'Ilgraith had watched Jak's efforts. When he moved away, she took over his spot while staying on the rocks. As a lynx, she preferred not to get her feet wet. A minute or so later, a swift swipe with a front paw hooked a fish. Grabbing it in her mouth, she returned to the shoreline, dropped the fish on the sand, and went back to the same spot. A few minutes later, she snagged another fish.

Long ago, H'Ilgraith had been obliged to learn how to fish on her long sojourns away from H'Aleth. All of her alternate species ate fish—especially the lynx and the great horned owl. The sharp, curved claws of a lynx and the talons of a raptor served her well. So she had become quite proficient in catching fish. Wolves, however, have relatively straight and blunted claws: their canines were better suited to snatch fish.

H'Ilgraith's success did not go unnoticed. Jak decided he would use a similar method. He began swiping at passing fish with his paw. When this procedure failed to work, he invented the swipe and bite technique. This only netted him a face full of water from his paw combined with the splash of an escaping trout. In the meantime, H'Ilgraith had snared yet another fish.

Thoroughly frustrated, Jak abandoned his effort and looked at H'Ilgraith. She took pity on him and, with a soft mew, beckoned him to join her feast.

An Odiferous Encounter

The two travelers had progressed well below the timberline and had reached territory that H'Ilgraith knew well. The region was completely new to Jak, and he wanted to explore it. So they did. Since it was sparsely inhabited, a wolf and a lynx could continue to travel together as long as they remained alert for any signs of human activity.

For the most part, H'Ilgraith followed Jak's lead as he explored the new terrain. This was not purely curiosity. Jak was making sure he knew the features of the area, which species inhabited it—especially other wolves—where he could find water and shelter, and how to find his way back again. From time to time, H'Ilgraith would issue a quiet call and signal a change in direction if they were traveling too far off course.

Late one innocuous afternoon, Jak crossed an animal he had not encountered in his territory. It looked a little bit like a badger. It had black fur with a white stripe starting from the top of its head that branched into two stripes, one along each side of its body, until they converged again at the base of the animal's tail. It had long foreclaws, not unlike those of a badger. *Probably used for digging*, Jak mused. This animal was more slender than a typical badger, and it had a tapered snout and a long, furry tail. *Perhaps it's a different species of badger*, he thought. As he moved closer, the animal became acutely aware of his presence. It turned to face him with a growl and raised its tail in a threatening posture.

H'Ilgraith immediately yowled a warning to Jak. She was well aware of this animal's defenses. One of her countrymen could transform into one. Jak turned his attention to the lynx and saw her backing away. He couldn't believe it. A lynx was retreating from an animal barely half her size. When he looked back at the animal, Jak was astounded that it was turning its back on a wolf easily ten times its size.

H'Ilgraith virtually screeched a yowl at Jak and bolted in the opposite direction. Jak couldn't understand it. Still, he turned around and ran after her. As he did so, he was nearly overwhelmed by a terrible, nauseating smell and the sensation of a wet substance striking his flank.

It was days before the odor of the skunk's musk faded. H'Ilgraith refused to get near him until the smell had diminished considerably. That was Jak's first encounter with a skunk, and he sincerely hoped it would be the last.

A Hidden Haven

After crossing into H'Aleth territory, H'Ilgraith located one of her dens, where she had stowed supplies. She ducked inside and, a minute later, came out with a robe for Jak. After she reentered the den, they both transformed into humans so they could finally converse again. As H'Ilgraith and Jak traveled through the northwest region of H'Aleth, known to H'Aletheans as the Caput Canis, H'Ilgraith came to a stop.

"Have you ever explored a cavern?" she asked Jak.

"I have," Jak replied. "Why do you ask?"

"There is a large, complex limestone cavern not far from here," she explained. "It is one of my favorite haunts. Would you like to see it?"

"I would," replied Jak, intrigued. So H'Ilgraith and Jak diverted from their appointed path. A few hours later, H'Ilgraith showed Jak an unimposing hole in the ground covered by vegetation. A shallow subsidence led to a passageway into the cavern. It was large enough for a fox to slip inside, but not a wolf or an adult human.

"You can't go," H'Ilgraith suddenly exclaimed. "The passageway is too narrow and steep," she said, clearly disappointed.

"Yes, I can," Jak replied. "I can change into a gray fox, which has come in handy on several occasions."

A short time later, two gray foxes slipped into the passageway.

H'Ilgraith had roamed in that cavern for many years and knew it well. Generations ago, it had sheltered a host of people and the many species of plants and animals they had brought with them after a gamma-ray burst struck Earth. Most living organisms directly exposed to gamma radiation perished. Those able to shelter deep underground in caves or caverns or in the ocean depths survived. Organisms with robust DNA repair mechanisms (extremophiles) also weathered exposure to the radiation.

The cavern itself was not without its perils. Many animals entering the passage would have quite a slide, careening down its length and encountering a rather rough landing at the end. Injuries were not uncommon. Two gray foxes, however, could traverse it without difficulty, even carrying their robes. Their claws were sharp and curved. Although designed for digging a den, they also provided traction. Once inside, however, both humans and animals could get lost in the cavern system. If they did not find their way back or could not be found, they would die. Others fell to their deaths after slipping into an unseen chasm.

The shallow passageway allowed barely enough light into the first room, where iridescent minerals were embedded in the cavern's walls. In the dim light, Jak saw H'Ilgraith trot a short way into the cavern and reach an outcropping. When she scratched the surface, a large patch of minerals lit up. She looked back at Jak and then curled up in her robe.

Jak recognized that she was going to transform again. *Into what species this time?* he wondered. *Human, I guess.* So Jak did the same.

When Jak awoke, he could hear the rustle of H'Ilgraith's robe. She had found the matchbox and hurricane lamp that she had brought years ago. She struck a match and lit a candle housed in the lamp. Suddenly, iridescent minerals lit up the room. Jak found it both eerie and surreal. *It's like looking out into the galaxy,* he thought.

"I hear water flowing and splashing," Jak said.

"An underground river flows through the cavern," responded H'Ilgraith. "Follow me and stay up against the wall," she admonished.

Using the hurricane lamp to light their way, they inched down a narrow passageway into the cavern system. It was pitch black everywhere else. When the wall they were hugging turned to the right, they had entered another room. Once again, the room fluoresced in the candlelight. Jak saw a waterfall spilling over a ledge near the top of the room with the glitter of minerals shining behind it. It was spectacular. He understood why H'Ilgraith liked to come here. It was peaceful. It also gave a false sense of security.

"I'm not the only one who has ever found this place," H'Ilgraith said as she recounted its history. "Both human and animal bones are found here. Still, the lack of natural light and narrow passageways have kept this room and the rest of the cavern a safe and undisturbed haven."

On the way back, Jak saw why they had to hug the wall. To get in or out, they had to pass a deep chasm, where another waterfall had flowed long ago. The ledge had enough room for a slender fox to slip in and out without too much risk. A much larger human needed to be very careful.

To return to the surface, Jak and H'Ilgraith had to transform back into foxes. They used their claws to climb the steep slope. It was a difficult climb, which explained why some visitors to the cavern never got out again.

Supplemental Notes and Citations
Extremophiles

Extremophiles are organisms capable of surviving and even thriving in environments once considered incompatible with life (Coker, 2016; Rampelloto, 2013). These include extremes of temperature, high levels of ionizing radiation (e.g., gamma rays), loss of all water from tissues (desiccation), and lack of oxygen (hypoxia) (Hashimoto & Kunieda, 2017; Jung et al., 2017; Makarova et al., 2001; Omelchenko et al., 2005; Pavlopoulou et al., 2016; Singh et al., 2013). They survive because they have developed antioxidant systems that protect them from tissue damage and sophisticated DNA repair mechanisms. Consequently, their cells do not die, their structures remain intact, and they do not develop genetic mutations. Yeast, a single-celled organism, can repair DNA damage within three hours

(Makarova *et al.*, 2001; Singh *et al.*, 2013). Research using DNA sequencing technologies is underway to discover how these repair mechanisms work.

Although most extremophiles are single-celled organisms, some multicellular animals (eukaryotes) can survive under extreme conditions. Tardigrades (e.g., *Milnesium tardigradum*) are microscopic invertebrate animals with species that thrive in extremes of temperature, radiation, and desiccation on Earth, and even in outer space (Beltrán-Prado *et al.*, 2015; Hashimoto & Kunieda, 2017; Nelson, 2002).

Effects of Ionizing Radiation

Ionizing radiation (e.g., gamma rays) is highly penetrating energy that can strip electrons from organic atoms and molecules (Xue *et al.*, 2009; Rendic & Guengerich, 2012). This action has both direct and indirect effects on cells and their DNA (Desouky *et al.*, 2015; Reisz *et al.*, 2014; Rendic & Guengerich, 2012). Direct effects occur when ionizing radiation strikes the cell, disrupting DNA, breaking chromosomes, and producing free radicals (e.g., reactive oxygen species and reactive nitrogen species).

Free radicals are charged particles, formed when ionizing radiation interacts with cell water. They are also highly reactive and cause the indirect effects of radiation, including damage to DNA and other cellular constituents (lipids and proteins). Injured cells can release free radicals into surrounding tissues, thereby spreading damage to cells that were not directly affected by the radiation.

The degree of damage depends upon the type of radiation (high versus low energy), how much radiation was released, the duration of the exposure, and the availability of DNA repair mechanisms (Reisz *et al.*, 2014).

DNA Repair Mechanisms

DNA breaks are not uncommon. If left unrepaired, they can lead to the transfer of DNA from one chromosome to another (translocations), carcinogenic changes, and cell death (Ceccaldi *et al.*, 2016.) Hence, DNA repair mechanisms are critical for maintaining the integrity of DNA sequences. There are mechanisms for reversing malformed, damaged, and or mutated DNA (Brooker, 2009d). Enzymes (e.g., endonucleases) remove the affected component (base pair, segment) while other enzymes make a new base pair (DNA polymerase) and reinsert it into its proper place (DNA ligase).

Double-stranded DNA breaks are more dangerous; however, they can be repaired as long as one member of the chromosome pair is undamaged (homologous recombination [Figure 1]) (Brooker, 2009d; Jasin & Rothstein, 2013; Moore *et al.*, 2014; Xue *et al.*, 2009). The damaged segment of DNA in the broken chromosome is excised. The comparable segment of DNA in the undamaged sister chromosome (chromatid) is temporarily excised and relocated to the broken chromosome. Enzymes that normally replicate DNA (e.g., DNA polymerase) make a copy of the substitute. The damage is repaired, and the borrowed DNA is returned

Fig. 1. Double-stranded DNA Repair Mechanisms:
Homologous Recombination

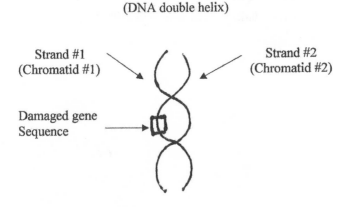

Chromosome
(DNA double helix)

Strand #1
(Chromatid #1)

Strand #2
(Chromatid #2)

Damaged gene
Sequence

to its original chromosome.

Figure 1: Double-stranded DNA Repair Mechanisms:

Homologous Recombination

In a DNA double helix, two complementary strands of DNA are loosely bound to each other and twisted around a single axis along their length. When a segment of DNA is damaged, an endonuclease can cut into the strand and separate a damaged DNA segment (e.g., a nucleotide) to allow editing or excision of the affected segment.

In homologous recombination, DNA polymerases make a copy of the corresponding DNA segment on the sister strand to use as a pattern (template) for making a new copy for the affected strand. Once the new copy is made, DNA ligase reattaches the newly fashioned DNA segment on both ends. The DNA strand is restored.

Rad51 is one of several proteins that are essential for homologous recombination in both somatic (mitotic division) and reproductive (meiotic division) cells (Machida *et al.*, 2015, Sung *et al.*, 2008, Vispe *et al.*, 1998.). It, too, is highly conserved, from yeast to humans (Sung *et al.*, 2008; Tashiro *et al.*, 2000; Vispe *et al.*, 1998). Rad51 directs the homologous exchange between the two DNA strands (Machida *et al.*, 2014; Prakash *et al.*, 2015). It works in conjunction with the tumor suppressor genes BRCA1, BRCA2, and p53 to stabilize genes and prevent mutations (Kolinjivadi *et al.*, 2017; Tashiro *et al.*, 2000). It also increases resistance to radiation damage in mammalian cells (Vispe *et al.*, 1998).

CHAPTER 13
JAK

After H'Ilgraith and Jak emerged from the cavern, they became a lynx and a wolf again to continue their journey. H'Ilgraith took Jak to a village where they could find human resources. Although the wolf was unknown, H'Ilgraith was recognized immediately. The villagers offered both of them a place to resume human form, fresh clothing, food, and shelter.

When H'Ilgraith, the consummate loner, returned with an unknown companion, word spread rapidly. This was unprecedented. Once the two travelers reached the estate, H'Ilgraith immediately sought out Weston and H'Assandra to introduce them to Jak.

H'Assandra, a bit more politic than her cousin, greeted Jak graciously. "I am H'Assandra, H'Ilgraith's cousin," she said. "This is Weston, our chief of security. Welcome to H'Aleth."

"Jak," answered Jak, shaking hands first with H'Assandra and then with Weston. "A pleasure to meet you," he said. Then he asked, "Who is H'Ilgraith?"

H'Assandra stood quietly and looked at H'Ilgraith, mentally shaking her head at her cousin.

"I am," answered H'Ilgraith.

Jak couldn't help himself. He burst out laughing and then said, "Hi," to H'Ilgraith.

Addressing Jak, Weston said, "Please tell us about yourself."

A Migrant Life

Jak could not remember a time when his family was not on the move. His parents were migrants and would spend time in one place before moving somewhere else. When he was about five years old, he learned that his parents used this strategy in part to keep from being discovered.

In most cases, the family moved with the season. They would travel into the montane forest during late spring through early fall, then to the woodlands further south from late fall into early spring. As a general rule, winter weather was milder there, although heavy snow and blizzards could occur. This migratory pattern also followed seasonal migrations of several prey species, including deer. Both parents could transform into gray mountain wolves, and they usually hunted as a pair.

Hence, both Jak and his brother learned at a very early age how to forage for fruits, nuts, berries, and edible native plants, including herbs and mushrooms. They learned which trees provided bark, dried leaves, and twigs to make a smokeless fire; how to build a fire; and how to roast meat on a spit. They also learned how to patch the few clothes they owned.

When not living near a settlement, his mother and father spent most of their time as wolves, especially in the winter. Their heavy winter coats kept the entire family warm when they nestled together in an underground den or a cave before a small fire.

From late spring to early fall, both parents would be in human form unless they were on a hunt. During warmer weather, the parents would teach their children to read, write, and do arithmetic. They also taught them a wide range of vocational skills to enable them to live independently.

Haunted

When Jak and his brother were very young, the family would settle temporarily near loosely scattered settlements of people who were trying to eke out a living from the land. These settlements did not engage in any kind of commerce other than to trade among themselves. Some would grow a few vegetables or forage for food while others made products from native plants or the hides of native wildlife killed for food. Then they would exchange their goods and services for the items they needed.

Dwellings were small and made of dried, matted grass, sticks, and mud. Bedding consisted of leaves and dried grass. There was rarely a fire for warmth or cooking. The risk was too great. A fire might spread, or its smoke might alert hunters to their presence and location. There were no permanent structures of any kind. These people knew that one day, they might have to abandon everything they had and flee for their lives. They were *H. transformans* and lived under the constant threat of being captured and possibly killed by bounty hunters. Many villagers were haunted by past raids and the loss of family members.

"Not all people are friendly," Jak's mother warned them. "There are some who would do us harm, so we must be prepared to pack up and leave quickly and quietly." This was graphically illustrated late one night.

A Midnight Raid

A sudden commotion arose within the settlement one night, which aroused Jak and his family. They could hear shouts, screams, and cries coming from the village. Both of Jak's parents leaped up from their floor mats. "Get your brother up and ready to move—now!" his father ordered. As Jak did so, he saw his mother snatch up three satchels, a bow, a sheath of arrows, and two knives. One knife, a satchel, and the bow and arrows she gave to his father. The other knife she kept for herself. She gave Jak one of the satchels and slung the other one over her back. "Hold onto your brother," she whispered to Jak. "We must run."

There was no time for the two adults to transform into wolves. Had they done so, their flight would have been much faster. The children would have ridden on their backs, holding onto the supplies they took with them. Instead, the family had to flee on foot as quickly as they could with their two boys running with them.

Fortune favored the family. They had established their dwelling beyond the settlement's perimeter, opposite from where the attack had begun. Their distance from the settlement and the clamor raised by the assault covered their escape. As they fled, they did not look back. They stopped only as needed for the boys to catch their breath while their parents surveyed the territory.

Several hours later, they reached the foothills of the northern mountains and began the climb into them. Both parents were looking for an escarpment, rockslide, crevice, or cave that would provide sufficient cover and shelter—at least temporarily. Everyone needed to rest. They found an opening among some boulders that had fallen long ago, creating a narrow passageway between two massive rock fragments. Just before the family ducked inside the opening, they looked back. A stream of dark smoke was rising in the distance, drifting toward the east. They knew then that the settlement had been burned to the ground.

"Did anyone else escape?" Jak asked.

"We do not know," his father answered.

Jak heard his mother whisper, "I hope so."

Once inside, both parents unloaded the family's few belongings and bundled their children together for warmth. It was cold among the rocks, and the wind crept through the crevice into their makeshift den. Soon afterward, they settled down and curled up to transform. The children were not old enough to do so. Yet, they were quite familiar with the chrysalis that formed around each parent. Soon, both parents would emerge as wolves and surround their children with thick winter coats.

A Change in Direction

After their narrow escape, the family decided to avoid any settlements. Both their sons were old enough to participate in sustaining a place to live. The couple had decided not to have any more children. They both felt it was too dangerous, and the strain on resources could jeopardize the two they already had.

As they traveled, the parents searched for a quasi-permanent den within the montane forest. It needed to be large enough for the whole family, including two growing youngsters, secluded and readily camouflaged, and sufficiently remote for there to be little human traffic. As they ranged further into more mountainous terrain, the father stumbled on an opening to a cave hidden by an overhang.

A brief investigation revealed stale air, the faint sound of running water in the distance, and no other inhabitants such as bats.

"Perfect," said both parents.

Too dark and gloomy, thought their offspring. They would be met with a pleasant surprise. The family had stumbled onto the entryway into a limestone cavern. A rockslide long ago had created the cave when boulders tumbled down atop each other. The force of the blow had also collapsed a section of the ground under them, opening the cavern's entrance. Both parents investigated and found it uninhabited except for troglobites, which live only in caves and caverns. They also discovered many blind alleys. Once the parents had ascertained that there were no predators in the cavern, supervised romping was allowed in the area where a little light filtered in from the cave's entrance and illuminated the iridescent minerals dotting the walls.

Jak's parents had finally found a well-hidden and secure location to raise their family. They did not have to move again. Like his parents, Jak and his brother could transform into gray mountain wolves. Jak could also become a gray fox. When both became proficient at transforming, their parents taught them how to live as wolves. They needed to learn to do so. The family was much safer working as a pack, and there was less risk of suspicion if they acted like native wolves.

After both of Jak's parents died, he and his brother struck out on their own. Jak became a lone wolf. He, too, had a restless spirit.

An Impregnable Fortress

After Jak had provided an abbreviated history of his life, H'Ilgraith described her travels and what she had observed along the way. She reported the mound of decaying humanoid and animal hybrid corpses. Then she provided an abbreviated account of her encounter with Jak. She also described the battle between the two gray dragons.

"Although I do not know why, I always assumed any battles between dragons would be aerial contests," she said. "Apparently, not. These two were battling on the ground."

Later, she would learn that wings and talons could get tangled in aerial fights—much like those of eagles. If they could not separate, they would crash from a very high altitude—lethally for both combatants. By contrast, aerial tests of strength, endurance, agility, and nerve were quite common. Dragons often tested their skills by flying through narrow canyons or crevices or racing at high altitudes and diving at high speeds in a game of chase.

H'Ilgraith's description of the Cassius Foundation fortress—its location and external fortifications—engendered the most interest. "Unfortunately, I was unable to see the inside of the fortress," she told her listeners. "None of my alternate species could have approached it without being spotted. I regret I cannot tell you anything more about it," she said.

"I can," said Jak.

Jak described the interior of the fortress in great detail (appendix D). "There are barracks for soldiers, multiple storerooms for supplies and equipment, and an armory of weapons and ammunition. Another armory has a large furnace and many forges. There are cages for both wild animals and for the animal hybrids that guard the grounds. I don't know much about the research building except for the dungeon in its cellar." Jak sketched the layout of the fortress, including the structures inside it. "There is also a boathouse with several barges and a large scaffolding," he added.

"How did you come to know all of this?" asked Weston.

"I was a guest there," Jak replied with a hint of sarcasm. "I was trading at a small marketplace used by villagers, in a region contested by Cassius and Biogenics. Both *H. sapiens* and *H. transformans* could go there to barter for goods. I brought bows and arrows that I had made. I could always exchange these items for just about anything I wanted. While I was there, the marketplace was attacked by well-trained huntsmen."

"How do you know they were well-trained?" asked Weston quietly. He was still skeptical.

"By the way they were able to converge on the market without being detected," Jak replied. "They were light-footed and wore soft boots, so they made little sound. They approached downwind so that those of us with heightened senses could not detect their scent or hear their approach. They also knew where to focus their attack. They must have known that *H. transformans* would be found there, which means they also had good intelligence."

Still cautious, Weston asked, "How were you captured?"

"Everyone was caught completely off guard, including me," Jak answered ruefully. "The hunters came prepared to capture *H. transformans,* which meant capturing everyone. They brought large nets that they shot overhead using bows and arrows. This method ensnared several people at one time. I was one of them."

"Why did no one suspect you of being an *H. transformans?"* Weston asked.

"There was no time for me to transform—fortunately," Jak replied. "The bows and arrows I had brought for trade were taken by the hunters. Since it was clear the weapons were handmade, they assumed I was an *H. sapiens.* When we arrived at the fortress, I was immediately designated as a laborer. Laborers work everywhere in the fortress, except in the research building."

Still troubled by Jak's tale, Weston asked, "If the fortress is as impenetrable as H'Ilgraith suggests, how did you get out?"

"An underground resistance had been welling up for quite some time," Jak answered. "I was approached by another laborer who told me others were planning an escape. He asked if I wanted to join them."

Weston continued to quiz Jak. "What did you say?" he asked.

"I told him he was crazy," Jak answered. "The sheer number of animal hybrids on the grounds precluded anyone or any species from escaping. I had been there for almost four months—plenty of time to scout out the place. I couldn't find any place where even a mouse could escape. I'm a pretty good fighter as both a human and a wolf, but as a lone wolf, I would not be able to battle my way past the hybrids."

"Then how did you escape?" asked Weston.

Jak replied, "When I learned what they planned to do and met the man planning the breakout, I realized there was a chance for some people to get out." Jak paused for a minute and seemed to drift away. Then he said grimly, "Many people died that night, sacrificing themselves so that others could escape," he said. *Including me,* he thought.

A reflective Weston asked Jak, "Does the fortress have any defenses?"

Jak answered, "Yes. Cannons are stationed along all sides, including the riverside. It's surrounded by a moat and an earthen embankment."

A Treasure Trove

The longstanding feud between the Cassius Foundation and the Biogenics Corporation was intensifying. Skirmishes between the two were becoming more frequent and more violent. Rex Cassius was releasing increasing numbers of deadly animal hybrids to infiltrate contested areas and any surrounding territories they could reach. Even the House of Erwina, well to the west of H'Aleth, had noticed an increase in animal hybrids crossing its borders. H'Ilgraith's description of the discarded and decaying hybrid corpses bespoke of Rex's attempts to accelerate the production of genetically engineered creatures.

Bounty hunters in the service of both Cassius and Biogenics were becoming bolder and more aggressive. Their attacks on villages in the contested region had spiraled upward. They were no longer making any attempt to differentiate between *H. sapiens* and *H. transformans*.

These threats crept ever closer to H'Aleth. It was only a matter of time before Rex set his sights on it. For the moment, his feud with Biogenics consumed most of his attention and resources. Even so, H'Aleth needed to remain vigilant.

Weston recognized the value of the store of information that Jak held. Jak knew Cassius territory far better than any of H'Aleth's scouts, including H'Ilgraith. He knew its geography, many of its people—*H. sapiens* and *H. transformans* alike—and had personal knowledge of the inner workings of the fortress. *A treasure trove indeed*, thought Weston, *and a timely one.* Yet Weston recognized that Jak's alternate species was a lone wolf. It was unlikely he would stay in any one place for long.

Part III
Revolution and Reprisal

CHAPTER 14
I, Cassius

Even before H'Aleth had been established, the Cassius Foundation had been a threat to any *H. transformans* and any *H. sapiens* suspected of being an *H. transformans*. Rex Cassius, a contemporary of H'Ilgraith, continued his family's tradition of conquering other territories, enslaving their people, and capturing *H. transformans* to expand their empire. H'Ilgraith and others of her generation had grown up under this threat.

Lord Cassius

Rex Cassius was the grandson of Angus Cassius, founder of the Cassius Foundation (appendix C). Like his grandfather, Rex could transform into a great horned boar. As soon as Rex was three years old, Angus immediately took over his rearing and education. Angus instilled in his grandson the mission to develop a royal lineage via the male line. When Rex inherited his grandfather's mantle as head of the Cassius Foundation, he continued the search for the combination that would ensure a male lineage. To this end, he bred his daughter to the next heir in line, Argus. This path brought the two branches of the family back together and produced two male *H. transformans* offspring, the eldest of which—Rafe—rapidly became dominant (Pedigree 2).

Rex had taken his grandfather's teachings to heart and followed in his footsteps. He governed all the regions annexed by the Cassius Foundation and everyone in them. "This land is mine," he asserted, declaring himself Lord Cassius. "Anyone living in my territory is under my rule," he proclaimed, and he set his sights on the territory held by the Biogenics Corporation. Granted, there were other territories to conquer, which could easily be overpowered. Biogenics was Rex's only real competition.

Pedigree 2:

Descendants of Angus Cassius

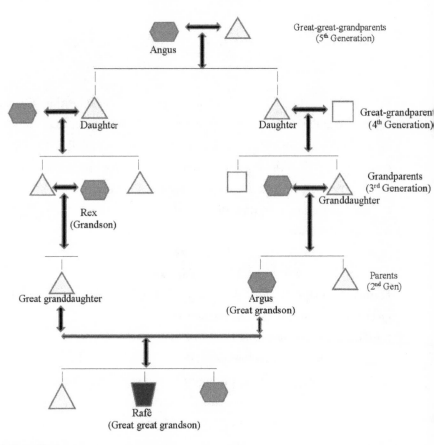

Key to Pedigree Chart

Homo sapiens female ⬭(HS)   Homo sapiens male ▭HS

Homo transformans female
with average capability △

Homo transformans male
with average capability ⬡

Homo transformans female
with extraordinary capability ◇

Homo transformans male
with extraordinary capability ▽

Marriage or coupling ⟷   Descendants ↕

As his grandfather had done, Rex continued to use *H. transformans* to fortify his ranks. He ensured their service by capturing their families and holding them hostage. Those whose alternate species were not powerful predators became genetic engineering test subjects. Perhaps by infusing their genomes with the genes of an apex predator, he could expand his army with more aggressive hybrid humanoids.

Prudently, Rex continued calling his empire the Cassius Foundation. This kept others from recognizing his true intent. People in the other territories would be lulled into complacency and more readily overcome if they thought he was conducting business as usual.

Chimera

Rex dreamed of fusing an *H. transformans* (himself) with a fire-breathing dragon to create a version of the legendary chimera. Instead of a lion's head and goat's body, he would have the head and tusks of a boar and the flight and fire-breathing capability of a dragon. Nothing—not even another dragon—would be more powerful than he. His dream drove him to discover new methods of genetic engineering and new combinations of genes and genomes, that could bring him closer to his final goal.

Rex was frustrated by his numerous unsuccessful attempts to create powerful hybrid humanoids of his design. These were to be the precursors before he hybridized himself with the genes of a dragon. He railed at the geneticists for failing to engineer viable specimens with the characteristics he wanted. The few that survived were malformed and could barely function. Most were mentally deficient. Those who could not comprehend language well enough to follow commands were destroyed. Those who could work were forced into labor either at the fortress or in a village.

In the meantime, Rex wanted to accelerate the production of animal hybrids imbued with deadly qualities. Fortunately, his geneticists were more successful at creating these types of hybrids, which included the moresistrurus and the harpyacalgryph. Although these and other successes buffered Rex's anger, they did not appease him.

A Guessing Game

For Cassius geneticists, trying to decide where to insert the genes became a guessing game. They were inserting DNA from one species into the genome of another species without a map. Since the inserted DNA was not native to the species receiving it, the geneticists had to make educated guesses where the genes should go—a trial-and-error method of genetic engineering.

The geneticists knew why most of their attempts to create hybrid humanoids failed. Often, the work they were directed to do broke chromosomes, which disrupted gene sequences and caused loss of genetic material. The damage was rampant, and there were no inherent DNA repair mechanisms to rectify it. When genes critical for development, growth, and survival (essential genes) were damaged beyond repair or lost, the outcome was lethal. Even many surviving humanoids suffered from severe disabilities.

Rex assumed that genetic engineering was a simple process. Just add genes for the desired characteristic and voilà. He did not know how genes worked or the factors affecting them—nor did he want to know. For a geneticist, these factors were critical and represented pitfalls in engineering.

In desperation, a geneticist attempted an explanation of pleiotropy. "One gene can have many different effects," he said. "It is impossible for us to predict in advance what effect, if any, a gene from one species will have when inserted into another species."

With this tidbit of information, Rex exploded with frustration. Then he eyed the geneticst and replied coldly, "If you can't figure out what to do, I don't need you."

The implications were clear and relayed to all the scientists and laboratory staff. Geneticists faced the constant threat that failure would endanger their lives and possibly those of their family. Thus, they felt compelled to produce viable animal hybrids and alter the genomes of *H. transformans* even though they knew these hybrids were victims of Rex's malice. They were trapped in a moral dilemma they could not resolve.

Initially, scientists devoted much time and effort to identifying genes and gene sequences that were lethal as well as those that caused the myriad deformities they saw. They were motivated both by science and by a desire to remediate, if not prevent, the terrible suffering of the vast majority of their subjects.

As geneticists learned what worked and what did not, some deliberately began to undermine Rex's intentions. They would produce a successful animal hybrid blend just often enough to keep him at bay. This reduced the number of new hybrids with exotic features designed to bolster their deadliness. They also elected not to develop remedies that would prevent damage to essential genes. They just told Rex, "We can't fix this problem. We are testing another approach." This precluded developing human and animal hybrids that were doomed to suffer and die from malformation.

Supplemental Notes and Citations
Broken Chromosomes

If a chromosome breaks, DNA repair mechanisms will usually—but not always—repair the break in native DNA. Breaks can heal in a way that alters the structure of the chromosome. This can lead to deletions, substitutions, and translocations of genetic material within and among chromosomes. It changes the structure of the affected chromosomes, displacing genes within or across them. Causes of chromosome breakage (clastogens) include ionizing radiation, chemicals, and viruses.

Deletion is the loss of a portion of a chromosome and the genes present in it.

Inversion is two breaks on the same chromosome that lead to a reversal of the gene's order. The genes may reattach in reversed order by repair mechanisms (e.g., AB*CDE*FG may become AB*EDC*FG).

Substitution is one gene sequence being substituted for another (see translocation below).

Translocation is a break in two or more different (nonhomologous) chromosomes resulting in the displacement of genes. The break causes the exchange and reattachment of genetic material between the two chromosomes.

Pleiotropy

The same gene can have multiple and variable effects on different tissues. When a gene appears or is inserted into a different location, it can result in a cascade of (unexpected) changes downstream.

Essential Genes

A gene is considered essential when it is needed for development, growth, and survival (Bartha *et al.*, 2018; Clowes *et al.*, 2014). The loss or dysfunction of an essential gene often precludes viability so that the embryo never develops. Whether or not a gene is essential may depend on where it is used. It may be essential in one developmental pathway without being essential in others (Rancati *et al.*, 2018).

Transgenic, Hybrid, and Chimeric Species

Transgenic species are created by inserting the genes of one or more other species into the host's genome (Brooker, 2009a; Murray & Maga, 2016; Niemann & Petersen, 2016; Petersen, 2017). For example, a jellyfish gene that codes for fluorescent green coloring (a bioluminescent protein), inserted into mice, enabled their skin and eyes to display a fluorescent green glow (Booker, 2009c). Technically, adding animal genes to an *H. transformans* would result in a transgenic species (versus a hybrid).

Hybrid species occur when two different species (e.g., a female horse and a male donkey) mate to produce offspring (e.g., a mule).

Chimeras result when different parts (e.g., intact cells, tissues, and organs) from different species of animals are blended into a single species (Bourret *et al.*, 2016; De Los Angeles *et al.*, 2018; Wu & Izpisua Belmonte, 2016). Had Frankenstein created his monster using organs from different animals, his creation would have been a chimera. By extension, when genes from one species are inserted into the genome of another species to induce characteristics of the former, theoretically, the result would be a chimera.

CHAPTER 15
A Lust for Power

In his desire to have powerful species at his command, Rex ordered his bounty hunters to find and capture *H. transformans* that could become powerful predators—wolves, bears, hyenas, wild boars, and others. These coveted characteristics would enable him to create an army that would crush any resistance. He also commanded his troops to capture apex predators whose features his scientists could transplant into another predator or whose eggs could be used to genetically engineer animal hybrids.

One predator was not subject to capture. The great gray dragons were too powerful to overcome, and reaching their aeries, high in the northern mountains, was nigh on impossible. The red dragons, on the other hand, were much smaller than the grays and could be killed by a large spear launched from a catapult. Their aeries were in the southwestern mountains and much easier to reach. Unfortunately (from Rex's point of view), the H'Aletheans, whose territory lay between Cassius territory and the southwestern mountain range, protected the red dragons.

Corporate Malfeasance

Over the years, Rex obtained most of his workforce and materiel by force of arms, kidnapping, and threatening to release his animal hybrids on anyone who refused him. He directed his bounty hunters to kidnap as many geneticists, genetic engineers, and laboratory technicians as they could find. "Bring them and their families to the fortress," Rex ordered. "Start with the Biogenics Corporation. They are well endowed with the sort of people I need." *And taking them from Biogenics could cripple its operations*, he thought.

Rex desperately needed to know which genes supported the capability to transform. His grandfather, Angus Cassius, had been unable to discover or steal the genetic code that made transformation in humans possible. Cassius Foundation geneticists could identify the genotype that coded for a specific species' phenotype; however, this was not enough.

Rex strongly suspected that Biogenics had found the genes that conferred this capability. To his frustration, his spies had failed to acquire this highly classified information. A kidnapped Biogenics geneticist might know which genes were responsible and their location on the chromosomes. If not, he or she would complement the geneticists conscripted from the companies he and his grandfather had already overrun. Unfortunately for Rex, the kidnappings were less than stellar successes. Most abductees had no knowledge of the sciences. Still, they had useful skills that could be redirected to provide the services and labor that he needed.

Corporate Malevolence

Over time, Cassius hunters had captured many *H. transformans* with alternate species that Rex deemed of lesser value—beaver, fox, raccoon, and others. These *H. transformans* were herded together and held in cells erected in the cellar beneath the research facility. They represented the majority of test subjects used in genetic experimentation. Rex wanted to see whether their capabilities could be boosted or new ones developed. Few of these people survived. Among those who did, their resulting deformities often left them crippled. Afterward, they were carted off to a village to work and eventually die. A few with capabilities Rex found useful were kept at the fortress, mostly for slave labor.

Many people that hunters trapped and caught in their raids on *H. transformans* turned out to be *H. sapiens*. Rex wasted no time or resources on genetic testing. He simply ordered his hunters to torture the new captives to see if they would transform in response to the stress. If they didn't, they were declared *H. sapiens*. All *H. sapiens* prisoners served as slave labor for the fortress.

The hunters never considered the possibility that some *H. transformans* could suppress the drive to transform. Hence, many *H. transformans* remained undiscovered. This would prove to be a critical oversight. In the not-too-distant future, two men—one who could transform into a powerful gray mountain wolf and another who could become a red deer—would be pivotal in undermining Rex's operations.

Rex gave little thought to the family members. They served as bonded servants and assured that workers would follow his orders to keep their families from harm. Most of the spouses were used as laborers or performed menial jobs. Even children were not exempt. They worked in the kitchen, laundry, and housekeeping services. Any child between five and eight years of age was assigned to assist with tasks that required little or no strength or dexterity. Children eight years of age and older performed unskilled labor. Not only did this augment the workforce for maintaining the fortress, but it also kept adult family members too busy to plot against their captors.

Or so Rex thought.

A Rare Prize

One day, a raid finally netted Rex a Biogenics geneticist and her family. "Bring them to me at once," Rex ordered. *She may know the genes that convey the ability to transform.*

Katrina, the kidnapped geneticist, had worked primarily with breeding protocols and outcomes. She specialized in rare recessive genes that caused disease. From her work, she understood the importance of pedigrees and inheritance patterns. She strongly suspected that the genes conferring the capability to transform resided in the X chromosome.

Katrina was an *H. sapiens*. Her husband, Randall, was an *H. transformans*. They had two children—a daughter Katelin, eight years of age, and a son Franklin, six years of age. While working at Biogenics, Katrina had examined the chromosomes (karyotype) of both of her children. Katelin had one normal-sized X chromosome and one markedly larger than average. Franklin had normal-sized X and Y chromosomes. Though Katrina was almost certain Katelin was an *H. transformans* like her father, she could not be sure. Katelin was too young to transform. Franklin, however, was likely an *H. sapiens* like his mother.

Upon her capture, Katrina kept silent about her suspicions. "My specialty is tracing pedigrees for recessive genes," she told Rex. "I use genetic engineering techniques to excise these genes and replace them with a normal variant," she added, hoping this would be enough to save herself and her family.

It was. Rex needed her skill and expertise in excising and inserting genes. *Perhaps her knowledge can identify the cause of the many failures wrought by my geneticists*, he thought. So he turned a blind eye to Katrina's species—for the moment. Then he focused on planning an outright assault on the Biogenics research facility.

Whispers

Like the other captured geneticists, Katrina abhorred the work she was forced to do. Yet she had a husband and two children to protect. Over time, she learned there were other geneticists and laboratory technicians who felt as she did. Some had also worked at Biogenics. All were desperate to find a means of escape.

Through his raids, Rex had bolstered the numbers—if not the loyalty—of his army, research staff, and workforce. Yet only the guards, supervisors, advisors, and military officers were loyal followers. The vast majority of his workers were unwilling conscripts and forced labor. Rex remained unconcerned. After all, he held their families hostage in an impenetrable fortress and used animal hybrids to hunt down and kill anyone trying to escape.

Rex's confidence was misplaced. With his forcible enslavement, he had brought into his fortress the seeds of revolt. His cruelty inadvertently abetted the developing resistance.

Family members brought back important information regarding activities, routines, and routes throughout the fortress. Katrina's husband was a case in point. Randall had been a structural engineer at Biogenics. Fortunately, he could control his ability to transform, even under duress. Thus, his species remained undiscovered when he was abducted with the rest of his family. Presumed to be an *H. sapiens,* Randall was considered an inferior species and designated to serve as a common laborer. His expertise went completely unrecognized. On a day-to-day basis, he worked wherever he was assigned, doing whatever he was assigned to do. This served him well. He was in a perfect position to observe and report who was working where, which activities were occurring when, and the strengths and weaknesses of every structure he encountered. Over time, he learned the operations of the entire fortress, except those within the walls of the research building. Katrina provided much of that information.

Thus, coworkers whispered what they had learned to each other. Even children reported what they had seen and heard. Useful information included schedules, placements of guards, gate openings and closings, dock operations, and other activities both inside and outside the research building. Eventually, the information reached the ears of a few key strategists who were trying to identify a way out. One of them was Randall.

Supplemental Notes and Citations
Karyotype

Karyotype is a display of the number and arrangement of chromosomes in a cell, as seen under a microscope. Individual chromosomes can be distinguished by their size and, upon staining, by the patterns of banding (Shemilt *et al.*, 2015). Many genetic defects, such as extra or missing chromosomes, chromosome breaks, fragments, and transpositions, can be seen in a karyotype. Initially, only relatively large defects were readily visible. Newer techniques can identify smaller defects not previously visible in a karyotype (Veerabhadrappa *et al.*, 2016).

CHAPTER 16
RESISTANCE

R ex was well aware of the resentment he had engendered. Numerous escape attempts, some by a lone individual and others by a small group of three or four people, had all failed. After each attempt, Rex tightened his control over his prisoners and those forced to work for him. He increased the number of guards, limited access to the fortress's grounds, and stationed hybrid animals where they could be released to intercept and kill anyone seen trying to escape. After a while, isolated escape attempts ceased. With that, Rex was satisfied he had finally suppressed his enslaved workers.

A Means of Escape

Unbeknownst to Rex, an underground resistance had welled up beneath him. Coworkers joined in seeking means for their entire families to flee. Several of the geneticists conspired with laboratory staff under the guise of working on a genetics problem. They knew the operations within the research building. Family members brought them information on operations in the rest of the fortress. Finally, leaders had enough information to begin examining options for escape. The goal was to free as many people as possible, including every family member.

One thing was clear from the start. "We certainly cannot scale the fortress walls and make a run for it," declared Randall. His background had designated him as the chief architect of the escape plan. "That would be suicide." So much for plan A.

"What about hijacking a barge and sailing it down the river?" suggested another strategist. That plan would entail spiriting a mass of people across the fortress unseen by guards on the ramparts and in the turrets, then through the dock with its guards, seizing control of a well-guarded barge, getting everyone aboard, and pushing off—all without being discovered. This notion was just as suicidal as scaling fortress walls. It, too, was discarded. "Does anyone even know how to steer a barge?" someone asked. It was an academic question.

"Can we swim across the river?" asked another person.

"No," replied Randall. "The river has a rapid flow rate and strong undercurrents. Even a strong swimmer would be at risk. Most of us would never make it, and the children certainly would not."

"What other options are there?" another asked. "We can't fly out."

"We can dig," replied Randall.

A Movement Underground

Digging was a definite possibility; however, several pragmatic questions quickly arose from this recommendation.

"Dig where?"

"In what direction?"

"How deep?"

"How will we shore up a tunnel?"

"What do we do with the dirt?"

"How do we get around the moat?"

"We don't," replied Randall to the last question. "We go under it. The moat is shored up with rock and mortar to keep it from eroding. The tunnel will be deep enough and shored up with mortar itself. Under these conditions, such a narrow section of the moat should not collapse."

Other questions addressed equally pressing issues.

"How do we get home?"

"What do we do about the people held in the dungeon? We can't just leave them here."

"Even if we get out, which way do we go?"

"Due north, if you are returning to Biogenics territory," said a man's voice. "Due east if you are going anywhere else."

"But Biogenics territory is west of Cassius territory," someone noted.

"So is the Taurus River," replied the man. "You can't cross it here, but further north, you can. Just beyond the westward bend in the river, there is a sandbar on the east side where the river slows as it makes a broad turn. A submerged rope bridge extends from the east side of the river to the west bank. If you can transform into a four-footed alternate species, you may be better off swimming across the river at that point."

The man described tripping over the bridge—literally—when traveling as a wolf along the western bank of the river. Left in disrepair, its moorings on both banks had fallen down and become covered by silt. The bridge itself had sunk below the waterline. When he attempted to use it to cross the river, he soon discovered that all four feet were getting tangled up in the bridge's ropes. He struggled just to keep his head above water. When he finally broke free, he decided swimming across the river would be easier—and faster. Later, as a human, he found that having bigger feet and two hands to grip the ropes allowed him to cross the river using the bridge.

"Once you cross the river, you can head west," the man continued. "You will be crossing through territory claimed by both Biogenics and Cassius. Along the Biogenics border of the contested region, there are scattered outposts hidden by camouflage. You will not be able to see them. If you are near an outpost, the sentries stationed there will see you and probably challenge you. Once you convince them you are not raiders, they will help you. Once inside Biogenics territory, there are scattered villages where you can get help, as well."

"How do you know all this?" asked Randall, who had thought that only he knew about the outposts.

"I lived in the contested area," the man replied.

Randall walked over to the man who had described the safest route to Biogenics territory. "I'm Randall," he said by way of an introduction.

"Jak," replied the man, as the two men shook hands.

Strategy

"What else can you tell me about the territory to the north and west of us," Randall asked. "We are looking for a place close to the north wall to dig a tunnel," he added.

"Dig your tunnel to the east into the forest," Jak said. "The forest will provide more cover. Once people reach it, they can scatter all through it, making it harder for guards and hybrids to chase them down. Anyone who can climb trees can hide their scent by moving from tree to tree. Most *H. transformans'* alternate species can easily outrun a human. Many alternate species may be unable to outrun an animal hybrid. The risk is taking the time to transform. If you can make your tunnel big enough for an adult to crawl through it, many people can go through as their alternate species."

But some can't, thought Randall ruefully. His alternate species was a red deer.

A laborer offered the solution regarding where to dig. Known as the dungeon, the cellar beneath the research building had been converted into a large jail with cells that could hold several people. "I was assigned to sweep out the guard quarters located adjacent to the cellar under the research building. I noticed that the guards avoided going into the dungeon unless ordered to bring someone out."

Having worked as a janitor, the laborer described going into the dungeon to remove much of the waste collecting in and around the cells. The guards allowed janitors to clean them because it reduced the stench that permeated their quarters. "It also brought a small measure of relief to the prisoners," he added.

To complete his task, the janitor had had to take a lighted torch into the otherwise unlit dungeon. In the farthest cell, he saw a corner where part of the mortar shoring up the cellar walls appeared to be eroding. The prisoners in that cell were scratching away at it. Those who could transform into an animal with claws were gradually digging through the cellar wall. "They are already trying to dig a tunnel," the janitor reported.

"This could be a place to start, but how do we get to it?" asked Randall.

"It might be easier than you think," replied the janitor. "There are many janitors. We are a humble lot and keep our heads low when approaching or nearing guards. They have grown accustomed to our deference and usually ignore us when we pass by."

"Do they keep count of how many come and go?" asked Randall.

"Not usually," answered the janitor. "Different janitors go to the cellars from week to week, ostensibly because the filth is overwhelming. So faces change. Usually, three or four of us go at one time and smuggle food and medicine into the prisoners," he said. "We have even smuggled in a healer from time to time to treat infections and wounds," he added.

"So if four went in but only three came out or vice versa, you don't think they would notice?" asked Randall.

"They haven't so far," the janitor replied. "We are very humble," he emphasized with a smile. "And to keep their goodwill, from time to time, we will abscond with libations taken from a root cellar and bring them wine (illustration 7)."

Illustration 7: The Dungeon

CHAPTER 17
INTO THE EARTH

The prospect of digging a tunnel out from the dungeon had numerous logistical issues. Questions about how deep, how big, and what to do with the dirt still needed addressing. At least now they had a way to rescue the people in the dungeon.

Size Matters

The strategists agreed the tunnel must be large enough to allow a 200-pound human or animal to crawl through it. This would accommodate nearly every adult human and the vast majority of alternate species represented among the *H. transformans*. Many species—foxes, wolves, otters, skunks, and especially badgers—had claws that could speed the digging. No shovels, pickaxes, or other equipment would be needed. Once through the cellar wall, they would descend twenty feet below the dungeon's floor before heading out horizontally beneath the compound itself. This eliminated the risk that anyone on the surface, including animal hybrids, could hear sounds of digging and scraping.

The issue of mortar and dirt removal had a similar solution. A woman who worked in the kitchen petitioned to plant a vegetable garden to grow food for workers and their families. "We will tend the garden and grow the vegetables ourselves," she said. Permission was granted, provided half the harvest was ceded to Rex to feed his family, advisors, and supporters.

Naturally, the best location for the garden was the expanse between the research building and the east wall. The relatively rich dirt from the tunnel was raked and folded into the soil, which disguised it. It added nutrients to the earth, which was a boon to the plants. In turn, they responded with a bumper crop that included vegetables, vine fruits, and rye grain. The stalks of grain and corn were dried, and janitors took them to the dungeon, ostensibly to provide bedding for the prisoners and absorb waste. They were stored in the tunnel in anticipation of preparing mortar.

A rough mortar consisting of mud from the tunnel dirt and crushed fibers from the dried plant stalks served to shore up the tunnel walls and keep soil from crumbling into the tunnel. With the garden above the tunnel, there was minimal foot traffic to disturb it. The research building was level and very stable, preventing any disturbance to delicate laboratory equipment and experiments.

A Matter of Sensibility

A new moon was chosen as the time for an escape. Fortunately, the outer wall of the fortress and the land beyond it had better lighting than its interior. Rex did not anticipate an attack from inside his fortress, which he deemed secure. Even so, people would need to move from shadow to shadow as quickly as possible to reach the research building undiscovered and then into the dungeon below.

"Even when you reach the forest, a dark moon is essential," Jak told them. "Moonlight is a powerful source of illumination. Most of the animal hybrids guarding the fortress will have nocturnal vision. Though people and animals will be leaving the tunnel under cover of trees, they can still cast a shadow or be seen in the moonlight."

"Speaking of hybrids, they also have excellent hearing and sense of smell," remarked one of the co-conspirators. "What do we do about them?"

"Feed them," said another conspirator. "They are only fed every few days to keep them hungry. Even then, they only get rotten food. Once released from their chains, they will attack almost anything that moves and eat it. They will fight each other to feed on the victim."

"What do we feed the dungeon guards?" asked another.

"Wine," answered the janitor. "They have come to expect it, and we will not disappoint them."

So laborers who worked where food was stored, cooked, or served remained alert to any opportunities to pilfer food from storage and scavenge any discarded food. Once a date for the escape was set, people took food and hid it a day or two early in preparation for throwing it out for the animal hybrids to find.

Exit Strategy

After many months of slow, painstaking excavation, the tunnel extended well beyond the forest line to the east. Massive tree roots made that clear. A new moon was only a few nights away. A mix of anxiety, anticipation, and exhilaration began to grow among the captives. These feelings needed quelling to prevent a slip of the tongue or unusual display of emotion. Plans were made for everyone to flee with the realization that not everyone could or would escape. This approach was taken so that people who wanted to risk an attempt would have the chance to do so.

"Why not let a few people go at a time?" asked one of the participants.

"Who would you suggest should go first?" asked Randall. This question was greeted initially with silence.

"That won't work," someone finally said. "A few people have tried to escape in the past, usually people with no family to consider. As far as we know, no one has ever succeeded. Anyone who made it past the wall was hunted down and killed."

Then Katrina spoke. "I agree, although for a different reason. The loss of any of the research staff would be recognized immediately," she said. "Especially a geneticist," she added.

"Any missing laborers and menial workers would be noticed, as well," the janitor added.

"Everyone needs to flee at the same time. Yet we can't all jam into the tunnel at once," Randall noted.

"Perhaps we can draw straws or lots and assign a time when people can go to the tunnel," someone suggested.

"I think that would be logistically impossible. It would require an extraordinary amount of coordination," replied Randall. "Plus, people may start to barter with each other for a different place in the line. Almost certainly, someone would be overheard, and we would be discovered. I really don't know how we are going to handle the volume of people trying to get into the tunnel," he said. He paused for a moment, then said quietly, "Not everyone is going to escape. There are simply too many of us."

"First come, first served," said a pragmatic Jak. "People go through the tunnel as they get to it. A backlog is inevitable, given the number of people who want to get out of this place. Still, the tunnel is large enough for people to move through it quickly."

"But if you don't make it, there will be no second chance," someone commented soberly.

"Perhaps there could be," mused Randall. The structural engineer thought for a moment. "I think we have to realize that many will be left behind. At some point, a guard will see something or recognize what is happening and sound an alarm. When guards and hybrids are heard entering the research building, those not yet in the tunnel will need to seal up its entrance."

"How?" someone asked.

"We can make a mat of leaves and stalks shaped to fit the tunnel's entrance and leave it with a pile of mortar inside the dungeon cell," Randall explained. Those still in the dungeon will put the mat into the tunnel's entrance and plaster the mortar over it. The last people to get into the tunnel will need to stay long enough to bolster the mat from the tunnel side while others apply the mortar. In the meantime, others left in the dungeon will need to cram into the cell, close the cell door, and latch it. When the guards arrive, prisoners can act excited but still captive."

The janitor then added, "Since guards rarely come into the dungeon, they will not know the prisoners. They won't recognize that they are not the same ones, and they won't be surprised to find the cell full."

"So there could still be a next time if the tunnel is not discovered," said a co-conspirator.

"Yes," answered Randall, "with only a few inches of mortar and matted reeds to breach."

"Assuming the exit from the tunnel is not found," Jak reminded them.

"There's another factor to consider," said Randall. "The more people who escape, the more resources Rex will have to expend chasing us down. He will have to choose between securing his fortress and chasing after us."

"I think he will empty out the fortress," commented another conspirator ruefully.

"Even if just a few of us can reach Biogenics, maybe the company will mount a rescue effort," offered a Biogenics technician.

"It's possible," said Randall. "Think of all the information we will be bringing back with us—the genetic engineering, the fortress, everything," he added. "That information is incredibly valuable. If Biogenics could raid the fortress, the corporation could have it all and could free the remaining captives."

"Perhaps Biogenics could find a way to help some of the hybrid humanoids, as well," suggested Katrina.

Supplemental Notes and Citations
Vision

The retinas of mammals contain cones, which operate in the daylight and support color vision, and rods, which are most active in dim light and support nocturnal vision. Diurnal mammals, including humans, have more cones than rods, whereas nocturnal mammals have more rods than cones. Both cones and rods have protein receptors (opsins) that are sensitive to light (photons). They absorb photons at different frequencies and convert them into signals (Borges *et al.*, 2018; Emerling *et al.*, 2015; Jacobs, 2009; Terakita, 2005). The genes that code for these receptors also specify the photopigments that react to light. Variations in a single position (single nucleotide polymorphism) within an opsin gene can alter the frequency to which a photopigment will react and the individual's perception of color accordingly. There are five families of opsin genes: four for cones and one for rods. The gene sequences in each family create opsins that absorb light along a band of frequencies.

Except for primates, modern mammals have opsins from only two cone gene families (Jacobs, 2009). This results in dichromatic vision, which decreases the ability of most mammals to discriminate color. Primates, including humans, have opsins from three cone gene families and, therefore, have a greater capacity to distinguish variations in color.

Deficiencies in red and green color perception are caused by mutations in opsin cone genes that code for red-green color perception (OPN1LW, a long-wavelength gene, and OPN1MW, a middle-wavelength gene). (Davidoff *et al.*, 2016; Patterson *et al.*, 2016). These genes are located on the X chromosome (Gardner *et al.*, 2016). Since they are X-linked traits, offspring can inherit them. Achromatopsia is the absence of a cone photoreceptor function (Michalakis *et al.*, 2017), caused by gene mutations (CNGA3 and CNGB3). This inherited disorder results in impaired vision from birth. Gene-replacement therapy, using adenoviruses as the method of delivering the missing genes, is under investigation.

The development of color vision comes at the expense of distinguishing objects in dim light. Increased visual sensitivity (e.g., color discrimination) comes at the expense of visual acuity (Heesy & Hall, 2010). Visual acuity is also strongly affected by eye size and length (Veilleux & Kirk, 2014). Mammals with larger eyes have greater acuity than those with smaller eyes. Those with both eyes facing forward have binocular vision, which also improves perception.

Hearing

Most mammals can hear at much higher frequencies than humans. They can also point their ears toward (or away from) a sound to increase (or decrease) sound reception (Heffner & Heffner, 2007). Since humans cannot hear above a certain frequency (20 kilohertz), they cannot detect sounds that other mammals can readily receive.

A vast array of sixty or more genes are involved in the process of hearing. They direct the structure of the inner and outer ear, the nerve pathways that receive sound from the ear and transmit it to the brain, and the areas in the brain that receive and interpret the sound (Angeli *et al.*, 2012). Genetic mutations are responsible for hearing loss in approximately 50%–60% of the population affected by hearing loss. Most hearing loss is due to a single gene mutation (monogenic) (Angeli *et al.*, 2012).

Smell

The ability to detect scent relies on the detection of chemical odors (Logan, 2014). Odor-receptor genes code for the receptors that react to these chemical signals (Keller & Vosshall, 2008; Ignatieva *et al.*, 2014; Verbeurgt *et al.*, 2014). Odor-receptor genes are highly variable not only between species but within a species (Keller *et al.*, 2007; Ignatieva *et al.*, 2014; Logan, 2014). Humans have about 700–900 odor-receptor genes. Other mammals have much higher numbers: e.g., 1,200–1,500 for rodents, 1,100 for dogs (Keller & Vosshall, 2008; DeMaria & Ngai, 2010). To compound the difference, nearly 50% of human odor-receptor genes are nonfunctioning due largely to gene mutations (DeMaria & Ngai, 2010; Verbeurgt *et al.*, 2014). Other species have a much smaller percentage of inactive genes (Keller & Vosshall, 2008). These differences likely account for the increased odor sensitivity of mammals other than humans.

There is also a wide range of variability in scent recognition among people smelling the same scent (Zhang & Firestein, 2007). Variations in a single position within a gene (single nucleotide polymorphism) can alter the perception of an odor from one individual to another (Keller & Vossall, 2008; Keller *et al.*, 2007; Ignatieva *et al.*, 2014; Nuno & Ferreira, 2016).

Single Nucleotide Polymorphism (SNP)

A change in a single nucleotide, such as swapping cytosine (a nucleotide) for guanine (another nucleotide), is the most common type of genetic variation (International SNP Map Working Group, 2001). It is the primary source of genetic variation (polymorphism) within a species, including humans. Most are benign and cause little or no change in a gene's function. In contrast, sickle cell disease is caused by a single-gene mutation (point mutation) in which thymine (a nucleotide) replaces adenine (another nucleotide) in the gene that codes for ß-hemoglobin (Pace *et al.*, 2012).

CHAPTER 18
A Break for Freedom

During the darkness afforded by the new moon, people began to slip out late at night and move toward the research building. If the escapees could make it that far, they could probably reach the dungeon. Even though research continued twenty-four hours a day, there was little foot traffic in the research building. Activity was limited to the labs on the upper floors.

Guards around the compound noted restlessness among the animal hybrids. Yet the hybrids soon were quieted by food tossed to them. Even some of the guards seemed remarkably relaxed. They had found some wayward bottles of wine carelessly dropped and left lying where the guards would not fail to see them.

Into the Woods

Once in the cellar, people and alternate species alike were able to race past the dungeon guards. They were sound asleep. Their wine had been supplemented by the addition of valerian to ensure they slept well.

An *H. transformans* whose alternate species was a badger had been designated to be the first one through the tunnel. When he reached the end of it, he peered out a small opening and looked around. For the moment, the coast was clear. The badger rapidly enlarged the opening so that the people and animals following behind him could get out and be on their way. For a time, the badger kept watch until he was relieved by a raccoon, another animal with excellent nocturnal vision.

For a while, everything was quiet, and many people moved through the tunnel and fled into the woods. It did not last.

An alarm sounded inside the compound. Suddenly, lights that had been illuminating the exterior of the fortress turned inward. The compound lit up to the sight of people and animals running toward the research building. One of them was a large gray mountain wolf.

Guards immediately began setting free their animal hybrids to run down the escapees. Several did not react. They were busy eating the food people had thrown out to them. Once freed, some of them began fighting with each other for the food. Many of the hybrids, however, were stimulated by the fleeing captives and began to chase them down.

Only a few of the laborers and genetics staff had been able to procure weapons by snatching small tools from workbenches or scalpels from labs. These utensils were of no avail against an armed guard or a hybrid. By contrast, the *H. transformans* pressed into service in the Cassius army did have access to weapons. Some had managed to pilfer bows and arrows on the eve of their escape. Other undiscovered *H. transformans* risked transforming into their alternate species, some of which were well endowed with weaponry. Jak was one of them. As a gray mountain wolf, he attacked an animal hybrid that was about to bring down a man trying to protect his wife and child. The hybrid was no match for the powerful wolf, which quickly dispatched it. Most of the hybrids were too thin and malnourished to overcome an adversary that was strong and fit.

More than once on his way to the research building, Jak interceded to bring down a guard or a hybrid about to overtake someone. Once he reached the building, he saw a black bear standing guard alone at its entrance. The bear allowed anyone trying to escape to go through it. As guards and hybrids raced toward the building, the bear braced to fend off their attack as long as possible. When Jak reached the entrance, he turned to guard the door alongside the bear. Between the two of them, they would hold back their attackers until relieved.

When archers appeared and began shooting people and animals down, Jak knew that he and the bear didn't stand a chance. He nudged the bear in an attempt to get him to back away and begin the run to the tunnel. It was too late. The bear had already been struck by multiple arrows and was making his last stand, barring the entrance with his body.

Jak would never know who the bear was. As he raced toward the tunnel's entrance and through it, he silently thanked him for his sacrifice. Jak was one of the last captives to get out before the tunnel entrance was sealed. Yet his fighting was not done.

Guards and animal hybrids, including musticani (illustration 8), serojacutas, and theracapracani, had been released through the eastern gate. The hybrids reached the forest well ahead of their guards and were already bearing down on people who were trying to disappear into the forest. Thus, it was hybrids Jak encountered as he sped through the area. He brought down any hybrid that attacked him and a few more hybrids in defense of other fleeing captives. Still, Jak could not battle the entire horde. So he raced away, sprinting at thirty-five to forty miles per hour, leaving the hybrids and their guards well behind him. Then he settled into a steady pace at five miles per hour. Wolves are distance runners, so Jak could keep up that pace for several hours. He was finally free.

The Crossing

Many people did not survive their flight from the fortress. They were too weak or too crippled to run or climb. Still, they wanted to try. In some respects, their sacrifice helped others to escape. Both guards and hybrids attacked the ones they could reach first, which allowed others to get away.

Many did escape, especially those who fled back to Biogenics territory (map 2). Katrina and her family were among those who did. Initially, they had fled on foot carrying their children. As Jak had recommended, once they reached the woods, they and others ran northward, keeping the northern mountains ahead of them and the river on their left. The alarm at the fortress had not yet sounded when Randall helped Katrina and the children climb into a tree for safety. Then he settled down to transform into a red deer. When he regained consciousness, the alarm at the fortress had been raised. Guards and hybrids were already in pursuit. Katrina, Katelin, and Franklin jumped onto their father's back and held on.

Illustration 8: Mustecanis

Map 2

ESCAPE FROM BONDAGE

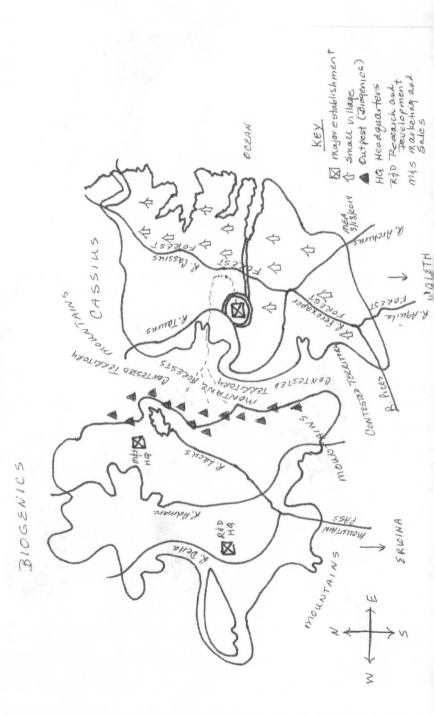

Unencumbered, a red deer could reach up to 40 miles per hour. Randall couldn't achieve this speed carrying his family on his back and dodging the trees all around. Still, he had enough of a head start and enough speed to keep ahead of their attackers. When they reached the river, the deer swam across, carrying his family with him.

Others who reached the sandbar found the submerged bridge Jak had described. The top ropes of the bridge were about a foot below the surface of the water. The first ones intrepid enough to try the bridge found themselves feeling their way across in about four feet of water. The bridge wobbled terribly under their feet until enough people got on it to help stabilize it. Fortunately, the river's bend slowed the flow of water at that point, so there was relatively little turbulence. Midway across the river, however, its current was much faster and threatened to wash some people away. Parents carrying children on their shoulders were at greatest risk. Meanwhile, those waiting to cross pulled on their end, trying to help steady it. The first ones to cross the bridge did the same on their end.

Unmitigated Fury

Rex was beside himself with rage. When the alarm was raised, he ordered the immediate release of hybrids to hunt down and kill any human they found outside the fortress. He didn't stop to think that many of them would elect to remain free in a place where food appeared plentiful, at least for the moment. Many never returned to the fortress. So Rex lost another significant resource.

Rex was not as concerned about the loss of common laborers and servants. There were plenty of hapless humans in the neighboring territories to replace them. The loss of the geneticists and laboratory personnel, however, had dealt him a severe blow. Most, if not all, of the projects they managed would wither and die without them. This was a major catastrophe.

It didn't occur to Rex or his guards that anyone fleeing to the east would turn back to the west. So most of the guards continued their pursuit eastward. Rex also did not know about the submerged bridge. It had been built long ago, before his grandfather had invaded the area. Thus, most of the people heading back to Biogenics territory were able to cross the river and reach safety. Jak was one of them.

Hindsight

Although Jak resented his capture and imprisonment at the fortress, he did not regret it entirely. His stay had been quite informative. He had become astute at identifying enemy agents, especially bounty hunters. He also learned to recognize a myriad of animal hybrids, including those released during the escape from the fortress.

After his escape, Jak leveraged his knowledge of Rex's operations to foil Rex's attempt to capture, intimidate, or coerce anyone else in his territory. This proved a boon for many *H. transformans* living in the contested region. Jak would warn them of an impending raiding party, giving them time to disappear into the surrounding territory.

Late one pivotal evening when Jak was patrolling his territory as a wolf, he intercepted a potential enemy agent whom he did not recognize. He spent the rest of the night discovering that he had encountered a lynx, a badger, a gray fox, and a great horned owl all rolled up into one determined *H. transformans* female.

Now what? he had asked himself.

CHAPTER 19

COUNTERSTROKE

The Cassius Foundation was not the only organization to dabble in genetic engineering. Its chief rival and adversary, the Biogenics Corporation, specialized in breeding *H. transformans* who could become powerful animals, especially apex predators. Its research and development division focused its efforts on breeding stronger and more powerful *H. transformans* among its own ranks. Eventually, the offspring would be enlisted to bolster the territory's defenses.

After Rex Cassius released human and animal hybrids in his assaults on Biogenics, the latter amended its operations to include modifying the genomes of *H. transformans*. Biogenics required countermeasures to defend their territory against Rex's living weaponry. So its genetic engineers enhanced the capabilities of *H. transformans* entering into its breeding programs and those of their offspring. They also focused on modifying genomes to strengthen the native abilities of other species.

Although some of Biogenics' tactics were less than beneficent, the company's practices lacked Rex's malevolence. Most of the geneticists' work focused on patterns of breeding and their outcomes. They augmented the genome of an *H. transformans* who had an incomplete set of genes for an alternate species. If the individual had at least 80% of the alternate species' genome, Biogenics could complete the set with fidelity (targeted genome editing). The organization was engaged in another highly classified project. It was working on a means to convert a natural X chromosome into a transforming X chromosome (XT).

A Historic Merger

In years past, the Eugenics Corporation and the Biogenetics Company had been two separate organizations. Biogenetics dealt in genetic research, whereas Eugenics specialized in sales and marketing for companies like Biogenetics. They were not competitors: each filled a different niche in their quest for a share of the genetics trade. On occasion, they even conducted business with each other to their mutual benefit.

When the two organizations realized that Angus Cassius was a threat to both of them, their respective leaders joined forces in a merger to challenge him. The two organizations became the Biogenics Corporation. The research and development division (formerly Biogenetics) continued to specialize in genetic research and maintained its former headquarters. Similarly, the marketing and sales division (formerly Eugenics) continued its operations and also assumed responsibility for personnel management for both divisions. It operated out of the former Eugenics headquarters.

This strategic move placed them in a stronger position to challenge Angus. The Biogenics Corporation's combined resources and geographic proximity made it a formidable opponent. Angus was enraged, and he passed his fury on to his grandson. From that point forward, a blood feud existed between Cassius and Biogenics.

Corporate Espionage

Both Biogenics and the Cassius Foundation engaged in corporate espionage to discover each other's research, development secrets, accomplishments, and methods. Since both had *H. transformans* in their service, there was no need for disguise—only deception. An *H. transformans* with the genome of a pet species could transform and infiltrate an employee's home as a pet to discover what idle conversation might reveal.

Spies also could infiltrate an organization simply by becoming an employee. Alternately, disgruntled and impoverished employees were subject to bribery. Biogenics found many such workers within the Cassius Foundation. Unfortunately, Rex cut off this information source when he incarcerated everyone within the Cassius fortress. All of these efforts came with the substantial risk of discovery and the torments that might follow.

After the kidnapping of a key geneticist, Calan, the head of the Biogenics research division, immediately took measures to prevent another raid on the company's scientists. He promptly ordered all of the Biogenics research staff and their families brought to the research division's headquarters. A hastily constructed barracks served as temporary housing until a secure dormitory could be built.

Members of the Biogenic's research council were deeply concerned that the kidnapped geneticist would be forced to reveal at least some of what she knew to protect her family. So they assumed the worst, that Rex would soon own all her knowledge, including the operations of Biogenics research laboratories and their location. Thankfully, she was not involved in any of their cutting-edge discoveries regarding the genes of transformation. Nevertheless, the council members of both divisions were more than furious. Rex's act would not go unanswered.

The Path to Retaliation

Biogenics began working on a strategy to disrupt Rex's operations. Sending more people to spy on him was clearly insufficient. None of their outpost spies had uncovered his plot to kidnap one of their geneticists, nor had they intercepted the raiding party.

"We must execute a raid of our own," insisted a board member.

"Where and with what?" asked Stokal, Biogenics' chief of security. At the time, Biogenics had two headquarters to protect—the research division and the marketing and sales division. Both had security forces. Neither had an army.

Hearing no reply to his query, Stokal voiced his own recommendations. "Increase the number of guards and outposts along the border with Cassius, and make sure they are armed. If you have any plans for invading Cassius territory, we had better start recruiting an army."

With the concurrence of the research division's council members, Calen directed that recruitment of an armed force begin immediately. "Emphasis should be on recruiting *H. transformans* whose alternate species are apex predators," he ordered. "*Homo sapiens* can be recruited as well, provided they have the physique to serve as fighters and can use weaponry," he added.

The council also approved establishing additional outposts inside the contested region to watch for any more incursions by Cassius agents. "All personnel should be armed and prepared to challenge and engage anyone who trespasses into our territory," commanded Calen. He further directed the procurement or building of facilities for producing weapons and staffing them with skilled armorers, bowyers, and fletchers. If Biogenics was going to have an army, its soldiers would need weapons, including cannons.

With the means of exacting retribution underway, identifying targets remained an outstanding issue. Biogenics' strategists were seriously hampered by their lack of intelligence regarding Rex's operations. So it was an enormous windfall when, months later, Biogenics scouts found several bedraggled people wandering in the wilderness and brought them to an outpost. The kidnapped geneticist and most of their technicians were among them. After security officers interrogated the refugees, they transported them with haste to Biogenics research headquarters.

Soon, Stokal knew what to attack and where. This knowledge left him with two major tactical problems: how to reach the fortress and how to breach it, if it could be breached. He could not send armed forces across a rope bridge. They would have to build a bridge of their own.

Biogenics structural engineers were quite proficient at building bridges across rivers. They had built several across the Della, Admare, and Maris. These bridges, however, were designed to support foot traffic and wagons pulled by oxen or horses. Building a bridge that would support troop movements across the River Taurus would be costly and time-consuming—not to mention dangerous. Yet the troops had to cross the Taurus to reach Rex's fortress. Given their destination, this bridge would have to be very well defended or readily blown up.

In the interim, Biogenics would continue attacking Cassius outposts in the territory they both claimed. These outposts were the staging areas for Rex's incursions into Biogenics territory. Targeting these locations would at least hamper if not stop his raids on Biogenics villages.

Tit for Tat

Thus began the tit for tat of skirmishes between Biogenics and Cassius. Rex would launch a raid into Biogenics territory. Biogenics would counterattack with a raid of its own. Initially, Biogenics raided both Cassius outposts and villages. Successful outpost raids yielded supplies of food, weapons, ammunition, and other useful items that the Biogenics Corporation would distribute among its own villages and use to supply its army.

After raiding a few Cassius villages, Biogenics realized that there was little return for this effort. The villages were too poor. If one had a cache of weapons, the raiders would seize them. It was not long before Biogenics raiders reported that the risk of raiding a village was as high as that of raiding an outpost. The guards would run away, after releasing animal hybrids to wreak havoc on invaders and villagers alike. This led to many casualties among both adversaries before some of the creatures could be killed. Many others escaped and slipped into the surrounding territory. The raiders quickly learned to differentiate those villages that housed weapons from those that did not. The former had more guards and hybrids. So Biogenics strengthened its attack force for any village that had a store of weapons and ordered its troops to avoid raiding any that did not.

When Rex learned of this strategy, he moved most of the guards and animal hybrids from villages without a store of arms to those that did. This benefited the inhabitants of villages without stores of weapons or ammunition. They could then overcome the remaining guards and gain access to any food stores.

Supplemental Notes and Citations
Targeted Genome Editing

Genome editing refers to a change in native DNA by artificial means (appendix E). Genetically engineered and programmable nucleases, enzymes designed to cut DNA, are new technologies that offer a highly specific method of artificially modifying an existing gene sequence (Baliou *et al.*, 2018; Batzir *et al.*, 2017; Guha & Edgell, 2017; Lee *et al.*, 2018). Nucleases such as transcription activator-like effector nuclease (TALEN), clustered regularly interspaced short palindromic repeats

(CRISPR), and other nucleases are currently in use. CRISPR has been used in genetically engineered animal models (Baliou *et al.*, 2018; Petersen, 2017; Ryu *et al.*, 2018).

The nucleases can isolate and cut double-stranded DNA precisely in a pre-specified location in the genome (Batzir *et al.*, 2017; Petersen, 2017; Ryu *et al.*, 2018). Subsequently, genetic modifications (e.g., excision of a defective gene and insertion of a normal gene) can be accomplished. The DNA strand is repaired using naturally occurring repair mechanisms (e.g., homologous DNA repair pathways). In effect, the edit results in an artificial change to a gene or gene sequence—the equivalent of a mutation—hopefully, with a desirable outcome.

Outstanding issues in the use of these methods include side effects, fidelity of delivery, and possible immune reactions (Lee *et al.*, 2018; Baliou *et al.*, 2018). Misplaced changes could disrupt a DNA sequence. The integration of foreign DNA could elicit an immune response. In addition, different nucleases have different applications. Hence, the most appropriate nuclease needs to be selected to ensure that the DNA is cut at the right place (on target) (Guha & Edgell, 2017).

CHAPTER 20
Measures and Countermeasures

Rex was determined to impose his will on any company with the word "gene" or "genetics" in its name. The Biogenics Corporation was too large for him to overpower without additional leverage. So when his agents kidnapped a Biogenics geneticist, he thought he would soon learn the secret of transformation. Then he could create an invincible army. When the revolt freed the geneticist, Rex changed his strategy.

A Passion for Personnel

Rex knew that the functions of the two divisions within Biogenics had not changed appreciably except for consolidating personnel. At first, he dismissed the marketing and sales division as of no significance. "Paper-pushers and salesmen," he snorted. "They are utterly useless." His attitude changed abruptly after a multitude of his enslaved workers escaped. He had lost count of the number of laborers that were killed or fled; however, he was acutely aware of the research staff he had lost.

Suddenly, Rex developed a passion for personnel matters. If he could access the information held at the old Eugenics headquarters, he would know who the researchers were and where to find them. Furthermore, Eugenics had always been well endowed with staff. Rex suspected that this had not changed with the merger. If he could conquer and occupy the Biogenics marketing and sales division headquarters, he could force its people into his service. They represented a significant boost in what had once been called "human resources," which he sorely needed. It would also provide a back door into the former Biogenetics territory and, ultimately, to Biogenics research and development facilities. Once Rex secured this territory, the Biogenics Corporation and all of its assets would be his.

An Initial Inquiry

Rex dispatched an agent to investigate the likelihood of a successful hostile takeover of the Biogenics marketing division and its surrounding territory. "You are not negotiating with the executives who operate this division," he emphasized to his agent. "You are to determine the number of personnel and material assets they have, how much territory they control, and how much resistance they can mount against me."

When Rex's agent arrived at Biogenics marketing and sales headquarters, he identified himself as an emissary from the Cassius Foundation. Given the emissary's unannounced arrival, the division's chief executive, Francesca, was surprised and suspicious. Initially, she greeted the envoy from the Cassius Foundation as if he were a potential customer.

The agent immediately began demanding strategic information. "Where are your laboratories and breeding facilities located?" he asked. "How many personnel are assigned to each one?"

"We are the marketing and sales division of Biogenics. We don't conduct any genetic research in this facility," Francesca responded. "We don't mix and match genes. We have no laboratories or other facilities for conducting genetic tests or dabbling in genetic engineering. We don't breed anybody. We do marketing and set up contracts between buyers and sellers."

The agent just looked at Francesca. Then he asked bluntly, "How many workers do you have, and where are they located? How many of them are *H. sapiens*, and how many are *H. transformans?*"

Given the agent's abrupt demeanor and his demands for information, Francesca began to suspect the emissary's intent. Before the merger, Eugenics territory had been north of Biogenetics territory, with which it shared its southern border. Biogenetics's former land had bordered Cassius territory to the east. It occurred to Francesca that Rex might be planning an incursion by trampling through the area that was once Eugenics. If he succeeded, he could easily strangle Biogenics economically or overrun it militarily. In either case, Francesca's division would be a casualty.

Francesca declined to answer the emissary's question and instead asked, "Why do you want to know?"

In a threatening voice, the agent replied, "Answer my questions, or I will report to Lord Cassius that you refused to cooperate."

Francesca recognized the implications of the agent's threat immediately. He was not negotiating with her. Rex was planning a hostile takeover of this division to gain control of it.

In a cold voice, she ordered, "Get out! Now!"

The Die Is Cast

Immediately after the emissary's departure, Francesca quickly apprised her council members of her suspicions and her basis for them. "We must alert the research division immediately," she said. The council agreed wholeheartedly.

Francesca dispatched a courier to Calen with an urgent message: "We need to meet. Rex Cassius may be marching on us. We have reason to believe he may try to go through us to get to you. I am on my way to your headquarters."

When Francesca arrived at the research division's headquarters, she met with its governing council.

She warned them bluntly, "I think we are in Rex's crosshairs."

Calen replied, "I know. We have already begun to build an army to counter his aggression. We are preparing for an incursion along our eastern border. Do you have information to the contrary?" he asked.

"Possibly," Francesca replied. She described her encounter with Rex's emissary.

Calen was surprised by the agent's boldness. "He wasn't very subtle, was he? What preparations are you making to defend your division and its surrounding territory from an invasion?"

"None—so far," Francesca replied. "We have security guards in all our facilities. We do not have an army. We have many *H. transformans* whose alternate species are quite formidable. As humans, however, our staff is not trained to fight in a war."

This information was met with a grim silence.

Suddenly, Francesca asked, "If you are building an army, perhaps we can send recruits to join it and become trained. This would augment your forces and create a unified army to fight wherever it is needed. We could build a common defense, which would be far more efficient and cost-effective. We might have enough forces to push Rex back."

Calen polled his council members. They concurred with Francesca's proposal with one proviso.

"*Can* you recruit people to join the army?" Calen asked.

"Given the circumstances, I doubt I will have any trouble finding recruits," Francesca replied.

A Wary Messenger

Rex's emissary was terrified to face him. He had returned without the information that Rex had demanded. Normally, this kind of report would have resulted in a fatality. When the emissary reported how the division's chairwoman had ejected him, Rex's fury instead turned toward Francesca.

"She dared to defy me?" Rex raged, while his agent anxiously sought cover. "She thinks her puny workforce can withstand my power? We shall soon see."

Rex then turned his attention to annexing the marketing and sales division of Biogenics and all its resources by force. "This should be an easy conquest," he told his lieutenants. "The old Eugenics territory is not far away, and they have no armed forces. We should be able to sweep through their territory and then attack the research facilities from Biogenics' northern flank."

Rex failed to consider that he might be spreading out his forces too thinly. One of his lieutenants cautioned against his strategy. "Our forces are already engaged on the east boundary of Biogenics, where they are being repelled. Dividing our forces to attack on a second front could spread them too far," argued the lieutenant.

Rex dismissed the lieutenant's concern. "We will have plenty of conscripts once we conquer their marketing and sales territory," he said.

"They won't know how to fight," offered the lieutenant in rebuttal.

"They won't need to know," snapped Rex, now quite angry. "They just need to take fire. Their job is to serve as a shield for the real army coming behind them."

A short time later, a new lieutenant joined Rex's retinue. His predecessor had been dispatched to supervise the guards in one of the most destitute Cassius villages.

The Plan of Attack

Against his lieutenants' counsel, Rex ordered an attack across Biogenics' northern border, focusing initially on its marketing and sales headquarters. Two raiding parties of *H. transformans* would be redeployed to the contested area nearest the headquarters. All members were trained in military arts and could transform into powerful and deadly animals.

Rex dictated a two-pronged attack. Each raiding party would attack and annihilate one of the two outposts nearest the headquarters. Then both groups would invade Biogenics' northern territory and converge on the headquarters. The combined forces would overwhelm it and take immediate control. After they had captured the division, Rex would lay claim to the entire northern region.

"How many people do they have?" asked one lieutenant.

"It doesn't matter. They are nothing but clerks and bookkeepers. They will offer no resistance," replied Rex. "But kill anyone who does," he added.

Then he remembered the woman who refused to meet his demands. "Kill the female who heads that division," he ordered, still fuming that Francesca had defied him.

Unbeknownst to Rex, Biogenics had been recruiting and training a host of recruits to form an army to protect their southern border. After basic training in scouting, surveillance, and archery, the recruits were deployed across the southern outposts to gain experience working with seasoned security officers.

Francesca had, indeed, rallied a large number of people to come to the defense of their territory. Rather than transfer these recruits to the southern region for training, Stokal sent skilled military staff to train recruits in the marketing and sales region. This bolstered the number of troops stationed at every outpost.

Stokal had a very long border to defend. Up to this point, most skirmishes had taken place on the southeastern front, where Rex was trying to capture the research and development division. When Francesca alerted Calen that Rex might be planning to attack their northeastern front, Stokal made a strategic decision to reinforce the outposts nearest to the marketing and sales division. He anticipated that Rex would attack what Rex thought was Biogenics' weakest point. Until recently, that would have been the case. Rex had torpedoed his own attack plan when he sent his agent to meet with Francesca.

Ambush

Soldiers at one of the Biogenics southern border outposts observed what appeared to be two raiding parties headed northwest. At first, the troops stationed at the outpost thought it was a party of hunters seeking to capture *H. transformans* for their bounty.

Yet this group was different. It appeared to be a well-organized and well-armed tactical attack force. Its members avoided individuals and small groups that a hunting party would normally assault. Instead, they made every effort to conceal their passage. Clearly, they were focusing on a different objective.

Word was sent via courier up the line to the northern outposts, alerting them to the likelihood that an armed force might be headed their way. Where and when it might attack was unknown. Without knowing the target of the attack, each outpost braced for an assault.

Biogenics scouts spread out to locate and track the armed force. To their consternation, they found it had disappeared. In consolidating their defenses at each outpost, Biogenics had left the territory between outposts largely unprotected except for scouts. The invaders had slipped past them—somewhere. Then began a frantic search for the enemy.

Unbeknownst to the defenders, the outposts were not Rex's intended target. At the behest of his lieutenants, Rex directed that the attack force deliberately avoid having any encounter with the armed outposts. This would alert Biogenics to the incursion and trigger defensive actions, which would endanger the operation.

Stokal had known the border was too long for outposts to counter a major offensive. If Rex's lieutenants overcame an outpost and captured any of its defenders alive, they could soon learn exactly where all the other outposts were and what their capabilities were. So Stokal planned another defense—a nearly invisible force that could overwhelm an unsuspecting invader.

Over the years, Biogenics had bred many *H. transformans* who could become powerful predators. Most of them had grown up in Biogenics territory and were loyal to the corporation. So Stokal had created a covert army comprising those who could transform into wolves, bears, boars, dholes, and other wild dogs. They were supported by *H. transformans* who could become very large and very dangerous mammals—moose and elk—and those who could become slender and stealthy animals—fox and weasel. He had positioned a large contingent of these *H. transformans*, as their alternate species, inside the northern border.

Only the Biogenics leadership knew of this plan. None of the people at the outposts were aware, and neither was Rex.

Thus, when Rex's attack force thought it had slipped by the Biogenics outposts undetected, it had not. After nightfall, one Cassius soldier after another was attacked and dispatched by an enemy they could not see. None of them had a chance to transform into their own alternate species to save themselves. The enemy did indeed disappear.

CHAPTER 21
A NOVEL STRATEGY

W hen the foray to acquire the Biogenics northern territory and its marketing division failed, Rex set his sights on a huge reservoir of *H. transformans*—H'Aleth. The possibility of augmenting his army and his laboratories with a wide array of formidable warriors and research subjects would tilt the balance of power in his favor. He would have all the resources he needed to defeat and subsume Biogenics into his empire.

An Intrusion

Rex sent *H. transformans* in his service to infiltrate H'Aleth and spy on their resources and defenses. His agents transformed into their alternate species with the expectation that they would travel throughout H'Aleth unnoticed or largely ignored by the inhabitants. This assumption was entirely incorrect.

H'Aleth's villagers knew the scouts that covered their region and even recognized them when transformed into their alternate species. Thus, villagers soon detected unfamiliar wildlife lingering suspiciously close to their homes and fields. Since most native wildlife kept its distance from human habitation, the behavior of these animals was dubious. Soon, the intruders found themselves accosted by the villagers and forced to retreat. It was not long before word of their incursion had spread throughout H'Aleth, and the intruders found themselves chased out of the territory altogether.

Rex's spies were able to report that H'Aleth's villagers were highly vigilant. Nevertheless, his agents were able to observe some villages, including a large one with a gated estate. "Most of the activities appeared to be agricultural," reported the lead spy. "We saw no guards, and only a few villagers carried bows and arrows—probably hunters," he added.

Nor did the interlopers see any sign of H'Aleth's scouts, who kept them under close surveillance even after they fled H'Aleth's territory. Once the intruders crossed into their home territory, the scouts knew they were Cassius spies.

A New Approach

Rex was pleased with his spies' report. He had several options for invading H'Aleth. He could sail his armed forces down the River Taurus, which bordered his fortress. Unfortunately for this plan, the river had numerous rapids. Portage around these rapids was an option for a small vessel, even one carrying cargo. Yet a flotilla of rafts, barges, rowboats, and kayaks was not what Rex had in mind. He wanted a warship.

Rex also considered sending his army over land to invade and conquer H'Aleth. His lieutenants advised that H'Aleth would be expecting this approach. The H'Aletheans kept a careful watch over their land and rivers. They would not be caught off guard if he sallied forth via either avenue of approach.

If Rex wanted to attack H'Aleth by surprise, it would have to be by sea. *But how?* he wondered. He could build a warship at his fortress; however, there were no rivers running east that were large and deep enough to sail a battleship down to the coastline. He could rig a transport to haul the ship overland to the east coast. This would require an enormous amount of human and animal power, and he had no seaport. It would take decades to excavate a location on his coastline, build another fortress and a seaport, and then build a ship.

"But I can build a canal," he told his lieutenants. He had already excavated a moat around his fortress, with both ends opening into the River Taurus. Locks at each end controlled the flow of river water into the moat. He could do the same to the east, widening and deepening one arm of it to support a galleon, then using a series of locks to control the flow of water. Rex would still need an enormous number of laborers to dig and haul dirt and rocks away to build his canal. He would need many more to quarry mountain granite to line it and prevent erosion.

"We will need the bounty hunters to increase the supply of both *H. sapiens* and *H. transformans*," Rex informed his lieutenants. "The former will serve as a source of labor. Any of the latter who can transform into a beast of burden—oxen, cattle, moose, buffalo, bears, and others—will be forced to do so. As their alternate species, they can be harnessed to haul equipment and materials." Native beasts of burden were rare within Cassius's borders. So Rex also authorized his bounty hunters to steal domesticated farm animals from other territories, provided they were large enough to carry supplies or haul a load. Rex did not hesitate to raid his own villages of laborers. Few guards were left except those needed to protect his stores of supplies.

So began two massive construction projects: one to build a warship (appendix F) and one to dig a canal big enough to accommodate a warship. Rex also initiated another equally massive development project. He needed to boost his supply of humanoids to serve as laborers and animal hybrids to serve as guards. Thus, his plan required a substantial increase in the genetic engineering of both.

Fair Winds and Flowing Seas

To man his warship, Rex would need capable people not only to man the sails but also to row in synchrony. "This should not be a problem," Rex told his lieutenants. "Once the canal is built, we will transfer the laborers from the canal to the ship. Both *H. sapiens* and *H. transformans* can hoist sails and row the boat." He neglected to factor in the training required to accomplish these tasks. It did not occur to him that many of his laborers were hybrid humanoids with features that precluded their performing either task.

It did occur to Gustavian, the ship's captain. "I would like to pick the crew slated to row and man the sails," Captain Gustavian said. "I will be able to tell which ones are better suited to rowing versus manning the sails."

Rex rarely allowed anyone else except himself to make a decision. In this case, however, he was satisfied to give that chore to Gustavian, as he had no intention of screening the crew. The lieutenants he assigned to sail on the ship would report on the crew's performance.

"Pick the right ones," he growled to Gustavian.

Later, one of the lieutenants asked, "Speaking of the crew, what if one or more of them decide to jump ship?"

"Shoot anyone who does," Rex replied without hesitation. "Guards will be armed with bows and arrows. Most likely, any deserter will be someone who has no family. In any case, tether the deserter to the ship—dead or alive—so that his body is hauled beyond the stern. Before long, predatory fish will attack it and begin consuming it. This will dispose of the deserter and serve as a deterrent to any others who might be thinking of abandoning ship."

The lieutenant said nothing. Even though the whole idea sickened him, he dared not reproach Rex. Later, he thoughtfully forgot to mention Rex's solution to Gustavian.

Another factor to consider was the length of time required for a round trip. This included rowing and sailing from the River Taurus into the canal and through it to a bay on the east coast, then over the ocean to the shore of H'Aleth, and back to the bay again. When asked, Gustavian replied, "I estimate an ocean voyage of ten to fifteen days, assuming fair winds." He had no idea how long it would take to sail or row the ship through the canal and all of its locks.

The shipbuilder, Surrelius, had another problem he dared not broach with Rex. The fortress was built on solid land, albeit one rocked from time to time by earthquakes. There had never been any seafarers in Rex's family nor among the people they had conquered. Hence, they had little knowledge of how to build a ship strong and steady enough to weather a severe storm at sea. The shipbuilder had to rely on history and his knowledge and experience in building crafts designed for rivers and lakes.

Gustavian was deeply concerned about the vessel's seaworthiness as well as his own skill in rough seas. He had never captained so large a ship nor any ship over an ocean. All of his boating experience was on rivers and lakes. He could handle category-three rapids in a barge or small boat and category-five rapids in a kayak. Together with the shipbuilder, he had built small sailing boats to traverse lakes. He, too, had to rely on history and his own experience.

The ship's first test of seaworthiness would come when it passed through the canal into the open sea, before reaching H'Aleth's coastline. This voyage would have to take place in good weather. Rex forbade a second trial run. "If they can sail the boat once, they can do it again," he asserted. The fitness of the ship and its crew in rough seas would not be known until they encountered a storm.

Welcome News

Fair winds supported the ship's maiden voyage past H'Aleth's southern coast. Given the size and weight of the warship, its captain could not sail it too close to shore. It needed a draught of at least twenty-four feet to avoid running aground. So when it passed by H'Aleth's coast, the captain ordered *H. transformans* with good long-distance vision and *H. sapiens* holding spyglasses to line up on the starboard side facing the shoreline. They were directed to look for and report any sign of human occupation—houses, barns, plowed land, farm animals, and people. The spotters reported only coastal birds and a few marine mammals. They saw no sign of human habitation. If anyone saw terrestrial mammals, no one spoke of it. There was a tacit conspiracy of silence among the shanghaied crew.

With the focus first on testing the seaworthiness of the ship and subsequently on reconnoitering H'Aleth's coastline, the captain and crew paid little attention to sea life other than sharks. So they remained unaware of another marine mammal that also patrolled the southern ocean. If disturbed, it could upend and wipe out any ship and all of its crew with fire, flipper, or tail (illustration 9). Subsequently, Gustavian reported a successful voyage with the ship proving seaworthy—much to his relief.

"Excellent!" chortled Rex, whereupon he promptly named the ship after himself.

A senior lieutenant continued the report. "There was no evidence of human occupation along H'Aleth's coastal border. The most common animals we saw on land were shorebirds—egrets, herons, seagulls, and other marine birds."

Upon hearing this news, Rex was delighted. "So the coast is uninhabited," he assumed. "Then we can anchor offshore and transport troops via barges or dinghies onto shore. We could probably do so in broad daylight," he boasted.

The lieutenant cautioned against this approach. "After dark or just before dawn is best, when there is just enough light to see the shore," the brave soul suggested. "This would allow us time to establish a beachhead before scouting out the terrain. If truly uninhabited, we would have time to build an outpost, establish a perimeter, and lay claim to the land. Then we could transport wood and other materials to erect a pier large enough and sturdy enough to support troop landings, heavy equipment, and armaments. Once we have fortified our position, we can begin moving inward." The lieutenant held his breath as he waited for Rex's reaction.

Rex appeared to agree with the recommendation. "If the area is uninhabited, the H'Aletheans won't even know we have landed. Even if anyone is present, though, I don't expect much resistance. We have seen no evidence to date that they have established any defenses." *My lieutenants envision a conventional military approach*, he thought. *I have another strategy to augment customary tactics.*

"Be sure to build a sturdy wall around your outpost and landing," Rex warned. "When I release a horde of hungry hybrids onto the land, they will eat any living thing they can reach, including humans. There will be no one to flee or report on our movements." So he thought.

Part IV
Revelation

CHAPTER 22
KINDRED SPIRITS

After H'Ilgraith and Jak had briefed H'Assandra and Weston, H'Assandra recognized that Jak was not an agent of Rex Cassius or anyone else. "You are welcome to stay here," she told Jak. "H'Ilgraith will take you to your quarters and show you where you can find food, water, clothing, and other necessities. She can show you around the estate and the village, as well," H'Assandra added.

A Change of Heart

For his part, Jak debated whether to stay or leave. When he and H'Ilgraith first arrived, he had observed that the estate was located just outside a well-established village, which appeared to have no fixed defenses. The estate's stone wall, surrounding its grounds, could be scaled or destroyed by cannon fire. It would impede archers trying to target someone; however, it would not stop a volley of arrows launched scattershot to strike whatever they might. From Jak's perspective, both the village and the estate were open to attack.

Jak and H'Ilgraith looked at each other. Jak gave the slightest shake of his head just once.

H'Ilgraith understood and was not surprised. Nevertheless, she asked Jak directly, "Do you want to stay?"

"Not really," Jak replied. "I keep watch over villages in my territory, and I trade there, but I don't live in them."

H'Ilgraith understood his position all too well. "Neither do I," she said. "Although this is my home, I spend as little time here as possible. I go to the villages in our territory, partly for surveillance and partly to tend to any illness or injuries afflicting the residents. Mostly, I travel throughout and beyond our territory, looking for the plants and minerals I want." She paused for a moment and then added softly, "I usually travel alone, but I would welcome your company."

Jak made no reply. He seemed to be scanning the horizon before him. H'Ilgraith stood by and waited to see what Jak would do. After a moment, she said quietly, "You told me once I was free to leave. So are you."

Jak looked at H'Ilgraith for a moment and made his decision. "I would like to explore this territory," he said. "I've never seen it."

"Then explore it we shall," declared H'Ilgraith emphatically. There may have been a tiny twinkle in her eye. "The two of us can conduct surveillance all across H'Aleth and explore any places you find interesting."

"When?" asked Jak, wondering how long he would be cooped up before they could leave.

"Tomorrow," said H'Ilgraith lightheartedly.

They did, indeed, set out the next day.

Becoming Better Acquainted

As they were starting out, Jak asked H'Ilgraith if she had a nickname. "Like mine," he added. "Jak for Jakovic."

"No," answered H'Ilgraith. The thought had never occurred to her. None of the sisters of the House of H'Aleth had nicknames.

"Well, you need one," Jak informed her.

H'Ilgraith was astonished. "Why? What is the matter with H'Ilgraith?" she demanded.

"Too many syllables," Jak replied. He wasn't about to tell H'Ilgraith he thought she had a really strange name. "I'll just call you Hil," he said. When H'Ilgraith glared at him, Jak hastily added, "Don't be offended. It is much more efficient. And, if we go beyond H'Aleth's borders, strangers are less likely to recognize that you are from H'Aleth."

H'Ilgraith had to concede the last point; however, she still didn't like her new nickname. It made her sound like a mound of earth. Even so, it did not take her long to adapt to it. It *was* more efficient.

Pairing up became enormously advantageous while traveling. As a general rule, Jak provided most of the security on their treks, and H'Ilgraith conducted most of the long-distance surveillance. In a woodland or montane setting, Jak would become a wolf. H'Ilgraith transformed into a great horned owl. From her vantage point in the trees, she could spot any movement. A soft hoot would alert Jak of any untoward activity.

In open terrain, a gray mountain wolf would stand out like a beacon. So Jak would become a gray fox while H'Ilgraith provided security as a lynx. If stealth was essential, both Jak and H'Ilgraith would transform into gray foxes. No matter where they were, they remained alert for the presence of any humans. Anyone who spotted a wolf traveling with a fox or a lynx would know immediately that both were *H. transformans*.

Prior to meeting H'Ilgraith, Jak had seen great horned owls from a distance; however, he had never actually encountered one. As a wolf, he dismissed owls as significant predators, and, as a human, he said as much. H'Ilgraith made no reply.

One pleasant day, Jak patrolled a wooded area as a wolf while H'Ilgraith conducted surveillance as an owl. While Jak was looking away, the owl lifted off silently. Suddenly she screeched, drawing the wolf's attention. When Jak turned toward the sound, he saw a sharp curved beak opened for a bite and long sharp talons fully deployed. They were aimed squarely at his head. He ducked to the ground just as the bird aborted her strike. The owl landed on a nearby branch and screeched at him again, saying, in effect, "Do not underestimate a raptor, even if it only weighs three and a half pounds." Jak got the message.

An Abiding Avocation

As the two of them continued their travels together, they grew comfortable in each other's company and came to rely on one another for support. They learned each other's respective strengths, weaknesses, and idiosyncrasies. Both of them liked to roam through uninhabited territory. Neither liked village life, nor were they ready to settle down and raise a family. Both were fully capable of defending themselves, and the talents of their alternate species complemented each other. Gradually, they became fond of each other and realized that they did not want to separate. As the bond between them deepened, they became espoused and only left each other's side when surveillance required it.

Since both of them could transform into a gray fox, this made traveling together easier and safer. Native foxes were social animals, and both males and females participated in raising a family. Hence a male and female fox working together would appear quite normal to an observer. As gray foxes, H'Ilgraith and Jak could communicate readily with each other through their barks, howls, and yelps. They could also mate without the risk of having offspring. In their alternate forms, they could not breed.

Though their reasons for roaming were not at odds, H'Ilgraith and Jak did not always have the same goals. Jak liked the challenge and thrill that came with spying on Biogenics and Cassius, especially the latter. He thwarted Rex's bounty hunters and hybrids at every opportunity. He was less than enamored with searching for plants and digging them up. *Boring*, he thought. Prudently, he said nothing of the sort to H'Ilgraith. Badgers tended to be short-tempered.

Despite H'Ilgraith's focus on plants, her searches took Jak into regions he had never seen. Then he enjoyed exploring what the area had to offer. After trekking through myriad countrysides, Jak finally asked H'Ilgraith, "Why are you so passionate about plants?"

"I use them in soups and other potions," H'Ilgraith explained. "I'm always searching for plants with nutritious, healing, or poisonous properties."

"Poisonous?" Jak inquired, suspiciously curious.

H'Ilgraith replied, "I have to know which plants or parts of a plant are poisonous. The pulps of many fruits are rich with nutrients and good to eat, but the seeds and pits of some contain amygdalin, which is poisonous. Some mushrooms contain amatoxin, a poison that can cause death in a day," H'Ilgraith continued. "So it is critically important to know which plants or parts of a plant are safe to eat or use and which are not," she advised.

A Rare Glimpse

H'Ilgraith and Jak had already traveled through H'Aleth's northwestern region en route to the estate. So H'Ilgraith led Jak to the prairies and mountains in its southwest. Jak enjoyed his sojourn through the grass, where he encountered a wide variety of familiar wildlife that had adapted to the region. One was a red wolf that neither attacked nor fled—a H'Aleth scout. The red wolf watched them briefly, then continued on her way.

When H'Ilgraith and Jak entered the foothills of the southwestern mountains, H'Ilgraith remarked, "This mountain range is quite different from your mountain forests and canyons. They are sunny with only a few fair-weather clouds, if any," she added.

Jak observed that H'Ilgraith had become especially vigilant. He became more watchful as well and asked, "What are you looking for, Hil?"

"Bounty hunters can be found in these foothills," she replied.

And dragons too, she thought. "What do you know about dragons?" she suddenly asked Jak.

"Very little," he replied. "They are enormous and deadly, and it is difficult to see them against the mountains. Fortunately, they rarely hunt in my territory."

"You are referring to the great gray dragons of the northern mountains," H'Ilgraith remarked.

"Of course," said Jak. Then it hit him. "There are dragons in these mountains." He looked at her, then scanned the sky. "What are we doing here?"

"Looking at the scenery," H'Ilgraith answered facetiously. Then she added, "Actually, many of the plants I use to treat illness and injury can be found here."

Jak sighed silently. "What do these dragons look like?" he asked grimly.

"They are beautiful," H'Ilgraith replied. "Southwestern dragons are smaller and more slender than their cousins to the north. Their scales are thinner and shine with iridescent colors in the sunlight. Red is the most common color, so we call them red dragons. Like their cousins, they have fire, long sharp talons, a long tail they can use for balance and for fighting, and wings that can generate powerful wind gusts."

"So you have seen them up close," Jak presumed.

"Very close," H'Ilgraith murmured, recalling her encounter with bounty hunters and the juvenile red dragon.

Jak was more than a little surprised by this revelation.

"They know all the scouts that keep watch here," H'Ilgraith continued, "But they do not know you. I want them to recognize you, as well."

Jak had zero interest in meeting a dragon of any color. His preferred modus operandi was avoiding them altogether. "Don't worry," he said. "I won't come into these foothills unless I'm traveling with you. The dragons are safe from me," he added with a hint of sarcasm.

"They are not safe from other humans," H'Ilgraith said quietly. "We do what we can to protect them. H'Aleth has devoted scouts to this region who watch for hunters and sound an alarm if any are detected."

Jak could hardly believe it. *Humans are protecting dragons? They've got the firepower!*

Not long after the two travelers had climbed higher into the foothills, a shadow passed overhead. A male red dragon had flown over them. Jak glimpsed the glitter of the dragon's iridescent scales in the sunlight. Unlike the drab gray dragons of the northern mountains, red dragons stood out. As H'Ilgraith and Jak looked up, the dragon turned back. Jak was alarmed at first; however, he saw that H'Ilgraith was not.

As the dragon passed by again, he did not strafe the two humans or create a wind gust. Instead, he rocked his wings slightly to acknowledge the two scouts. "This dragon now knows you are one of us," H'Ilgraith told Jak. "Soon, the rest of his clan will know as well."

"That's a relief. Are we done here?" Jak asked, hoping to descend back into the plains.

"Not yet," H'Ilgraith replied. "Red dragons usually avoid contact with humans; however, they will prey on other animals. A wolf would be a tasty morsel for an adult, and a fox would make a fine snack for a chick. So they still need to be introduced to your alternate species."

Fantastic, thought Jak with resignation.

Supplemental Notes and Citations

Most plant chemicals evolved to protect the plants from insects, animals, and even other plants that attack them. Most of these compounds are produced in such small amounts that they are not harmful to humans until they are distilled and concentrated. Amygdalin and amatoxin are among the most poisonous to humans.

Amygdalin

Amygdalin is a naturally occurring substance found in apricot kernels and the seeds of several other fruits, including apples, cherries, plums, and peaches (Konstantatos *et al.*, 2017; Sauer *et al.*, 2015; Senica *et al.*, 2017). A species of bacteria in the human intestinal tract has enzymes that convert amygdalin to hydrogen cyanide, which is absorbed into the bloodstream, resulting in cyanide poisoning (Jaswal & Palanivelu, 2018).

Amatoxins

Most fatal poisonings are caused by mushrooms that contain amatoxins (amanitins, phallotoxins) (Diaz, 2018; Wołoszyn & Kotłowski, 2017). Many species of mushrooms contain these compounds. The death cap mushroom (*Amanita phalloides*) causes the majority of fatalities (90%) due to acute fulminant liver failure (Diaz, 2018; Li *et al.*, 2018). Polymerase chain reaction (PCR) methods have been developed to identify the genes coding for these agents (Wołoszyn & Kotłowski, 2017).

CHAPTER 23
Tempting Fate

Ater exploring H'Aleth's southwestern territory, H'Ilgraith and Jak traveled to H'Aleth's northeastern region and ventured back into Biogenics and Cassius territories. Other than brushes with large horned herbivores and native apex predators, dangerous encounters were relatively few in Biogenics territory. The same could not be said for Cassius territory or the contested regions. Violent and often deranged animal hybrids roamed throughout those areas, and in abundance in or around any Cassius village along with hybrid humanoids.

Another Point of View

H'Ilgraith's forays frequently took the two of them close to a Cassius village. *Too close*, Jak thought. His prior experiences with Rex's hybrids had invariably been violent. The animal hybrids attacked on sight. The humanoids could be just as fierce if provoked. As far as he was concerned, all of them were deadly.

"Why do you want to get so close to these villages?" he asked.

"Two reasons," H'Ilgraith replied. "First, I want to learn as much about the inhabitants as I can. I have learned a great deal from studying the myriad human and animal hybrids I see in these villages. This information helps H'Assandra and Weston and H'Aleth's scouts, who keep watch over our borders. They need to know what Rex Cassius is brewing.

"Second, not all hybrids are violent," she continued. "Almost all of the humanoids are disabled because of their deformities. They are used as forced labor and live in appalling squalor. Unless they are a Cassius guard, there is very little food other than what they can forage or kill and no clean water. Escape is not an option for them. Anyone who tries to run away is hunted down and slaughtered by one or more of the animal hybrids."

As Jak listened, he became increasingly concerned about the risks H'Ilgraith was taking. "While I was a prisoner in the Cassius fortress, I saw the violence of his humanoid and animal hybrids. They are extremely dangerous and designed to kill," he warned.

H'Ilgraith considered Jak for a moment. "You saw the hybrids Rex used as guards or released onto the land to terrorize the people living there," she remarked. "Perhaps you should see the ones that live in his villages."

Village Life

So the two of them set out for a village that H'Ilgraith knew well. It lay north of the narrow strip of land between H'Aleth and Cassius territory, and south of the confluence of the rivers Feroxaper and Cassius. As they traveled, H'Ilgraith described conditions in a typical Cassius village.

The soil in and around a village was fouled, as was any nearby stream. The immediate area surrounding it was barren of vegetation. Villagers—mostly hybrid humanoids—had stripped away any nearby plants, including saplings. They spared large, mature trees only because they lacked the ability, strength, or tools to cut them down. Humanoids could not have any tools that could be used as weapons against the guards. "That is why I can observe the inhabitants remotely from one of the taller trees," H'Ilgraith explained.

When H'Ilgraith and Jak reached the narrow strip separating H'Aleth from Cassius territory, H'Ilgraith transformed into an owl and Jak into a mountain wolf. H'Ilgraith stayed aloft, watching for danger and guiding the wolf. As they neared the village, she flew to an oak tree from which she had watched the inhabitants previously. She landed beside the tree, gave a soft hoot, and flew up to the lowest branch.

Jak understood. He located a patch of brush and leaf litter amid some fallen branches. It was enough to shelter him. Unlike H'Ilgraith, Jak could not transform directly from one alternate species to another. First, he had to resume human form. Shortly afterward, he transformed again into a gray fox. Unlike wolves, gray foxes were quite adept at climbing trees.

H'Ilgraith had already ascended high into the oak. She had selected two neighboring branches that would support them and had enough foliage to conceal them. From this vantage point, the two of them could observe the inhabitants and their activities. Jak quickly scaled the tree and joined H'Ilgraith on her perch. Then they began their silent watch.

H'Ilgraith quickly spotted hybrid humanoids in the distance. They were quarrying large stone blocks cut from a granite outcropping. Both humanoids and beasts of burden were hauling them north. *Why?* she wondered. *What are they going to do with them?*

A Case in Point

While H'Ilgraith studied the activities at the quarry, Jak observed the village. He saw an entirely different world of impoverished, starving, sickly, and downtrodden humanoids. He was struck by the differences between these and the humanoids he had encountered at the fortress and in his territory. Their deformities and disabilities were striking. Many had sores and unhealed wounds. He could smell the fetid odor of infection. *These human hybrids cannot be a threat to anyone,* he thought. He saw some of them scouring the ground beyond the village's perimeter. He would learn later why they searched there.

The guards were humanoids without significant disabilities. In contrast to the rest of the villagers, they were in good physical condition. They abused those weaker than themselves and fought each other for a share of the provisions. One guard clearly dominated the others. He was an ursoxinoid, the largest humanoid in the village.

A serojacuta and a theracapracanis were among the animal hybrids guarding the village and its storeroom. Jak recognized both of them. The theracapracanis was pacing in its cage. It looked just like the one that had attacked him. *Is it the same one,* he wondered, *or just one of many?* The serojacuta, a powerful blend of hyena and wild boar, was chained to the storeroom. The hybrid lunged at anyone and anything that came too close to it. Only the ursoxinoid could approach the beast. He was the serojacuta's sole source of food and water. Everyone else gave it a wide berth.

Suddenly Jak nudged H'Ilgraith to get her attention. A crippled humanoid had stumbled and fallen too close to the serojacuta. It attacked instantly. The hobbled humanoid was just out of the hybrid's reach. He was having difficulty getting up, which aroused the hybrid even more.

Over time, the serojacuta's repeated lunges took a toll on the bolt that anchored its chain to the storehouse. It finally gave way. Once freed, the serojacuta attacked and mauled the helpless humanoid.

The initial attack bought precious minutes for other villagers to get away. Some huddled in their huts. Several scattered into the surrounding territory. A few who could climb trees fled into the forest and scaled the nearest one they could reach. One humanoid was just two trees away from a tree harboring a great horned owl and a gray fox. He was so focused on the serojacuta, he never noticed his neighbors.

When the serojacuta became preoccupied with a second victim, the ursoxinoid managed to catch hold of its chain. He yanked on it to pull the hybrid away. At first, the aroused serojacuta continued to lunge forward. Then it suddenly turned around, grabbed the chain in his powerful jaws, and pulled back. Thus began a test of strength—a tug of war between the serojacuta and the ursoxinoid, which the latter dared not lose.

The contest ended abruptly when another guard tossed a piece of meat to the hybrid. It released its grip on the chain to seize the food. Keeping a judicious distance, the guard continued tossing chunks of meat along a path leading to a cage. Once the serojacuta was enticed to enter it, the guard quickly tossed its chain into the cage, latched the door, and jumped away.

There was no need for the last step. The hybrid had had more food than it would have received in a month. Its belly full, it promptly settled down and went to sleep.

Precious Bounty

H'Ilgraith and Jak continued to keep watch on the village well into the night. When all was quiet to an owl's ears, H'Ilgraith flew down to the ground and waited while Jak descended from the tree. Then she led him to a location remote from the village, where they found a freshwater stream, bushes loaded with berries, and plenty of acorns and pine cones scattered on the ground. H'Ilgraith used her beak to break off clusters of berries. Next, she hooted softly to Jak and scratched at the roots of some vegetation. He understood and began to dig up the plants. As the owl hopped along the ground to other plants, Jak would dig them up. Between the two of them, they harvested roots, berries, nuts, herbs, and edible mushrooms. Using her beak, H'Ilgraith put the items into the satchel they carried, while Jak held it open in his jaws. All the while, both remained alert for the sight, scent, or sound of anyone or anything approaching nearby.

When they finished foraging, the two returned to the tree and the perch that had served as their village watch post. From that height, H'Ilgraith took the satchel in her talons. She gave Jak a soft hoot and flew closer to the village's boundary. There, she spilled the fruits of their labors upon the ground while keeping a tight grip on the satchel. She dared not let it fall to the ground. If found, it would alert the villagers and their guards to the presence of an intruder.

That is why the humanoids were foraging at the village's edge, Jak realized.

H'Ilgraith returned quickly to Jak. It was time to go. She kept a sharp eye on the village for signs of any activity as Jak descended from the tree. Both of them then fled the area as quickly and quietly as possible. H'Ilgraith remained aloft until they were far away from the village and had found a safe place where both of them could transform again. Shortly thereafter, a wolf and a lynx sprinted across the boundary separating H'Aleth from Cassius territory.

Many H'Aleth scouts kept watch over that border. They recognized the lynx, if not the wolf. When they saw the two animals running abreast of each other, the scouts knew the wolf was neither an enemy nor a predator.

A Delicate Balance

Later, H'Ilgraith described to Jak the conditions and situations she had seen at other times and in other villages. She wanted him to understand her sympathy for the beings forced to live in them. "Their huts are little more than mud and straw and barely provide any shelter from the elements," she told him. "There is no heat in the winter. So the humanoids will crowd together to stay dry and warm. Any who fall from illness or injury will be fed to the animal hybrids that guard the village. The *guard* hybrids are just as violent as the ones you encountered in the fortress."

H'Ilgraith was quiet for a moment. Then she added, "The villagers are prisoners not only of their own deformities but also of the armed guards who keep them captive. Although most of the guards are hybrid humanoids themselves, they are much more capable and receive food and clean water as a reward for their services. They fight each other for a portion of the supplies while the villagers, who are starving, receive nothing. The inhumanity is more than I can stand. So I forage at night, mostly as a badger, to find food for them and leave it nearby."

Jak was taken aback. If H'Ilgraith were caught or attacked by an animal hybrid, she would be killed. Period. As a badger, she could neither fly away nor run away fast enough. *She might have a chance to get up a tree*, he thought. *But if she can't get away, she will put up a fight and be torn apart*. Jak was horrified by the possibility, and the vision sickened him. His first impulse was to tell her to stop foraging for Cassius villagers. He knew better.

Instead, he took a deep breath and asked quietly, "How long do you think you can keep doing this without getting caught?"

"I have no idea," H'Ilgraith replied. Then she sighed and added, "I've dug so many dens in Rex's territory, it's a wonder the earth hasn't subsided beneath him."

"Don't you think you are tempting fate?" Jak asked.

H'Ilgraith did not reply. Both of them already knew she was.

CHAPTER 24
A Change of Venue

After the thoroughly depressing visit to a Cassius village, H'Ilgraith took Jak to the coastal regions of H'Aleth. H'Ilgraith had spent little time in this area, so most of it was new to her as well. To her delight, she found an abundance of plants she had not encountered elsewhere in H'Aleth. Coastal reeds were plentiful and strong. *So this is where our villagers get the material for their wicker products*, she thought.

Seventh Heaven

Water birds were plentiful, drawn by the wide variety of inshore fish—snapper, sea bass, trout, shad, and many others—upon which they fed. Occasionally, dolphins could be seen just offshore. Of course, dragonflies, caddisflies, and a host of other insects were prevalent. Many freshwater streams fed into these coastal waters. Fresh water, fresh air, a nice breeze, and a fabulous array of vegetation and wildlife all around resulted in a serene setting.

H'Ilgraith was in seventh heaven. She became completely immersed in her study of the plant and animal species in this habitat. She examined each type of reed and noted its characteristics. She also made a mental catalog of the animal species she observed: egrets, herons, seagulls, amphibians and turtles, fish, and a large underwater animal slowly swimming below the waterline. She would learn later that this animal was a manatee. There were so many different species that she couldn't keep track of them all. *Good*, she thought. *I will just have to come back here again—several times.*

"Hil, get down!" Jak's voice called out.

H'Ilgraith immediately ducked down into the reeds. She turned to look for Jak but could not see him through the thick vegetation. Knowing the direction from which his shout had come, she began moving toward him slowly, as if she were a lynx stalking prey, pausing to wait for a breeze to jostle the grasses before she inched closer. She still did not know the nature of the danger. She had not heard or seen an aerial predator. *Hunters,* she thought.

They could have spotted her, in which case she would be in serious danger. If hunters were present, this was not a good time to be a human female—*H. sapiens* or *H. transformans.* Except for the knife she carried, she was unarmed. If she could transform into a lynx, she could easily disappear into the reeds. The hunters could walk right by her and never see her. *But do I have enough time?*

H'Ilgraith could hear someone approaching. It was Jak, crouching low in the grasses yet paying no attention to how much he disturbed them. H'Ilgraith was appalled. "Hunters can see you moving through the grass," she whispered urgently.

"I haven't seen any hunters," Jak responded. "There is a ship just off the coast."

Surprised, H'Ilgraith asked, "What kind of ship?"

"I'm not sure," replied Jak. "It is a long ship with sails—a seafaring ship, I would guess," he added.

Both stayed low as they moved through the grass and then through the reeds to get a closer look at the vessel. Jak pointed out the portholes on the starboard side of the ship facing them. H'Ilgraith's vision was more acute than Jak's, and she could see a little more detail.

"There is something inside them," she said, "something round with a dark center."

For a moment, Jak was silent. Then he said, "Cannons. It's a battleship. So that is what Rex was building on the river."

H'Ilgraith was shocked by this announcement. "Are you sure?" she asked.

"Almost positive," Jak declared. "I saw the skeleton of a ship this shape being built. At the time, I didn't know what it would become. Rex used barges to move supplies and people along the river."

"We have to warn the village closest to us and the estate," said H'Ilgraith, then added, "You will have to warn them. As a wolf, you can run faster than I can. You are also an easier target if you stay here. I will remain behind as a lynx. No one will see me in the grass and reeds."

Jak was accustomed to providing most of the security, and he voiced his firm displeasure at this plan. "I have no intention of leaving you here alone."

"I won't be alone for long," H'Ilgraith said. "When you reach the closest village, find any scouts who are there or someone who can find them. Tell them about the ship. Scouts will arrive here soon after to begin a close watch on it."

Jak soon departed on his mission, taking his robe with him. Not long afterward, a lynx spied two scouts threading their way through the grass and into the reeds: Latransa, as a tawny brown coyote, and Balthorean, as a red wolf. They had arrived to keep watch. Both spotted the lynx and recognized her. The three of them spread out to cover as much of the coastline as their combined visual fields would allow.

The ship remained offshore for several hours. *Could it be conducting surveillance, as well?* H'Ilgraith wondered. Yet no one came ashore to investigate. Finally, the ship moved away, heading further down the coastline. Latransa and Balthorean followed it as it moved away. *Could it be a fishing ship?* H'Ilgraith wondered. Still, she had a sickening feeling that the people on the ship knew the area was inhabited. *Bounty hunters*, she thought.

A New Threat

When Jak reached the estate, his report of what appeared to be a warship off H'Aleth's southern coast raised alarm bells for Weston and H'Assandra. Until someone had sighted the seafaring ship, they had considered the ocean to be one of their barriers, protecting their southern border from Cassius to the east. It was theoretically possible the ship belonged to another group of seafaring people hitherto unknown. That notion was all but dismissed after Jak's report of seeing a ship being built at the fortress (appendix F).

When H'Ilgraith returned to the estate, Jak was waiting for her. "H'Assandra wants to see us," he said. Subsequently, Weston, Agora [ă-*gōr*-ă], H'Aleth's chief architect and engineer, and Navikolas [năv-*ĭk*-ō-lăs], H'Aleth's shipwright, joined Jak and H'Ilgraith as they met with H'Assandra.

Navikolas asked Jak, "When you were at the fortress, could you see how the shipboards were laid out?"

"Yes," answered Jak. "Boards were placed lengthwise from the front of the ship to the back. Other boards were laid out from side to side and looked like ribs."

This information was followed by silence. Rex had found a way to invade H'Aleth from the south.

"Our southern border from east to west is no longer secure," H'Assandra announced. She turned to Weston. "We must increase surveillance of the coastline throughout the day and night. Who do you have to spare?" she asked.

"All of our experienced scouts are deployed," Weston told her. "We have several apprentice scouts we can send to relatively safe settings as long as one experienced scout is within their reach. That will free up three or four scouts. The apprentices should be deployed in pairs to back each other up. They still lack experience. Two pairs of eyes will provide an extra measure of safety for them."

H'Assandra then turned to H'Ilgraith and Jak. "Will you help us?" she asked.

"Of course," they exclaimed, virtually in unison.

"Then we will need both of you to return to the southeast coastline," said H'Assandra. "That will allow us to assign other scouts to the southwest coastline."

H'Ilgraith noted the irony. It was just the place she had wanted to be. Yet instead of exploring the area, she would be watching for invaders.

Tactical Plans

When finally on their way back to the southeast coast, H'Ilgraith told Jak about the two scouts she had left behind. "They and I can blend into the vegetation. So could you, as a gray fox. You just wouldn't be able to see anything. As a wolf, you can see what is happening and can provide the strongest defense if we are attacked. You would also stick out like a sore thumb and attract attention. Which species do you want to assume?" she asked.

"Human," Jak replied. "I can blend into the grass, too," he said. "And I will have a strong bow and many arrows," he added. "If an armed force comes ashore, I can draw their fire, taking at least one or two of them out of the fight, while you and the other scouts circle them in an ambush."

"And if the armed force is an army?" asked H'Ilgraith.

"We will have to switch to plan B," offered Jak.

"What is plan B?"

"I have no idea. Maybe your two compatriots can come up with one."

As it turned out, the four scouts had plenty of time to consider plans B, C, D, and E after resuming human form. Their musings were interrupted temporarily when the ship reappeared on its return trip. This time, it did not linger as it passed by. Nevertheless, the scouts continued their watch for several days in case the ship returned. Finally, H'Ilgraith renewed her inspection of the flora and fauna of the area. When Balthorean returned to H'Aleth with his report, Jak and Latransa teamed up to maintain surveillance should the ship return.

It did not. There was no need. Rex's ship had made its successful maiden voyage. He now only needed to plot how and when to use his new warship.

CHAPTER 25
A Road Less Traveled

Given the sighting of a battleship along the southern coastline and Jak's description of a warship under construction, it became imperative to discover how Rex managed to sail a battleship from an inland location—the fortress—to the ocean. H'Aleth's strategists generated several hypotheses.

The River Hypothesis

"You mentioned that Rex was building what appeared to be the skeleton of a warship on land adjacent to a river," Weston noted. "It seems logical that he would sail the ship down that river."

H'Ilgraith sketched out a map of the territory surrounding the fortress. When she was an owl, she had the spacial mapping ability inherent in all owls. She had used this ability to map Cassius territory as she flew through it and discovered the Cassius fortress.

"That river flowed north to south," reported H'Ilgraith. "It then curved westward in a wide bend," she added.

"If we are thinking of the same river," offered Jak, "then it curves back to the east. A high mountain range rises in the east. If the river continues its run eastward, the mountains will force its flow to the south."

"Then any rivers that flow east to the ocean would have to originate in those mountains," said Weston.

"Two rivers, the Aguila and the Arcturus, flow through our territory from north to south," said H'Assandra. "If the river to which you are referring flows into either one or simply continues as one of them, then Rex's warship could still reach H'Aleth. He would not need to reach the ocean."

"The ship would never make it," said Navikolas. "There are few places along either river where a ship of that size would not run aground. Furthermore, it would break up trying to cross the rapids—and there are many rapids. The ship's captain would have to portage around them—something he could not do with a warship. Finally, a vessel of that size sailing down a river would not pass by unnoticed," he said wryly.

A notion suddenly occurred to Jak. "The moat," he exclaimed. "There is a moat around the fortress, which connects to the river at both ends. If Rex could build a moat around his fortress, could he not also build moats around the rapids?" Jak asked.

"Not in secret," Weston responded. "I would think the level of effort to create so many waterways around the rapids would be prohibitive. Once in H'Aleth's territory, they would be subject to sabotage," he added.

"He could build a canal," said Navikolas grimly, "and if he can build a canal, he can excavate a riverbed," he added. He thought for a moment and then decided, "The latter effort might prove unwise. Rivers take their own course, and riverbeds are constantly shifting."

Then H'Ilgraith spoke. "While Jak and I were observing one of the Cassius villages, I saw humanoids, oxen, and other animals in the distance struggling to haul large stone blocks from a quarry toward the northwest. It looked as though they were headed for the River Aguila," she said. "Could Rex use blocks of stone to keep the riverbed even?" she asked.

"It is conceivable," replied Navikolas, "but I don't think it is feasible. That wouldn't help him get his ship over the rapids."

A few minutes passed before anyone spoke again. Then Navikolas suddenly spoke sharply, "Let me see the map of the northern territory along with H'Ilgraith's sketch." A moment later, he said quietly. "If Rex could find a place for his warship to cross the River Cassius, he could reach the sea by building a system of canals."

Retracing Steps

"We need to go back," Jak concluded grimly.

H'Ilgraith agreed. "We can return to the place where we first saw the stone being quarried and track it to its destination. Perhaps the stone is being used to build another structure inside the fortress," she suggested.

"It's possible," said Jak, "but I think another stone structure would have to be built outside the fortress. The inside is already crowded. The research building has a huge footprint. Even though Rex built a bridge across that river, I doubt it would hold up under the weight of those blocks unless it has been reinforced," he added.

"The problem is not only where they're taking the stones," said Weston, "but how they're using them. If it is for another building at the fortress, then so be it. If it is for a canal to the sea, then we need to assess the structure for any weaknesses and defenses."

"A moment," spoke H'Assandra. "H'Ilgraith's journey to find the fortress was nearly a fatal one. I will not sanction another such excursion," she added firmly.

"We may not need to get close to the fortress," offered Weston. "Even if the stones are headed in that direction, a raptor could spot it nearly two miles away," he added, looking directly at H'Ilgraith.

"H'Ilgraith and I can go back," offered Jak. "Between the two of us, we have already seen much of the western and southern regions of Cassius territory. Woodland owls are very common, as are wolves," he added.

"May I join you?" asked Weston.

"Of course," answered H'Ilgraith. Then she turned to Jak and said, "Weston also transforms into a gray mountain wolf."

"That raises another possibility," offered Jak. "Wolf packs are also common. Can anyone else become a gray wolf?" he asked.

"Yes," replied H'Assandra. "Edrian's alternate species is a gray mountain wolf, and he is the lead scout for our northern regions."

"So are Mavelov and Ilsa. Mavelov conducts surveillance in the northwestern region. Ilsa does the same for the northeastern region." said Weston.

"Would they be willing to come with us?" asked Jak.

"They wouldn't miss it," Weston assured Jak.

Wolf Pack

The four men met with Ilsa and H'Ilgraith to determine the best paths to take into Cassius territory. Petramonte [pĕt-ră-*mŏn*-tĕ], H'Aleth's chief geographer and mapmaker, joined them to create a map based on the information each member could provide. He, too, was an *H. transformans.* Though it would have been ideal to have a mapmaker join the group, Petramonte's alternate species was a bighorn sheep. His presence among a pack of wolves would not go unnoticed, especially since the latter would not hesitate to prey on the former.

H'Ilgraith provided the locations of the villages she had observed. Both she and Jak provided information about the hybrid animals they had seen and where they had seen them. They also described the hybrids' characteristics, especially their weaponry.

Having mapped out their strategy, five wolves set out at a steady trot with an owl providing aerial surveillance. They traveled as a pack, with Edrian taking the lead. H'Ilgraith flew a discrete distance away from them while still keeping them in sight. An owl flying in tandem with wolves would betray their true nature. She kept an eye on their immediate surroundings while scanning the territory ahead. She stayed alert for any animal that did not flee from the path of a wolf pack. Her chief concerns were hunters that attack by ambush and hybrids that attack with abandon.

Their travel through H'Aleth's northern territory and across the border into the southern region of Cassius was uneventful. This was due, in part, to additional scouts who flanked the wolves until they had penetrated deep into Cassius territory. Once they were well inside the montane forest, H'Ilgraith could fly closer to them without being spotted by someone from the ground. Nevertheless, she still needed to be alert for aerial predators that might attack her. She had not forgotten her encounter with the harpyacalgryph and the moresistrurus.

Since this wolf pack had left its own territory, it traveled mostly during the day, from early dawn to late twilight, to identify landmarks and keep on course. The wolves bedded down during the deep of the night. Two wolves always stood watch until relieved by two more.

H'Ilgraith also slept at night; however, as an owl, she would slip into a light sleep for minutes at a time. Even when sleeping, she could hear the movements of an owl's prey species. So she could readily detect the movement of anything larger. One night, everyone heard something crashing through the underbrush.

The Hunt

The wolf pack had bedded down in underbrush near a mound of rubble when they heard the pounding footfalls of a biped heading their way. The wolves jumped up immediately and spread out under cover to avoid being detected and to mount an attack on an adversary, if necessary. Edrian and Jak jumped atop the mound to get on high ground and hunched down in the rubble to avoid being seen. H'Ilgraith flew aloft.

A waning moon, low in the night sky, provided limited light. Even though wolves had excellent nocturnal vision, the darkness in the forest was hiding both themselves and whatever was barreling toward them. Soon they also heard many other bipeds running toward their position. Something was being chased.

Suddenly, the screech of an owl warned the wolves of imminent danger. A moment later, something ran past the mound and then paused. For a brief moment, it revealed itself. The weak moonlight fell upon a creature as it stood partially upright to look back over its shoulder. It appeared to be a large, stooped, hybrid humanoid with abnormally long arms, long fangs, and a loud snarl (illustration 10).

The humanoid suddenly ducked into the underbrush and crouched down. The wolves heard a salvo of loosed arrows fly past them and the hybrid humanoid. Hunters! Edrian and Jak immediately jumped down to the rear of the mound. Under its shadow, they waited and listened. *Where is Hil?* Jak wondered.

An overeager hunter raced ahead to locate the creature. He was certain he and his comrades had brought down the beast. The humanoid immediately ambushed the lone hunter and killed him. The victim's cries alerted his comrades that the creature was still alive. As the remaining hunters raced ahead, the humanoid quickly disappeared. When the hunters

Illustration 10: Papiopanoid

came upon the body of their slain comrade, they were not dismayed. It just meant there was one less person to share a bounty.

"We've lost track of it," said the first hunter. "We need to get out of here before it ambushes us, too."

"But the bounty on this hybrid is really high," countered a second hunter. "We should keep looking for it."

"In these woods with this little light, we will never find it. But it could find us," admonished the first hunter.

"We could come back with torches," offered a third.

"It will be long gone before we get back," replied the first hunter. "Besides, a torch will only serve as a beacon for any hybrid around to find us and ambush us."

"We should still look for it," argued the second hunter. "Maybe one of our arrows wounded it. If so, we can find it, bring it back, and collect the bounty."

The first hunter made a mental note to divest himself of the two idiots flanking him. He knew that if they failed to bring down the humanoid in a hail of arrows, it would kill all three of them. "If the two of you want to keep hunting the hybrid, go right ahead. I'm leaving."

All three hunters turned back empty-handed. The wolves waited for the sounds of the hunters to fade and for any sounds suggesting the humanoid was still in the area. A soft hoot told them that the coast was clear. Jak breathed a mental sigh of relief. H'Ilgraith was right behind them. She had flown into the canopy where she could watch the movements of the hunters, the humanoid, and her companions.

She recognized the humanoid. She had seen it in a Cassius village. It was a papiopanoid [păp-ē-ō-*păn*-oid], an *H. transformans* whose alternate species was a chimpanzee. The genes of a baboon had been added to his genome. As soon as she resumed human form, she would tell her comrades what she knew about it.

Supplemental Notes and Citations
Spatial Mapping in Owls

Owls rely on both vision and hearing to locate prey. They use their exquisite hearing to localize sound and their long-distance vision to create a topographical map of their surroundings. Their brains integrate both visual and auditory signals to locate and target their prey (Hazan *et al.*, 2015). Since owls are primarily nocturnal predators, they rely predominantly on auditory mapping when hunting at night (Pena & Gutfreund, 2014). The accuracy of their auditory map is honed further by visual acuity, which is more reliable in adequate light (Carr, 2002).

CHAPTER 26
In the Belly of the Beast

After their near-encounter with the bounty hunters, H'Ilgraith suspected the papiopanoid had escaped the quarry. Its powerful physique revealed a humanoid that had been developed to serve as a guard or a laborer. Although it appeared to be a violent creature, no one knew if it truly was. The papiopanoid was being hunted and chose to try to escape rather than ambush the remaining hunters. H'Ilgraith had seen many humanoids in Cassius villages that looked formidable yet were nonviolent. She also had seen bodies with a similar appearance in the mound of decaying carcasses. *It seems Rex was finally successful in creating one that survived,* she thought.

Still, the wolf pack would need to remain alert for other possible encounters with more of Rex's creatures. The closer they drew to the quarry and the fortress, the greater the risk. H'Ilgraith realized that other animal hybrids might have survived. She had not yet described the many decaying corpses she had seen. Her companions needed to know what other creatures might rise up before them.

A Word to the Wise

When the pack reached a particularly dense part of the forest, H'Ilgraith dropped in front of a large oak and hooted at the wolves. They promptly looked 360 degrees around their location. There was no sign, scent, or sound of any danger, so Weston and Jak turned back to look at the owl while the others continued their watch. H'Ilgraith scratched at Jak's satchel. She grabbed a robe in her beak and then flew from the ground directly up into the tree. The wolves took advantage of the brief respite as they waited for H'Ilgraith to reappear.

Does she expect us to transform, too? Jak wondered. In the absence of a loud squawk from the tree, he decided that she did not.

The wolves would not need to transform to hear what H'Ilgraith would tell them. They could still understand human language. They just could not speak it as wolves. Since none of her companions could transform as quickly as she could, it was safer for them to remain wolves. As a pack, they could bring more power to bear should something untoward approach. When she descended from the tree, H'Ilgraith described the characteristics of the partially decomposed creatures she had seen.

"Many were humanoid; however, most seemed to be animal hybrids. Nearly all of them were much larger than the normal species upon which they were based, and nearly all had deformities that would have crippled them had they lived. Many had large canines, fangs, horns, and even thick scales, which were not native. Most of these features were misaligned, at best, and usually misplaced on some part of the body, rendering the feature useless." She paused for a moment and then added quietly, "The humanoids must have been *H. transformans*. I cannot imagine what they suffered at Rex's hands."

For a moment, the wolves remained silent. Then Edrian abruptly set out at a quickened and determined pace. The others promptly followed. H'Ilgraith would catch up after she transformed into an owl.

Secret Surveillance

The wolves continued to travel northwest a few more days until they could hear the sounds of laborers. H'Ilgraith dropped down in front of them again. She hopped along the ground, leading them slowly to a mound of rocks, which had fallen long ago. She ducked briefly into an opening and, shortly thereafter, emerged with a soft hoot. This break in the rocks provided a suitable location from which a wolf could observe activities in the quarry. It would also hide the wolf that occupied it. The rest of the pack promptly found several more breaks among the rocks. Those that provided a good vantage point were quickly occupied.

H'Ilgraith ascended into the trees to keep watch over the surrounding area. Given her keen eyesight, nothing would get past her. She could give the wolves advanced warning should anyone or anything head their way.

So the wolves watched as a variety of mostly hybrid humanoids labored to cut blocks of rock out of the mountainside and load them onto a wagon. Bisalcesoids, bovicervids, papiopanoids, and ursoxinoids served to carve out the blocks of stone. Oxen, moose, bears, and other large animals hauled them away. Clearly, the latter were *H. transformans* who had these animals as their alternate species. Serojacutas and other animal hybrids served as guard animals. Oddly, there were no humans supervising the project. Hybrid humanoids served to muster the laborers and keep them working.

In watching the proceedings at the quarry, it quickly became evident that operations were less than well organized. The disarray led to numerous altercations among the workers. The bisalcesoids and ursoxinoids were particularly quarrelsome. Edrian and company saw a demonstration of their capabilities when a fight broke out between two of them. Although they were evenly matched in size and weight, the ursoxinoid had the advantage. The bisalcesoid was designed to be a beast of burden. The ursoxinoid was designed to be a fighter, had horns that could gore an opponent, and a bony plate covering its forehead. It likely would have been the victor had the serojacutas not joined the fray. They were aroused by the fight and began attacking both combatants indiscriminately. With this new assault, both humanoids had to break off their struggle to defend themselves against a violent creature with formidable tusks. Remarkably, this brief outburst restored calm to the quarry.

The watchers noticed that the bovicervids and papiopanoids avoided the fight. *Not all Cassius creatures are inherently violent*, thought Weston.

After watching the quarry and the hybrids working in it, Edrian backed out of his hideaway, signaling the others that they were moving on. He turned his attention to the stones as they were taken away from the quarry. It soon became clear that the caravan was not headed toward the River Aguila or the fortress. It had turned eastward.

A Looming Shadow

Many endless treks hauling stones through the forest had eroded the forest's floor and created a coarse roadway. Since the caravan extended way beyond their line of sight, the pack decided to pick up its pace until the wolves reached the caravan's head or the end of the roadway. They could stay well within the forest, where they would remain unseen by those they followed.

Thus far, the weather had favored the wolf pack and the owl. As they headed in a northeasterly direction, parallel to the caravan of stones, the weather changed. Storm clouds formed, and the air cooled. As dark clouds built up, eddies and currents swirled in them, forming surreal shapes to tantalize the imagination. Gale-force winds followed one of these shapes. Jak knew all too well what had caused them. He snapped a deep growl and sank to the ground as he watched the sky overhead. Hearing the warning, the other wolves followed his lead. They, too, watched the sky as did H'Ilgraith. Despite the wind, she flew higher into the canopy of a nearby tree. She wanted to see what had alerted Jak. She saw nothing amid the darkening clouds.

We are not the only ones keeping watch, Jak thought. A great gray dragon had passed overhead, undetected by the rest of the travelers below. Its dark gray blended with the brewing storm clouds.

As wind and rain began buffeting the wolves, some regretted leaving the shelter of the rock mound. Nevertheless, they forged ahead. H'Ilgraith, however, needed to seek shelter or transform. Her feathers were not waterproof—the price of silent flight. They would become saturated by the rain. She quickly found a sheltered nook in the tree where she transformed into a lynx. She still wouldn't be happy about getting wet, but she would be able to keep pace with the wolves.

The pack slogged through the rain, keeping the caravan within sight to their left. The rain was actually a boon for them. It washed away any sign or scent of their passage, leaving no trail for anyone to follow. Yet the great gray dragon could have taken note earlier. Dragons had raptor-like vision.

Did he see us? Jak wondered. *Probably. He might dismiss a pack of wolves in the forest, but I doubt it.* Jak was worried. Normally, wolves would not travel so close to hybrids of any kind.

When it finally stopped raining and the pack paused for a brief respite, Jak stepped aside, taking his satchel with him. Not long afterward, he rejoined his comrades as a human to warn them. "A great gray dragon flew over during the storm. I do not know why, but I suspect he was patrolling the area. There is no doubt he saw the caravan, and I have little doubt that he saw us. Dragons consider wolves and other mammals as prey species and may view animal hybrids the same way. He could have been looking for prey, although I doubt it. A heavy rainstorm is not the best time to be on a hunt." Jak paused for a minute and then added, "We could be attacked by a dragon. What do you want to do now that we have come so far?"

Edrian stood up and thrust his head toward the east. Weston and the others quickly joined him. They were ready to continue their mission. Jak nodded in agreement and said, "I'll join you shortly."

CHAPTER 27
Waterway to the Sea

Now that they were in dragon territory, additional surveillance of the sky overhead was imperative. Hence, H'Ilgraith transformed back into a great horned owl. She divided her time between watching for hybrids and other predators within the forest and flying high into the canopy to look for gray dragons. *Would a dragon try to make a meal of an owl?* she wondered. *What would a dragon do with a mouthful of feathers?*

The Canal

Fortunately, no other gray dragons made an appearance. The remainder of their journey following the caravan was uneventful. In fact, it had become rather tedious until H'Ilgraith dropped to the ground with a soft hoot. They were nearing a human-made boundary of the forest. The wolves promptly slowed down and began a stealthy approach, as if they were stalking prey. As they approached the forest's edge, they sank to the ground to conceal their shape and crept forward. When they were close enough to have a clear view of the terrain in front of them, they stopped.

The vista before them was astounding. A massive canal, deep and wide, was set in an east-west direction. It spread out before them as far as they could see in either direction. They now knew how a warship built on the River Taurus could reach the east ocean. What they could not see was where, along the eastern shore, the canal emptied into the sea.

The far wall of the canal was shored up by large blocks of quarried stone. No doubt the canal's entire surface was covered by blocks of stone.

Locks had been installed at intervals to control the flow of water. Jak recognized them as the same locks he had seen in the moat at the fortress.

Even though the canal was complete, there was still a need to protect the massive project. Small fortresses that looked like freestanding turrets were being built along both sides of the canal. The turrets alternated so that their crossfire would cover its full length. The few finished turrets showed cannon mounts and alcoves for archers. This construction explained the ongoing need to quarry stone. It also explained the large contingent of humanoids and beasts of burden similar to the ones they had seen at the quarry.

As with Rex's fortress, the dirt and stones dug up to create the canal were used to make an embankment on both sides of it. An enemy crossing over the embankment would be an easy target for both cannon and arrow. Last but not least, there were two additional locks—one on either side of the canal—that could be opened to flood the area between the embankment and the canal, creating a moat like the one for the fortress. Rex wasn't taking any chances.

Strategies

The wolf pack retreated deeper into the forest to consider what actions its members could take, if any. Before doing so, they first had to find a well-hidden and secure location to resume human form. Once more, H'Ilgraith took flight to search for a suitable site. With all the other hybrids present, she was concerned that many others could haunt the forest to intercept any intruders. Finally, she spotted a rocky overhang created by the erosion of the softer rock layers below it. The cavity formed by the overhang was deep. Scrub vegetation had grown at its base, providing additional cover. Unfortunately, there was relatively little cover between the trees and the overhang. So the wolves waited until nightfall before darting inside the makeshift cave. There they waited, silent and unmoving, listening for sounds that their presence had been detected. H'Ilgraith planned to remain an owl and position herself outside the overhang for wider surveillance. Her plan changed when a large paw landed on her tail feathers. It was Weston, saying, in effect, *No you don't.*

It was cold under the ledge, so the pack decided to remain as wolves, with their undercoat of warm fur, until the sun heated the air the next day. H'Ilgraith took advantage of the opportunity to nestle among her comrades and stay warm. The wolves took turns, in pairs, serving as sentries, allowing the others to indulge in a light sleep. Throughout the night, the only signs of activity were from the canal site. It seemed construction continued twenty-four hours a day, with torches lighting the work area at night.

The next morning, they took turns again changing back into human form and donning their robes. They needed to strategize their next steps.

"What can we do?" asked Ilsa. "It looks like only cannons or high explosives could possibly damage the canal."

"We didn't get close enough to detect any weaknesses in the construction," Edrian said. "We need to get closer."

"No," Jak warned. "There is no cover around either side of the canal. If you reach the top of the embankment, the animal hybrids will see you and attack immediately." Jak thought for a minute and then explained, "Not because you are an enemy. They will attack because you are a source of food. Rex keeps his guard animals hungry so they will attack anything that moves outside a given boundary." With this grim news, the notion of looking for weaknesses in the construction was discarded.

"We could continue to follow the canal to where it reaches the ocean," offered Mavelov.

"I would be interested in knowing this, as well," Weston said. "Unfortunately, it may be of no strategic value. Since we have no warship of our own, we cannot take the battle to Rex and intercept his ship before it reaches our shores."

"We can maintain surveillance," said Edrian. "At any point where a scout sees a warship in the canal, he or she needs to relay the alert to H'Aleth. At least in that way, we can have some advance warning."

"This area is a long way from home and deep in Cassius territory," Ilsa reminded Edrian. "It took us weeks to get here."

"She has a point," said Mavelov. "The ship could set sail and reach H'Aleth before we received a report."

"Not if the scout has wings," offered H'Ilgraith.

"There are six of us, five wolves for support and an owl for aerial surveillance," Edrian said. "To maintain that level of support, we would have to leave the rest of our borders unsecured. Furthermore, our scouts know the portion of Cassius's territory that borders H'Aleth. They do not know this region. It is too dangerous to leave a lone scout here."

"I can stay," offered Jak. "I already know the region to the west. Learning the geography and wildlife in this region will not pose a problem. I know most of the hybrids, too."

"Then I, too, will stay behind to keep watch," said H'Ilgraith. "If the time comes, I can fly back to H'Aleth to give warning."

Weston dreaded telling H'Assandra about these arrangements. "I would prefer a different plan—one that does not include leaving even one powerful *H. transformans* within the reach of Rex Cassius," he said. "I am unwilling to leave anyone here. Our resources would be better used keeping watch on the southeastern coast. Everyone is going back," he added firmly.

"I agree," said Edrian. "We have learned what we needed most to know. We must expect an attack across any of our borders and, possibly, from more than one approach. We need to prepare defenses where we thought none were required. We cannot leave valuable resources here to sit and wait."

H'Ilgraith felt disappointed. Despite the danger, there was much to explore in this territory.

For once, Jak was satisfied to return. He had not forgotten what had flown overhead in the storm.

Sabotage

The pack members transformed once again into wolves for the trip back. Just as they left the outcrop, they heard a deep rumble and the sound of rocks loosening. Earthquake! Dirt and stones began to fall as the wolves bolted into the forest. The trees would buffer a rockslide.

A moment later, they heard a thunderous crash behind them. When they looked back, the outcrop had broken off, leaving a shower of rocks in its wake.

Then they heard another deep rumble. This one was louder and closer. Both H'Ilgraith and Jak recognized the sound. H'Ilgraith shrieked a warning and flew low over the wolves, trying to lead them away. All but one wolf got the message and turned to leave the area. Jak headed toward the forest's edge and the canal. Just inside the edge, he crouched down and waited.

H'Ilgraith was frantic. She flew back to him and tried to get him to leave. She even pecked at his tail and then on his head. Jak shook his head, *no.*

Puzzled, the rest of the pack waited for H'Ilgraith and Jak to join them. When the two did not, the pack turned back. *What is he waiting for?* wondered Weston. *What is he looking for?* wondered Edrian.

Meanwhile, the number and intensity of the rumbles had increased. Soon their effects could be seen as the turrets began to sway and their mortar to crumble. It looked and sounded like an earthquake, yet the ground was not heaving, and no cracks were opening up.

As the turrets began to tumble, the humanoid and animal hybrids ran from the stone structures on the verge of collapsing. Many were not quick enough to avoid being struck by the turrets as they fell. Ironically, the canal itself appeared undisturbed.

By this time, H'Ilgraith had given up trying to lead her comrades away. She perched on a tree limb overhead to maintain some degree of surveillance as the wolves watched events unfold. Suddenly, a gale-force wind blew across the area, bowling over all the hybrids and hastening the destruction of the turrets. This time, there was no storm. The wolves watched as a great gray dragon descended and landed beside the canal. With a whip of his massive tail, he struck down any turrets that had not yet crumbled.

The dragon paused for a moment and watched as the animal hybrids and humanoids fled from his attack. He made no attempt to stop or harass them. Then he looked directly at the wolves waiting just inside the forest. *He sees us!* Weston realized, holding his breath.

The dragon took several lumbering paces as he lifted off and became airborne again. At first, it looked as though he was flying away. The wolves were about to breathe a sigh of relief when they saw the dragon bank to come back around. The pack took their chance and fled. H'Ilgraith took off with them. As the dragon made his approach, the wolves couldn't resist looking back to see what he would do. After all, they were still human.

The pack watched as the dragon spewed searing fire across that entire section of the canal (illustration 11). It melted the mortar holding any stones in place, including those in the canal. As the canal walls gave way, stones crashed into its basin. Finally, dragon fire fused any collapsed stones in a heap, including those from the turrets and those now littering the canal. The entire structure was in ruins.

The dragon made one more pass to examine his handiwork before landing again. Using the claws of his back feet, he dug up the embankments. Then he used his tail to whip the dirt over top of the burning stones. Not only was the fire contained, but there was now also a ton of dirt and rocks lying atop the ruins. No ship would pass through this section of the canal. His work done, he lumbered into a takeoff and was soon gone.

As the pack watched the dragon, they were mesmerized by his power. Even after seeing two of the behemoths engaged in mortal combat, H'Ilgraith and Jak were transfixed. His firepower was breathtaking.

With the dragon's departure, the intruders also turned to go home. Their journey home would be more hazardous because of the many hybrids that had fled into the surrounding forest. Hopefully, most were headed back in a westerly direction, toward the quarry. It was likely, however, that some would elect to remain free. So in the hope of avoiding encounters with any of them, Weston led the group further eastward before turning south toward H'Aleth.

CHAPTER 28
A CALL TO ARMS

The Trek Home

I nitially, the wolf pack continued to follow the canal. Beyond the section destroyed by the dragon, it remained intact. Finally, they had to turn south if they were ever going to get back to H'Aleth. Weston still wondered where the canal had connected to the ocean and where the battleship was berthed. *Rex probably parked it in a bay somewhere along the coastline*, he thought.

The destruction of at least one section of the canal precluded sailing any more ships past that point. Two questions remained. Had any other ships passed through the canal already, and, if yes, had they already reached the coastline?

The trek back to H'Aleth was not entirely uneventful. Cassius villages dotted the landscape. Edrian and Weston created a mental map of each village they encountered and the resources it held. This information would be priceless in assessing the Foundation's strength and ability to launch an attack over land or to resupply a battleship. H'Ilgraith kept an aerial map. When the pack returned to H'Aleth and resumed human form, they and H'Ilgraith would work with Petramonte to refine their maps of the Cassius northeast territory.

H'Ilgraith, Edrian, and Jak were familiar with Cassius villages. Weston, Mavelov, and Ilsa were not and were shocked by the conditions they saw. Still, they committed to memory the locations of villages with substantial storerooms, suggesting a stockpile of supplies. As dismayed as they were by the villages, they were amazed by the numbers of humanoid and animal hybrids they saw. Many looked identical. *They are being cloned*, Weston thought.

Ramping Up Defenses

Weston knew that H'Aleth was ill-prepared to fend off a cloned hybrid horde. He snapped a growl at the other members of the pack and promptly picked up the pace. They must return to H'Aleth as soon as possible. H'Aleth needed to ramp up its defenses on its northern and eastern borders and prepare the defenses of its southern coastal regions.

Periodically, the pack alternated bursts of speed with a steady trot. This routine allowed them to continue traveling with relatively few rest periods. Yet when nearing any sign of human or hybrid activity, stealth became imperative. Sometimes, the pack had to stop and wait for an enforced rest before resuming their trip back home.

In the meantime, H'Aletheans had not been idle. H'Assandra and her brother Edward set aside most civil affairs, focusing on the defense of H'Aleth from invasion. Serena and Tragar, both experienced scouts, were dispatched to warn every northern and southern village, respectively, of the risk and guide them on how best to prepare for an invasion. Each community needed to decide how to hold a defensive position, mount a counterattack, and escape if overwhelmed. Other scouts who worked in those regions also participated in the preparations.

Craftsmen and women from each village who knew how to fashion bows and arrows, knives, spears, and swords were asked to travel to the main village adjacent to the estate. Their skills and additional hands would increase the production of these armaments for subsequent distribution among all villages.

Hidden outposts were established across the southern coastal borders. Each blended into the vegetation native to its area. They were made from native plants woven at the base, leaving their tops free to move in the breeze. A small cache of weapons could be stowed there for anyone in human form to use. Traps were set for anyone or anything weighing over forty pounds. Most of the native animals found among the coastal reeds were small and light; they could walk or scurry over a trap and not sink into it. Larger animals or humans would find their legs quickly entangled in a quagmire of twisted reeds. They would not drown; however, it would take a long time for them to dig, cut, bite, or chew their way out. Fortunately, larger animals, such as deer, rarely wandered into the area unless a predator was chasing them.

The training of scouts intensified. Normally, it took four or five years for a scout to become fully seasoned, not only in stealth but also in combat. This could not be expected of younger recruits; however, their observational skills could be developed quickly. An experienced scout was given three or four young adults as apprentices instead of the usual one or two. All recruits had to be proficient in two things: the use of a bow and arrows and using the capabilities of their alternate species.

Finally, nearly every child who had come of age could develop the skills inherent in their alternate species. Thus, children twelve to fourteen years of age, who had grown up in H'Aleth, spent additional time in their alternate species. The children were delighted with the opportunity. At first, they did not understand that survival might depend upon their abilities. It occurred to H'Assandra that H'Aleth's youngsters could be paired with age-matched youngsters from other territories, especially the contested regions. The latter brought life experiences with them from these areas, not hypothetical ones. Their somber tales of life before they came to H'Aleth imparted a seriousness to H'Aleth's youngsters that no adult could convey.

Fight or Flight

When the wolf pack returned to H'Aleth, Weston briefed the security council on what they had seen. The only good news he could impart was the great gray dragon's destruction of a section of the canal system.

"Why the dragon did this, we do not know," he reported. "Strangely, he did not attack any of the hybrids, nor did he attack us. He seemed focused on destroying that segment of the canal." Weston turned to Jak. "What do you know about the relationship between the dragons and the Cassius Foundation?" he asked.

"Not a thing," Jak replied. "I never saw a dragon while I was a prisoner in the fortress, and I have never seen one so close." That was the reason Jak had stayed behind. He wanted to see what the dragon would do, and he had already known that they would not have escaped if the dragon had chosen to attack them.

"My biggest concern," Weston continued, "is the large number of hybrids—human and animal—that we saw at the quarry, at the canal, and in the villages we observed on the way back. Rex must have thousands of them. Although we saw a variety of hybrids, there were many with the same characteristics. I suspect he is cloning them. If he turns his workforce into an army, we could be overwhelmed."

For a moment, no one spoke. Then Weston said what no one wanted to hear. "We may have to flee farther into the southwestern region, perhaps into the mountains or west into the desert."

"Leave this fertile land and the forests and rivers that abound here?" spoke a councilman in disbelief. "Not without a fight!"

"We do not have an army, nor was it ever our founders' intent to have one," said H'Assandra. "Still, I believe it is incumbent upon us to protect this land, which has harbored us, and all the life that lies within it. At the same time, we must find a haven for the youngest of our members and those among us too frail to mount a defense. Our elders still can nurture our children. Any child twelve years of age or older should be able to assume many adult duties in caring for the very young and the very old."

H'Assandra tasked Balthorean with finding places in the foothills and lower ranges of the southwestern mountains where H'Aletheans could shelter. "These places must not impose upon the red dragons' range," she insisted. "It would not be wise to intrude upon their territory." She also tasked Valeria with identifying places in the southwestern plains and desert, where people could find safety should Rex invade.

The Best Defense

Both Jak and H'Ilgraith offered to serve as scouts beyond the northern boundary of H'Aleth's territory. "Jak knows the contested territory very well, and I know Cassius southern territory along our border," said H'Ilgraith.

H'Assandra knew better than to argue with her cousin. "Be careful," she warned, looking at Jak.

Jak nodded to H'Assandra. He understood what she meant. Yet he had no idea how he was going to keep H'Ilgraith from getting into trouble in Cassius territory or anywhere else for that matter. *One can aught but try*, he thought.

Sometimes the best defense is a good offense. Weston began recruiting for anyone skilled in armaments who would be willing to defend H'Aleth's territory. Many new immigrants volunteered their services. H'Aleth was their home now. No longer were they obliged to be constantly on the move, fleeing from Cassius bounty hunters and barely able to eke out a living. Many more displaced people flooded into H'Aleth every day. They brought with them valuable intelligence about Rex's activities and the creatures he was releasing into the contested regions. Given the hybrids' success at driving people out of those areas, it seemed logical that Rex would eventually use the same tactic against H'Aleth's population.

"Not if we can ambush them," Weston told H'Assandra. "We can station archers in the trees to spot and bring down any attackers. We can excavate earthen dugouts beneath the prairie grass that can hide an archer until an enemy passes by. If the hybrid is an animal with a good sense of smell, the archer can shoot an arrow into the beast as it attempts to enter the dugout." Weston tasked his scouts with identifying other hidden places where an ambush could be set or another trap laid. The H'Aletheans had to outsmart their enemy.

The House of H'Aleth had one other major advantage that Rex greatly desired and did not possess. Every sister of the House of H'Aleth could transform into a raptor. With the extraordinary visual range and acuity of raptors, virtually anything that moved would be seen, whether in daylight or dark of night. There would be few, if any, sneak attacks.

Supplemental Notes and Citations
Somatic Cell Nuclear Transfer (SCNT)—Cloning

Somatic cell nuclear transfer was the method used to clone a sheep named Dolly in 1996 (Turner, 1997), a horse in 2003 (Gambini & Maserati, 2017), a dog named Snuppy in 2005 (Lee *et al.*, 2018), and other farm animals (Saini *et al.*, 2018). The process uses a fertilized egg that has had its nucleus removed (an enucleated oocyte) (Simões & Rodrigues Santos, 2017). The nucleus is replaced by the nucleus of a somatic (nonreproductive) cell from the same species that donated the egg. The modified oocyte proceeds to develop into an embryo and ultimately into a fully grown adult.

This process is not as simple as it sounds. The somatic nucleus must be reprogrammed by factors in the oocyte's cytoplasm so that the somatic nucleus behaves like the nucleus of a fertilized egg (Loi *et al.*, 2016; Simões & Rodrigues Santos, 2017). A somatic cell nucleus has a full complement of 46 chromosomes and all the genes contained therein. A reproductive cell—an ovum or a sperm—has only half a complement, 23 chromosomes. When a sperm merges its half complement with an ovum's half complement, the resulting fertilized oocyte then has a full complement of 46 chromosomes—as does a somatic cell. The cytoplasm of a fertilized egg contains substances that promote the growth and development of an embryonic cell and an embryo. The cytoplasm of a somatic cell supports the maintenance of a mature cell.

The use of SCNT in humans is laced with ethical implications. The Ethics Committee of the American Society for Reproductive Medicine (2016) determined that the practice of SCNT in humans is unnecessary and unethical.

CHAPTER 29
Voyage of the Rex Cassius

Rex remained unaware of the damage the great gray dragon had inflicted on his canal. No one told him about it, and no one was going to tell him. His lieutenants who had visited the site to observe and report on the progress pretended to know nothing about it. Fortunately for them, Rex assumed all was well. His warship had reached the ocean, and he never intended for it to return inland. He did intend to build another ship someday. "One day, I will have an armada," he declared. His shipbuilders glanced at each other and said nothing.

Outfitting the Warship

Rex had settled on his plan to invade H'Aleth by sea. Surveillance reports from his battleship's maiden voyage indicated that the southern coast of H'Aleth was uninhabited by humans or land mammals of any kind. A plethora of birds, insects, fish, and small reptiles abounded. These would pose no threat nor impede an invasion.

For the ship's maiden voyage, the crew was limited to the captain, Gustavian, crewmen to man the sails, rowers, and a few lieutenants, spotters, and archers. There were no cannoneers or animal hybrids aboard. There were only enough supplies in the hold to provide for the skeleton crew. The weather was good, and the voyage went smoothly.

Conditions became a bit more complicated when the ship was outfitted for war. With his battle plan established, Rex ordered it be readied to set sail for H'Aleth. Food, water, handheld armaments, and supplies needed for the rigging were loaded on one side of the hold. Cannon supplies, materials for building a dock, and an array of small, cramped cages were placed on the other side of the hold. The cages held the hybrids intended for release onshore in advance of his fighting force's embarkation. All of these items provided ballast for the ship. None were properly secured.

Rex's fighting force consisted of cannoneers, archers, and powerful hybrid humanoid laborers transferred from the quarry and the canal. From the last group, Gustavian selected humanoids to man the oars. He picked *H. sapiens* and *H. transformans* forced into service to handle the sails. Rex placed additional lieutenants on board to oversee all operations. They were tasked with selecting other humans, both men and women, to serve as stewards aboard ship. These people manned the galley, cleaned the crew's quarters, and performed any other duties set before them.

In an extraordinary arrangement, the lieutenants answered to Rex— not to the ship's captain. Even so, the lieutenants knew that their best hope of surviving the ocean voyage lay with following Gustavian's orders.

Mayhem Below Deck

Gustavian ordered the rowers to maneuver the warship out of the waters where it had been moored. Once the ship reached the open waters of the ocean, he ordered the sails raised. The winds were already blustery. As the ship headed south, Gustavian eyed the southern sky warily. Far in the distance, he could see clouds billowing, harbingers of a possible storm. He ordered the ship under full sail. He wanted to reach H'Aleth as quickly as possible. Its coastline bent inward like a shallow bay. The waters would be quieter there unless a tropical storm struck the coast. Even though it was the time of year when tropical depressions developed, Rex would not wait to launch his invasion of H'Aleth.

Gustavian would have preferred to sail relatively close to land. Unfortunately, he had to give the east coast of H'Aleth a wide berth to avoid detection. He could not afford to alert any H'Aletheans who might see the ship. This meant sailing in more southerly waters, where ocean waves were choppier, especially with the threat of a storm.

The maiden voyage had not prepared anyone for rough seas. More importantly, the animal hybrids were not prepared for an ocean voyage at all. They had spent their lives on *terra firma*. The way ocean waves and swells tossed the ship created turmoil below deck. The cages shifted and listed with every roll of the ship, flinging the animals around in their cages. They were trapped and terrified. Their distress increased with the size of the swells, which became ever greater as wind speed increased.

Finally, the inevitable happened. As the cages crashed against each other, some of the locks broke. The freed hybrids found themselves in even worse straits. They could gain no foothold anywhere, and their cages no longer protected them. Some were able to scramble on top of supply crates that were only slightly more secure. Others died when crushed by colliding cargo. Although the crew could hear the mayhem and the hybrids' frantic cries below, no one went down there.

An Impending Storm

With the onset of heavy seas and a darkening sky, Gustavian was certain a storm was coming. *I might be able to manage a tropical storm,* he thought, *but a hurricane is another matter.* Although they were not far from H'Aleth's coastline, he knew he should not head for shore. The ship could be tossed onto hidden rocks in the shoals and become wrecked. It was safer in open water.

He ordered all hands, except for the cannoneers and rowers, on deck. "Secure all cargo on the ship, including the animal cages, and batten down the hatches," he shouted to the crew. He ordered the bowmen to help the crew trim the mainsails and rig the storm sails. He charged the cannoneers with making sure all lashings were secure on the kegs of gunpowder, boxes of cannonballs, and the cannons themselves so that they could not shift. He ordered the rowers to cover their positions.

When crewmen opened the hatch to the hold, two animal hybrids atop a cascade of cargo leaped onto the open deck. Of those who had broken out of their cages, these were the only two who had survived. They immediately attacked the first crewmen they encountered. Their attack was short-lived. The heaving of the ship tossed them across the deck. They went overboard and quickly disappeared.

The crew struggled to secure the cargo, to no avail. It had not been lashed properly, and heavy seas had tossed and scattered crates, barrels, and cages. Fortunately, in doing so, the cargo had tumbled around the hold until it was jammed up and could shift no more.

Out of the Depths

Gustavian watched the weather, the wind, and the swells closely. He noted that some swells in the distance were much higher than others, and they were coming closer. Unbeknownst to the captain and his crew, an unknown marine mammal was approaching the ship. It had encountered the two animal hybrids tossed into the ocean and found them a suitable snack. Perhaps there was more prey ahead. The animal issued a series of clicks that bounced off any objects in its path. One of these was the warship. The animal did not view this object as food; however, prey could be harboring inside it.

When a huge swell approaching the ship suddenly disappeared, Gustavian knew that no wind had caused that motion. *It has to be a whale*, he thought, hoping the animal had diverted its path away from the ship and had not gone under it. Gustavian thought it odd that he did not see the whale's fluke when it dived.

Suddenly, the entire ship seemed to rise out of the water. Then it slammed back down on the ocean's surface. A seafaring blue dragon had nearly upended the ship (illustration 12). The upheaval threw overboard anyone on deck not holding on tightly or lashed to the boat—just as it had thrown the hybrids. Barges, canoes, rafts, and some of the rigging were torn away from the ship. The debris was scattered over the water like so much flotsam. The *odontoceti* surfaced long enough to swallow the hapless sailors and humanoids in the water. It simply viewed these life-forms as food. Given its size, power, and striking similarity to a dragon, Gustavian knew this was no whale. It was all the motivation he needed to head for the nearest shoreline.

A few of the canoes appeared to be intact. Once the sea dragon submerged again, Gustavian ordered any crewmen that could swim to fetch them back to the ship. To keep crewmen from being washed away, they were tethered by rope so that they could be pulled back with the canoe in tow. Gustavian could not afford to lose any more hands—human or humanoid. He needed every hand and lifeboat he had left.

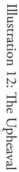

Illustration 12: The Upheaval

Despite the damage to the ship, especially the rigging, it was still afloat. Gustavian suspected it was barely seaworthy and little more than a glorified rowboat. He ordered the rowers back to their stations. The crew salvaged enough rigging to hoist a few small sails. "Head for the nearest coastline with all available speed," he ordered. Gustavian watched as the *odontoceti* followed until the warship drew too close to the shoreline. Then it had to turn away. It needed deeper draft than the ship.

Final Disposition

Gustavian anchored the warship just off H'Aleth's eastern coast. Even if he could get the ship back home, he knew he could not go back empty-handed. Rex would certainly kill him and probably the lieutenants for the damage to the vessel, the loss of so many hybrids, and the failure of the invasion. The lieutenants knew it, too. Gustavian mustered the crew, including the hybrid humanoids, most of whom would understand his announcement.

"We cannot go back," he told them. "The ship is no longer seaworthy, and we must destroy it. Once we scuttle the ship, we must go our separate ways, perhaps two or three together, and meld into this territory. It would be unwise for all of us to stay together. This would arouse suspicion."

"What about the hybrids in the cargo hold?" asked a crewman.

"Release them," ordered Gustavian, "but feed them first. They should frighten away any inhabitants near our landing site."

Every animal hybrid still alive was crazed. This did not bode well for the crew tasked with bringing them topside and ferrying them to shore. Fortunately, they were still caged until released on land. As Gustavian predicted, they quickly disappeared.

Rex never learned what happened to his ship. His shipmasters suggested it was likely lost at sea in a storm. This assumption in no way abated his fury.

Part V
H'Ilgraith's Decision

CHAPTER 30
Ursuscro!

H'Aleth's scouts had observed the ship's demise and overheard Gustavian's plan for the crew. The scouts kept watch as many crew members stayed in H'Aleth and eventually integrated into the villages. They were relieved to be beyond Cassius's reach. Those who had families still held hostage passed through H'Aleth's territory in an attempt to return to them. Their fate was unknown. The animal hybrids invariably attacked someone and were killed. The hybrid humanoids disappeared into the wilderness, finally free of their enslavement.

The threat of an impending attack on H'Aleth's southern coastline was averted. A sea dragon had assured that outcome. For the moment, the H'Aletheans had some respite from the threat on their southern shore. Nevertheless, the possibility of an invasion by sea still existed. So they remained alert and kept their watch over the coastline.

Still, the greatest threat of invasion came from the north. Fortunately, many newly trained scouts patrolled H'Aleth's territory. Weston now had a depot of weapons, which he could deploy on a moment's notice. H'Aleth was much better prepared to repel invaders. To provide a measure of advanced warning, H'Ilgraith and Jak returned to Cassius territory to resume their watch.

A Familiar Odor

During one of their forays into a heavily forested region of the northern mountains, Jak, as a wolf, caught the scent of a bear that had recently traversed the area. Although the smell was characteristic of a species of *Ursus*, it also carried an odd and unfamiliar odor. Jak realized that something about this bear was unnatural.

H'Ilgraith, as an owl, was perched on the branch of a nearby tree. She observed the intensity with which Jak investigated the scent of another animal. She gave a short, soft hoot to draw Jak's attention then flew higher in the canopy to get a wider view of the surrounding area. From this new vantage point, she observed a paucity of native animals, most of them small mammals and reptiles and a few birds. She thought it odd that she saw no large species, such as deer, nor did she see any other predators, such as lynx, foxes, or wolves. Something was amiss.

Before H'Ilgraith descended from the canopy, she transformed into a badger. She had seen no sign of any humans, so there was no one to notice that a wolf and badger were working together. Both H'Ilgraith and Jak continued to track the scent for some distance.

H'Ilgraith also found the scent disturbing. For her, there was a hint of familiarity. *Where have I smelled something like this before?* she wondered. She finally sat down on her rump, her forepaws across her belly, and pondered. Suddenly, she caught the sound of another animal approaching. Her badger's relatively poor eyesight discerned the shape of a bear. It was stalking her.

Ambush

Jak had moved a hundred yards away, still tracking the scent. He turned back when he heard several low-pitched growls from H'Ilgraith. He saw her retreating from a large animal, built like a bear yet with the head of a boar and fangs like those of a tiger. While H'Ilgraith was distracted, an ursuscro had approached downwind and caught her by surprise.

Jak knew instantly that H'Ilgraith did not stand a chance against this beast. With a loud and aggressive growl, he launched himself toward the ursuscro, drawing its attention away from H'Ilgraith and onto himself. The ursuscro turned and immediately charged his challenger (illustration 13).

As a badger, H'Ilgraith knew she would not be effective in this fight. *But a lynx can be*, she thought. Even though the lynx's bite force was much less than that of the wolf or bear, sharp claws and canines could be very potent if properly applied. The badger ducked behind a large boulder.

Illustration 13: A Sudden Onset

During her transformation, H'Ilgraith was unaware of the fierce battle between Jak and the hybrid bear, which was more than a match for a lone wolf. Moments later, a lynx lunged atop the boulder and sprang onto the hybrid's back. It was down on all four feet, facing away from her with its head down. H'Ilgraith could not see that it was standing over the body of a wolf. As her claws and canines sank into the creature's flank, it roared and reared up on its back legs.

It bucked and wrenched in an attempt to shake off the lynx. Its efforts were to no avail. Its neck was too short and thick for it to reach back and bite or gore its attacker. Suddenly, the beast slammed into a large tree behind him, jarring both himself and the lynx.

H'Ilgraith, stunned by the blow, loosened her grip. She was barely able to leap onto the tree trunk as the ursuscro threw her off. She scrambled up the trunk just as the creature launched a counterattack. Its tusks barely missed goring her flank. Once she reached a limb that would support her, she renewed her attack. Bears could climb trees, too; however, they were not as nimble as cats. *If he attempts to climb the tree, I will have him*, she vowed to herself. She would ravage his head as he climbed toward her.

The ursuscro had not escaped his battle with the wolf unscathed. The wolf had inflicted deep bite wounds on the ursuscro's neck, shoulder, and forelegs. These wounds impaired his ability to climb. He snarled and lunged at the lynx, who struck back with claws that ripped into his snout and struck at his eyes.

The ursuscro seemed to realize the cat's advantage. With a frustrated and angry snarl, he dropped back down on all fours and hobbled away.

Then H'Ilgraith saw Jak's mangled body. She was horrified. Instantly, she jumped down from the tree. When she landed next to the wolf's body, she froze. Jak was dead.

The harrowing sound of a lynx's scream echoed through the mountains. H'Ilgraith had lost her soul mate.

Fury

Grief-stricken, H'Ilgraith laid down beside Jak's body for a long while. She could not leave him lying where he fell, exposed to scavengers.

Neither could she carry him back to H'Aleth. *He would not want to be buried there anyway*, she told herself. *He loved the mountains.* She looked at the boulder that had sheltered her. She transformed into a badger once more and began to excavate a steep tunnel—one large enough to hold a wolf. She started where the wolf lay and delved deep beneath the boulder. Once she reached a depth of ten feet, she excavated a den large enough to accommodate both a badger and a wolf. Once she finished, she hauled the wolf's body into the tunnel. The slope was steep enough for a wolf's body to slide readily down the tunnel, almost crushing the badger.

Once Jak's body was settled in the den, H'Ilgraith climbed out and began to fill the den and then the tunnel with the dirt she had excavated. Jak's body was buried deep enough to prevent any scent from rising to the surface. Nevertheless, the badger scavenged for rocks and stones, which she piled atop of the opening to the tunnel. She also scratched up and disrupted the place where Jak's body had lain, scattering dirt and debris everywhere and effectively dispersing the scent of all three animals over a wide area.

It took her a day to accomplish her tasks. Bone-tired, H'Ilgraith paused only long enough to transform back into a lynx. Then she began tracking the hybrid while its scent remained fresh. As a master of stealth, she could both track her quarry efficiently and reengage it without transforming again. H'Ilgraith was certain the bear was an animal hybrid—probably one engineered by the Cassius Foundation. Then she realized why his scent had seemed familiar. The mound of carcasses she had encountered on a previous foray carried a similar odor.

As H'Ilgraith pursued her adversary, she also plotted her plan of attack. She would be confronting an animal far larger than herself with formidable weapons of its own. So how does a twenty-two-pound cat bring down an 800-pound bear? *With cunning*, she told herself.

The lynx's large, padded paws supported a silent approach. If she maneuvered herself upwind, she could ambush him. *But not from the ground*, she decided. She estimated that the beast was about eight feet tall. Leaping onto its back again would not suffice. *Its head will*, she determined. *It will be greatly hampered if it is blind. Then I can attack it at will and tear out its throat.*

CHAPTER 31

RETRIBUTION

A great gray dragon heard the fearful cry of the lynx and wondered at it. He had been keeping watch over his terrain when he heard the tormented sound. Soon, a high mountain crag shuddered and shifted, yet no stones fell. The dragon, perfectly blended into the mountain, lifted off. He immediately set forth to search for its source. Something dangerous and deadly had entered his domain.

A pair of dragon chicks, perched on the ledge of their aery, also heard the cry. They too became alert and looked toward the sound. Their mother abruptly called to them from the cave that housed their nest, and they promptly scurried inside. Then the dragoness positioned herself at the entrance to her cave. There she watched and waited—her deadliest weapon at the ready.

Vengeance

As the gray dragon soared over his territory, his raptor-like vision detected many animal species native to the mountains and their montane forests. He also spotted a large bear-like creature, clearly a hybrid. Not infrequently, unnatural creatures encroached on his territory. As long as they entered and left without posing a threat, the gray dragons treated them like any other prey species. Those that did pose a threat were quickly dispatched.

The gray dragons knew the source of these unnatural creatures. Humans had built a fortress close to the River Taurus, where they produced many corrupted creatures. Although the dragons could readily destroy the structure with everything and everyone in it, they did not. There were many innocent animals, including humans, housed there. Furthermore, the fortress had the means to kill a great gray dragon—cannon fire. So the grays kept watch from a prudent distance.

The dragon's sharp eyes also caught sight of a lynx carefully picking its way through the underbrush and over rocky terrain. Clearly, it was stalking prey; and its trajectory was taking it toward the hybrid bear. If the lynx were to stumble upon it, the encounter could be fatal for the lynx. *Should I intervene?* the dragon wondered. He decided to alight silently on a nearby rocky escarpment, where he could meld into its formation, and watch events as they unfolded.

Great gray dragons are long-lived. There is little an adult gray dragon has not seen or encountered within its territory. So the dragon was astonished when the lynx suddenly broke from its stalk, ran straight at the hybrid, leaped onto a nearby boulder, and vaulted onto the beast's shoulders in a direct and deliberate attack. This was so bizarre, the dragon knew immediately that the lynx was not a native species. He was certain that the cat had uttered the fearful cry he had heard.

H'Ilgraith's grief had turned to fury, and she redoubled her determination to avenge her mate's death. From the beast's shoulders, she immediately launched her upper body onto its head, sinking her canines into its forehead and her claws into its face. Once again, the ursuscro tried to dislodge the lynx and swiped at her with his front paws. This time, she had a better grip, yet she was not inflicting enough damage. In attacking from the rear, she had missed getting her claws into his eyes. The ursuscro was able to turn his head enough to strike her upper body with his tusks.

As the two mortal enemies clashed, the dragon knew that the lynx was outmatched. The cat was being battered by the hybrid's attempts to gore and dislodge its attacker. Certain of the bear's origin, the dragon climbed down from the escarpment.

Engrossed in their battle, the two combatants failed to notice the deepening shadow that drew near as the dragon crept closer. When the ursuscro became aware of a larger creature encroaching upon him, he abruptly aborted his counterattack against the lynx and charged the new entrant. Either the hybrid did not recognize the nature of this second adversary or he had no regard for it. Seconds later, the ursuscro lay dead in the dragon's jaws. With a swift whip of his head and neck, the dragon tossed the carcass aside.

A Proposal

H'Ilgraith was shocked by the sudden appearance of a great gray dragon and was certain she would be his next target. Exhausted and in despair, she made no move to flee from him. Her vengeance satisfied with the death of the ursuscro, she lay down upon the ground and slipped into a twilight sleep.

For his part, the dragon had no intention of killing the lynx. The cat had the scent of a transformed being, so he waited. Soon, a chrysalis formed around her. Not long afterward, the chrysalis evanesced, and a badger could be seen laying where the lynx had been.

The dragon knew then that he had encountered an *H. transformans* with truly extraordinary capabilities. The situation posed an interesting question and an intriguing opportunity. *Is it possible for our species to ally with this species of human?* he mused. *Could we be aligned against a common enemy?* The dragon encircled the badger with his massive tail, which both entrapped and protected her.

Sometime later, the badger morphed once again to resume human form. When H'Ilgraith finally awoke, she was surprised to find herself encompassed by the dragon's tail. She was appalled at having no robe. Fortunately, the dragon's tail covered her effectively; however, it also enclosed her completely. *Now what do I do?* she wondered.

H'Ilgraith heard a barely audible, low-pitched rumble. Oddly, she was able to distinguish the words from the tonal sounds she heard. As she listened carefully to discern them, she realized, *Dragons do know our language.*

"Why did you attack a creature that was well beyond your ability to vanquish?" rumbled the dragon.

"It killed my mate," H'Ilgraith replied. Once again, overcome by sorrow, she finally could grieve in a way the lynx could not. Tears began to flow.

The dragon interceded with another query. "Do you know the creature's origin?" he asked.

"I suspect it," H'Ilgraith replied, regaining her composure. "It is likely a hybrid, genetically engineered by the Cassius Foundation."

"We agree," the dragon responded. "Many such creatures find their way into our territory. The humans occupying a fortress in that region have tried to kill our chicks and steal our eggs. Their attempts have failed. They are no match for us. So they release unnatural beings in the hope that one of their creations can accomplish what they cannot. What of your people?"

H'Ilgraith replied, "We, too, are hunted for our abilities to transform. My ancestors left their home to flee from bounty hunters hired to kill or capture us. My people settled in a distant land, far from those who would persecute us. We just want to live in peace. Yet the hybrids are a reminder that danger is never far away." *And they are creeping closer,* she thought.

"My clan and others of my kind wish the same," the dragon remarked. "It would seem we share a common adversary. Perhaps our two species could reach an accord."

The dragon then proposed an agreement whereby his clan would protect and defend any of H'Ilgraith's kin who entered the gray dragons' realm. In return, H'Ilgraith's kin would protect and defend any dragon eggs or wayward chicks they encountered until they could be fetched home. Each one would warn the other if either became aware of an impending danger that threatened their survival.

The dragon's proposal held great appeal for H'Ilgraith. Even if the agreement were informal, such an alliance would strengthen security across the northern lands.

"I cannot speak officially for my clan," H'Ilgraith responded. "I believe they would be a willing ally in this matter, as would I. I must return home as quickly as possible to report what has happened here and relay your proposal." Then it occurred to H'Ilgraith, "How will I find you again?"

"You need only resume your form as a lynx, ascend onto a rocky outcrop, and call to us," the dragon replied. "Our sentinels will recognize your cry, determine its vector, and find you."

Then H'Ilgraith told the dragon her origin. "I am H'Ilgraith of the

House of H'Aleth. My kin includes those of the House of Erwina to the west of H'Aleth and the House of Gregor in the far arctic north."

"I am Theovolan [thē-ō-*vō*-lăn]," the dragon responded.

"With your permission, I will use the shelter of your tail to transform for my return home," H'Ilgraith said. Theovolan consented, and, a short time later, a great horned owl lifted off and began its flight back to H'Aleth.

Impressive, thought Theovolan. He already knew that this *H. transformans* female could become more than one mammal; however, he was surprised to see an avian species appear before him. *This clan of* H. transformans *is a powerful one.*

Supplemental Notes and Citations
Tonal Language

Pitch is an important cue in tonal languages (e.g., Mandarin Chinese) (Jain *et al.*, 2017; Deroche *et al.*, 2019; Ortega-Llebaria *et al.*, 2017). Changes in pitch alter the meaning of a word. In non-tonal languages (e.g., English), changes in pitch can relay emotion. They do not change meaning. Patterns of emphasis and the speed of tonal changes can even alter the meaning of a syllable within a word (Antoniou *et al.*, 2018). The brain translates these differences into meaningful constructs (Deroche *et al.*, 2019.) Thus, listeners must be very attentive to changes in pitch when listening to a tonal language (Braun & Johnson, 2011).

CHAPTER 32
An Accord

A s weary as she was, H'Ilgraith could not afford to let down her guard. She had already encountered one deadly avian hybrid. With the Cassius fortress not far away, the likelihood of other unnatural avian predators was high. Fortunately, her return to H'Aleth proved uneventful.

H'Ilgraith flew directly to the manor house, where she sought out H'Assandra, who was in her chambers. When a great horned owl landed directly in front of her, H'Assandra knew exactly who it was.

The owl issued a sharp shriek—a warning call to alert H'Assandra to a matter of urgency. Then the owl slipped into one of H'Assandra's robes. While awaiting H'Ilgraith's transformation, H'Assandra sent word via a courier to Weston and any senior scouts at hand. "H'Ilgraith has returned with a warning. I do not yet know its nature. Join us in the arboretum. H'Ilgraith and I will arrive shortly."

H'Assandra immediately recognized that Jak was not with her. Once H'Ilgraith resumed human form, H'Assandra asked, "Where is Jak?"

"Dead," replied H'Ilgraith without saying another word.

An Enlightening Report

At the council meeting, H'Ilgraith described the creature that had killed Jak. She said nothing of Jak's death or its manner. Her grief would not allow this part of the tale to be told. Instead, she next described her encounter with the great gray dragon. She abridged her report, saying, "I saw him kill the creature that would have killed me had he not intervened."

Then she recounted her unusual conversation with him. "The gray dragons have been persecuted by the Cassius Foundation, as well. The Foundation has used animal hybrids in an attempt to steal their eggs and kill their chicks. The dragon offered to protect my clan if we enter his territory, provided we protect any lost dragon eggs or chicks we encounter."

The council members were astonished. "So the rumors are true," offered Mavelov, the lead scout and wildlife specialist. "We have long known that most animal species, including dragons, have a means of communicating with other members of their own species even if we cannot discern it. Until now, we have not encountered a nonhuman species that appears to understand language as we know it," he added. "I wonder how dragons learned our language?" he mused out loud.

"They were here long before we were," said H'Assandra. "I suspect they learned our language by listening to us and mimicking our vocalizations—just as we have learned the myriad sounds that other animal species make and how to mimic them," she added.

Weston had more pressing issues to address—namely, the potential ramifications of engaging with great gray dragons. "How do you know all this?" he asked H'Ilgraith.

"Of my own knowledge, only that he killed the hybrid and did not kill me," replied H'Ilgraith. "Neither did he attack me while I rested nor when I resumed human form. Somehow, he sensed I was not an enemy. As for his history of persecution, I can only relay what he told me."

"I can believe his story," said Mavelov. "Because of the Foundation's persecution of the red dragon species, I have had to assign extra scouts to that region to protect them."

The irony of the red dragon's situation did not escape Weston. Yet he knew that cannons and catapults could kill a dragon. His scouts, at their own peril, had managed to thwart Cassius bounty hunters by sabotaging their weapons.

Then H'Assandra spoke to H'Ilgraith. "You have spoken to a gray dragon who offers us an alliance. Would you like to serve as our liaison to his species and return to confer with them?"

H'Ilgraith's initial thought was, *Not in the least.* She recoiled from the idea of passing through the area where Jak had been killed. Her memory of his fallen body was much too vivid. She also disliked the notion of serving as an intermediary. She just wanted to get away.

Yet she also valued an alliance with a powerful ally that might destroy the Cassius Foundation someday. Serving as liaison would provide an opportunity to learn much more about great gray dragons. She realized the ursuscro was not at fault for killing Jak. The person who had created him was to blame.

"Yes," H'Ilgraith agreed.

"Then as soon as Edrian arrives, you will meet with us again in council to deliberate how we should proceed. I have dispatched Serena to fetch him back to the estate," H'Assandra added. "I will also send word to Erwina and Gregor."

H'Ilgraith nodded and braced herself for the onslaught of chatter she would have to endure.

Deliberations

With the return of Edrian, the council met again in the arboretum. The members from H'Aleth included H'Assandra, Edrian, H'Ilgraith, Weston, Mavelov, and Petramonte. Leliana [lä-lē-*ă*-nă], Erwina's chief of security, and Andronovich [ăn-*drŏn*-ō-vĭch], Gregor's chief of security, also were present.

H'Assandra opened the meeting, saying, "A chance encounter between H'Ilgraith and a great gray dragon has raised the possibility of our entering into a mutual agreement for the protection of both our clans. I am seeking your counsel on this matter." The newest arrivals were stunned by this revelation. "Yes," H'Assandra continued in response to their reaction. "They understand the common language and can communicate with us."

Considerable discussion centered on the prospect of negotiating anything with a dragon. The debate swirled around the gray dragons' reputation as a dangerous species, the practicality of such an alliance, and any relationship the dragons might have with Cassius or Biogenics. H'Ilgraith had remained silent during what seemed to her to be an endless debate. Finally, she spoke.

"When the gray dragon and I *considered* the possibility of an agreement, I informed him that Erwina and Gregor were also part of my clan. He is expecting an accord with our three houses. That offer is what I intend to take back to his clan," she said firmly. "I already know he considers the Cassius Foundation an enemy. I have no idea what his clan's attitude might be toward the Biogenics Corporation."

H'Ilgraith's assertion was met initially with silence.

Finally, H'Assandra spoke. "I, too, believe we should consider the possibility of an agreement with the gray dragon clan. To do so would require that we send an emissary to them." Then she looked directly at H'Ilgraith. "H'Ilgraith will be our liaison with the gray dragons. She will convey our thoughts and considerations regarding an arrangement with our three houses. Perhaps at some point in the future, she can ask them about Biogenics. For now, we need to identify what we would like covered by an agreement."

"Keep it as simple as possible," advised Weston. He proceeded to outline his priorities: 1) Maintain surveillance over Cassius territory. 2) Report any mass movement of Cassius forces. 3) Report any new hybrid— humanoid or animal—including a description of it and where it was seen. 4) Report finding any member of either species who is lost, including offspring and eggs. 5) If possible, protect a member of either species until his or her own species can recover him or her. 6) Take care and approach each other with all due respect.

H'Ilgraith breathed a sigh of relief. *Finally, a practical person*, she thought.

"Does anyone have a recommendation to add to Weston's proposal?" asked H'Assandra.

"I do," H'Ilgraith replied. "We have scouts. Dragons have the equivalent, which they call sentinels. We should make arrangements for our scouts to recognize their sentinels and vice versa, just as we do for the red dragons. The scouts can confer with each other when someone is lost or found, when a new hybrid has been detected, or when there is unusual activity."

"If the dragons agree, we can make those arrangements," said Weston. "And if they also agree to our recommendations, we will have an accord."

CHAPTER 33
A Sojourn with Dragons

O nce more, H'Ilgraith gathered her robe and flew off to the foothills of the northern mountains where she first encountered Theovolan. When she reached the timberline, she transformed into a lynx to begin her ascent into the lower rocks. Upon reaching a ledge where she could be seen, she yowled. Then she waited. It was reminiscent of her encounter with the red dragons.

A Startling Encounter

H'Ilgraith did not have long to wait. A great gray dragon soon appeared. To H'Ilgraith's consternation, this was a different dragon. His coloring was much darker than that of Theovolan. As he headed toward her, he looked as if he was stalking her. H'Ilgraith suddenly thought, *He thinks I'm prey!* She bolted immediately down the rocks in an attempt to reach the tree line, where she might have a chance to escape.

The dragon anticipated the lynx's reaction and moved to block her escape. He landed a short distance in front of her. At nearly thirty feet tall, he towered over her tiny frame. With a wingspan of forty-five feet, his wings spread out and overlapped, surrounding her (illustration 14). H'Ilgraith was trapped. Faced with the massive size and visage of a great gray dragon, she could only await her fate.

They both waited. Finally, H'Ilgraith issued a soft mew. The dragon cocked his head a little, then rumbled, "I am your escort." H'Ilgraith then realized that the dragon recognized her and had responded to her call. As a lynx, however, she could not reply to him. So she stood up and gave him a definitive mew.

Illustration 14: Encircled

H'Ilgraith realized that the dragon's wings would shelter her if she transformed. *Perhaps, he is waiting for me to resume human form so we can communicate*, she surmised. H'Ilgraith had come prepared for such an event. So she pawed her satchel open, took out her robe, and curled up inside it. A short time later, H'Ilgraith emerged, clothed. In the absence of a proper introduction, she thought it best to confirm her identity: "I am H'Ilgraith of the House of H'Aleth," she said, introducing herself to the dragon.

"I am Fenovartan [fĕn-ō-*vär*-tăn]," the dragon replied. "Theovolan told us to watch for you." Then he extended a talon to grasp H'Ilgraith. She stepped inside it just as she had done once before with a red dragon. When she was secure, the dragon lumbered to lift off the ground. Unlike the smooth takeoff of a red dragon, this takeoff was jarring. H'Ilgraith felt every bone in her body rattle until the dragon became airborne. Once aloft, the flight was smooth and short.

Fenovartan took H'Ilgraith to an enormous tectonic cave system recessed deeply into the mountainside. The twists and turns along passageways formed by fracture lines sheltered the system from the frigid north winds. It was kept warm by periodic bursts of dragon fire to heat the walls.

Theovolan was away. So H'Ilgraith spent the first few days listening to dragon rumbles, discerning the different tonal inflections, and learning how to recognize the sound of words used in the common language when uttered by a dragon. Although H'Ilgraith attempted to replicate some of the rumbles she heard, she was unable to pitch her voice correctly.

H'Ilgraith also had the opportunity to observe more than one family living in the cave system. Their social interactions were virtually identical to those of the red dragons. *These two species are related*, she concluded.

Discourse with Dragons

Once Theovolan returned, the two of them met. H'Ilgraith had learned he was the head of this clan of great gray dragons. She relayed her people's recommendations for maintaining surveillance, protecting clan members, and exercising caution when encountering other members of their respective species. She also suggested that their scouts and sentinels learn to recognize each other.

Theovolan added that members of their species who were not scouts should keep a discreet distance. "There are many clans of humans and dragons," he rumbled. "It will be difficult to discern which of us is friend or foe, predator or prey, unless we know each other in advance. Idle curiosity could result in a fatal mishap," he cautioned.

"I will forward your reply to my kinsmen," H'Ilgraith said. "I believe we have an accord. Sometime soon, we should arrange for our scouts to meet one another."

Shortly thereafter, H'Ilgraith was airlifted back to the foothills of the northern mountains. This time, the takeoff was smooth. A smaller, female dragon only had to launch herself off a ledge to achieve flight immediately.

When H'Ilgraith reached the forest, her sadness returned. For a brief moment in time, her interest in the gray dragons had distracted her. Once she reported to H'Assandra, her task would be done. Then she could leave the confines of the estate and be on her own once more. She quickly transformed into an owl for the return flight to H'Aleth.

Upon her return to H'Aleth, H'Ilgraith advised H'Assandra and Weston of Theovolan's concurrence with the accord. When she turned to leave, H'Assandra approached her with another task.

"You have learned to understand the gray dragons' vocalizations and how best to speak to them in our language. Now teach me, Edrian, and Mavelov."

H'Assandra explained why. "Your brother leads the scouts who watch over our northern borders and the territories beyond it. He, his scouts, and Mavelov are the ones most likely to find dragon chicks and eggs. If a great gray dragon sees any of them collecting an egg or encountering a chick, they must be able to convince the dragon that they are not hunters."

H'Ilgraith had to admit that H'Assandra's points were valid. Then H'Ilgraith mentioned another experience involving a red dragon. "Once I thought I understood what an adult red dragon was saying. I wonder whether both red and gray dragon species share the same tonal language. If they do or are merely using another dialect, we could have the means to communicate with both species. I would like to find out before I try to teach anyone how to understand the dragons' rumbles."

H'Assandra nodded her assent. "Very well. Balthorean is the lead scout in the southern region of H'Aleth. If you find that red dragons use the same or similar speech, then Balthorean and his scouts will need to learn how to listen as well."

H'Ilgraith soon discovered there was little difference in the tonal patterns used by red and gray dragons. So she taught Edrian, Mavelov, Balthorean, and H'Assandra how to listen to dragon rumbles and their tonal inflections to discern words in the common language. She also taught them how to pitch their voices as low as possible. This would help the dragons to discern the words humans were using. With these tasks completed, H'Ilgraith's work as an emissary was finished. It was up to H'Assandra and her advisors to maintain the relationship with the red and gray dragons—albeit remotely.

CHAPTER 34
SURCEASE OF SORROW

H'Ilgraith remained disconsolate after Jak's death. She retreated from most social contacts. When in residence at the estate, she kept to herself unless there was a threat or other significant issue that required her attention. Her family was well aware of her melancholia and tried to provide her with a measure of solace. Yet, H'Ilgraith could not be consoled. She buried herself in her herb gardens and in preparing nutritional and medicinal potions (appendix G).

A Solitary Soul

H'Ilgraith continued to forage throughout H'Aleth and the regions beyond for many years hence. As she roamed far afield in search of ingredients, she was absent from the estate for months at a time. She would return when she had significant information to report or required resources to make her potions. Thus, her fellow sisters never knew if or when she might reappear.

When challenged by H'Assandra for neglecting some of her duties as a sister, H'Ilgraith fired back. "Some people are too sick to come here. . I can travel to their villages. Besides, I conduct surveillance wherever I go."

H'Assandra replied with a sigh, "Please try to spend a little time with us in council. Since we have moved more scouts to the southern coast, the northern scouts are spread thinly. Your surveillance reports would be invaluable. We are seeing more animal hybrids, and more people are fleeing into our territory. Many of these people may need your care. You could learn more by being in their midst than our scouts can by observing or mingling with them."

H'Assandra had an ulterior motive for making this recommendation. It might keep H'Ilgraith inside H'Aleth's territory, where roaming would be safer. As long as H'Ilgraith stayed within or near H'Aleth's boundaries, Weston could keep track of her through the scouts. They often spotted her in small villages and camps where she might spend a few days. She brought nutritional potions to the villagers and treated their ailments and maladies as best she could. Her travels also took her into the southwestern mountains to obtain the plants that grew there and visit the red dragons. Then there were times when she simply disappeared. When this happened, both Weston and H'Assandra suspected H'Ilgraith had slipped across H'Aleth's northern border and entered Cassius territory.

H'Ilgraith did not hesitate to invade the lands claimed by Rex Cassius. By watching the activities in Cassius villages, she could observe any new humanoid or animal hybrids. She continued to provide some relief to the suffering she saw in these villages. From time to time, she returned to the fortress, looking for weaknesses and a way to get inside without being seen. She searched in vain for the escape tunnel Jak had described. All the while, she risked encountering hunters or hybrids. Although she did not seek dangerous encounters, neither did she avoid them. When faced with a menacing hybrid, she did not hesitate to engage it. She was fey and seemed not to care about the risks she took.

A Narrow Miss

In fact, H'Ilgraith was responsible for many of the people immigrating to H'Aleth. She spent considerable time in the contested areas that Jak had once patrolled, trying to protect the people who were living there as he had done. Alas, she lacked the power of a gray mountain wolf to bring down hybrids and hunters. So she patrolled the area as an owl, providing advanced warning of any dangers that threatened the people there.

Before long, people learned to recognize the warning shriek of a great horned owl. The animal hybrids never picked up on it. Unfortunately, the bounty hunters did. Before long, they were hunting the owl that had foiled so many of their raids. They knew the bird had to be an *H. transformans* female and a valuable prize if it could be caught or killed.

One day, a small group of *H. transformans* were approaching H'Aleth's border when they heard an owl shriek. When they looked toward the sound, they saw a band of seven bounty hunters racing toward them. Most of the group began running toward the border as fast as they could. Some of the hunters loosed a volley of arrows at the fleeing people while the other hunters turned and shot arrows at the bird, trying to bring it down.

The hunters had not anticipated a fight from the bedraggled group. So they were surprised when a few of them, also armed with bows and arrows, stayed behind to hold off the hunters. Then the hunters who had turned on the bird rejoined their comrades to overpower the defenders.

The hunters met with yet another surprise. Suddenly, one was struck down by a well-aimed arrow that seemed to have come out of nowhere. Two H'Aleth scouts had observed the small group approaching the border and saw the hunters' attack. One of them was a highly skilled archer who rarely missed her target. The other was an apprentice who was quite capable. The scouts immediately engaged the hunters with the senior scout, quickly bringing down a second one. Suddenly, the band of seven hunters were five, facing an effective armed force. Unprepared to risk their lives, they quickly fled the scene.

H'Ilgraith did not escape the incident unscathed. She could not avoid the volley of arrows the hunters aimed at her from different directions. Much older now, she could not react as quickly as she once could. One arrow nipped her left leg and another one her right wing when she banked to avoid the arrows. She fell unseen by the hunters after they had become otherwise engaged. H'Aleth's scouts, however, knew exactly where she landed and who she was. Once the hunters had fled, the scouts ran to pick up the wounded owl who was struggling to limp along on the ground.

Grounded

Much to her dismay, H'Ilgraith had to be carried back to the estate to recover from her injuries. She was wounded in her right arm and left leg. Although the wounds were not serious, they hampered her abilities. Having resumed human form, she could not transform again until her wounds were fully healed. To do so would jeopardize her alternate species and possibly result in permanent damage. She was finally stuck at the estate. At least, she could recover in her own cottage where she would have peace and quiet.

Not for long. When H'Ilgraith saw H'Assandra approaching the cottage, she recognized immediately that her cousin was coming with a new task.

H'Assandra came straight to the point. "You have been developing and preparing medicinal potions for decades," she said to H'Ilgraith. "When you pass from this life, what will happen to all the knowledge you have stowed in your head? Will it be lost forever? Or will you leave your recipes to those who follow you?" she asked.

"What would you have me do?" demanded H'Ilgraith in return. She dreaded the thought of having to write down every recipe. *This I will not do*, she thought, *but I will write out the most important ones.*

As it turned out, H'Assandra's proposal was far worse than H'Ilgraith had imagined.

"Teach others how to prepare your recipes," H'Assandra replied. "Our children and grandchildren must know how to treat the maladies they surely will encounter. We must not leave them bereft of the knowledge you have."

H'Ilgraith stifled a glare and looked at H'Assandra suspiciously.

"You need not change anything that you do now. Just describe what you are doing and why," H'Assandra continued. "Your apprentices will learn by watching you prepare the recipes. They can write down the ingredients, how to prepare them, and how to mix the recipe, along with any explanations. Finally, they can prepare the recipes themselves under your tutelage. Once the recipes are written, we will have recipe books to pass on."

"It's more than just preparing potions," H'Ilgraith said adamantly. "Several recipes use highly toxic ingredients. If not used judiciously, these potions can be deadly."

"Then it is crucial that you convey this information to your apprentices for them to record in the recipes," H'Assandra stated. "Perhaps you can task them to categorize the recipes from easiest to most difficult, and from least to most toxic."

Once again, H'Ilgraith was resigned to her fate. Even so, certain conditions would have to be met.

"I will have no one under the age of twelve preparing potions, and only those who are mature and responsible," H'Ilgraith insisted. "Anyone preparing potions must be fully proficient in arithmetic and have suitable penmanship for transcribing the recipes. Finally, anyone transcribing a recipe or preparing a potion must attend diligently to the task at hand. I will not tolerate idle chatter or inattentiveness," she concluded.

"Agreed," said H'Assandra.

So began H'Ilgraith's tenure as a teacher of potions (app G). Over time, she slipped into the role of mentor for those students who demonstrated a high level of understanding and proficiency. Two of her students, in particular, showed great interest in learning about the plants from which the ingredients were derived. They sought out Floberius to learn how to grow them. Subsequently, they helped H'Ilgraith tend her gardens.

Once the recipe books were finished, H'Ilgraith offered an apprenticeship to these two students. They accompanied her to villages within H'Aleth to administer potions to people who needed them. This allowed her apprentices to observe the effects of potions on the malnourished or those suffering maladies. New immigrants frequently offered such opportunities.

H'Assandra almost fainted when she learned of H'Ilgraith's offer. *This is truly a remarkable change*, she thought. She did not realize how weary her cousin had become. H'Ilgraith had an ulterior motive. One day, she planned to leave H'Aleth and never return. In mentoring her apprentices, she would leave two young adults with her expertise to tend to H'Aleth's expanding population. Her people would continue benefiting from her knowledge long after she was gone.

Supplemental Notes and Citations
Cyanogenic Compounds

Many plants and some insects produce cyanogenic compounds (e.g., amygdalin) to fend off other species that prey on them (Alitubeera *et al.*, 2019; Jensen *et al.*, 2011; Zagrobelny *et al.*, 2018). Many of these compounds can be found in the seeds of fruits (e.g., apricots), in tubers (e.g., cassava), and in arthropods (e.g., beetles). If eaten or used in excess, cyanide poisoning can result (Alituberra *et al.*, 2019; Sauer *et al.*, 2015).

Methylazoxymethanol (MAM)

The seeds of cone-bearing plants are a food source both for humans and other animals. One of their constituents is metabolized into a toxic substance, MAM, known to cause DNA damage and induce genetic changes associated with the development of cancer in nonhuman primates (Bode & Dong, 2015).

Digitalis purpurea

The leaves of many plants have been used to brew teas (e.g., lavender, comfrey, mint, chamomile, and many others). Historically, the leaves of the foxglove plant were used in tea to induce diuresis in people with dropsy (congestive heart failure). Foxglove leaves contain digitalis. Even in tiny amounts, this agent can be toxic to the heart and cause death, usually due to an irregular heartbeat (cardiac arrhythmia) or to a suppressed heartbeat (Janssen *et al.*, 2016; Wu *et al.*, 2017).

CHAPTER 35
H'Eleanora's Secret

Once H'Ilgraith's protégés had developed the knowledge and skill needed to function independently, H'Ilgraith retreated into her cottage. She was alone again and could prepare to leave H'Aleth and return to the contested territories. She did not expect to come back home. Eventually, she would have one last deadly encounter with a hunter or a hybrid. Her plan changed abruptly when one of her sisters, H'Eleanora, sought her help.

A Secret Request

H'Ilgraith's younger kinswoman, H'Eleanora, had two sons. Yet she wanted another child—a daughter—one who would continue H'Eleanora's line. So she approached her elder cousin with the notion of entering a breeding program that engaged *H. transformans* males.

"My husband will not entertain having another child," H'Eleanora told H'Ilgraith. "He claims to be too busy with his sons." She paused for a moment and then added, "I suspect he has no interest in having a daughter. So I must find other means."

H'Eleanora had chosen the TransXformans Company, which specialized in breeding offspring with desired characteristics, including the specific gender requested. The company could identify and select sperm from an *H. transformans* male that contained a transforming X chromosome (XT) and fertilize H'Eleanora's ovum with it. This would ensure that H'Eleanora would have a powerful daughter with two transforming X chromosomes (2XT) (figure 2). The male's genes for an alternate species need not be considered.

Fig. 2. High Probability of a Female *H. transformans* Offspring
with Two X^T Chromosomes

H'Eleanora
All eggs have an X^T
(transforming chromosome)

X^T X^T

Unknown X^T	X^T X^T	X^T X^T
Male $\quad$ Y	X^T Y	X^T Y

H. transformans

Key: X^T = transforming X chromosome
      Y = male chromosome

As an *H. transformans* female with two transforming X
chromosomes (2XT), all of H'Eleanora's ova would carry an X^T
chromosome. A male *H. transformans* would have sperm with either
an X^T chromosome or a Y chromosome. A pairing of a male X^T sperm
with any one of H'Eleanora's ova would ensure a female offspring
with two X^T chromosomes.

H'Ilgraith sensed H'Eleanora's loneliness and understood it well.
Even after so many years, the loss of Jak still haunted her. Nevertheless,
she advised against taking such an action.

"Have you lost your mind?" she asked H'Eleanora. "There are too
many unknowns. Are you determined to go down this path?"

"Yes," H'Eleanora asserted. "But no one must know of it," she
admonished her older cousin.

H'Ilgraith just looked at H'Eleanora. "Exactly how will you keep your
pregnancy a secret?" H'Ilgraith demanded.

"Before it becomes apparent, I must find a safe and secluded place to
stay," H'Eleanora replied. "Given your travels, I thought you might know
of such a place."

"And when you return home with a newborn baby, what will you tell
your husband and the rest of your family?" asked H'Ilgraith.

"I don't know," H'Eleanora admitted. "I have no doubt I will be faulted for my actions. No one should dare fault my infant," she declared adamantly. "As my daughter, she will be a sister in the House of H'Aleth, and I will defend her. I will raise her in the manner befitting a sister."

"If you insist on carrying out this plan, I will go with you and watch over you," said H'Ilgraith. "But I do not approve of it."

Fortunately, H'Ilgraith had been schooled in midwifery at Gregor and could attend to H'Eleanora's needs—especially as the latter insisted upon absolute secrecy.

"I know of several places you can stay," H'Ilgraith said. "There are remote villages in the southwest where I am known. I can introduce you as a newly widowed woman with child. The people are friendly, and most of them are *H. transformans*. They will offer you a place to stay and will look out for you, as will I. *You,* however, must devise a reason for leaving that will satisfy H'Assandra."

Gray Guardians

As fate would have it, H'Eleanora became ill early in her pregnancy and could not leave the estate. She stayed in H'Ilgraith's cottage, where her pregnancy would remain concealed. As it advanced, H'Eleanora developed an ever-worsening toxemia that H'Ilgraith was powerless to abate. After sending an urgent message to the House of Gregor, H'Ilgraith made arrangements to transport H'Eleanora overland to Gregor. Fortunately, it was late spring. The passes through the northwest mountains and the pass to Gregor would be open. Even so, the journey would be perilous due to an increasing number of animal hybrids roving throughout the territories.

H'Ilgraith arranged for the two women to join a party of traders traveling to Gregor. A few days prior to their departure, she transformed into a great horned owl, grasped a short robe in her talons, and flew into the northwest mountains to seek out the clan of great gray dragons she had encountered in the past. Even at a flight speed of forty miles per hour, it took her two days to reach the northern mountains, where their aeries could be found. The presence of a woodland owl at these altitudes caught the attention of sentinels whose deep rumblings promptly reported the remarkable sighting. When she reached an outcropping, H'Ilgraith transformed into a lynx and yowled. One dragon knew immediately who she was. Theovolan met the exhausted lynx and took her once again into the warmth of his nest. The lynx slipped into her robe and promptly fell unconscious.

Not long afterward, H'Ilgraith awoke, having resumed her human form. "I have a great favor to ask of you and your clan," she said. "A kinswoman of mine is gravely ill. She carries a female child in her womb, whom she has named H'Ester. Her sickness threatens both their lives. In two days hence, we will begin the journey north to Gregor in the hope that their physicians can save both mother and child. We must pass through your territory and then north through the southern pass. I ask that you and your clan and any kin you have in the far north watch over us until we reach our destination."

Theovolan did not hesitate. "This we will gladly do. You and your clan have been steadfast in keeping watch over the lands to our south and alerting us to dangers that approach our territory."

"Thank you," responded H'Ilgraith gratefully. "Now, I must leave and return to my kinswoman as quickly as possible."

"If you wish, I will carry you as far as the edge of the foothills," Theovolan replied. "From there, you must continue on your own."

H'Ilgraith thanked Theovolan again. She was relieved. The lift would save her an enormous amount of time and effort.

Two days hence, two women, with assumed names, began their trek to the House of Gregor. The traders with whom they traveled never knew they had an armed escort flying far above them.

The Passing of H'Eleanora

Once they reached Gregor, H'Eleanora received the care H'Ilgraith had been unable to provide. Both hoped that Gregor's physicians would reverse her toxemia or at least bring it under control. Alas, they could do neither. All their knowledge and skill were to no avail.

When H'Eleanora became aware she would not live to raise her daughter or even see her, she impressed upon H'Ilgraith the care and tutoring her child would need. She was fearful of what might happen to her daughter without a sister to support and guide her. With the onset of labor, H'Eleanora's condition deteriorated rapidly. The baby was taken by Caesarean section as her mother slipped away.

H'Ilgraith felt profound sorrow at the death of H'Eleanora. She had become close to her younger cousin as both of them strived to carry her pregnancy to term and deliver a healthy newborn. Now H'Ilgraith was left with a slight female infant who survived the onslaught of the illness that had wracked her mother's body. In fact, upon examination, the physicians at Gregor pronounced her healthy.

Yet H'Ilgraith felt a deep sense of foreboding. *What do I do with this child?* she wondered. She was at a loss.

CHAPTER 36
A Foundling

The Gregorians fully expected H'Eleanora's infant to be returned to her remaining family. Yet H'Ester had no immediate family. *She is essentially an orphan,* thought H'Ilgraith. *Still, she is a sister of the House of H'Aleth, albeit of unknown paternal parentage.*

H'Ilgraith knew she would face many questions when she returned to H'Aleth without H'Eleanora and with a newborn infant. For some of them, she could provide a suitable answer. For others, she could not.

H'Ilgraith's Dilemma

H'Ilgraith could explain H'Eleanora's death. She had died of shock. Her ashes would not reveal any secrets. *But how do I explain this child?* H'Ilgraith asked herself.

Should I reveal her origin? No one but she and H'Eleanora were supposed to know the child's parentage until H'Eleanora addressed it. It was not H'Ilgraith's place to do so.

Who will raise her? Certainly not H'Eleanora's wedded husband, already immersed in raising his two sons. *Even if I reveal her origin, it is unlikely he will have any interest in her.* The infant was not his offspring.

Once her origin is revealed, who will defend her standing? For the child's heritage to be recognized, at some point, her family would have to know who she was. Yet the child might be spurned if people learned her sire was unknown. H'Eleanora would have defended her child as innocent of how she was conceived. H'Eleanora would have protected her standing as a sister in the House of H'Aleth. H'Eleanora would have dealt with all of these concerns.

So H'Ilgraith returned to her original question. *What do I do with this child?* She felt kinship with H'Eleanora, who, in dying, had lost the chance to have the daughter she so desperately wanted. H'Ilgraith also felt a sense of duty toward the infant—to keep her safe until someone stepped forward to raise her.

H'Ilgraith considered several options. Raising the child herself was not one of them. She had never had any desire to raise children. She and Jak had been happy with the freedom both of them enjoyed. So H'Ilgraith had never entertained any thoughts of having offspring. In fact, she found rowdy, raucous children running to and fro and underfoot irritating. They were a plague and a pestilence and another good reason to go on scouting expeditions. It would seem that her maternal instinct genes were either missing or turned off.

Perhaps I can find a kind family in one of the villages to raise the child, H'Ilgraith thought. *Perhaps the House of Erwina would accept her as an orphan and raise her.*

Yet neither of these options would provide the training that the child would need to defend her kin or assume the role of mistress of the House of H'Aleth should the need arise. H'Ilgraith also knew that H'Eleanora had wanted her child raised at H'Aleth.

As she bundled up the newborn infant and procured an ample supply of goat's milk, a more pressing question arose. *How do I get this baby back to H'Aleth?*

The Return Home

The traders with their horses and mules had left Gregor long ago. Summer in the far north had begun to wane. H'Ilgraith knew she needed to go as soon as possible to get through the pass. Since she and the infant would be traveling without an escort, Gregor provided her with a horse to ease and speed her return to H'Aleth.

As she left the House of Gregor and headed toward the southern pass, H'Ilgraith noticed a shadow passing over her and the child. An arctic dragoness flew overhead (illustration 15). She saw an old woman riding alone through the plains and noted that she carried a small bundle in her arms.

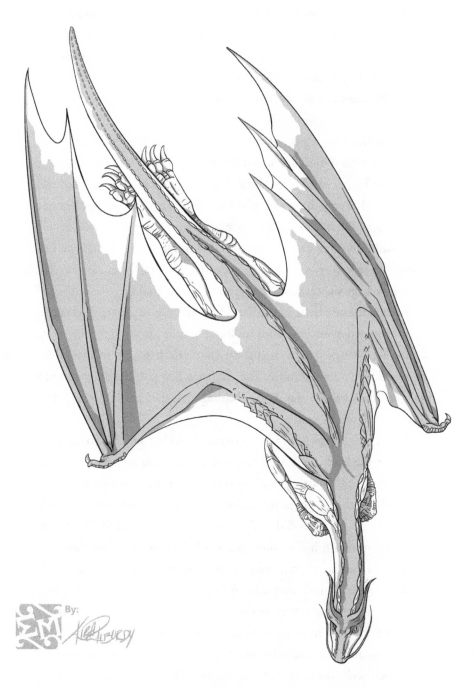

Illustration 15: Dragonensis arcturus alba

Her clan had been told of two women traveling through their territory—one of whom was with child. Now only one woman was returning, and she carried an infant. H'Ilgraith saw the dragoness bank and turn in a full circle until she aligned her path with H'Ilgraith's direction. H'Ilgraith knew at once the dragon was not a threat. She and the infant would have an escort after all.

Sometime later, a great gray dragon keeping watch over the north face of the northern mountains noted the flight of an arctic dragoness. She was much farther south than usual. Something must have triggered this rare event. The gray dragon lifted off and flew northward along the same trajectory as the dragoness. He soon spotted the reason for the latter's flight path. The gray dragon had been told to expect two women and an infant. He saw only one, and she appeared to be traveling alone except for the package she carried. As he grew closer, he could see the outline of an infant. He knew then who it was. H'Ilgraith was returning to H'Aleth.

The gray dragon continued his flight toward his arctic cousin. As he neared her, he rocked his wings lightly. The arctic dragoness acknowledged his signal with a similar move. The gray then flew past the dragoness in a wide arc to assume her trajectory. The dragoness then performed the same maneuver to return home.

The gray dragon flew over H'Ilgraith, making sure his shadow fell upon her. He landed a short distance in front of her and waited for her to approach. H'Ilgraith knew she could not make the trip across the mountains with a newborn infant, even on horseback. She was also fairly certain the dragon intended to fly them over the mountains. She set the horse free to return home and approached the dragon. When she stood before him, he reached out with a talon and grasped her as she stepped inside it. After a lumbering takeoff from the ground, the dragon flew them through the mountains at a relatively low altitude so that his charges would not become too cold or hypoxic. After a short flight through the mountains and over the montane forest, the gray dragon landed in a large glade well within H'Aleth's territory. There, he released H'Ilgraith to complete her journey home within a few days.

H'Aleth's scouts kept a careful watch throughout the territory and readily intercepted any dangerous creatures that might enter it. Most likely, one or more scouts would find H'Ilgraith—especially after seeing a great gray dragon fly overhead and land. This event would command their immediate attention since dragons rarely came so close to areas inhabited by humans. Indeed, two scouts found H'Ilgraith quickly. One of them could transform into an elk to carry her and the infant back to the estate. The other transformed into a wolf and raced back to apprise H'Assandra that H'Ilgraith had returned.

"She carries an infant with her," he reported.

A Foundling

As soon as H'Ilgraith arrived in the village adjacent to the estate, several of its inhabitants accosted her. Word had spread rapidly that she was carrying a baby. Such an aberration warranted inspection. Soon, she was swamped by people asking questions about the infant. Most of them she ignored. For a few, she had a sharp retort.

"Whose baby is it?"

"Where did you get the baby?"

"Is this your baby?"

"Certainly not," H'Ilgraith snapped.

"Is it a boy or a girl?"

"How old is the baby?"

"When did you have your baby?"

"I didn't!" H'Ilgraith fumed.

A short time later, matters became serious when she met with H'Assandra.

"First, where is H'Eleanora?" H'Assandra asked. Although her demeanor was calm, she was deeply concerned.

H'Ilgraith recounted the story of the illness that took H'Eleanora's life, despite her will to live and the efforts of those who cared for her. "Her death came suddenly. I had no chance to send word to you or her husband. Her body was cremated at Gregor." Then she added stiffly, "I have her ashes. Please give them to her husband with my condolences."

"Perhaps you should tell him what happened and give her ashes to him," suggested H'Assandra.

"No," H'Ilgraith replied firmly. "During the time I cared for her in my cottage, he never once appeared." H'Ilgraith paused and then added coolly, "Perhaps he was too busy with his sons."

In that moment, H'Ilgraith made her decision.

H'Assandra accepted the small wooden box containing H'Eleanora's ashes. Then she asked, "And the infant?"

"A foundling," H'Ilgraith replied.

"Do you know her species?" asked H'Assandra.

"Human," H'Ilgraith answered, knowing full well that this designation would be interpreted as *H. sapiens.*

"Shall I make the arrangements to find a home for this child?" inquired H'Assandra.

"No," replied H'Ilgraith. "I will tend to her."

H'Assandra studied H'Ilgraith for a moment. She knew that H'Ilgraith disliked being hampered by children. *Something remarkable must have happened for her to take on this child*, H'Assandra surmised. She knew H'Ilgraith often omitted many details from her scouting reports. Still, H'Assandra wanted to be sure that H'Ilgraith was determined to raise the child herself.

"You are making a lifelong commitment," H'Assandra warned.

"I know," H'Ilgraith responded. *I will raise this child,* she vowed to herself. *A well-trained child will earn the respect of her fellow sisters. Then I will reveal her origin and defend her mother.*

Supplemental Notes and Citations
Mothering

Maternal instinct or mothering refers to a mother's attitudes and actions that reflect caring for and protecting her offspring (Barrett & Fleming, 2011; Bell *et al.*, 2014; Ebstein *et al.*, 2012; Elmadih *et al.*, 2014; Mehta *et al.*, 2016; Tombeau Cost *et al.*, 2017). Oxytocin is a hormone that is produced during and after pregnancy. Although it is most closely identified with lactation (breastfeeding), it is strongly associated with maternal behaviors of caring (e.g., infant bonding) in both animals and humans. Its influence may persist for forty-eight months after delivery.

The genetic code for the genes known to produce oxytocin may vary from one woman to another (genetic polymorphisms) (Ebstein *et al.*, 2012; Tombeau *et al.*, 2017). These variations could influence the degree to which a mother may be favorably disposed toward her infant. Environmental influences, including cultural norms and experience with pregnancy and child-rearing, also influence maternal behaviors (Feldman *et al.*, 2016). Thus, there is no single gene governing mothering or maternal instinct. There are multiple influences on maternal behavior.

Genetic Variants (Polymorphisms)

It is quite common for a gene to have "siblings" that perform the same function. These variations may have no effect whatsoever on the performance of the gene. For example, there are four variations on the genetic code for the amino acid valine. All variants produce the same product.

On the other hand, some variations may cause subtle differences in how the gene performs its function. For example, variations in the genetic code for liver enzymes that break down (metabolize) alcohol affect the efficiency of the enzymes. Some produce enzymes that metabolize alcohol quickly, whereas others produce enzymes that do so slowly.

EPILOGUE

A young, slight girl trotted behind an old woman, who was walking at a brisk pace. The child was perhaps six years of age. She had dark brown hair and amber eyes. The two had left their living quarters within H'Aleth's estate and passed through its northernmost gate. "Where are we going, Mistress?" the child asked.

"We are going into the forest to find valerian," the old woman replied. Then she bade the child, "Describe the appearance of the valerian flower."

"It is pink and white with many tiny flowers," the child answered correctly. "Can we bring some of the flowers back with us? They have a sweet scent."

"Possibly," the old woman replied and then asked, "Where will we find the plant?"

"Where the dirt is dry and rocky," the child responded.

The old woman continued to quiz the child. "What part of the valerian plant is used for medicine?"

"The root," replied the child, who then asked, "Will you become a badger and dig up the roots?"

"Certainly not," the old woman answered sharply. "We will dig up the roots by hand using the trowels we brought." Then the old woman admonished, "Enough idle chatter. We must attend to the tasks at hand."

"Yes, Mistress."

APPENDICES

APPENDIX A

In the House of H'Aleth

Life in a New Territory

After arriving in a new territory, the H'Aleth family and their friends surveyed it. Their people identified its geographic characteristics, different species of wildlife, and those species' habitats. They recognized their mutual interdependence with other species, including plants and insects—with the possible exception of mosquitos. Later, they learned that some species of bats feed on mosquitos. As humans, they built settlements that were discreet, in part to avoid discovery and in part to minimize their intrusion into the territories of other species. When conducting surveillance across their territory, scouts who could transform into species native to that region would keep watch over it.

Given the range of species into which *H. transformans* could change, most H'Aletheans had a great appreciation and a healthy respect for other animal species, both domestic and wild. Hence, they did not hunt other animals for food. They raised domestic animals for the products they provided (e.g., eggs, milk, wool). H'Aletheans carefully preserved habitats for all species, including themselves, and minimized any intrusion upon other species.

Gardening was a common activity. Vegetable, herb, and fruit gardens provided most of the food sources. Both gardening and animal husbandry provided products that H'Aletheans could trade. Given the active lifestyle required by their environment, few H'Aletheans suffered premature death due to disease. Bounty hunters caused the majority of early deaths.

Childhood in the House of H'Aleth

Children began school as early as four years of age. As soon as they could transform safely (came of age), all children started lessons in scouting and self-defense. They lived under the constant threat of being hunted and captured. Early scouting lessons taught children to be alert and secretive from a young age. The Biogenics Corporation and the Cassius Foundation vied to acquire additional genomes—especially those of female *H. transformans*. Everyone's safety rested on constant vigilance and surveillance and the ability to flee or engage an adversary, as appropriate. The children of H'Aleth had to grow up quickly.

Many after-school activities involved scouting, both as humans and as their alternate species. Tiberius, H'Aleth's wildlife biologist and veterinarian, taught children who were coming of age the strengths and weaknesses of their alternate species. They needed a clear understanding of what their species could and could not do to avoid endangering or injuring themselves.

Despite the potential dangers, H'Aleth's children could still enjoy life and have fun. At first, even scouting was fun. The risk of danger was exhilarating until the threat became real. So too, was transforming and romping as their alternate species. Still, all of these activities had to be tempered with caution. Tiberius kept a close watch over children who were just learning to transform. He could intervene quickly if one were injured. When injuries occurred, they often served as a life lesson for the other children.

As soon as children demonstrated proficiency in basic scouting competencies, they were allowed to go on field trips. To learn about their homeland, children accompanied by at least one set of parents would tour each region—the grasslands, mountains, forests, and plains (map 3). They learned the features of these lands, the species that inhabited them, and the potential resources available. Where there was a village, they would stay for several days to meet the people living there, observe how they lived, and learn which products they made and which services they could provide. In this manner, the children learned about available resources,

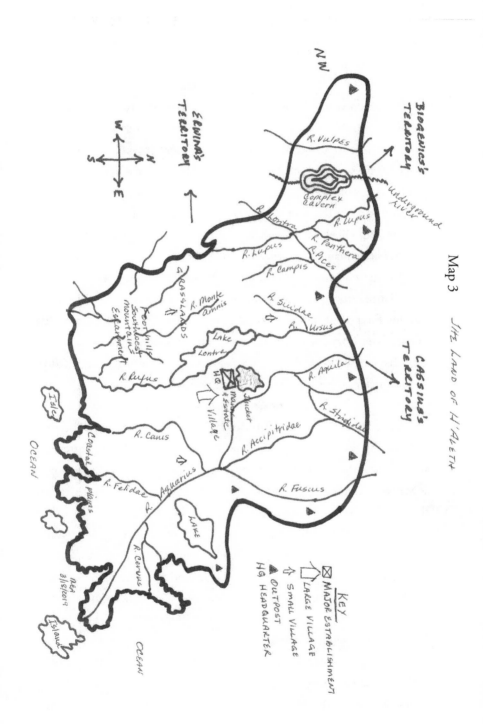

Map 3 *The Land of Hialeth*

where they could be found, and any dangers they should avoid. Equally important, the children learned how to locate a village without a map. There were no roads in H'Aleth.

Young Adulthood

By sixteen years of age, a youth was considered a young adult. Each individual would have identified a trade or service of special interest to him or her. For many, it was scouting. For others, it was a vocation, one of the sciences, or the arts. For a few, it was history or governance. Once identified, people with extensive knowledge in each specialty worked with each young adult to foster their interest and help them develop expertise in what would likely become their field of endeavor. Apprenticeships with a master craftsman were available to hone skills.

Anyone who desired to become a scout had to demonstrate mastery of surveillance techniques and skill in using at least one weapon. Part of the training for a scout included expeditions to conduct surveillance outside H'Aleth's territory, including incursions into areas contested by Biogenics and Cassius. Such expeditions were extremely dangerous. Scouts had to be prepared and ready for an encounter with an enemy force.

Descendants of Ruth and Edvar

All direct descendants of Ruth and Edvar received the same education and training as did any other child in H'Aleth (pedigree 3). They attended school with other children their age to study the subjects typically taught at school. Yet the school day did not end there for those who traced their lineage back to Ruth and Edvar. Even before coming of age, they were learning the duties and responsibilities of preserving their house and protecting its people. As young adults, they were expected to become involved in governance and in the strategies and tactics needed to mount a defense should their territory come under attack. By this time, most of them had had at least one close encounter with hunters in the employ of Cassius or Biogenics, if not both.

Although females had greater capabilities for transformation, both Ruth and Edvar realized that someday, the female line could fail, leaving males as their only direct descendants. Consequently, age-matched brothers, sisters, nieces, nephews, and cousins descended from Ruth and Edvar were raised and educated as a group in preparation for the possibility they would become mistress or master of the House of H'Aleth. All of them learned the principles and practices of governance and acquired the knowledge they would need to make decisions for the welfare of their people. Given Ruth and Edvar's extended family, rarely was any offspring raised alone.

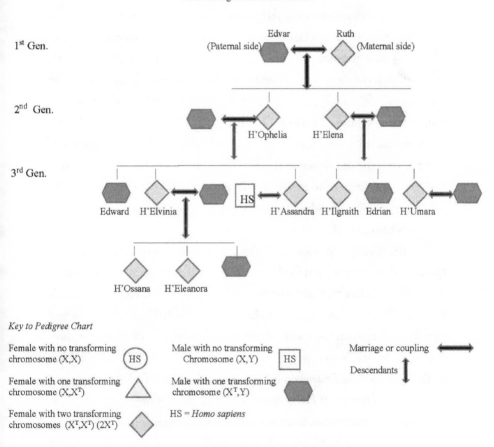

Ped. 3. Descendants of the House of H'Aleth
First through Third Generations

Key to Pedigree Chart

Female with no transforming chromosome (X,X)	Male with no transforming Chromosome (X,Y)	Marriage or coupling
Female with one transforming chromosome (X,X^T)	Male with one transforming chromosome (X^T,Y)	Descendants
Female with two transforming chromosomes (X^T,X^T) (2X^T)	HS = *Homo sapiens*	

APPENDIX B

EVOLUTION AND MIGRATION OF DRAGONENSIS DRAGONIS

Evolution and Migration of Monotremes

Dragons are classified as monotremes (taxonomy). The monotremes are one of the three lineages of mammals surviving to the present day. They evolved from a common ancestor (clade), the cynodont that existed about 260 million years ago during the late Jurassic period (Deakin, 2017; Koina *et al.*, 2006) (Table 1). Subsequently, the eutriconodonts evolved and eventually diverged, initially into the monotremes (cladogram 1) and then into the marsupial and placental lines (cladogram 2). *Dragona* was the first branch off the monotreme line and subsequently diverged into terrestrial and aquatic species (cladogram 3).

As the species expanded, many migrated across territories in search of space, suitable climate, and food sources. Some of the earliest descendants of the monotreme line migrated into the landmass that ultimately became South America. When volcanism created a bridge between the South American and the North American landmass (Laurentia), descendants of *Monotrematum sudamericanum* (Davis *et al.*, 2002; Kielan-Jaworowska, 1992; Weisbecker & Beck, 2015) and *Dragona* crossed into southwestern regions.

Migratory Patterns of Dragonensis dragonis

Ancestral migrations of terrestrial dragon lineages spread throughout tropical, arid, temperate, and subarctic tundra regions. As a rule, dragons do not migrate seasonally. They are social animals and establish a home territory. They do not move from it unless conditions become untenable.

Thus, epigenetic effects secondary to environmental conditions shaped their adaptations and, therefore, their distinctive phenotypes.

Dragonis rubra adapted to arid and semiarid regions. They developed reflective scales that deflected sunlight and decreased the influence of the sun's radiation on their body temperature. Their aeries were high in southern mountains where cooler air and winds also moderated the heat from the sun's rays. Their reddish-brown scales also reflected the myriad colors seen in the southwestern mountains, which helped to camouflage them. Their only known predators were humans who hunted them for their colorful scales, curved horns, and eggs. They were on the brink of extinction before they came under the protection of the House of H'Aleth.

Dragonis fuscus magna migrated into temperate and mountain regions. They are the largest of the terrestrial dragons. Their size helped them withstand the harsh climate conditions in the higher mountain ranges.

Those with dark-colored scales had another survival advantage. Unlike *D. rubra*, the gray dragons' scales absorbed ultraviolet radiation from the sun, which kept their surface scales warmer. Thus, over the ages, the dragons' scales darkened, becoming a gray to charcoal black color. This coloring also helped them to blend into rocky terrains and be less visible to prey species.

Dragonis alba spread into the subarctic and arctic regions. Although a terrestrial dragon, *D. alba* was an excellent swimmer. Its relatively thin scales were gray on its dorsal surface (top of the head, back, and top of wings) to absorb radiation from the sun. They were almost pure white on their ventral surface (chest, underbelly, and under the wings) for camouflage.

Dragonensis odontoceti was monotreme. It traversed the eastern and southern ocean waters. Its scales were different shades of blue, so it was called a "blue dragon" in the common language. Both *D. alba* and *D. odontoceti* had an exquisite sense of electroreceptivity that allowed them to target and catch prey underwater.

Radiation Resistance in Dragonensis dragonis

Terrestrial dragons lived at considerably higher elevations than did most human populations. Thus, in theory, dragons should have been exposed to higher levels of gamma radiation and its attendant risks. Yet this was not the case. First, dragons often nested deep within crevices and caves, especially when they had young chicks. Hence, they were protected from much of the radiation as long as they sheltered under sufficient layers of bedrock. Aquatic species that lived in the ocean depths were largely unaffected.

Second, *Dragona* was an ancient family within the *Monotrematum* order (cladogram 3). The recent gamma-ray burst was not the first one their species had endured. Like some species of tardigrades, *Dragona* was naturally radiation-resistant. They evolved with the genetic mechanisms that repaired the double-stranded DNA breaks caused by exposure to intense ionizing radiation. These mechanisms efficiently and effectively restored the integrity of the genome. Unfortunately for the marsupial and placental mammals that followed, this ability was gradually lost.

Supplemental Notes and Citations
Taxonomy

Taxonomy is the hierarchical system wherein plants, animals, and other forms of life are grouped according to their physical characteristics and, more recently, based on genetic analysis (phylogenetics). Class is a taxonomy of animals that share common characteristics. A class of animals encompasses the families of animals and the species that fall under it. Mammals (Mammalia) and birds (Aves) are two different classes of animals within the animal kingdom.

Within a class, animals are further subdivided into families with more closely related characteristics: e.g., *Hominidae* (humans), *Canidae* (wolves, dogs, foxes, etc.), *Felidae* (cougar, lynx, house cat, etc.), *Mustelidae* (badgers, weasels, otters, etc.). Genus is the category of taxonomy that falls between family and species: e.g., *Hominidae* (family), *Homo* (genus), *sapiens* (species).

Clade

A clade is a group of organisms that includes all descendants with a common ancestor. Birds, dinosaurs, and crocodiles all have a common egg-laying ancestor. Even more remotely, birds, reptiles, and mammals have the same ancestor with four extremities (tetrapod). A cladogram is a phylogenetic schematic that traces the development of species over time (see cladograms 1, 2, and 3).

Evolution of Mammals

Approximately 310 million years ago, the sauropsid and the synapsid lines branched. The sauropsids branched again into lines that led to birds and reptiles. The synapsid line began the path to the development of mammals.

The earliest mammals descended from cynodonts, the common ancestor for the three branches of mammals (Kielan-Jaworowska, 1992); however, the evolution of mammals was not linear (Luo, 2007). Multiple additional branches diverged, many of which eventually became extinct. The eutriconodont branch diversified even further. One of its branches ultimately led to present-day mammals.

Since most mammalian characteristics are seen in soft tissues, there is little fossil evidence. The features that can be observed from fossils include a hinged jaw (detached from the skull), middle ear bones (separated from the jaw), and the development of molar teeth (Flannery *et al.*, 1995; Kielan-Jaworowska, 1992; Luo, 2007).

Continental Drift

Approximately 200 million years ago, the supercontinent Pangaea began to break apart to form two smaller continents: Gondwana and Laurasia (Weisbecker & Beck, 2015). Under the influence of continental drift, Laurasia drifted north. About 145 million years ago, Gondwana began to break up into landmasses that would become Antarctica, Australia, New Zealand, Africa, and South America. Similarly, the Laurasian landmass also separated to form the European-Asian landmass and the Laurentian landmass (North America and Greenland).

About 105 million years ago, the African continent separated from South America (Davis *et al.*, 2002; Weisbecker & Beck, 2015). About 65 million years ago, South America drifted north, and a bridge formed between the North and South American continents. Maps illustrating continental drift may be found at the United States Geological Survey website https://www.usgs.gov/.

Ancestral Migration of Mammals

Monotremes are the last remaining members of an ancestral spread of mammals from Gondwana (Weisbecker & Beck, 2015). Fossil evidence of monotremes and other flora and fauna from Gondwana has been found both in South America (Argentina) and North America (Texas) (Flannery *et al.*, 1995; Weisbecker & Beck, 2015). Eventually, the monotreme line in the Americas became extinct. Only the platypus (one species) and echidna (four species) survive in Australia and New Zealand.

Epigenetic Influence on Gene Functions

These are internal (e.g., biochemical) and external (e.g., environmental) factors that can have a direct effect on gene expression and how a gene functions, if at all (Duncan *et al.*, 2014; Pal & Tyler, 2016; Potaczek *et al.*, 2017). These factors become attached to the target gene; yet, they do not alter its structure—only its function. Some of these factors can be inherited by offspring (Pal & Tyler, 2016).

Electroreceptivity

Electroreceptivity was well developed in monotremes from the early cretaceous period; however, it was more pronounced in aquatic monotremes (e.g., the platypus) (Asahara *et al.*, 2016).

Table 1

Geologic Timeline

Approximate Timeline (mya*)	Era	Period	Notes
2.6 to present		Quaternary	
23–2.6	Cenozoic	Tertiary	Spread of fauna from South America across isthmus of Panama to North America ~3 mya
65–23		Paleogene	
146–65	Mesozoic	Cretaceous	Echidna/Platypus branch of monotremes emerged ~75–50 mya
			Laurentia (North America) separates from Eurasia ~80 mya
			Marsupial lines diverged from placental lines ~90 mya
			Dragona branch of monotremes diverged ~95–75 mya
208–146		Jurassic	Monotremes diverged from therian (marsupial/placental) mammals ~166mya
			Eutriconodonts emerged ~186–163
245–208		Triassic	Pangaea begins to separate into Gondwana and Laurasia
			Pangaea formed ~225 mya
			Mammaliaforms appeared ~230 mya
286–245		Permian	Cynodonts diverged from synapsid line ~265-260 mya
360–286	Paleozoic	Carboniferous	Synapsid line diverged from Sauropsid line ~310–320 mya
410–360		Devonian	
440–410		Silurian	
505–440		Ordovician	
544–505		Cambrian	
4500–544	Pre-Cambrian		
4500			Approximate time of the "big bang" (4.5 billion years ago)

*million years ago (mya)

Divergence of Eutriconodonts
Cladogram 1

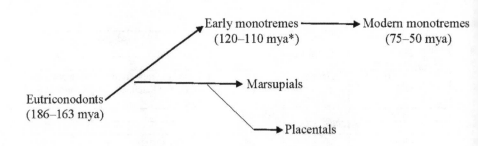

*million years ago (mya)

Divergence of Monotremes
Cladogram 2

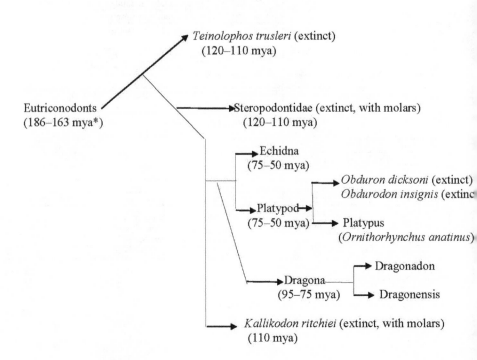

*million years ago (mya)

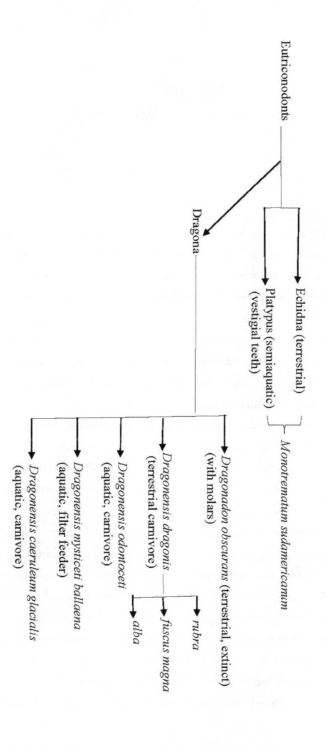

Divergence of *Dragona*
Cladogram 3

Eutriconodonts

Dragona

Echidna (terrestrial)

Platypus (semiaquatic) (vestigial teeth)

Monotrematum sudamericanum

Dragonadon obscurans (terrestrial, extinct) (with molars)

Dragonensis dragonis (terrestrial carnivore)

rubra

fuscus magna

alba

Dragonensis odontoceti (aquatic, carnivore)

Dragonensis mysticeti ballaena (aquatic, filter feeder)

Dragonensis caeruleum glacialis (aquatic, carnivore)

APPENDIX C
The Cassius Foundation

Angus Cassius was an *H. transformans*. He was born and raised at a time when this characteristic was both feared and spurned. When he came of age and could transform, he decided that being spurned would not be his fate. *But I will be feared*, he vowed.

Angus's alternate species was a great horned boar—an omnivore. At first, he railed against those genes. He wanted the capability to become an apex predator. He soon learned, however, that the wild boar was a powerful and aggressive animal with impressive tusks that could give an apex predator second thoughts about attacking it.

Subsequently, he considered his species, *H. transformans,* far superior to that of an ordinary *H. sapiens*. "Plain humans are genetically inferior," he declared. "They are just another mammalian species of no special merit, although they are useful as a source of labor." He actively suppressed the knowledge that the base genome of *H. transformans* was *H. sapiens*.

Angus refused to associate himself with mere humans. So he surrounded himself with *H. transformans* who would accept him as the dominant male. They deferred to Angus largely because they were afraid of him. He was quite capable of goring anyone who opposed or even annoyed him. Consequently, Angus accumulated many subordinates, a very few tactful advisors, and no friends. He did have a family, and he taught his family members to be just as aloof as he. He instructed his offspring, "*H. sapiens* are suitable for two purposes: to work and die." This included any relatives unfortunate enough to fall into that category.

The Foundation

Angus created the Cassius Foundation to foster his drive to dominate society. He built it on the premise that he could use genetic engineering to make *H. transformans* more powerful and bend them to his service. He lured many *H. transformans* with a promise of enhancing their characteristics. The potential to create animal hybrids also fueled his pursuit of domination.

The genes conferring the ability to transform had not yet been identified. The Biogenetics Company, which later merged with the Eugenics Corporation, was actively pursuing research to identify them. Angus was content to let his rival competitor expend its resources. Once the genes were discovered, he would take whatever steps were necessary to obtain the research. He did not hesitate to engage in corporate espionage.

In the meantime, Angus engaged in hostile takeovers of smaller genetics companies through intimidation. In this manner, he accumulated geneticists, technicians, supplies and equipment, and the knowledge acquired through their work. He lured other scientists into his fold by offering them a state-of-the-art research facility in which to further their study of genetics and by promising housing for their families. Indeed, Angus did provide such a facility. He just neglected to mention it was inside a well-fortified fortress that also would serve as their prison.

Legacy

To cement his self-appointed station as an absolute ruler, Angus wanted to establish his lineage as royalty. Since both he and his wife were *H. transformans,* they should have been able to produce both male and female progeny who were also *H. transformans* (figure 3). They had two healthy daughters, both of whom were *H. transformans.* They were born with one normal X chromosome and one transforming X chromosome. To their parents' disappointment, neither daughter had two transforming X chromosomes, which would have afforded them much greater capability. Far worse, Angus and his wife had no sons at all. Consequently, Angus bred with many other female *H. transformans* with the same outcome—female offspring with one transforming X chromosome—no male offspring.

Fig. 3. Low Probability of a Female *H. transformans* Offspring
with Two Transforming X Chromosomes

Wife / Consort

Egg with an X^T Egg with a plain X
(transforming)   (non transforming)
chromosome   chromosome

	X^T	X
X^T	X^T, X^T	X, X^T
Y	X^T, Y	X, Y

Angus Cassius

H. sapiens   H. transformans

Key: X^T = transforming X chromosome
      X = maternal or paternal nontransforming X chromosome
      Y = male chromosome

In this pattern, the mother has only one X^T. For each pregnancy, there is a 50% probability the child will inherit one X^T and be *H. transformans*—25% that a female child will have an X^T, X and 25% that a male child will have an an X^T, Y. There is a 25% probability that a female child will have two X^T and chromosomes. There is a 25% probability that a male child will have no X^T chromosome (an *H. sapiens*).

The lack of a male heir haunted Angus and drove his search for a suitable male *H. transformans* to breed with his daughters. Patterns of inheritance were critically important in his effort to establish his desired lineage. So he actively sought out and did not hesitate to kidnap any male *H. transformans* who could become a large, powerful animal—especially an apex predator. His oldest daughter consented to marry her father's selection and had three children, one of whom was a son named Rex (Angus's grandson). The younger daughter defied her father and married an *H. sapiens* man. This infuriated Angus, who banished both of them. Ironically, it was the banished daughter's female offspring (Angus's granddaughter) who would marry an *H. transformans* man and produce another male *H. transformans* heir, Argus (Angus's great-grandson).

Supplemental Notes and Citations
Sex Chromosomes

Females have two X chromosomes, and males have one X and a Y chromosome. Normally, each female egg (ovum) will carry one X chromosome, whereas each male sperm will carry either an X chromosome or a Y chromosome. Hence, females will always transmit an X chromosome to the offspring, whether the child is male or female. Males will transmit either an X chromosome for a daughter or a Y chromosome for a son.

Male Infertility

Infertility in males may be caused both by chromosome and gene abnormalities (Coban *et al.*, 2018; Mateu *et al.*, 2010; Piomboni *et al.*, 2014). Even in fertile males, sperm that fail to develop properly can have an abnormal number of chromosomes (aneuploidy). This can result in sperm with two reproductive chromosomes where there should be only one— either an X or a Y—or none at all. If an aneuploid sperm fertilizes an egg (ovum), the resulting embryo may inherit three reproductive chromosomes (trisomy) or only one reproductive chromosome (monosomy). If the sole reproductive chromosome is an X (XO genotype), a female embryo will develop, albeit with some deficiencies, and grow to be an adult. If the sole reproductive chromosome is a Y (YO genotype), the male embryo will not develop at all. The YO genotype is incompatible with life.

Even in sperm that have a Y chromosome, genetic defects (microdeletions) in the chromosome can prevent the development of an embryo (Mateu, 2010). In the latter case, it may be possible for the male to have normal female offspring, yet be unable to produce male offspring.

APPENDIX D
The Fortress

The Cassius Foundation fortress (illustration 16) was located about midway between its northern and southern borders. It lay to the east of a broad bend in the River Taurus along the western border of the Foundation's territory. Thus, it was within easy reach of the river's waterway. Angus Cassius had selected the remote location for its secrecy as well as access to a major river. Not only did the river provide a means of transport, but it also offered an upstream source of freshwater, a power source for generators, and an avenue to discharge waste downstream.

Security

The mammoth fortress sat on a rise in a wide-open area devoid of trees, shrubs, or any other vegetation that could hide anyone or anything that might approach it—accidentally or otherwise. It was bordered on three sides by a ten-foot earthen embankment built by dirt dug from a deep moat beyond it. The moat wall nearest to the fortress was braced by stone blocks to prevent erosion. The land between the moat and the forest boundary was covered by a short variety of zoysia grass that might hide a small rodent. These defenses impeded an army's forward movement and kept cannons at a distance, limiting the effectiveness of both.

The side of the fortress facing the river lacked any barriers. Instead, the moat extended to the river on the northwestern and southwestern edges of the fort. There, locks had been built which, when opened, allowed water from the river to flood the moat. When both locks were opened simultaneously, the onrushing waters would slam into each other with deadly force, creating violent turbulence in their wake. Any men, machines, or animals caught in the trench would be crushed and drowned by the torrent.

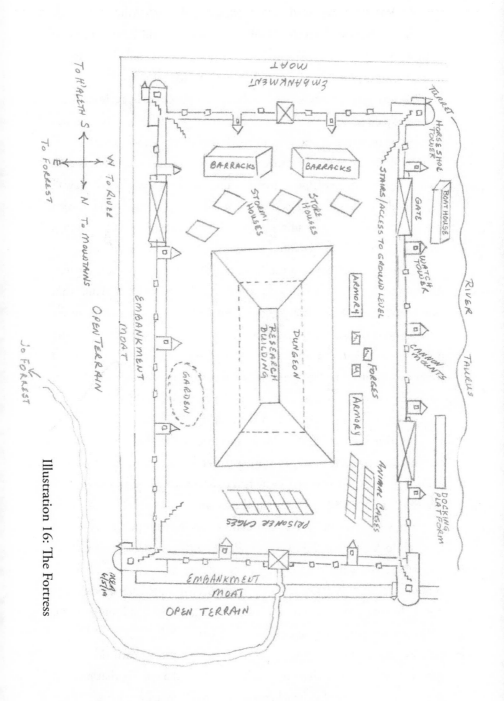

Illustration 16: The Fortress

The fortress's outer wall, which encased other structures, was built with stone. Nearly thirty feet high and eight feet thick, it supported cannon mounts. Guards patrolled the wall, and archers could be stationed there. Cutouts punctuated the wall at intervals for cannons.

The fortress's corners were built wider to support the large, horseshoe-shaped towers. Each horseshoe tower hosted a turret from which archers could rain arrows down upon an enemy. Two large watchtowers were placed midway along the eastern and western walls. Two smaller watchtowers were built along the northern and southern walls, equally spaced along each wall between the corner towers. Additional small watchtowers stood between the larger towers and also adjacent to each large gate. Each had openings on all sides, which allowed a full view of the fortress inside and out.

The only entrances into the fortress were through heavy iron gates. All gates were equipped with a drawbridge and large wooden planks that could be extended over the embankment and the moat to allow access to and egress from the fortress. Small gates were located midway on the northern and southern walls. The moat along the northern wall had a small unreinforced bridge that would support foot and wagon traffic. In the event of an attack, the bridge would be washed away by the turbulent flow of water from the river when the locks were opened.

The eastern wall had one large gate located midway between the central tower and the southeast-corner tower. It accommodated overland troop movements. The western wall had two large gates. The northwestern gate was located midway between the northwest-corner tower and the center tower. It received goods and materials delivered to a large, covered loading dock built on the riverbank. The southwestern gate was located halfway between the middle tower and the southwest-corner tower. It supported troop movements via the river. A boathouse and docking area was built along the riverbank across from this gate. The boathouse was the only enclosed structure built outside the fortress walls.

All gates had two exterior guardhouses with one on each side of the gate. Guards stationed there inspected anyone and anything that reached the gate. In the event of an attack, a short enclosed passageway between each guardhouse and the gate allowed guards to get inside the gate under cover.

The stone used to build the fortress likely was quarried from the mountains. Lumber for wooden structures almost certainly came from trees nearby, leaving a large clearing around the fortress. The clearing provided a broad and clear view of anyone or anything that dared to approach it.

Research and Development

Several structures inside the walls included barracks for soldiers, storerooms for supplies and equipment, two armories—one for housing weapons and ammunition and one for forging them—cages for wild animals and hybrids, and an outdoor prison for anyone they had captured alive—mostly *H. transformans.* The Cassius Foundation had no intention of taking enemy forces alive unless they could transform.

A massive stone structure about sixty feet tall was the fortress's centerpiece. Shaped like a broad ziggurat, the outer walls of each layer were two feet thick, hardening them against cannon fire. Hence, there were no windows. This building housed the labs, the generators that powered them, and the geneticists and genetic engineers who worked in them. For the staff's convenience, it also housed a dungeon below ground for the subjects of breeding programs and genetic experimentation.

The people working in the research laboratories were essentially incarcerated in the research building. Several floors were contained dormitories that housed both the workers and their families, most of whom had been kidnapped. There was a single central staircase that inhabitants could use to reach where they worked or to leave the building if they were laborers working elsewhere in the fortress. The building's exits were secured by guards and could be bolted from the inside and the outside.

Rex Cassius had apartments for himself and his family members on the top floors of the building. Access to these floors was barred to anyone, save a known family member. From this lofty perch, Angus and his descendants enjoyed a clear 360-degree view of the fortress and the surrounding territory. Although they could see the expanse of forest beyond the fortress, they could not see through its canopy. Hidden staircases on all four sides of the building provided access to their apartments. The doorway into an individual apartment could be bolted from within. Doorways leading to and from the staircases were guarded. They were not bolted. Family members felt assured of their safety except for the risk of fire.

Steam-driven generators provided the continuous supply of energy needed to power the research building and the rest of the fortress. River water and coal served to make steam. Laborers—humans, animals, and hybrids alike—mined the coal, loaded it onto barges for transport to the fortress, unloaded it upon arrival, and shoveled it into the furnaces that fired the generators.

APPENDIX E
Genetic Engineering and Hybridization

Rex's desire for ever more dangerous and deadly hybrids fueled his drive to embellish both humans and animals with additional weaponry and increase their aggressiveness. To this end, he harnessed genetic engineering to embed animal weaponry and instill ferociousness in his hybrids.

Human Hybrids (Hybrid Humanoids)

Breeding—especially, inbreeding—is one way to develop *H. transformans* with the desired alternate species (e.g., apex predators, beasts of burden). Individuals with the known ability to transform into a desired species would be selected for breeding programs. The disadvantage of breeding is the time required to gestate the offspring (average nine months) and the development of his or her capability (average eleven to twelve years). This required raising *H. transformans* children. Thus, breeding programs were resource-intensive and prohibitive for someone who wanted immediate results.

Consequently, children under the age of eleven were safe from kidnapping. Their parents, however, were not. Many young children were orphaned when their parents were captured. Unless other people sheltered these children, they would die of exposure, malnutrition, and disease.

Development of a new alternate species required the use of genetic engineering in an adult *H. transformans*. Inserting the genes (or balance thereof) of another species into the genome of an *H. transformans* could be accomplished quickly using the proper method (e.g., a viral vector). A relatively short period (days) was required to integrate the new genes. A period of observation (days to weeks) was required to observe the host's reaction. Ill effects typically foreboded a failed experiment and often the death of the recipient. In the absence of ill effects, the genetically modified *H. transformans* was forced to transform. If the transformation was successful and the animal was normal for that species, then the genetic modification was deemed a success.

The development of specific animal features also required genetic engineering in an adult *H. transformans*. For many captured *H. transformans*, the hybridization process was modified to create a genetic hybrid humanoid with characteristics of several different animal species. If successful, then the humanoid would develop the phenotypic features found in those species while still maintaining his or her basic human form. The genes coding for one or more specific characteristics (e.g., horns, claws, enlarged canines, fangs with venom) would be inserted and the host observed. If there were no adverse reactions to the genes, then the *H. transformans* would be forced into a transformation. Typically, the chrysalis would be stripped away to observe which features developed. If the desired features appeared, the transformation would be artificially aborted. The *H. transformans* would be trapped permanently in his or her new form, along with any other changes that occurred as a consequence of genetic modification.

Frequently, the outcome was lethal. In most cases, the lethality was due to the abrupt termination of the transformation. Even if the affected *H. transformans* survived, the hybrid humanoid almost invariably demonstrated additional unplanned and unexpected characteristics. Many of these untoward effects caused disability and often led to the humanoid's demise.

Animal Hybrids

Native animal species could not transform; however, their gestational and growth periods were much shorter. Thus, native apex predators could be bred in a relatively short period. Genetic engineering was required to endow these predators or other species of animals with additional dramatic features. The intent was to create a powerful, predatory hybrid animal that would be even more lethal than the native species. Interspecies breeding was entertained for a brief period; however, these were almost uniformly unsuccessful. In lieu thereof, genetic modifications of fertilized eggs were undertaken.

Shortly after breeding, a fertilized ovum would be harvested. The genes of the desired feature would be inserted into the developing egg. Often, the genes for growth factors were added to increase the size of the offspring. Then the embryo would be reimplanted and its development monitored. If an offspring failed to develop the desired characteristics or acquired malformations incompatible with life, then the developing embryo or fetus would be destroyed. The results were far more successful for animal hybrids than for hybrid humanoids and much less resource-intensive.

Success in both human and animal hybrids was determined by whether or not the hybrid developed the desired characteristics, survived to adulthood, and could function in the role for which it was developed. After developing an animal hybrid successfully, the Cassius Foundation could clone it. This streamlined the production of useful hybrids without the disasters associated with cut and paste genetic engineering.

Supplemental Notes and Citations

Genetic engineering uses artificially created (programmable) specialized enzymes (nucleases) to alter a specific segment of a gene. These enzymes can identify a particular gene, gene sequence, or gene component, excise a portion of a gene, insert another gene segment, and join gene segments together. Many of these enzymes are clones of naturally occurring enzymes reproduced via genetic engineering (Brooker, 2009a).

Multiple genes for a particular characteristic need not be contiguous or even located on the same chromosome. Many may be dispersed at different places along the same chromosome or across multiple chromosomes (Brooker, 2009d). Polymerase chain reaction (PCR) can locate and reproduce copies of a desired gene or gene sequence.

Polymerase Chain Reaction

Polymerase Chain Reaction (PCR) uses a naturally occurring nucleic acid enzyme (DNA polymerase) to make multiple copies of a designated DNA sequence (Brooker, 2009d; Garibyan & Avashia, 2013). PCR can tease out a specific piece of DNA from other strands of DNA. Hence, it is of great value in identifying a particular gene sequence or even a single base. This technique can identify variations and mutations of a single component (nucleotide) of a gene (single nucleotide polymorphism, SNP) or of a gene sequence (Matsuda, 2017). Recently, digital PCR (dPCR) has honed the precision with which PCR can detect mutations in DNA, including cancer markers released into plasma and other body fluids (free DNA) (Olmedillas-López et al., 2017; Tong et al., 2017). It is also used in prenatal testing for blood typing and the identification of selected genetic disorders (Nectoux, 2018).

Clustered regularly interspaced short palindromic repeats and CRISPR-associated protein 9 (CRISPR-Cas9)

A specialized type of genetic material (ribonucleic acid, RNA), is genetically engineered to target a specific sequence of DNA (Batzir et al., 2017; Doetschman & Georgieva, 2017; Heinz & Mashreghi, 2017; Jiang & Doudna, 2017; Stella et al., 2017; Zhang et al., 2018). With an endonuclease (Cas9, an enzyme) in tow, the RNA binds to the designated sequence of DNA. The endonuclease cuts the DNA (double-stranded DNA) at a predetermined location. After cutting the DNA, one can insert or delete genes to repair a damaged DNA segment (e.g., replace an abnormal sequence with a normal one). Often, the cell's own DNA repair mechanisms (e.g., homologous DNA repair) will repair the break (Salsman & Dellaire, 2017).

CRISPR/Cas9 can be used to edit stem cells and germ (reproductive) cells (Zhang et al., 2018; Ormond et al., 2017). The potential to alter germ cells and change the direction of embryonic development is fraught with peril (Rossant, 2018; Shinwari et al., 2018). The American Society of Human Genetics developed recommendations for germline editing. It advised against it unless there is a compelling clinical indication for doing so and evidence to support its therapeutic use (Ormond et al., 2017).

APPENDIX F
The Warship

The warship itself was a hybrid. In designing the ship, Rex Cassius had to avoid using any mechanical devices to power it. The sounds of an engine would startle native wildlife and alert his adversaries. So he could not use steam to power his vessel. A galleon could attain a speed of eight knots, provided the prevailing winds cooperated. In a dead calm, it might as well be grounded. A galley could attain a speed of two to four knots. So Rex decided to blend a galleon with a galley (illustration 17). He ordered his shipbuilder to add a deck with a single bank of oars on both sides, above water level and below the gun deck. Powerful hybrid humanoids would row the oars and keep the ship moving forward—albeit slowly. This modification did not change the weight of the vessel significantly. The addition of heavy rowers offset the weight of a steam-powered engine. There was no longer any need to stow large loads of coal in the ship's hold.

There were four decks on the ship (not including the hold). The lowest deck housed the oars and was reserved for hybrid humanoids who served as rowers. They were not quartered and remained at their station. When not rowing, they could eat or sleep. The gun deck housed cannons on both sides with barrels of gunpowder and crates of cannonballs between each pair of cannons. As a rule, only a watchman was stationed here to sound an alarm if the guns became displaced or friction sparked a fire.

Archers, cannoneers, stewards, and crewmen who handled the sails were quartered mid-deck. There they eked out a place to bed down. Some of the cannoneers bedded down on the gun deck despite the risks. The quarterdeck was reserved for the lieutenants who were given hammocks. Only the captain's cabin had a bunk bed.

Illustration 17: The Warship

The upper deck was open. Spotters and lookout sentries watched and reported changes in the weather, sightings of any other ships, and sightings of any sharks or killer whales. Archers would be deployed to the upper deck if their services were needed before going ashore. Guards were everywhere. Most of them were hybrid humanoids who would become an army once ashore.

A small crow's nest near the top of the mast provided a 360-degree view around the ship. In fair weather, this was the only peaceful place on it. In foul weather, it was preferred over being assigned to work in the hold.

On each side of the ship, barges and canoes hung upside down from the rigging. Ostensibly, they would bring scouts and troops and caged hybrids ashore. Multiple rafts dangled from each side of the ship, where there were no cannon portholes. These would ferry the materials for building a dock and establishing an outpost on H'Aleth's coast. These craft could also be used as lifeboats or life rafts, although that was not Cassius's intent.

Fire was a major hazard on any ship. Wood was used to build ships and boats along with the crates, barrels, and other items used aboard. Pitch and tar lined the hull and barrels to waterproof them. Thus, few lanterns were allowed on the ship. The captain's cabin and the quarterdeck each had one, though, and a few handheld lanterns were available to use below deck. Large barrels of sand were stationed in quarters and on each deck, which provided a place to set down a lantern, if necessary. Anyone caught leaving a lantern unattended risked being keelhauled.

Supplemental Notes and Citations

Keelhaul is a barbaric act of punishment wherein the offender is tied to the ship and thrown overboard to be dragged under the ship's keel. It was used on seafaring vessels on or about the 17th century. It often proved lethal and was used as a form of execution.

APPENDIX G
Potages, Potions, and Poultices

Most of H'Ilgraith's recipes were well known to those who practiced the healing arts. Nonetheless, care had to be taken. Not all recipes were easy to prepare, and some were dangerous, if not used judiciously.

Potages

H'Ilgraith prepared a wide variety of soups and chowders with grains, beans, and other vegetables that provided vitamins, minerals, vegetable protein, and carbohydrates (appendix K). She seasoned her potages with spices and herbs—especially, thyme, oregano, and basil—for flavor and their potential health benefits. She did not use meat in any of her preparations.

Prepare tomato base in potable water.

Season with oregano, thyme, and basil.

Add one or more of the following grains or legumes as sources of vegetable protein and B vitamins—barley, buckwheat, lentils, chickpeas, kidney beans, pinto beans, peas, etc. Add white potatoes and corn for a chowder.

Add one or more of the following for additional sources of vitamin A—carrots, squash, sweet potato, tomato, etc.

Add one or more dark-green, leafy vegetables for additional sources of vitamins and minerals—chard, kale, spinach, broccoli, onions, etc.

Add edible mushrooms.

H'Ilgraith also prepared custards with eggs (Miranda *et al.*, 2015; Soliman, 2018) and goat's milk (Zenebe, 2014), which provided protein, vitamins, minerals, and carbohydrates. She added human breast milk for additional nutrients and to inoculate the goat's milk with *Bifidobacterium* and *Lactobacillus* (Dror & Allen, 2018; Murphy *et al.*, 2017). Finally, she would add freshly picked berries for an additional source of vitamins, minerals, and fiber.

Preparation of milk custard

Heat goat's milk, stirring continuously till it begins to thicken, then allow it to cool.

Decant excess water, if any, to the consistency desired.

Add human breast milk.

Add one or more of the following fresh fruits, whole or crushed (strained for infants), as sources of vitamins, minerals, and fiber— blueberry, strawberry, raspberry, grapes, cranberry, etc.

Preparation of egg custard

Mix milk, eggs, sugar, and desired spice, if any (e.g., cinnamon).

Mix thoroughly, heat, and stir continuously until desired consistency is reached, then cool.

Potions

The majority of H'Ilgraith's potions were medicinal. She prepared a wide variety of herbal extracts and essential oils. Herbal extracts are highly concentrated liquid extracts of an herb, usually administered in drops. They can be further diluted to prepare tinctures and elixirs.

Preparation of herbal extracts and tinctures

For herbal extracts, combine equal amounts of herb (dry measure) with equal amounts of liquid (usually alcohol). Herbs are soaked in alcohol to extract any constituents which would dissolve in it.

For herbal tinctures, fill a glass jar with fresh leaves of the desired herb. Pour alcohol into the jar until the herb is completely covered.

Store extracts and tinctures in a dark closet or cabinet for four to six weeks. Shake the jar periodically to redistribute the alcohol so that it comes in contact with all surfaces of the herb. Strain the liquid into a clean jar or bottle. Label the container with the type of solution, the date of preparation, and the ingredients used. Store in a cool, darkened area, away from sunlight.

Preparation of fruit and honey elixirs

Preparation is similar to tinctures except that elixirs are typically made from fruit with or without honey added to sweeten them. Elixirs may be used to provide nutritional supplements or to make extracts and tinctures more palatable.

Fill a jar ½ to ¾ with crushed fruit. Strain the crushed fruit first for infants.

Add alcohol or wine till the fruit is completely covered.

Store in a cool, dark closet or cabinet for four to six weeks.

Strain the liquid into a clean jar.

If honey is desired, add it to the mixture and mix thoroughly.

Store in a cool location.

Essential Oils

Essential oils were a major component of H'Ilgraith's medicinal armamentarium. When used in aromatics and salves, they brought considerable relief from suffering (Eckert *et al.*, 2018). When applied to wounds, some herbal preparations would promote healing and decrease the incidence of infection (Piatkowska & Rusiecka-Ziółkowska, 2016; Rai *et al.*, 2017). H'Ilgraith frequently prepared essential rose oil and oils of basil, oregano, or thyme to use in ointments and balms. She rarely made lotions or creams. Water-based preparations are quickly absorbed and do not persist on the skin, as would an oil-based preparation.

H'Ilgraith could prepare vegetable oil by hand from peanuts (a legume). The procedure was tedious and very time-consuming, yet it was simpler and easier than trying to extract oil from nuts. Villages that had gristmills could prepare vegetable oil from nuts, seeds, and corn. So whenever H'Ilgraith visited a village where these products were made, she would acquire a jar of vegetable oil. Whenever she ventured into Cassius territory or the contested territory, she always carried a tiny supply of essential oil and a few leaves of oregano, basil, and thyme in her satchel.

Preparation of peanut oil

Crush shelled peanuts in a small amount of water until the mixture is smooth. Add small amounts of water, as needed, so that the resulting mixture is completely homogenous. (Note: This step is very time-consuming.)

Pour the mixture in a jar and cover it.

Allow the mixture to set until the oil separates.

Decant the oil. This fraction of the oil will be the most clarified.

Strain the mixture to extract additional oil, if desired.

Use the remaining peanut mixture as a food item.

Select the aromatic spice (e.g., cinnamon, cloves), aromatic flower (e.g., rose, lavender, peppermint), or medicinal herb (e.g., oregano) to add to the oil.

Crush the spice, bruise flower petals, or chop leaves.

Prepare an infusion by placing the desired constituent in a jar and adding oil to cover it. Seal the container tightly and shake the contents so that oil is in contact with all of the constituent.

Allow it to set for twenty-four hours.

For aromatics, open the container and test the aroma. If not strong enough, strain the oil and repeat the process above with a fresh batch of constituent. Repeat the process as often as necessary to obtain the desired intensity of fragrance.

Put the essential oil in a dark glass container that has a tight seal, and store it in a dark, cool location.

Preparation of balms and ointments
(oil- or wax-based preparations)

H'Ilgraith used honey both as a nutritional supplement and in the preparation of salves. Although the estate usually kept a supply of honey on hand, H'Ilgraith preferred to procure a fresh jar from the villages that kept honeybees. The villagers also would provide her with beeswax, which she used to prepare balms and ointments for topical application.

Combine beeswax and oil in a 1:4 ratio for a balm or in a 1:5 ratio for an ointment.

Heat the two constituents together slowly over low heat, stirring continuously until the beeswax has melted and blended with the oil.

Test consistency by allowing a drop to cool. Balms are usually thicker than ointments. Add more beeswax or oil, as needed, to achieve the desired consistency.

Allow the preparation to cool without thickening, then add the essential oils for scent or therapeutic use if desired. When adding honey to a balm, mix it in thoroughly.

Poultices

H'Ilgraith would use poultices to apply medicated dressings to intact skin or wounds (no author, 1887). They provide moist heat to increase circulation to the area, draw out pus and toxins, and provide a means of delivering medicinal ingredients topically.

Preparation of poultices

Prepare a soft, moist, and often warmed pomace of bran, oatmeal, or dried bread to provide warmth.

Add essential oils, herbs, or honey to treat infected wounds, reduce inflammation, and promote healing.

Add aloe or menthol to relieve pain.

Apply the preparation directly onto the skin or wound and then wrap or place a clean cotton cloth on top to keep the pomace in place and secure. Alternatively, spread the pomace directly onto the dressing and then apply it.

APPENDIX H
Cast of Characters
(In alphabetical order)

Agora [ă-*gōr*-ă]—*H. transformans* (XT, Y), architect, and engineer.
Biography: His grandparents fled with Edvar and Ruth to a new territory. He learned his craft during the building of the research facility adjacent to the manor house. He was instrumental in designing and building the wall around the estate.
Transformed within *Canidae* family. Alternate species: labrador.

Andronovich [ăn-*drŏn*-ō-vĭch]—*H. transformans* (XT, Y), chief of security at Gregor.
Biography: An H. transformans of unknown parentage, he was rescued by another family when raiders killed his parents. His new family took a chance and fled to Gregor. Gregor became his home.
Transformed within *Ursidae* family. Alternate species: black bear.

Balthorean [băl-*thŏr*-ē-ăn]—*H. transformans* (XT, Y), lead scout in the southern region of H'Aleth.
Biography: An offspring of parents who carried the gene for red hair, his hair was a dark auburn color. He had inherited the genes for red hair from both parents. This characteristic carried over to his alternate species and allowed him to blend into the southwestern plains and mountains. He was the red wolf that joined in the surveillance of a warship off the southern coast of H'Aleth.
Transformed within *Canidae* family. Alternate species: red wolf, red fox.

Calen [*kā*-lĕn]—*H. sapiens* (X, Y), chairman of the governing council for the research division of Biogenics.

Cassius, Angus—*H. transformans* (XT, Y), the original owner of the Cassius Foundation.

Biography: Founded one of the two largest organizations researching the genetics of *H. transformans,* Initially, Angus used the abilities of *H. transformans* to gain control of other companies and their resources. Subsequently, he extended his reach to encompass entire territories. Ultimately, he intended to establish himself as absolute ruler over all territories. The Biogenics Corporation became his chief competitor and archrival.

Transformed within *Suidae* species. Alternate species: wild boar.

Cassius, Rex—*H. transformans* (XT, Y), head of the Cassius Foundation.

Biography: Grandson of Angus Cassius, he took over the management of the Cassius Foundation after the death of his grandfather. He continued to expand the Foundation's territories and resources, largely through hostile takeovers and intimidation. He continued to pursue his grandfather's dream of absolute rule over every territory and of establishing a royal family lineage. The Biogenics Corporation remained the Cassius Foundation's archrival.

Transformed within *Suidae* species. Alternate species: wild boar.

Edrian [ĕd-rē-ăn]—*H. transformans* (XT, Y), chief scout of the northern territory.

Biography: H'Ilgraith's brother, first cousin of H'Assandra, and eligible to become master of the House of H'Aleth. He and H'Ilgraith learned their scouting and surveillance skills together from the same master scout and developed their expertise under his guidance. Edrian maintained a close relationship with family members and had strong ties with the people of H'Aleth.

Transformed within *Canidae* family. Alternate species: gray mountain wolf, gray fox.

Edward—*H. transformans* (XT, Y).

Biography: Son of H'Ophelia and H'Assandra's brother, he was eligible to become master of the House of H'Aleth. He served with H'Assandra to manage civil affairs for the House of H'Aleth and became instrumental in coordinating defensive measures.

Transformed within *Canidae* family. Alternate species: gray mountain wolf, gray fox.

Fenovartan [fĕn-ō-vār-tăn]—*Dragonensis dragonis fuscus magna.*

Biography: A member of Theovolan's clan, he recognized H'Ilgraith's yowl when she returned to the northern mountains to arrange an accord with Theovolan and his clan. Fenovartan was H'Ilgraith's escort and transported her into the clan's aery.

Floberius [flō-*ber*-ē-us]—*H. transformans* (XT, Y), plant biologist, and arborist.

Biography: He and his family once lived in the contested area. They fled their home when a clash between Biogenics and Cassius encompassed their farm. They immigrated to H'Aleth, where Floberius was recognized as an expert botanist. He often assisted H'Ilgraith with the identification of plants, their constituents, and their uses.

Transformed within *Cervidae* species. Alternate species: mule deer.

Francesca—*H. sapiens* (X, X), chairwoman of the governing council for the marketing and sales division of Biogenics.

Gustavian—*H. transformans* (XT, Y), captain of Rex's warship.

Biography: His family had long lived under Cassius' rule. His parents had been unable to escape when the Cassius Foundation overtook the region in which they lived. His father apprenticed him to a shipbuilder so that he would have a valuable skill and a better life than his parents.

Transformed within *Cervidae* family. Alternate species: mule deer.

H'Assandra [hă-*săn*-dră]—*H. transformans* (2XT), Mistress of the House of H'Aleth.

Biography: daughter of H'Ophelia, sister to Edward, and granddaughter of Ruth—the first mistress of the House of H'Aleth (Ped 3). H'Assandra accepted the mantle of mistress from her mother, H'Ophelia.

Transformed across mammalian and avian classes. Alternate species: gray wolf, red fox, lynx, red-tailed hawk, and golden eagle.

H'Eleanora [*hĕl*-ĕ-an-*or*-ah]—*H. transformans* (2XT).

Biography: Second daughter of H'Elvinia, she was eligible to become mistress of the House of H'Aleth. She died from complications of childbirth, leaving her newborn infant, whom she named H'Ester, an orphan.

Transformed across mammalian and avian classes. Alternate species: red fox, cougar, white-tailed deer, long-eared owl.

H'Elena [hĕl-*ĕ*-nah]—*H. transformans* (2XT).

Biography: Daughter of Ruth and H'Ilgraith's mother, she was eligible to become mistress of the House of H'Aleth. Her older sister, H'Ophelia, accepted the role of mistress.

Transformed across mammalian and avian classes. Alternate species: gray wolf, red fox, lynx, Cooper's hawk, great horned owl.

H'Ilgraith [hil-*grăy*-ĭth]—*H. transformans* (2XT).

Biography: Daughter of H'Elena, sister to Edrian, and granddaughter of Ruth, she was eligible to become mistress of the House of H'Aleth. She spent considerable time in the presence of red and gray dragons, learning about their communities and their tonal language. Espoused to Jak, she was widowed when a hybrid ursuscro killed him. After Jak's death, she became withdrawn and spent most of her time alone searching for plant and mineral constituents she used in her potions. Later in life, she fostered a foundling who was fated to become mistress of the House of H'Aleth. She had no children of her own.

Transformed across mammalian and avian classes. Alternate species: gray fox, badger, lynx, and great horned owl.

H'Umara [hu-*mar*-a]—*H. transformans* (2XT).

Biography: Daughter of H'Elena, sister of H'Ilgraith and Edrian, and granddaughter of Edvar and Ruth, she was eligible to become mistress of the House of H'Aleth. She studied medicine at the House of Gregor and became a physician. Later, she married into the House of Erwina.

Transformed across mammalian and avian classes. Alternate species: gray fox, cougar, and Cooper's hawk.

Ilsa—H. *transformans* (XT, X), scout in the northeastern region of H'Aleth.

Biography: The second of two children, her family had immigrated to H'Aleth before she was born. Her father was an *H. sapiens,* her mother an *H. transformans.* They fled their farm with her brother when hunters raided a nearby village where they often traded their crops. Ilsa was disinclined to engage in farming and chose scouting as her vocation. She would return to the farm to help prepare for sowing seeds in the spring and harvesting crops in the fall.

Transformed within *Canidae* family. Alternate species: gray wolf.

Jak (Jakovic [*jak*-ō-vĭc])—*H. transformans* (XT, Y), lone scout in the contested region.

Biography: Born into a migrant family of unknown heritage, he became H'Ilgraith's companion and husband. Jak was the eldest of two children and became the family patriarch at age sixteen when his father was killed. Both parents could transform into gray mountain wolves. Jak developed the ability to become a gray wolf and gray fox at age thirteen. Once he was sufficiently proficient at transforming and had adapted to his alternate species, he joined his parents on patrols and subsequently on hunts to learn these skills. As a young wolf, Jak was neither large enough nor strong enough to bring down a large prey animal alone; however, he could assist his parents and gained valuable experience in doing so.

One day, all three were on a hunt. They spotted a female boar and were about to bring her down when a large male boar attacked. His father tried to fend off the male and was gored. Jak and his mother abandoned the female and tried to distract the male boar away from his father. Their persistent and coordinated attacks finally drove him off. They returned to the father only to find him dead.

The family was devastated. Jak's mother resumed her human form and never transformed again. The following winter was harsh, and it took its toll. His mother fell ill, stopped eating, and died late one night. Shortly thereafter, Jak and his brother parted and became lone wolves. Jak spent most of his adult life as a wolf, as did both of his parents, until he encountered an extraordinary badger. Husband of H'Ilgraith, he was killed defending her from a hybrid ursuscro.

Transformed within *Canidae* family. Alternate species: gray mountain wolf, gray fox.

Katrina—*H. sapiens* (X, X), genetic engineer for the Biogenics Corporation.

Biography: Kidnapped by Rex Cassius with her husband Randall, daughter Katelin, and son Franklin, she was forced to work in Rex's genetic engineering labs. She escaped with her family and many other kidnapped captives during a bold escape engineered in part by her husband.

Latransa [lă-trăn-să]—*H. transformans* (XT, X), scout.

Biography: She conducted scouting and surveillance throughout H'Aleth's territory. She was the coyote who joined in the surveillance of a warship off the southern coast of H'Aleth.

Transformed within the *Canidae* family. Alternate species: coyote.

Leliana [lă-lē-*ă*-nă]—*H. transformans* (2XT).

Biography: Chief of security at the House of Erwina, she was related to Ruth via the paternal line.

Transformed across mammalian and avian classes. Alternate species: gray fox, lynx, and prairie falcon.

Mavelov [*măv-ĕ-lof*]—*H. transformans* (XT, Y), a lead scout and wildlife specialist.

Biography: He conducted scouting and surveillance primarily in the northwestern region of H'Aleth. He also taught the children of H'Aleth about wildlife and assisted those who were *H. transformans* to learn the characteristics and skills of their alternate species.

Transformed within the *Canidae* family. Alternate species: gray wolf, gray fox.

Navikolas [năv-*ĭk*-ō-lăs]—*H. transformans* (XT, Y), an experienced shipwright.

Biography: He built watercraft for the lakes and rivers of H'Aleth, including steam-powered and sailing vessels. He was a skilled rower, canoer, rafter, and kayaker who could traverse category five rapids. He taught scouts how to navigate rivers and rapids using a variety of watercraft.

Transformed within *Ursidae* family. Alternate species: black bear.

Petramonte [pĕt-ră-*mŏn*-tĕ]—*H. transformans* (XT, Y), chief geographer and mapmaker.

Biography: He fled the mountainous areas of the contested region when he came under attack by hunters. His knowledge of the region's geography and skills as a mountain climber allowed him to elude his attackers. Later, he made his way into H'Aleth, where he promptly learned its geographic regions and provided accurate maps of the territory north of H'Aleth.

Transformed within *Ovidae* family. Alternate species: bighorn sheep.

Randall—*H. transformans* (XT, Y), structural engineer.

Biography: Husband of Katrina, he also worked for Biogenics Corporation. Kidnapped by Rex Cassius with his wife and children, he was forced to work as a laborer in the fortress. He was the chief architect of an escape plan and a tunnel built to free as many captives as possible.

Transformed within *Cervidae* species. Alternate species: red deer.

Serena—*H. transformans* (2XT), scout.

Biography: Both parents were *H. transformans* of unknown lineage. She was a scout in the north and northeastern territory of H'Aleth. She knew the villages located in that region and the people who lived there. She was sent to the northern villages to help them prepare for a potential invasion by Cassius forces. As a Cooper's hawk, she could spot an incursion from a long distance away and alert all her villages quickly.

Transformed across mammalian and avian classes. Alternate species: gray fox, cougar, Cooper's hawk.

Stokal—*H. transformans* (XT, Y), chief of security for the Biogenics Corporation.

Biography: Initially, he handled security for the research and development division, planning and conducting operations to counter the Cassius Foundation's sorties into Biogenics' southern region. Later, he organized an army to defend both divisions.

Transformed within the *Canidae* family. Alternate species: gray wolf.

Surrelius [sĭr-rā-lē-ŭs]—*H. sapiens* (X, Y), chief architect and builder of the warship *Rex Cassius*.

Theovolan [thē-ō-vō-lăn]—*Dragonensis dragonis fuscus magna*.

Biography: The leader of the clan of great gray dragons with whom the H'Aletheans reached an accord. Together, they would maintain surveillance over the Cassius Foundation and protect their respective clan members from being killed or captured by hunters and hybrids.

Tiberius—*H. transformans* (XT, Y), wildlife biologist and veterinarian.

Biography: A native H'Alethean, his mother had immigrated to H'Aleth when he was a very young child. He was a trained scout; however, his alternate species did not allow the stealth required for scouting. So he specialized in wildlife and trained as a veterinarian at Gregor.

Transformed within *Ursidae* family. Alternate species: brown bear.

Tragar—*H. transformans* (XT, Y), scout.

Biography: He immigrated to H'Aleth and became a scout in the southeastern territory of H'Aleth. He settled in one of the villages located in that region, quickly learned where the other villages were located, and grew to know the people who lived there. He was sent to the southern villages to help them prepare for a potential invasion by Cassius forces from the southeast, including its coastline. As a red deer, his alternate species stuck out like a sore thumb in the southern terrain. Yet he could race at nearly forty miles per hour to reach even remote villages quickly. The villagers would definitely see him coming and be alerted.

Transformed within *Cervidae* species. Alternate species: red deer.

Valeria—*H. transformans* (2XT), apprentice scout.

Biography: Born in H'Aleth, both parents were *H. transformans* of unknown origin who fled to H'Aleth. Under the mentorship of Balthorean, she conducted scouting and surveillance throughout H'Aleth's southwestern region. She was tasked by H'Assandra to scout the plains and desert for potential places where H'Aletheans could evade Cassius forces.

Transformed within the *Canidae* and *Felidae* families. Alternate species: lynx, desert gray fox.

Weston—*H. transformans* (XT, Y), chief of security.

Biography: An *H. transformans* of unknown origin, his grandparents belonged to one of the families who left with Ruth and Edvar when they fled their original home to found a new one, the House of H'Aleth, in a more remote territory. He became a skilled scout, archer, and swordsman and served within every region in H'Aleth's territory. He also mentored apprentice scouts and taught youngsters how to watch and wait unseen, both as humans and as their alternate species. When H'Assandra became mistress of the House of H'Aleth, the position of security chief was open. She appointed Weston as her chief of security.

Transformed within the *Canidae* family. Alternate species: gray wolf.

APPENDIX I
Alternate Species
(in alphabetical order by class)

Mammals

Badger (*Mustelidae*)—omnivore, predominantly carnivore.

The badger's coat is brownish-black with distinctive alternating white and black bands on the head and face. It has huge claws on its forefeet for digging, can dig faster than any other species, and can excavate a burrow within minutes. Badgers have a wide range of vocalizations, including low-pitched growls associated with aggression, high-pitched squeaks, and a purring sound. Normally nocturnal, badgers forage mostly at night. Larger species of badgers often hunt and forage on the ground. They can climb trees to reach honey and nuts; however, they are awkward. They can run at fifteen to twenty miles per hour. A powerful and aggressive animal, badgers can fend off larger predators, especially from the safety of a den. Although badgers can swim, they avoid doing so, if possible.

Boar, wild (*Sus scrofa*) —omnivore

The boar's fur coat is grayish–brownish to black. They have a large head and shoulders, a narrow hind, and thin legs with hooves. Males can weigh up to 400 pounds, may be six feet long, and stand four feet high at the shoulder. Both males and females have tusks—long canines that extend four to five inches and curve outward. Hence, they are often called a great horned boar. They have relatively poor eyesight; however, they have an excellent sense of smell. They can run up to 30 miles per hour.

Caracal (*Caracal caracal*)—carnivore

Caracals are small-to-medium size slender cats with tall tufted ears that taper, long legs, and long canines. Its long legs allow it to leap nearly ten feet into the air to catch birds. Females weigh about twenty to thirty pounds, so it is comparable in size to the harpy eagle.

Cougar (*Puma*)—carnivore
Cougars are one of the larger species of wild cats. Females have an average weight of 100 pounds, whereas males can weight 120–200 pounds. They can reach speeds of forty to fifty miles per hour. Cougars can range to about 10,000 feet above sea level.

Deer, Red (*Cervus elaphus*)—herbivore
Also known as elk, they are among the largest species of deer. Males stand three and one-half to four and one-half feet at the shoulder and weigh 350–450 pounds. They can run up to approximately 40 miles per hour. They can swim if necessary and ford a river.

Dragon (*Dragonensis*)—carnivore

Great gray dragons (*Dragonis fuscus magna*) (illustrations 6, 11, 14)—omnivore, predominantly carnivore
Great gray dragons are so named because their scales are dark gray to black and blend into the granite of the northern and northeastern mountains where they have their aeries. They range up to 14,000 feet. They rarely appear in the foothills; however, they are known to hunt in montane forests and to investigate violent or tumultuous incidents. They are the largest and most powerful of the land dragons. Their fire ranges from 1,600–2,200 degrees Fahrenheit, roughly the equivalent of a blast furnace. (Note: The melting temperature of granite is approximately 2,200–2,300 degrees Fahrenheit.)

Red dragons (*Dragonis rubra*) (illustration 2)—carnivore.
Red dragons are so named because their scales reflect a red to reddish-brown color. They live in the southern and southwestern mountains and range from 9,000–11,000 feet. A relatively slender animal by dragon

standards, they are the smallest of the dragon species. They are more lithe and agile than their larger cousins, and their bodies are more flexible and nimble. Their slender shape is also more aerodynamic; therefore, they can attain greater flight and diving speeds than the gray dragons.

Blue dragons (*Dragonis odontoceti*) (illustrations 9, 12)—carnivore.

Blue dragons are named for the deep blue scales extending from the top of their head, over their back, to the top of their tail. Their underside is white. They are the dragon equivalent of an orca. They have the characteristic head and neck of a dragon; however, their body is streamlined for speed underwater. Their fins are modified wings with characteristics of both. A long tail serves as both rudder and whip. Using both their wings and their tail, they can achieve speeds of nearly 50 miles per hour (approximately 43 knots) underwater. Although they cannot fly for sustained periods, their modified wings and a whip of their tail can launch them out of the water and over most fishing boats, in either a breach or an attack. They breathe fire mostly above water. They can breathe fire underwater; however, its power and distance are compromised.

Arctic dragons (*Dragonis arcturus alba*) (illustration 15)—so named because of the almost pure white on most of their body. They have gray coloring on the tops of their head, back, and wings, and white coloring on the chest, underbelly, and under the wings. Their body is streamlined for diving, so they are somewhat smaller than the gray dragons. Their scales are thinner and tapered so they can overlap when compressed during a dive. Their wingspan is thirty to forty-two feet; however, they can fold their wings tightly against their body for diving. Their soaring speed is 150–180 miles per hour, and their diving speed in the air is 230–260 miles per hour.

Fox, gray fox (*Urocyon cinereoargenteus)*—omnivore

The gray fox has a coat of various shades, predominantly gray with a mix of white and black. It is the second-largest fox and has a long tail. It is usually nocturnal and sleeps during the day. The gray fox is well adapted for montane forests and can climb trees that are fifty to sixty feet high and jump from tree to tree if the trees are close. Although foxes can swim, their fur is not waterproof. It becomes saturated and can weigh the fox down; hence, it prefers not to get wet. It can run at speeds up to thirty-five to forty miles per hour. Its claws are sharp and curved, like those of a lynx, except they are much shorter. Like a badger, the fox uses its claws to dig a den. All species of fox have a wide range of vocalizations. They can bark, yip, growl, and screech. Many behaviors serve as visual cues (e.g., an aggressive versus a submissive posture), and scent-marking indicates their territorial range and sex status.

Leopard (*Panthera pardus*)—carnivore

Of the five species of big cats—lion, tiger, leopard, jaguar, cougar—leopards are the smallest. An adult's body length is typically three to *six feet* long. Their tail adds another two to three and one-half feet to their overall length. They stand two to two and one-half feet tall at the shoulder. Males and females vary in weight. While males weigh eighty to 200 pounds, females weigh sixty to 130 pounds. A leopard can run about thirty-five miles per hour and jump about ten feet high. Bite force is about 1000 pounds per square inch. Leopards are skilled in climbing trees and are strong swimmers.

Lynx (*Lynx canadensis*)—carnivore

The male adult lynx is about three feet long and weighs twenty to thirty pounds. Females are much smaller, measuring between two and two and one-half feet long and weighing between ten and fifteen pounds. Claws are one and a quarter to one and one-half inches long. Canine teeth are about four inches long, which are large for the lynx's size. Some species of mountain lynx can range up to about 18,000 feet.

Striped skunk (*Mephitis mephitis*)—omnivore

The skunk is a small animal, weighing from five to twelve pounds with a body length of eight inches to one and one-half feet. Their tails can add another five to fifteen inches. Males are larger than females. They can spray a strong repugnant oil from two anal scent glands up to ten feet away. Their musk has a sulfur-like odor and is extremely irritating to the eyes. They eat a wide variety of small animals, including insects, rodents, frogs and snakes, birds, and eggs. They also eat berries, roots, nuts, and some plant leaves.

Wolf, gray mountain (*Canis lupus irremotus*)—*carnivore*
The gray mountain wolf is the largest species of wolf, with an average weight of eighty to one hundred pounds; however, a large male can weigh up to 180 pounds. Normally (e.g., when feeding), a wolf's bite force is about 400 pounds per square inch; however, in a battle, a large wolf can have a bite force over 1000 pounds per square inch. Wolf howls can be heard over relatively long distances. Normally, wolves use howling to stay in contact with other members of their pack. The range of a contact howl is about five miles in forested areas and about ten miles in open territory. Wolves have good visual acuity and wide peripheral vision, which enables them to see prey at long distances.

Birds

Condor (*Gymnogyps californianus*)—carnivore (scavenger).
Body size is about three and one-half to four and one-half feet. They weigh between eighteen and twenty pounds. They have a wingspan of nine to ten feet, from tip to tip. This allows the condor to soar for long distances in open space. They can reach altitudes of 15,000 feet.

Golden eagle (*Aquila chrysaetos*)—carnivore
One of the largest eagles, this bird is slightly smaller than the bald eagle. It is also among the most powerful eagles. Its talons can exert a pressure of 400 pounds per square inch. Its flight speed is twenty-eight to thirty miles per hour, and it can soar up to 10,000 feet.

Great horned owl (*Bubo virginianus*)—carnivore
This species can be found almost anywhere, although they prefer

wetlands and forests and do not range above the tree line in the mountains. It is a powerful bird for its size. Its talons can extend as wide as four by eight inches and can exert approximately 300 pounds per square inch. It can carry prey up to eight to nine pounds (almost three times its weight). It can attain a flight speed of twenty to forty miles per hour. All owls have binocular vision. Although an owl's eyes are fixed in their sockets, the owl can turn its head 270 degrees in either direction. This gives the bird a wide range of vision. Owls have sharp visual acuity, even in low light. They are farsighted and can see objects nearly two miles away in daylight. Both their sight and hearing are exquisitely sensitive to movement. They have directional hearing, an unusual ability to locate prey precisely by sound. If a prey species is hidden and does not move, an owl may not see it. Their calls include deep and soft hoots, whistles, shrieks, and coos, among other sounds.

Harpy eagle (*Harpia harpyja*)—carnivore

The harpy is the largest eagle. Females are about three to three and one-half feet long and weigh between twelve and twenty pounds. Their talons are five inches long and among the largest and strongest of raptors. Their wingspan is about six to six and one-half feet. Despite their size, harpy eagles can maneuver through the forest canopy. Their plumage consists of dark gray feathers on their wings and back with white breast feathers. They have an additional tuft of gray-to-white plumage on the top of the head. When raised, the plumage resembles tufted ears.

APPENDIX J
Hybrid Species

Ybrids were human or animal species in which the genes of one species were mixed with those of one or more other species via genetic engineering methods. In human-animal hybrids— known as hybrid humanoids—the base genome was *Homo transformans,* with the genes of one or more animal species inserted, usually via a viral vector. The *H. transformans* was forced into a transformation, which was abruptly stopped when the desired characteristics become apparent. If the victim survived, he or she could not transform again and remained trapped in his or her transformed state.

In animal-animal hybrids, the base genome belonged to one animal with other animal genes added. Native animals could not transform into another species. Consequently, their genomes were altered by inserting genes into a fertilized egg or a developing embryo.

By convention, the names of human-animal hybrids ended in -id or -oid, which reflected the human base genome mixed with another animal. The names of animal-animal hybrids were composites of their species' names. The first component represented the primary species to which other species' genes were added.

Human-Animal Hybrids (Hybrid humanoids)

Bisalcesoid [bĭs-ăl-cēs-oĭd] (illustration 1)

Genetics: the genes of a bison (*biso*–iso genes of a bison (s of human-ani *H. transformans* who could transform into a moose (*–alces*)

Description: A large *H. transformans* male weighing close to 500

293

pounds. He had humanoid facial features with a hairless face. He had the dark, leathery skin of a bison with the latter's heavy coat of hair on his upper torso and upper extremities. He had stringy, patchy human hair hanging from his scalp. His teeth were molar (consistent with an herbivore). He had a huge human head with vestigial antlers and no horns. His ears, eyes, nose, and mouth were like a bison's, and his dentition consisted of the even, large teeth of an herbivore. He had the goatee of a buffalo dangling below his chin. His back legs were human with hooved feet. His arms were like a bison's front legs, with massive hands shaped like paws. His fingers were shortened and thickened with long, straight, and blunted nails. His enlarged torso was similar to the upper body of bison. So as a hybrid, he was hunched backed and bent far forward, which made him top-heavy. He could rear up on his back (hind) legs like a human but could not sustain an upright stance due to his heavy, enlarged torso.

Purpose: created to be a beast of burden—to haul heavy objects such as blocks of stone chiseled from a mountain or a wagon of logs from felled trees.

Bovicervid [bōv-ĭ-cerv-ĭd].

Genetics: the genes of bighorn sheep (*-ovis*) were spliced into the genome of a male *H. transformans* who could transform into an elk (*-cervus*).

Description: an *H. transformans* who was forced into a permanent transformation as an elk with no visible human characteristics. His skull was thickened, especially over the forehead. He had a thickened, heavier, and much stronger six-point rack that increased the lethality of a blow. Unfortunately, the rack was so heavy that his neck muscles were unable to hold his head fully erect. Nevertheless, he could still ram an opponent with lethal force. As an elk, he weighed 700 pounds and stood five feet tall at the shoulder. He had an elk's long legs and could run at twenty-five miles per hour, accelerating up to forty-five miles per hour in a burst of speed. He had the concave, elastic hooves of a bighorn sheep, which increased his agility on rocky mountain slopes.

Purpose: intended for fighting and hard labor, especially in rocky terrains, and served as a laborer hauling blocks of stone in a quarry.

Papiopanoid [păp-ē-ō-*păn*-oid] (illustration 10)

Genetics: the genes of a baboon (*papio–*) were spliced into male *H. transformans* who could transform into a chimpanzee (*–pan*).

Description: an *H. transformans* who was forced to begin transformation into a chimpanzee. The transformation was interrupted when the desired characteristics of the baboon appeared. The intent was to produce a hybrid with the strength of a chimpanzee, the fangs of a baboon, the aggressiveness of both, and the height and dexterity of a human. The result was a tall humanoid that could sit upright but not stand upright. He had long arms and hands like those of a chimpanzee, the strength of a chimpanzee, the fangs of a baboon, the ability to run almost as fast as a chimpanzee, and the aggressiveness of both the chimpanzee and the baboon.

Purpose: engineered specifically to attack and fight.

Ursoxinoid—[er-*sŏx*-in-oid].

Genetics: the genes of an ox (*–bos*) were spliced into an *H. transformans* who could transform into a bear (*–ursus*)

Description: an *H. transformans* who was forced to begin transformation into a bear. The transformation was interrupted as soon as features of an ox appeared. He developed into a larger and stronger humanoid with greater strength and endurance, weighed approximately 350 pounds, and stood nearly eight feet tall. He could walk upright or on all four extremities. Additional features included a small pair of curved horns and the bony forehead of an ox.

Purpose: engineered for the purposes of serving both as a beast of burden and as a ferocious fighter.

Animal-Animal Hybrids

Harpyacalgryph [*hăr*-pē-ă-*căl*-grĭf] (illustration 3)

Genetics: the genes of a vulture (*–grif*) and a caracal cat (*–cal*) were spliced into the fertilized egg of a harpy eagle (*harpia*–ar

Description: the hybrid had the body of a harpy eagle with the wings of a condor, the long tufted and tapered ears of a caracal cat, and the broad beak of a vulture, which housed the canine teeth and tongue of a caracal cat. Its larger wingspan improved its ability to soar in open space; however, it made flight more difficult when lifting off from the ground and impeded its ability to fly through forest canopy.

Purpose: designed to be an aerial predator.

Moresistrurus [*mōr*-ā-sĭs-*trū*-rŭs)] (illustration 4)

Genetics: the genes of the pit viper (*−sistrurus*) were spliced into the base genome of a newly hatched green tree python (*more*−or

Description: a much larger than normal green tree python, enhanced by growth hormone, that had the fangs and venom of a pit viper. It could lurk in a tree, hidden by the foliage, strike out and hold its unsuspecting prey in its coils, and inject it with venom.

Purpose: an ambush predator designed to protect territories that Rex Cassius claimed by terrorizing anyone who entered them. Rex unexpectedly lost some of his hybrids to this creation.

Mustecanis [must-ĕ-*căn*-is], plural musticani (illustration 8)

Genetics: the genes of a weasel (*muste*−) were inserted into the nucleus of a fertilized red fox (*−canis*) ovum.

Description: the body of a weasel was enhanced to the size of a coyote with features of the red fox. It had the lithe body of a weasel; however, it was covered with red fur and had the bushy tail of a red fox. It was armed with the long and extremely sharp canine teeth and sharp claws of the red fox. It had the agility of a weasel and the speed of a fox and was nearly impossible to catch if it escaped. Its physical features, coupled with the ferocity of the weasel, raised it to the level of an apex predator.

Purpose: engineered to be a cunning, ferocious, and often unseen guard animal for storerooms and weapons caches; also used for digging, if needed.

Serojacuta [sĕr-*ō*-jă-*cū*-tă] (illustration 7)

Genetics: the genes of a boar (*seroja*−) were inserted into the genome of a developing hyena embryo (*−crocuta*).

Description: a shorter hyena with the stocky build of a boar, especially around its upper body and neck. Its neck was shorter and heavier than that of a native hyena. It still had the head, jaws, and bite force of the hyena—about 1,100 pounds per square inch—with the addition of the tusks of the boar. Its forelegs were shorter and stockier so that it no longer had the sloped back of a typical hyena. The front feet were paws while the back feet had developed into hooves. Due to its increased size and weight, its maximum speed was reduced to twenty-five miles per hour.

Purpose: engineered to be deadly and used as an attack or guard animal.

Theracapracanis [*thĕr*-ah-căp-rah-*căn*-ĭ̆], plural theraparacani (illustration 5)

Genetics: the genes of a jackal (–*canis*) and an ibex (–*capra*) were inserted into the nucleus of a fertilized leopard (–*thera*) egg to create an enhanced animal hybrid.

Description: the figure was a large, cat-like creature with the body of a leopard. Its coat was that of a leopard, except for the swath of black hair on it back, a gift of its jackal genes. Its head was shaped like that of a jackal. It had two spiked horns like that of a Nubian ibex, only longer and angled forward. If the creature charged in a direct attack, it would gore its opponent. The creature also had exaggerated leopard canines, which would rend flesh. It had the sure-footedness of the leopard and ibex.

Purpose: engineered to be an aggressive hybrid that would prey on any species, including humans.

Ursuscro [ur-*sŭs*-crō] (illustration 13)

Genetics: the genome of a bear (–*ursus*) was augmented with the genes of a boar (–*scro*) to create an especially aggressive animal hybrid.

Description: this hybrid had the size and form of a brown bear with the snout, tusks, and disposition of a wild boar. Its upper and lower canines were enlarged also.

Purpose: engineered to kill anything it attacked. The architecture of its brain was distorted as a consequence of its hybridization, and the hybrid eventually became deranged.

APPENDIX K
Medicinal and Nutritional Plants

There is limited evidence for the effectiveness of herbal remedies. Most of the research has been conducted in a laboratory setting. The lack of studies in humans prevents verifying these agents as safe and effective (Sharifi-Rad *et al.*, 2017). Many of these agents interact with other agents and may have significant side effects (Asher *et al.*, 2017).

Acorns—a source of essential fatty acids and oleic acids (e.g., monounsaturated omega-9 fatty *acid) as well as protein, vitamins, and minerals (Akan* et al., 2017; *Papoti* et al., 2018).

Aloe vera—anecdotal reports suggest it soothes wounds and may be effective as a temporary treatment for them (Bitter & Erickson, 2016); however, there is insufficient evidence to support wound healing.

Basil, essential oil—thought to have antioxidant, anti-inflammatory (Jamshidi & Cohen, 2017; Li *et al.*, 2017), and antibacterial (Sakkas & Papadopoulou, 2017; Zareen *et al.*, 2014) properties.

Berries, wild—reported to produce bioactive phytochemicals that have antioxidant, anti-inflammatory, and antiatherosclerotic effects (Li *et al.*, 2016; Wu *et al.*, 2018; Yuan & Zhao, 2017; Zhu *et al.*, 2018).

Calypso bulbosa (cypripedium)—reported to have numerous medicinal properties, including neuroprotective properties (Singh *et al.*, 2012). It has been used in tribal medicine to treat a wide range of symptoms, including nervous system symptoms such as tremors, convulsion, headache, and nerve pain (Wilson, 2007).

Carrot—a significant source of vitamin A (Olalude *et al.*, 2015).

Clover—reported to have bioactive chemicals (flavonoids, polyphenols, and vitamins) that provide antioxidant and antimicrobial effects (Kolodziejczyk-Czepas, 2016). [Note: Red clover is known for its estrogenic effects.]

Grains (e.g., buckwheat)—contain a flavonoid, rutin, also found in many fruits (e.g., apricots, blueberries, oranges, grapes, etc.) purported to have anti-inflammatory, antioxidant, and neuroprotective effects (Enogieru *et al.*, 2018; Ganeshpurkar & Saluja, 2017; Ghorbani, 2017; Kreft, 2016).

Hawthorn—reported to relieve symptoms of heart failure, angina, high blood pressure, and cardiac arrhythmias (Edwards *et al.*, 2012; Holubarsch *et al.*, 2018), possibly due to the presence of flavonoids (Dahmer & Scott, 2010).

Honey—reported to be active against bacterial, viral, and fungal infections and possess anti-inflammatory and antioxidant properties (Ahmed *et al.*, 2018; Cianciosi *et al.*, 2018). These effects are associated with the flavonoids and phenolic acids it contains (Cianciosi *et al.*, 2018). It may be effective as a temporary treatment for wounds (Bitter & Erickson, 2016).

Legumes—have phytochemicals (e.g., flavonoids) that provide an anti-inflammatory effect (Swiatecka *et al.,* 2011; Zhu *et al.*, 2018). They are also a significant source of protein and B vitamins (Wallace *et al.*, 2016). When combined with grains, the two food groups supply almost all essential amino acids.

Menthol—a topical alcohol derived from the peppermint plant. Cools the skin and decreases pain (Pergolizzi *et al.*, 2018).

Mushrooms, edible—possess constituents that may promote the growth of beneficial (i.e., symbiotic) microorganisms in the gastrointestinal tract (Jayachandran *et al.*, 2017).

Oregano, essential oil—found to have antiviral, antibacterial, antifungal, antiparasitic, and antioxidative effects in laboratory tests (Lee *et al.*, 2017; Leyva-López *et al.*, 2017; Liu *et al.*, 2017; Negut *et al.*, 2018; Sakkas & Papadopoulou, 2017; Sharifi-Rad, 2017); however, its mechanism of action is unknown. Carvacrol and thymol are major phytochemicals associated with some of these effects. [See also Thyme.]

Peanuts—provide high-grade vegetable protein, unsaturated fat; fiber; vitamins; minerals including iron; and flavonoids (Arya et al., 2016).

Pecans—a diet rich in pecans is associated with improvements in indicators of cardiovascular risk, including some factors affecting diabetes risk (McKay *et al.*, 2018). (See also Walnuts.)

Pectin—sources include pears, apples, apricots, plums, citrus fruits, green bananas. Pectin is a form of soluble fiber purported to help retain fluid in the bowel and decrease the degree of diarrhea. Some types of pectin may aide in lowering cholesterol (Brouns *et al.*, 2012).

Peppermint oil—reported to ease abdominal pain and other symptoms associated noninfectious gastrointestinal symptoms (Alammar *et al.*, 2019; Anheyer *et al.*, 2017).

Potato peel—potato skin contains bioactive (phenolic) compounds purported to have antioxidant and antimicrobial effects (Akyol *et al.*, 2016; Silva-Beltran *et al.*, 2017). The plant produces these substances to protect its tuber from bacteria, fungi, viruses, and insects. It may be effective as a temporary dressing for wounds (Bitter & Erickson, 2016).

Rose, essential oil—petals provide the majority of fragrance in roses and other flowers (Guterman *et al.*, 2002). Inhalation and application to the skin are reported to have analgesic and antidepressant effects (Mohebitabar *et al.*, 2017).

Saint John's Wort— there is some evidence of its effectiveness in treating mild to moderate depression; however, evidence is limited due to the short duration of trials (one to three months) (Ng *et al.*, 2017). It has significant drug interactions and can alter the effects of several other drugs, including selected anticancer drugs, warfarin, oral contraceptives, and others (Chrubasik-Hausmann *et al.*, 2019; Soleymani *et al.*, 2017).

Sweet potato—a significant source of vitamin A (Low *et al.*, 2017).

Thyme, essential oil—the phytochemical thymol has been found to have antibacterial and antifungal activity in laboratory tests (Lee *et al.*,

2017; Liu *et al.*, 2017; Sakkas & Papadopoulou, 2017; Sharifi-Rad *et al.*, 2017). [See also Oregano.]

Tomato—rich source of flavonoids, carotenoids (vitamin A), vitamin C, and lycopene (an antioxidant) (Chaudhary et al., 2018).

Valeria roots—inconsistent evidence of effectiveness in inducing sleep, with no single active compound identified to induce sleep; however, several of the plant's chemical constituents combined may have a sedative effect (https://ods.od.nih.gov/factsheets/Valerian-HealthProfessional/#en20).

Walnuts—a diet rich in walnuts was associated with improvements in lipid levels (i.e., cholesterol), may have a beneficial effect on reducing the risk of developing cardiovascular disease (Bamberger *et al.*, 2017; Bamberger *et al.*, 2018; deSouza *et al.*, 2017; Ros, 2010), and have a beneficial influence on microorganisms in the gastrointestinal tract (Bamberger *et al.*, 2018).

Yarrow—fresh, moist leaves may decrease nosebleeds and heal superficial injuries to the skin (Akram, 2013; Lakshmi *et al.*, 2011).

GLOSSARY

Amino acid—an organic compound that, when combined with other amino acids, forms a protein.

Amniotes—species whose embryos are enclosed by an amniotic sac (mammals, birds, and reptiles).

Analogous—having similar structure and function via a different evolutionary ancestor (e.g., mammalian hair follicles are analogous to avian feather follicles).

Chimera—a blend of two or more animals from different species into a single animal.

Chromatid—one of two identical (or nearly identical) strands of DNA, which together comprise a chromosome.

Chromosome—two strands of DNA (a large group of genes clustered together in a predetermined sequence) twisted around each other and bundled together.

Chrysalis—a protective covering within which a juvenile form of an animal, usually an insect (e.g., a caterpillar), has entered the pupa stage and is undergoing metamorphosis into its adult form.

Clade—a group of organisms that include all descendants with a common ancestor. Birds, dinosaurs, and crocodiles all have a common egg-laying ancestor.

Cladogram—schematic demonstrating the evolutionary lineage of a species.

Class (taxonomy)—a group of organisms that have a common genetic background yet are genetically distinct from each other. Bacteria, reptiles, fish, dinosaurs, insects, mammals, birds, etc., all represent different classes within the animal kingdom.

Cloning—production of an identical copy of DNA either by natural (e.g., cellular mitosis) or artificial (e.g., genetic engineering) means.

302

Complementary strands—two strands of DNA paired up so that the nucleotides on each strand are matched up in a conventional manner: adenine with thymine (A-T) and cytosine with guanine (C-G).

Corm—a round underground bulb that stores nutrients for a plant (e.g., an onion). The visible stalk of the plant extends above ground from the top of the bulb, while the plant's roots extend downward from the bottom of the bulb.

Crown group—comprised of all species that share a common ancestor.

Deletion (of a chromosome)—loss of a portion of a chromosome and the genes present in it.

Desiccation—the removal of all water from something that normally has water (e.g., plants, animals).

Deoxyribonucleic acid (DNA)—genetic material comprising gene sequences (nucleotides) supported by a sugar and phosphate backbone.

DNA double helix—two complementary strands of DNA are loosely bound to each other (for ease of separation), twisted around each other along their length.

DNA polymerase—a group of enzymes that can replicate an exact copy of a DNA strand, then proofread and edit it for errors, making corrections along the way.

DNA ligase—an enzyme that (re)attaches DNA gene segments together, including broken edges.

Ecdysis—the process whereby old skin is shed (e.g., in snakes) or the outer casing is cast off (e.g., in insects).

Electroreceptivity—the ability to sense electrical impulses generated by muscle movement.

Endonuclease—an enzyme that can cut into a DNA strand and separate a damaged DNA segment (e.g., a nucleotide) to allow editing or excision of the affected segment.

Epigenetic—an external or internal influence that, when attached to a gene, affects the function of the gene without altering its structure.

Epigenetic factors—nongenetic agents, typically biochemical substances (e.g., vitamins, toxins), that influence gene functions (e.g., altering the expression of a gene) without altering the gene itself.

Eukaryote—a cell that contains specialized organelles not found in more primitive organisms (prokaryotes), including a nucleus in which DNA is organized as chromosomes.

Eutriconodont — an order of early mammals that continued to evolve into modern orders of mammals (e.g., primates).

Extremophiles—organisms capable of surviving in environments once considered incompatible with life (i.e., extremes of temperature, ionizing radiation, desiccation, etc.).

Gene—the basic building block of genetic matter. Coding genes determine the physical composition of a component used in building a biologic structure (e.g., an amino acid). Noncoding genes influence the function of other genes.

Gene, Dominant—the member of a gene pair that is active (expressed) in the phenotype.

Gene, Essential—a gene that is necessary for an organism to develop, function, and survive.

Gene, Imprinted—the member of a gene pair that carries a "stamp" or a "tag" that effectively turns off that gene.

Gene, Recessive—the member of a gene pair that is not active in the presence of a dominant gene.

Gene expression—the physical reflection in both structure and function of an organism's genetic code (genotype).

Genetic engineering—the artificial manipulation of genes to achieve a goal.

Genetic homology—gene sequences with a shared ancestry that are conserved and reused among multiple classes within the animal kingdom and a few even shared across kingdoms (e.g., animals and plants).

Genetic polymorphism—naturally occurring variations in the structure of a gene. Two different versions of the same gene may be paired together. These differences may or may not be expressed.

Genotype—an individual's overall genetic composition, whether or not it is expressed as an observable characteristic.

Genus (plural **genera**)—groups of species whose genomes are very similar yet remain distinct: e.g., the genus Homo includes the species *H. habilis, H. erectus, H. neanderthalensis,* and *H. sapiens.*

Hominid—any member of the primate family *Hominidae,* including humans and apes.

Homologous—having the same or similar structure and function derived from a common ancestor (e.g., genetic homology).

Homologous recombination—damaged or missing parts of DNA (e.g., nucleotides) are restored by copying and inserting similar or identical parts to repair double-stranded DNA.

Humanoid—a being with the appearance or character of a human.

Hybrid—a plant or animal comprising two or more different varieties; the result of crossbreeding between two different species of plant or animal.

Inversion (of a chromosome)—two breaks on the same chromosome leads to reversal of the gene order (e.g., AB*CDE*FG may become AB*EDC*FG).

Invertebrates—animals without a bony skeleton—specifically, lacking a backbone.

Karyotype—the number and appearance of chromosomes as seen under a microscope.

Maleficence—deliberate acts of harm or evil.

Malfeasance—deliberate acts or behaviors that violate accepted standards of conduct.

Messenger ribonucleic acid (mRNA)—a single strand of genetic material that is a complementary form of DNA used to transport the instructions contained within a DNA sequence.

Metamorphosis—the radical change of an organism into an altogether different shape, form, and function (e.g., from a caterpillar into a butterfly).

Monotreme (prototheria)—oldest mammals that lay eggs to produce their young (e.g., duck-billed platypus, spiny anteater).

Morphogenesis—gradual changes in structure, form, and function as an organism grows and develops into its final adult form.

Multifactorial—genes can be affected by multiple external factors (e.g., environmental), including those that can cause mutations (e.g., radiation, chemotherapy, etc.).

Nuclease—an enzyme that can isolate and cut double-stranded DNA at specified locations within the genome.

Neurotransmitter—a biochemical substance released by nerves to induce a specific response (e.g., act as a stimulant or a suppressor).

Nucleotide—a building block of DNA that consists of *one* of following four molecules—cytosine, adenine, guanine, or thymine—bound to a sugar molecule (deoxyribose) and a phosphate molecule. DNA consists of long strands of nucleotides.

Oocyte—an immature egg (ovum)

Ovum—an egg (plural: ova).

Penetrance—the extent to which a specific genotype is displayed in an individual's phenotype.

Phenotype—an individual's observable manifestations (physical characteristics) of genetic composition.

Physiognomy—physical features that suggest an origin or the character of an individual, including genetic, ethnic, and familial origins.

Phylogenetics—the study of the development of animals according to their evolutionary ancestry from a common ancestor to all its descendants.

Polymerase Chain Reaction (PCR)—procedure that can identify genes and where they are located and can be used to make copies of a specific DNA sequence.

Radioresistance—organisms that are able to withstand the effects of ionizing radiation.

Single Nucleotide Polymorphism (SNP)—the most common type of genetic variation, it represents a difference in a single nucleotide (e.g., swapping a C for T).

SNPs provide the basis of genetic diversity both within groups and across populations.

Somatic cell nuclear transfer (SCNT)—the process used to clone an identical offspring by inserting the animal's own DNA into one of its own fertilized ova and implanting the ova. (See also cloning.)

Stem ancestor—ancestor at the base of a branch.

Taxonomy—in biology, a hierarchical organization wherein plants, animals and other forms of life are grouped according to their physical characteristics and, more recently, on genetic analysis. The farther down the hierarchy an organisms falls, the more closely related it is to other similar life forms.

Tetrapod—in biology, an animal with the equivalent of four extremities (four-footed) or two pairs of limbs, including wings.

Transcription factor—an agent that directs whether or not a copy of a specific sequence of genetic code (DNA) will be made for subsequent use in building a structure (e.g., a protein).

Transformation—a radical change in structure, form, and function. When applied to living organisms, it is also known as metamorphosis.

Transgenic—an organism that has had genes from another species integrated into its genome.

Translocation (of genetic material)—the movement of a section of genetic material (or part of a chromosome) within a chromosome or across nonhomologous chromosomes, usually due to chromosome breaks.

Transposon (Transposable Element)—a small DNA sequence that can insert itself into other places in the genome in a cut and paste fashion thereby altering the function of the DNA at the new location.

Troglobites—animals that live only in caves and caverns where there is no light (versus those who shelter or nest in caves): e.g., cave crickets, cave fish, etc.

Vector—in physics, the characteristic of having direction and magnitude, which aids in locating a point in space relative to another point in space. In biology, an organism that carries and can transmit other organisms (e.g., bacteria, viruses, parasites).

Vertebrates—animals with a bony skeleton—specifically, a having backbone (vertebral column).

Viral vector—in genetic engineering, the use of a virus to transport genetic material (e.g., DNA) into a living organism.

REFERENCES
GENERAL REFERENCES FOR GENETICS

Brooker, R. J. (2009a). Biotechnology (Chapter 19). *Genetics: Analysis and Principles*, 3rd edition. McGraw-Hill (Higher Education).

Brooker, R. J. (2009b). Developmental Genetics (Chapter 23). *Genetics: Analysis and Principles*, 3rd edition. McGraw-Hill (Higher Education).

Brooker, R. J. (2009c). Overview of Genetics (Chapter 1). *Genetics: Analysis and Principles*, 3rd edition. McGraw-Hill (Higher Education).

Brooker, R. J. (2009d). Recombinant DNA Technology (Chapter 18). *Genetics: Analysis and Principles*, 3rd edition. McGraw-Hill (Higher Education).

Brooker, R. J. (2009e). Recombination and Transposition at the Molecular Level (Chapter 17). *Genetics: Analysis and Principles*, 3rd edition. McGraw-Hill (Higher Education).

Preface *(Wolf-Rayet stars)*
Crowther, P. A. (2008). Properties of Wolf-Rayet Stars. In: F. Bresolin, P.A. Crowther, J. Puls, (eds). Massive stars as cosmic engines. *Proceedings IAU Symposium*, No. 250, International Astronomical Union. doi: 00.0000/X000000000000000X.

Hambaryan, V. V., and Neuhäuser, V. V. R. (2013). Galactic short gamma-ray burst as cause for the ^{14}C peak in AD774/56. *Monthly Notices of the Royal Astronomical Society*, 430(1) 32–36.

Hashimoto, T., and Kunieda, T. (2017). DNA protection protein, a novel mechanism of radiation tolerance: Lessons from tardigrades. *Life*, 7(26). doi: 10.3390/life7020026.

Melott, A. L., Lieberman, B. S., Laird, C. M. *et al.* (2004). Did a gamma-ray burst initiate the late Ordovician mass extinction? *Int. J. Astrobiol,* 3(1), 55–65. doi.org/10.1017/S1473550404001910.

Melott, A. L., and Thomas, B. C. (2011). Astrophysical ionizing radiation and Earth: a brief review and census of intermittent intense sources. *Astrobiology,* 11(4), 343–361. doi: 10.1089/ast.2010.0603.

Thomas, B. C., and Goracke, B. D. (2016). Ground-level ozone following astrophysical ionizing radiation events: an additional biological hazard? *Astrobiology,* 16(1), 1–6. doi: 10.1089/ast.2015.1311.

Tuthill, P.G., Monnier, J. D., Gayley, J. D. (2008). The prototype colliding-wind pinwheel WR 104. *The Astrophysical Journal,* 675(1), 698. doi: 10.1086/527286.

Chapter 1. A Pleasant Outing (Genes, Body size).

Alina, D., Muste, A., Beteg, F., Briciu, R. (2008). Morphological aspect of tapetum lucidum at some domestic animals. Bulletin UASVM, *Veterinary Medicine,* 65(2).

Andrade, A. C., Jee, Y. H., Nilsson, O. (2017). New genetic diagnoses of short stature provide insights into local regulation of childhood growth. *Horm Res Paediatr,* 88(1), 22–37. doi: 10.1159/000455850.

Gokhale, R. H., Shingleton, A. W. (2015). Size control: the developmental physiology of body and organ size regulation. *Wiley Interdiscip Rev Dev Biol,* 4(4), 335–56. doi: 10.1002/wdev.181.

Kemper, K. E., Visscher, P. M., Goddard, M. E. (2012). Genetic architecture of body size in mammals. *Genome Biol,* 201213, 244. doi: 10.1186/gb4016.

Ollivier, F. J., Samuelson, D. A., Brooks, D. E. *et al.* (2004). Comparative morphology of the tapetum lucidum (among selected species). *Veterinary Ophthalmology,* 7(1) 11–22.

Schwab, I. R., Yuen, C. K., Buyukmihci, N. C. *et al.* (2002). Evolution of the tapetum. *Trans Am Ophthalmol Soc*, 100, 187–200.

Singh, R. K., Kumar, P., Mahalingam, K. (2017). Molecular genetics of human obesity: A comprehensive review. *C R Biol*, 340(2), 87–108. doi: 10.1016/j.crvi.2016.11.007.

Chapter 2. H'Ilgraith (Genotype, Phenotype, Genetic homology, Conservation of genes).

Brooker, R. J. (2009c). Evolutionary Genetics (Chapter 26). *Genetics: Analysis and Principles*, 3rd edition. McGraw-Hill (Higher Education).

Gardner, P. P., Fasold, M., Burge, S. W. *et al.* (2015). Conservation and losses of non-coding RNAs in avian genomes. *PLoS One*, 10(3), e0121797. doi: 10.1371/journal.pone.0121797.

Jorde, L. B. (2010). Genes and Genetic Diseases. In: K. L. McCance, S. E. Huether, V. L. Brashers, V.L., and N. S. Rote, *Pathophysiology: The Biologic Basis for Disease in Adults and Children* (7th edition)., Chapter 4. St. Louis: Mosby/Elsevier.

Kanherkar, R. R., Bhatia-Dey, N., Csoka, A. B. (2014). Epigenetics across the human lifespan. *Front Cell Dev Biol*, 2, 49. doi: 10.3389/fcell.2014.00049.

Lappin, T. R. J., Grier, D. G., Thompson, A. *et al.* (2006). Hox genes: seductive Science, mysterious mechanisms. *Ulster Med J*, 75(1), 23–31.

Lescat, L., Herpin, A., Mourot, B. *et al.* (2018). CMA restricted to mammals and birds: myth or reality? *Autophagy*, 14(7), 1267–1270. doi: 10.1080/15548627.2018.1460021.

Van de Pol, I., Flik, G., Gorissen, M. (2017). Comparative physiology of energy metabolism: fishing for endocrine signals in the early vertebrate pool. *Front Endocrinol (Lausanne)*, 8, 36. doi: 10.3389/feno.2017.00036.

Chapter 3. Far Afield
(Gene Expression, Conservation of Genes)

Elbarbary, R. A., Lucas, B. A., Maquat, L. E. (2016). Retrotransposons as regulators of gene expression. *Science*, 351(6274), aac7247. doi: 10.1126/science.aac7247.

Erwin, D. H. (1993). The origin of metazoan development: a palaeobiological perspective. *Biol J Linnean Soc*, 50(4), 255–274. doi: org/10.1111/j.1095-8312.1993.tb00931.x.

Goffinet, A. M. (2017). The evolution of cortical development: the synapsid-diapsid divergence. *Development*, 144(22), 4061–4077. doi: 10.1242/dev.153908.

Hueber, S. D., and Lohmann, I. (2008). Shaping segments: Hox gene function in the genomic age. *Bioessays*, 10, 965–979. doi: 10.1002/bis.20823.

Medstrand, P., van de Lagemaat, L. N., Dunn, C. A. *et al.* (2005). Impact of transposable elements on the evolution of mammalian gene regulation. *Cytogenet Genome Res*, 110(1–4), 342–352.

Nakayashiki, H. (2011). The trickster in the genome: contribution and control of transposable elements. *Genes Cells*, 16(8), 827–841. doi: 10.1111/j.1365-2443.2011.01533.x.

Pérez-Pérez, M. E., Couso, I., Crespo, J. L. (2017). The TOR signaling network in the model unicellular green alga Chlamydomonas reinhardtii. *Biomolecules*, 7(3). pii: E54. doi: 10.3390/biom7030054.

Suh, A., Churakov, G., Ramakodi, M. P. *et al.* (2014). Multiple lineages of ancient CR1 retroposons shaped the early genome evolution of amniotes. *Genome Biol Evol*, 7(1):205–217. doi: 10.1093/gbe/evu256.

Tatebe, H., Shiozaki, K. (2017). Evolutionary conservation of the components in the TOR signaling pathways. *Biomolecules*, 7(4). pii: E77. doi: 10.3390/biom7040077.

Chapter 4. Into the Fray (Metamorphosis, Morphogenesis).
Bayer, C., Zhou, X., Zhou, B. *et al.* (2003). Evolution of the Drosophila broad locus: the Manduca sexta broad Z4 isoform has biological activity in Drosophila. *Dev Genes Evol*, 213(10), 471–476.

Belles, X., and Sanos, C. G. (2014). The MEKRE93 (Methoprene tolerant-Krüppel homolog 1-E(#) pathway in the regulation of insect metamorphosis, and the homology of the pupal stage. *Insect Biochem Mol Biol*, 52, 60–68. doi: 10.1016/j.ibmb.2014.06.009.

Casaca, A., Santos, A. C., Mallo, M. (2014). Controlling Hox gene expression and activity to build the vertebrate axial skeleton. *Dev Dyn*, 243(1), 24–36.

Hiruma, K., and Kaneko, Y. (2013). Hormonal regulation of insect metamorphosis with special reference to juvenile hormone biosynthesis. *Curr Top Dev Biol.* 2013; 103:73–100.

Hueber, S. D., and Lohmann, I. (2008). Shaping segments: Hox gene function in the genomic age. *Bioessays*, 10, 965–979. doi: 10.1002/bis.20823.

Huether, S. E. (2010). Pain, Temperature Regulation, Sleep, and Sensory Function. In: K. L. McCance, S. E. Huether, V. L. Brashers, V.L., and N. S. Rote, *Pathophysiology: The Biologic Basis for Disease in Adults and Children* (7th edition)., Chapter 15. St. Louis: Mosby/Elsevier.

Mallo, M., Wellik, D.M., Deschamps, J. (2010). Hox genes and regional patterning of the vertebrate body plan. *Dev Biol*, 344(1), 7–15. doi: 10.1016/j.ydbio.2010.04.024.

Matfin, G. Disorders of Endocrine Control of Growth and Metabolism. In: Porth, C. M., and Matfin (eds)., *Pathophysiology: Concepts of Altered Health States* (8th edition)., Chapter 41. Lippincott Williams and Wilkins.

McCance, K. L. (2010). In: K. L. McCance, S. E. Huether, V. L. Brashers, V.L., and N. S. Rote, *Pathophysiology: The Biologic Basis for Disease in Adults and Children* (7th edition)., Chapter 1. St. Louis: Mosby/ Elsevier.

Minakuchi, C., Namiki, T., Shinoda, T. (2009). Krüppel homolog 1, an early juvenile hormone-response gene downstream of Methoprene-tolerant, mediates its anti-metamorphic action in the red flour beetle Tribolium castaneum. *Dev Biol*, 325(2), 341–350.

Mukherjee, A. Alzhanov, D., Rotwein, P. (2016). Defining human insulin-like growth factor I gene regulation. *Am J Physiol Endocr Metab*, 311(2):E519–E529. doi.org/10.1152/ajpendo.00212.2016.

Nicol, N. H., and Huether, S. E. (2010). Structure, Function, and Disorders of the Integument. In: K. L. McCance, S. E. Huether, V. L. Brashers, V.L., and N. S. Rote, *Pathophysiology: The Biologic Basis for Disease in Adults and Children* (7th edition)., Chapter 44. St. Louis: Mosby/Elsevier.

Nutt, D. (2006). $GABA_A$ Receptor: Subtypes, regional distribution, and function. *J Clin Sleep Med*, 2(2), S7-S11.

Oh, J. W., Lin, S-J., Plikus. M.V. (2015). Regenerative metamorphosis in hairs and feathers: follicle as a programmable biological printer. *Exp Dermatol*, 24(4), 262–264. doi: 10.1111/exd.12627.

Pineault, K. M., Wellik, D. M. (2014). Hox genes and limb musculoskeletal development. *Curr Osteoporos Rep*, 12(4), 420–427. doi: 10.1007/s11914-014-0241-0.

Rotwein, P. (2017a). Diversification of the insulin-like growth factor 1 gene in mammals. *PLoS ONE*, 12(12), e0189642. doi.org/10.1371/journal.pone.0189642.

Rotwein, P. (2017b). Large-scale analysis of variation in the insulin-like growth factor family in humans reveals rare disease links and common polymorphisms. *J Biological Chem*, 292, 9252–9261.

Rux, D. R., Wellik, D. M. (2017). Hox genes in the adult skeleton: novel functions beyond embryonic development. *Dev Dyn*, 246(4), 310–331.

Sigel, E., and Steinmann, M. E. (2012). Structure, function, and modulation of $GABA_A$ receptors. *J Biol Chem*, 287(48), 40224–40231. doi: 10.1074/jbc.R112.386664.

Simandle, G. (2009). Structure and Function of Skin. In: Porth, C. M., and Matfin (eds)., *Pathophysiology: Concepts of Altered Health States* (8th edition)., Chapter 60. Lippincott Williams and Wilkins.

Shimomura. Y., and Christiano, A. M. (2010). Biology and genetics of hair. *Annu Rev Genomics Hum Gene*, 11, 109–132. doi: 10.1146/annurev-genom-021610-131501.

Soshnikova, N. (2014). Hox genes regulation in vertebrates. *Dev Dyn*, 243(1), 49–58.

Ureña, E., Manjón, C., Franch-Marro, X., Martín, D. (2014). Transcription factor E93 specifies adult metamorphosis in hemimetabolous and holometabolous insects. *Proc Natl Acad Sci USA*, 13; 111(19):7024–7029.

Chapter 5. In the Realm of the Red Dragon (Language, Foxp2 gene).

Fisher, S. E. (2017). Evolution of language: lessons from the genome. *Psychon Bull Rev*, 24(1), 34–40. doi: 10.3758/s13423-016-1112-8.

Graham, S. A., and Fisher, S. E. (2015). Understanding language from a genomic perspective. *Annu Rev Genet*, 49, 131–160. doi: 10.1146/annurev-genet-120213-092236.

Mozzi, A., Forni, D., Clerici, M. *et al.* (2016). The evolutionary history of genes involved in spoken and written language: beyond *FOXP2*. *Sci Rep*, 6: 22157. doi: 10.1038/srep22157.

Staes, N., Sherwood, C. C., Wright, K. *et al.* (2017). *FOXP2* variation in great ape populations offers insight into the evolution of communication skills. *Scientific Reports*, 7(16866). doi: 10.1038/ s41598-017-16844-x.

Webb, D. M., and Zhang, J. (2004). FoxP2 in song-learning birds and vocal-learning mammals. *Journal of Heredity*, 96(3), 212–216. doi. org/10.1093/jhered/esi02.5.

Chapter 6. On Dangerous Ground
(Genetic engineering, Gene therapy).

Haas, S. A., Dettmer, V., Cathomen, T. (2017). Therapeutic genome editing with engineered nucleases. *Hamostaseologie*, 37(1):45–52. doi: 10.5482/HAMO-16-09-0035.

Kim, J. S. (2016). Genome editing comes of age. *Nat Protoc*, 11(9), 1573–1578. doi: 10/1038/nprot.2016.104.

Prakash, V., Moore, M., Yáñez-Muñoz, R. J. (2016). Current progress in therapeutic gene editing for monogenic diseases. *Mol Ther*, 24(3), 465–474.

Wang, D., and Gao, G. (2014). State-of-the-art human gene therapy: part II. Gene therapy strategies and clinical applications. *Discov Med*, 18(98), 151–161.

Wood, M., Yin, H., McClorey, G. (2007). Modulating the expression of disease genes with RNA-based therapy. *PLoS Genet*, 3(6), e109.

Chapter 7. A Narrow Escape.
No references.
Chapter 8. Calypso (Seizures, Genetic epilepsy).

Boss, B. J. (2010). Alterations in Cognitive Systems, Cerebral Hemodynamics, and Motor Function. In: K. L. McCance, S. E. Huether, V. L. Brashers, V.L., and N. S. Rote, *Pathophysiology: The Biologic Basis for Disease in Adults and Children* (7th edition)., Chapter 15. St. Louis: Mosby/Elsevier.

Brunklaus, A., Zuberi, S. M. Epilepsia. (2014) Dravet syndrome--from epileptic encephalopathy to channelopathy. *Epilepsia*, 55(7), 979–984. doi: 10.1111/epi.12652.

Helbig, I., Heinzen, E. L., Mefford, H. C. *et al.* (2016). Primer Part 1-The building blocks of epilepsy genetics. *Epilepsia*, 57(6), 861–868. doi: 10.1111/epi.13381.

Helbig, I., and Lowenstein, D. H. (2013). Genetics of the epilepsies: where are we and where are we going? *Curr Opin Neurol*, 26(2), 179–185. doi: 10.1097/WCO.0b013e32835ee6ff.

Hirose, S., Scheffer, I. E., Marini, C. *et al.* (2013). SCN1A testing for epilepsy: application in clinical practice. *Epilepsia*, 54(5), 946–952.

Jiang, T., Shen, Y., Chen, H. *et al.* (2018). Clinical and molecular analysis of epilepsy-related genes in patients with Dravet syndrome. *Medicine (Baltimore)*, 97(50), e13565. doi: 10.1097/MD.0000000000013565.

Lopez-Santiago, L., and Issom, L. L. (2019). Dravet Syndrome: a developmental and epileptic encephalopathy. *Epilepsy Curr*, 19(1), 51–53. doi: 10.1177/1535759718822038.

Medical Letter. (2018). Cannabidiol (Epidiolex) for epilepsy. *The Medical Letter on Drugs and Therapeutics*, 60(1559), 182–184.

Myers, C. T., and Mefford, H. C. (2015). Advancing epilepsy genetics in the genomic era. *Genome Med*, 7, 91. doi: 10.1186/s13073-015-0214-7.

Nissenkorn A., Levy-Drummer R. S., Bondi O. *et al.* (2015). Epilepsy in Rett syndrome--lessons from the Rett networked database. *Epilepsia*, 56(4), 569–576. doi: 10.1111/epi.12941.

Poduri, A. (2017). When should genetic testing be performed in epilepsy patients? *Epilepsy Curr*, 17(1), 6–22. doi: 10.5698/1535-7511-17.1.16.

Schutte, S. S., Schutte, R. J., Barragan, E. V., O'Dowd, D. K. (2016). Model systems for studying cellular mechanisms of SCN1A-related epilepsy. *J Neurophysiol*, 115(4). 1755–1766. doi: 10.1152/jn.00824.2015.

Steinlein, O. K. (2008). Genetics and epilepsy. *Dialogues Clin Neurosci*, 10(1), 29–38.

Symonds, J. D., Zuberi, S. M., Johnson, M. R. (2017). Advances in epilepsy gene discovery and implications for epilepsy diagnosis and treatment. *Current Opinion in Neurology*, 30(2), 193–199. doi: 10.1097/WCO.0000000000000433.

Tarquinio, D. C., Hou, W., Berg, A. (2017). Longitudinal course of epilepsy in Rett syndrome and related disorders. *Brain*, 140(2), 306–318. doi: 10.1093/brain/aww302.

Zerem, A., Haginoya, K., Lev, D. (2016). The molecular and phenotypic spectrum of IQSEC2-related epilepsy. *Epilepsia*, 57(11), 1858–1869. doi: 10.1111/epi.13560.

Zhou, R., Jiang, G., Tian, X., Wang, X. (2018). Progress in the molecular mechanisms of genetic epilepsies using patient-induced pluripotent stem cells. *Epilepsia Open*, 3(3):331–339.

Chapter 9. Unexpected Encounters.
No references.

Chapter 10. Truce.
No references.
Chapter 11. Immanis.
No references.
Chapter 12. Fellow Travelers (Extremophiles, Radiation, Repair mechanisms).

Beltrán-Pardo, E., Jönsson, K. I., Harms-Ringdahl, M. *et al.* (2015). Tolerance to gamma radiation in the tardigrade *Hypsibius dujardini* from embryo to adult correlate inversely with cellular proliferation. *PloS One*, 10(1). doi: 10.1371/journal.pone.0133658.

Brooker, R. J. (2009d). Gene Mutation and DNA Repair (Chapter 16). *Genetics: Analysis and Principles*, 3rd edition. McGraw-Hill (Higher Education).

Ceccaldi, R., Rondinelli, B., D'Andrea, A.D. (2016). Repair pathway choices and consequences at the double-strand break. *Trends Cell Biol*, 26(1), 52–64. doi: 10.1016/j.tcb.2015.07. 009.

Coker, J. A. (2016). Extremophiles and biotechnology: current uses and prospects. F1000Research, 5, F1000 Faculty Rev-396. doi: 10.12688/f1000research.7432.1.

Desouky, O., Ding, N., Zhou, G. (2015). Targeted and non-targeted effects of ionizing radiation. *J Rad Res Applied Sci*, 8, 247–254. doi. org/10.1016/j.jrras.2015.03.033.

Hashimoto, T., and Kunieda, T. (2017). DNA protection protein, a novel mechanism of radiation tolerance: Lessons from Tardigrades. *Life*, 7(26). doi: 10.3390/life7020026.

Jasin, M., and Rothstein, R. (2013). Repair of strand breaks by homologous recombination. *Cold Spring Harb Perspec Biol*, 5, a012740.

Jung, K. W., Lim, S., Bahn, Y. S. (2017). Microbial radiation-resistance mechanisms. *J Microbiol*, 55(7), 499–507.

Kolinjivadi, A. M., Sannino, V., de Antoni, A. *et al.* (2017). Moonlighting at replication forks – a new life for homologous recombination proteins BRCA1, BRCA2 and RAD51. *FEBS Lett*, 591(8), 1083–1100. doi: 10.100/1873-3468.12556.

Machida, S., Takaku, M., Ikura, M. *et al.* (2014). Nap1 stimulates homologous recombination by RAD51 and RAD54 in higher-ordered chromatin containing histone H1. *Sci Rep*, 4, 4863. doi: 10.1038/srep04863.

Makarova, K. S., Aravind, L., Wolf, Y. I. *et al.* (2001). Genome of the extremely radiation-resistant bacterium *Deinococcus radiodurans* viewed from the perspective of comparative genomics. *Microbiol Mol Biol Rev*, 65(1), 44–79.

Moore, S., Stanley, F. K., Goodarzi, A. A. (2014). The repair of environmentally relevant DNA double strand breaks caused by high linear energy transfer irradiation – no simple task. *DNA Repair (Amst).*, 17, 64–73. doi: 10.1016/dnarep.2014.01.014.

Nelson, D. R. (2002). Current status of the *Tardigrada*: evolution and ecology. *Integrative and Comparative Biology*, 42 (3), 652–659. doi. org/10.1093/icb/42.3.652.

Omelchenko, M. V., Wolf, Y. I., Gaidamakova, E. K. *et al.* (2005). Comparative genomics of *Thermus thermophilus* and *Deinococcus radiodurans*: Divergent routes of adaptation to thermophily and radiation resistance. *BMC Evol Biol*, 5, 57.

Pavlopoulou, A., Savva, G. D., Louka, M. *et al.* (2016). Unraveling the mechanisms of extreme radioresistance in prokaryotes: Lessons from nature. *Mutat Res Rev Mutat Res*, 767, 92–107. doi: 10.1016/j. mrrev.2015.10.001.

Prakash, R., Zhang, Y., Feng, W., Jasin, M. (2015). Homologous recombination and human health: the roles of BRCA1, BRCA2, and associated proteins. *Cold Spring Harb Perspect Biol*, 7(4), a016600. doi: 10.1101/cshperspect.a016600.

Rampelotto, P. H. (2013). Extremophiles and extreme environments. *Life*, 3, 482–485. doi: 10.3390/life3030482.

Reisz, J. A., Bansal, N., Qian, J. *et al.* (2014). Effects of ionizing radiation on biological molecules – Mechanisms of damage and emerging methods of detection. *Antioxid and Redox Signal*, 21(2), 260–292. doi: 10.1089/ars.2013.5489.

Rendic, S., and Guengerich, F. P. (2012). Summary of information on the effect of ionizing and non-ionizing radiation on cytochrome P450 and other drug metabolizing enzymes and transporters. *Curr Drug Metab*, 13(6), 787–814.

Singh, H., Kim, H., Song, H. *et al.* (2013). A novel radiation-resistant strain of *Filobasidium* sp. Isolated from the West Sea of Korea. *J Microbiol Biotechnol*, 23(11), 1493–1499.

Sung, P., Krejei, L., von Komen, S., Sehorn, M. G. (2008). Rad51 recombinase and recombination mediators. *J Bio Chem*, 278(44), 42729–42732. doi: 10.1074/jbc.R300027200.

Tashiro, S., Walter, J., Shinohara,, A. *et al.* (2000). Rad51 Accumulation at sites of DNA damage and in postreplicative chromatin. *J Cell Biol*, 217(9). doi: 10.1083/jcb.150.2.283.

Vispe, S., Cazaux, C., Lesca, C., Defais, M. (1998). Overexpression of Rad51 protein stimulates homologous recombination and increases resistance of mammalian cells to ionizing radiation. *Nucleic Acids Res*, 26(12), 2859–2864.

Xue, L., Yu, D., Furusawa, Y. *et al.* (2009). Regulation of ATM in DNA double strand break repair account for the radiosenstivity in human cells exposd to high linear energy transfer ionizing radiation. *Mutat Res*, 670(1–2), 15–23. doi: 10.1016/j.mrfmmm.2009.06.016.

Chapter 13. Jak.

No references.

Chapter 14. I, Cassius (Chromosomes breaks, Essential genes, Pleiotropy, Transgenic species et al)..

Bartha, I., di Iulio, J., Venter, J. C., Telenti, A. (2018). Human gene essentiality. *Nat Rev Gene*, 19(1), 51–62. doi: 10.1038/nrg.2017.75.

Bourret, R., Martinez, E., Vialla, F. *et al.* (2016). Human-animal chimeras: ethical issues about farming chimeric animals bearing human organs. *Stem Cell Res Ther*, 7(1), 87. doi: 10.1186/s13287-016-0345-9.

Brooker, R. J. (2009a). Biotechnology (Chapter 19). *Genetics: Analysis and Principles*, 3rd edition. McGraw-Hill (Higher Education).

Clowes, C., Boylan, M. G., Ridge, L. A. *et al.* (2014). The functional diversity of essential genes required for mammalian cardiac development. *Genesis*, 52(8), 713–737. doi: 10.1002/dvg.22794.

De Los Angeles, A., Pho, N., Redmond, D. E. Jr. (2018). Generating human organs via interspecies chimera formation: advances and barriers. *Yale J Biol Med*, 91(3), 333–342.

Murray, J. D., Maga, E. A. (2016). Genetically engineered livestock for agriculture: a generation after the first transgenic animal research conference. *Transgenic Res*, 25(3), 321–327. doi: 10.1007/s11248-016-9927-7.

Niemann, H., Petersen, B. (2016). The production of multi-transgenic pigs: update and perspectives for xenotransplantation. *Transgenic* Res, 25(3), 361–374. doi: 10.1007/s11248-016-9934-8.

Petersen, B. (2017). Basics of genome editing technology and its application in livestock species. *Reprod Domest Anim*, 52(Suppl 3), 4–13. doi: 10.1111/rda.13012.

Rancati, G., Moffat, J., Typas, A., Pavelka, N. (2018). Emerging and evolving concepts in gene essentiality. *Nat Rev Genet*, 19(1):34–49. doi: 10.1038/nrg.2017.74.

Wu, J., and Izpisua Belmonte, J. C. (2016). Interspecies chimeric complementation for the generation of functional human tissues and organs in large animal hosts. *Transgenic Res*, 25(3), 375–384. doi: 10.1007/s11248-016-9930-z.

Chapter 15. A Lust for Power (Karyotype).

Shemilt, L., Verbanis, E., Schwenke, J. *et al.* (2015). Karyotyping human chromosomes by optical and X-ray ptychography methods. *Biophysical journal*, 108(3), 706–713. doi: 10.1016/j.bpj.2014.11.3456.

Veerabhadrappa, S. K., Chandrappa, P. R., Roodmal, S. Y. *et al.* (2016). Karyotyping: current perspectives in diagnosis of chromosomal disorders. *Sifa Med J*, 3:35–40. doi: 10.4103/2148-7731.182000.

Chapter 16. Resistance.
No references.
Chapter 17. Into the Earth (Vision, Hearing, Smell).

Angeli, S., Lin, X., Liu, S. Z. (2012). Genetics of hearing and deafness. *Anat Rec (Hoboken)*, 295(11), 1812–1829. doi: 10.1002/ar.22579.

Borges, R., Johnson, W. E., O'Brien, S. J. *et al.* (2018). Adaptive genomic evolution of opsins reveals that early mammals flourished in nocturnal environments. *BMC Genomics*, 19: 121. doi: 10.1186/s12864-017-4417-8.

Davidoff, C., Neitz, M., Neitz, J. (2016). Genetic testing as a new standard for clinical diagnosis of color vision deficiencies. *Transl Vis Sci Technol*, 5(5), 2.

DeMaria, S. and Ngai, J. (2010). The cell biology of smell. *The Journal of Cell Biology*, 191(3), 443–452. doi: 10.1083/jcb.201008163.

Emerling, C. A., Huynh, H. T., Minh A. *et al.* (2015). Spectral shifts of mammalian ultraviolet-sensitive pigments (short wavelength-sensitive opsin 1) are associated with eye length and photic niche evolution. *Proceedings of the Royal Society B*, 282 (1819). doi: 10.1098/rspb.2015.1817.

Gardner J. C., Michaelides, M., Hardcastle, A. J. (2016). Cone opsins, colour blindness and cone dystrophy: Genotype-phenotype correlations. *S Afr Med J*, 106(6 Suppl 1), S75–S78. doi: 10.7196/SAMJ.2016.v106i6.11001.Go to:

Heesy, C. P., and Hall, M. I. (2010). The nocturnal bottleneck and the evolution of mammalian vision. *Brain Behav Evol. 75(3):195–203.* doi: 10.1159/000314278.

Heffner, H. E., and Heffner, R. S. (2007). Hearing ranges of laboratory animals. *J Amer Ass Lab Animal Sci*, 46(1), 20–22.

Ignatieva, E. V., Levitsky, V. G., Yudin, N. S. *et al.* (2014). Genetic basis of olfactory cognition: extremely high level of DNA sequence polymorphism in promoter regions of the human olfactory receptor genes revealed using the 1000 Genomes Project dataset. *Front Psychol*, 5, 247. doi: 10.3389/fpsyg.2014.00247.

International SNP Map Working Group. (2001). A map of human genome sequence variation containing 1.42 million single nucleotide polymorphisms. *Nature, 409*, 928–933.

Jacobs, G. H. (2009). Evolution of colour vision in mammals. *Philos Trans R Soc Lond B Biol Sci*, 364(1531), 2957–2967. doi: 10.1098/rstb.2009.0039.

Keller, A., and Vosshall, L. B. (2008). Better smelling through genetics: mammalian odor perception. *Curr Opin Neurobiol*, 18(4), 364–369.

Keller, A., Zhuang, H., Chi, Q. *et al.* (2007). Genetic variation in a human odorant receptor alters odour perception. *Nature*, 449 (7161), 468–472.

Logan, D. W. (2014). Do you smell what I smell? Genetic variation in olfactory perception. *Biochem Soc Trans*, 42(4), 861–865. doi: 10.1042/BST20140052.

Michalakis, S., Schön, C., Becirovic, E., Biel, M. (2017). Gene therapy for achromatopsia. *J Gene Med*, 19(3). doi: 10.1002/jgm.2944.

Pace, B. S., Ofori-Acquah, S. F., Peterson, K. R. (2012). Sickle cell disease: genetics, cellular and molecular mechanisms, and therapies (editorial). *Anemia*, 2012, 143594. doi: doi.org.10.1155/2012/143594.

Patterson, E. J., Wilk, M., Langlo, C. S. *et al.* (2016). Cone photoreceptor structure in patients with X-Linked cone dysfunction and red-green color vision deficiency. *Invest Ophthalmol Vis Sci*, 57(8), 3853–3863. doi: 10.1167/iovs.16-19608.

Nuno, T. and Ferreira, S. (2016). Unravelling the olfactory sense: from the gene to odor perception. *Chemical Senses*, 41(2), 105–121. doi. org/10.1093/chemse/bjv075.

Terakita, A. (2005). The opsins. *Genome Biol*, 6(3), 213. doi: 10.1186/gb-2005-6-3-213.

Veilleux, C. C., and Kirk, E. C. (2014). Visual acuity in mammals: effects of eye size and ecology. *Brain Behav Evol*, 83, 43–53. doi: 10.1159/000357830.

Verbeurgt, C., Wilkin, F., Tarabichi, M. *et al.* (2014). Profiling of olfactory receptor gene expression in whole human olfactory mucosa. *PLoS One*, 9(5):e96333.

Zhang, X., and Firestein, S. (2007). Nose thyself: individuality in the human olfactory genome. *Genome Biol*, 8(11), 230.

Chapter 18. *The Break for Freedom.*
No references.
Chapter 19. *Quid Pro Quo (Targeted genome editing).*
Baliou, S., Adamaki, M., Kyriakopoulos, A.M. *et al.* (2018). CRISPR therapeutic tools for complex genetic disorders and cancer (Review). *Int J Oncol*, 53(2), 443–468. doi: 10.3892/ijo.2018.4434.

Batzir, N. A., Tovin, A., Hendel, A. (2017). Therapeutic genome editing and its potential enhancement through CRISPR guide RNA and Cas9 modifications. *Pediatr Endocrinol Rev*, 14(4):353–363. doi: 10.17458/per.vol14.2017.BTH.Therapeu.

Guha, T. K., and Edgell, D. R. (2017). Applications of alternative nucleases in the age of CRISPR/Cas9. *Int J Mol Sci*, 18(12). pii: E2565. doi: 10.3390/ijms18122565.

Lee, S. H., Kim, S., Hur, J. K. (2018). CRISPR and target-specific DNA endonucleases for efficient DNA knock-in in eukaryotic genomes. *Mol Cells*, 41(11), 943–952. doi: 10.14348/molcells.2018.0408.

Petersen B. (2017). Basics of genome editing technology and its application in livestock species. *Reprod Domest Anim*, 52, Suppl 3:4–13. doi: 10.1111/rda.13012.

Ryu, J., Prather, R. S., Lee, K. (2018). Use of gene-editing technology to introduce targeted modifications in pigs. *J Anim Sci Biotechnol*, 9:5. doi: 10.1186/s40104-017-0228-7.

Chapter 20. *Measures and Countermeasures.*
No references.
Chapter 21. *Warship.*
No references.Go to:
Chapter 22. *Kindred Spirits (Amydalin, Amatoxin).*
Diaz, J. H. (2018). Amatoxin-containing mushroom poisonings: species, toxidromes, treatments, and outcomes. *Wilderness Environ Med*, 29(1), 111–118. doi: 10.1016/j.wem.2017.10.002.

Jaswal, V., and Palanivelu, J. C. R. (2018). Effects of the gut microbiota on amygdalin and its use as an [alternative] anti-cancer therapy: substantial review on the key components involved in altering dose efficacy and toxicity. *R Biochem Biophys Rep*, 14, 125–132. doi: 10.1016/j.bbrep.2018.04.008.

Konstantatos, A., Shiv Kumar, M., Burrell, A., Smith, J. (2017). An unusual presentation of chronic cyanide toxicity from self-prescribed apricot kernel extract. *BMJ Case Rep*, 2017, pii: bcr-2017-220814. doi: 10.1136/bcr-2017-220814.

Li, Y., Mu, M., Yuan, L. *et al.* (2018). Challenges in the early diagnosis of patients with acute liver failure induced by amatoxin poisoning: Two case reports. *Medicine (Baltimore)*, 97(27), e11288. doi: 10.1097/MD.0000000000011288.

Sauer, H., Wollny, C., Oster, I. *et al.* (2015). Severe cyanide poisoning from an alternative medicine treatment with amygdalin and apricot kernels in a 4-year-old child. *Wien Med Wochenschr*, 165(9–10), 185–188. doi: 10.1007/s10354-014-0340-7.

Senica, M., Stampar, F., Veberic, R., Mikulic-Petkovsek, M. (2017). Fruit seeds of the *Rosaceae* family: a waste, new life, or a danger to human health? *J Agric Food Chem*, 65(48), 10621–10629. doi: 10.1021/acs.jafc.7b03408.

Wołoszyn, A., and Kotłowski, R. (2017). A universal method for the identification of genes encoding amatoxins and phallotoxins in poisonous mushrooms. *Rocz Panstw Zakl Hig*, 68(3), 247–251.

Chapter 23. Tempting Fate.
No references.
Chapter 24. A Change of Venue.
No references.
Chapter 25. A Road Less Traveled (Spacial mapping).

Carr, C. (2002). Sounds, signals and space maps. *Nature*, 415(6867), 29–31. doi: 10.1038/415029a.

Hazan, Y. Kra, Y., Yarin, I *et al.* (2015). Visual-auditory integration for visual search: a behavioral study in barn owls. *Front Integr Neurosci*, 9(11). doi: 10.3389/fnint.2015.00011.

Pena, J. L., and Gutfreund, Y. (2014, February). New perspectives on the owl's map of auditory space. *Curr Opin Neurobiol*, 0, 55–62. doi: 10.1016/j.comb.2013.08.008.

Chapter 26. In the Belly of the Beast.
No references.
Chapter 27. Waterway to the Sea.
No references.
Chapter 28. A Call To Arms (Cloning).

Ethics Committee of the American Society for Reproductive Medicine. (2016). Human somatic cell nuclear transfer and reproductive cloning: an Ethics Committee opinion. *Fertil Steril*, 105(4), e1–e4. doi: 10.1016/j.fertnstert.2015.12.041.

Gambini, A., and Maserati, M. (2017). A journey through horse cloning. *Reprod Fertil Dev*, 30(1), 8–17. doi: 10.1071/RD17374.

Lee, S. H., Oh, H. J., Kim, M. J. *et al.* (2018). Dog cloning-no longer science fiction. *Reprod Domest Anim*, 53(Suppl 3), 133–138. doi: 10.1111/rda.13358.

Loi, P., Iuso, D., Czernik, M., Ogura, A. (2016). A new, dynamic era for somatic cell nuclear transfer? *Trends Biotechnol*, 34(10), 791–797. doi: 10.1016/j.tibtech.2016.03.008.

Saini, M., Selokar, N. L., Palta, P. *et al.* (2018). An update: reproductive handmade cloning of water buffalo (*Bubalus bubalis*). *Anim Reprod Sci*, 197:1–9. doi: 10.1016/j.anireprosci.2018.08.003.

Simões, R., Rodrigues Santos, A. Jr. (2017). Factors and molecules that could impact cell differentiation in the embryo generated by nuclear transfer. *Organogenesis*, 13(4), 156–178. doi: 10.1080/15476278.2017.1389367.

Turner, L. (1997). A sheep named Dolly. *CMAJ*, 156(8), 1149–1150.

Chapter 29. Voyage of The Rex Cassius.
No references.
Chapter 30. Ursuscro!
No references.
Chapter 31. Retribution (Tonal language).

Antoniou, M., and Chin, J. L. L. (2018). What can lexical tone training studies in adults tell us about tone processing in children? *Front Psychol*, doi.org/10.3389/fpsyg.2018.00001.

Braun, B., and Johnson, E. K. (2011). Question or tone 2? How language experience and linguistic function guide pitch processing. *Journal of Phonetics*, 39 (4), 585–594. doi.org/10.1016/j.wocn.2011.06.002.

Deroche, M. L. D., Lu, H-P, Kulkarni, A. M. *et al.* (2019). Tonal-language benefit for pitch in normally-hearing and cochlear-implanted children. *Scientific Reports,* 9(109).

Jain, S., Ajay, Kumaraswamy, S. (2017). Categorical perception of pitch: influence of language tone, linguistic meaning, and pitch contour. *J Indian Speech Lang Hear Assoc*, 31, 66–67.

Ortega-Llebaria, M., Nemoga, M., Presson, N. (2017). Long-term experience with a tonal language shapes the perception of intonation in English words: How Chinese–English bilinguals perceive "Rose?" vs. "Rose". *Bilingualism: Language and Cognition*, 20(special issue 2), 367–383. doi.org/10.1017/S1366728915000723.

Chapter 32. An Accord.
No references.

Chapter 33. A Sojourn with Dragons
No references.

Chapter 34. Surcease for Sorrow (Cyanogenic compounds, Methylazoxymethanol, Digitalis purpurea).

Alitubeera, P. H., Eyu, P., Kwesiga, B. *et al.* (2019). Outbreak of cyanide poisoning caused by consumption of cassava flour – Kasese District, Uganda, September 2017. *MMWR Morb Mortal Wkly Rep*, 68(13), 308–311. doi: doi.org/10.15585/mmwr.mm6813a3.

Bode, A. M., and Dong, Z. (2015). Toxic phytochemicals and their potential risks for human cancer. *Cancer Prev Res*, 8(1), 1–8. doi: 10.1158/1940-6207.CAPR-14-1060.

Janssen, R. M., Mattias, B., Oyakim, D. H. (2016). Two cases of cardiac glycoside poisoning from accidental foxglove ingestion. *CMAJ*, 188(10): 747–750. doi: 10.1503/cmaj.150676.

Jensen, N. B., Zagrobelny, M., Hjerno, K. *et al.* (2011). Convergent evolution in biosynthesis of cyanogenic defense compounds in plants and insects. *Nat Commun*, 2, 273. doi: 10.1038/ncomms1271.

Sauer, H., Wollny, C., Oster, I. *et al.* (2015). Severe cyanide poisoning from an alternative medicine treatment with amygdalin and apricot kernels in a 4-year-old child. *Wien Med Wochenschr*, 165(9–10), 185–188. doi: 10.1007/s10354-014-0340-7.

Wu, I. L., Yu, J. H., Lin, C. C. *et al.* (2017). Fatal cardiac glycoside poisoning due to mistaking foxglove for comfrey. *Clin Toxicol (Phila)*, 55(7):670–673. doi: 10.1080/15563650.2017.1317350.

Zagrobelny, M., de Castro, E. C. P., Moller, B. L., Bak, S. (2018). Cyanogenesis in arthropods: from chemical warfare to nuptial gifts. *Insects*, 9(2), pii: E51. doi: 10.3390/insects9020051.

Chapter 35. H'Eleanora's Secret.
No references.

Chapter 36. A Foundling (Maternal instinct).

Barrett, J., and Fleming, A. S. (2011). Annual research review: all mothers are not created equal: neural and psychobiological perspectives on mothering and the importance of individual differences. *J Child Psychol Psychiatry*, 52(4), 368–397. doi: 10.1111/j.1469-7610.2010.02306.x.

Bell, A. F., Erickson, E. N., Carter, C. S. (2014). Beyond labor: the role of natural and synthetic oxytocin in the transition to motherhood. *J Midwifery Womens Health*, 59(1), 35–42. doi: 10.1111/jmwh.12101.

Ebstein, R. P., Knafo, A., Mankuta, D. *et al.* (2012). The contributions of oxytocin and vasopressin pathway genes to human behavior. *Horm Behav*, 61(3), 359–379. doi: 10.1016/j.yhbeh.2011.12.014.

Elmadih, A., Wan, M. W., Numan, M. (2014). Does oxytocin modulate variation in maternal caregiving in healthy new mothers? *Brain Res*, 1580, 143–150. doi: 10.1016/j.brainres.2014.01.020.

Feldman, R., Monakhov, M., Pratt, M., Ebstein, R. P. (2016). Oxytocin pathway genes: evolutionary ancient system impacting on human affiliation, sociality, and psychopathology. *Biol Psychiatry*, 79(3), 174–184. doi: 10.1016/j.biopsych.2015.08.008.

Mehta, D., Eapen, V., Kohlhoff, J. *et al.* (2016). Genetic regulation of maternal oxytocin response and its influences on maternal behavior. *Neural Plast*, 2016:5740365. doi: 1155/2016.5740365.

Tombeau Cost, K., Unternaehrer, E., Plamondon, A. *et al.* (MAVAN Research Team). (2017). Thinking and doing: the effects of dopamine and oxytocin genes and executive function on mothering behaviours. *Genes Brain Behav*, 16(2), 285–295. doi: 10.1111/gbb.12337.

37. Epilogue.
No references.
Appendix A. In the House of H'Aleth.
No references.

Appendix B. Evolution and Migration of Dragonensis dragonis (Evolution of mammals, Epigenetic influence on gene functions).

Asahara, M., Koizumi, M., Macrini, T. E. *et al.* (2016). Comparative cranial morphology in living and extinct platypuses: Feeding behavior, electroreception, and loss of teeth. *Sci Adv*, 2(10), e1601329. doi: 10.1126/sciadv.1601329.

Davis, C. C., Bell, C. D., Mathews, S. *et al.* (2002). Gondwanan disjunctions: evidence from *Malpighiaceae*. *Proc Natl Acad Sci U S A*, 99(10), 6833–6837. doi: 10.1073/pnas.102175899.

Deakin, J. E. (2017). Implications of monotreme and marsupial chromosome evolution on sex determination and differentiation. *Gen Comp Endocrinol.* 244, 130–138. doi: 10.1016/j.ygcen.2015.09.029.

Duncan, E. J., Gluckman, P. D., Dearden, P. K. (2014). Epigenetics, plasticity, and evolution: how do we link epigenetic change to phenotype? J *Exp Zool B Mol Dev Evol*, 322(4), 208–220. doi: 10.1002/jez.b.22571.

Flannery, T.S., Archer, M., Rich, T.N., Jones, R. (1995). A new family of monotremes from the cretaceous of Australia. *Nature*, 377, 418–420.

Kielan-Jaworowska, Z. (1992). Interrelationships of mesozoic mammals. *Historical Biology*, 6, 185–205.

Koina, E., Fong, J., Graves, J. A. (2006). Marsupial and monotreme genomes. Genome Dyn, 2, 111–122. doi: 10.1159/000095099.

Luo, Z-X. (2007). Transformation and diversification in early mammal evolution. *Nature*, 450 (13), 1011–1019. doi: 10.1038/nature06377.

Pal, S., and Tyler, J. K. (2016). Epigenetics and aging. *Sci Adv*, 2(7), e1600584. doi: 10.1126/sciadv.160058.

Potaczek, D. P., Harb, H., Michel, S. (2017). Epigenetics and allergy: from basic mechanisms to clinical applications. *Epigenomics*, 9(4), 539–571. doi: 10.2217/epi-2016-0162.

Weisbecker, V., and Beck, Robin. M. D. (2015). Marsupial and Monotreme Evolution and Biogeography (Chapter 1). In: A. Klieve, L. Hogan, S. Johnston, P. Murray (eds)., *Marsupials and Monotremes*. Nova Science Publishers. ISBN: 978-1-63482-973-1.

Appendix C. The Cassius Foundation (Male infertility).

Coban, O., Serdarogullari, M., Onar Sekerci, Z. *et al.* (2018). Evaluation of the impact of sperm morphology on embryo aneuploidy rates in a donor oocyte program. *Syst Biol Reprod Med*, 64(3), 169–173. doi: 10.1080/19396368.2018.1428384.

Mateu, E., Rodrigo, L., Martínez, M. C. *et al.* (2010). Aneuploidies in embryos and spermatozoa from patients with Y chromosome microdeletions. *Fertil Steril*, 94(7), 2874–2877. doi: 10.1016/j.fertnstert.2010.06.046.

Piomboni, P., Stendardi, A., Gambera, L. (2014). Chromosomal aberrations and aneuploidies of spermatozoa. *Adv Exp Med Biol*, 791, 27–52. doi: 10.1007/978-1-4614-7783-9_3.

Appendix D. The Fortress.

No references.

Appendix E. Genetic Engineering and Hybridization (PCR, CRISPR/Cas9).

Brooker, R. J. (2009a). Biotechnology (Chapter 19). *Genetics: Analysis and Principles*, 3rd edition. McGraw-Hill (Higher Education).

Brooker, R. J. (2009d). Recombinant DNA Technology (Chapter 18). *Genetics: Analysis and Principles*, 3rd edition. McGraw-Hill (Higher Education).

Garibyan, L., and Avashia, N. (2013). Research Techniques made simple: Polymerase chain reaction (PCR). *J Invest Dermatol*, 133(3), e6. doi: 10.1038/jid.2013.1.

Matsuda, K. (2017). PCR-based detection methods for single-nucleotide polymorphism or mutation: real-time PCR and its substantial contribution toward technological refinement. *Adv Clin Chem*, 80, 45–72. doi: 10.1016/bs.acc.2016.11.002.

Nectoux, J. (2018). Current, emerging, and future applications of digital PCR in non-invasive prenatal diagnosis. *Mol Diagn Ther*, 22(2), 139–148. doi : 10.1007/s40291-017-0312-x.

Olmedillas-López, S., García-Arranz, M., García-Olmo, D. (2017). Current and emerging applications of droplet digital PCR in oncology. *Mol Diagn Ther*, 21(5), 493–510. doi: 10.1007/s40291-017-0278-8.

Tong, Y., Shen, S., Jiang, H., Chen, Z. (2017). Application of digital PCR in detecting human diseases associated gene mutation. *Cell Physiol Biochem*, 43(4), 1718–1730. doi: 10.1159/000484035.

CRISPR/Cas9

Batzir, N. A., Tovin, A., Hendel, A. (2017). Therapeutic genome editing and its potential enhancement through CRISPR guide RNA and Cas9 modifications. *Pediatr Endocrinol Rev*, 14(4), 353–363.

Doetschman, T., and Georgieva, T. (2017). Gene editing With CRISPR/Cas9 RNA-directed nuclease. *Circ Res*, 120(5), 876–894. doi: 10.1161/CIRCRESAHA.116.309727.

Heinz, G. A., and Mashreghi, M.F.Z. (2017). CRISPR-Cas system as molecular scissors for gene therapy. *Rheumatol*, 76(1), 46–49.

Jiang, F. and Doudna, J. A. (2017). CRISPR-Cas9 structures and mechanisms. *Annu Rev Biophys*, 22 (46), 505–529. doi: 10.1146/annurev-biophys-062215-010822.

Ormond, K. E, Mortlock, D. P., Scholes, D. T. *et al.* (2017). Human germline genome editing. *Am J Hum Genet*, 101(2), 167–176. doi: 10.1016/j.ajhg.2017.06.012.

Rossant, J. (2018). Gene editing in human development: ethical concerns and practical applications. *Development*, 145(16), pii: dev150888. doi: 10.1242/dev.150888.

Salsman, J., and Dellaire, G. (2017). Precision genome editing in the CRISPR era. *Biochem Cell Biol*, 95(2), 187-201. doi: 10.1139/bcb-2016-0137.

Shinwari, Z. K., Tanveer, F., Khalil, A. T. (2018). Ethical issues regarding CRISPR mediated genome editing. *Curr Issues Mol Biol*, 26, 103–110. doi: 10.21775/cimb.026.103.

Stella, S., Alcon, P., Nomtoya, G. (2017). Class 2 CRISPR–Cas RNA-guided endonucleases: Swiss army knives of genome editing. *Nature Structural & Molecular Biology*, 24, 882–892.

Zhang, Y., Sastre, D., Wang, F. (2018). CRISPR/Cas9 genome editing: a promising tool for therapeutic applications of induced pluripotent stem cells. *Curr Stem Cell Res Ther*, 13(4), 243–251.

Appendix F. The Warship.

No references.

Appendix G. Potages, Potions, and Poultices (Essential oils).

See also Appendix K.

Dror, D. K., and Allen, L. H. (2018). Overview of nutrients in human milk. *Advances in Nutrition*, 9(suppl. 1), 278S–294S. doi.org/10.1093/advances/nmy022.

Eckert, M., Amarell, C., Anheyer, D. *et al.* (2018). Integrative pediatrics: successful implementation of integrative medicine in a German hospital setting-concept and realization. *Children (Basel)*, 5(9), pii: E122. doi: 10.3390/children5090122.

Miranda, J. M., Anton, X., Redondo-Valbuena, C. *et al.* (2015). Egg and egg-derived foods: effects on human health and use as functional foods. *Nutrients*, 7, 706–729. doi: 10.3390/nu7010706.

Murphy, K., Curley, D., O'Callaghan, T. F. *et al.* (2017). The composition of human milk and infant faecal microbiota over the first three months of life: a pilot study. *Sci Rep*, 7, 4059. doi: 10.1038/srep40597.

No author. (1887). X. – Poultices. *The Hospital*, 1(20), 336.

Piątkowska, E., Rusiecka-Ziółkowska, J. (2016). Influence of essential oils on infectious agents. *Adv Clin Exp Med*, 25(5), 989–995. doi: 10.17219/acem/31287.

Rai, M., Paralikar, P., Jogee, P. *et al.* (2017). Synergistic antimicrobial potential of essential oils in combination with nanoparticles: emerging trends and future perspectives. *Int J Pharm*, 519(1–2), 67–78. doi: 10.1016/j.ijpharm.2017.01.013.

Soliman, G. A. (2018). Dietary cholesterol and the lack of evidence in cardiovascular disease. *Nutrients*, 10(6), pii. doi: 10.3390/nu10060780.

Zenebe, T. (2014). Review on medicinal and nutritional values of goat milk. *Acad J* of *Nutrition*, 3(3), 30–39.

Appendix H. Cast of Characters.
No references.
Appendix I. Alternate Species.
No references.
Appendix J. Hybrid Species.
No references.
Appendix K. Medicinal and Nutritional Plants (Herbs, fruits, vegetables, nuts, etc).

Ahmed, S., Sulaiman, S. A., Baig, A. A. *et al.* (2018). Honey as a potential natural antioxidant medicine: an insight into its molecular mechanisms of Action. *Oxid Med Cell Longev*, 2018, 8367846. doi: 10.1155/2018/8367846.

Akan, T., Gokce, R., Asensio, M. *et al.* (2017). Acorn (*Quercus* spp). as a novel source of oleic acid and tocopherols for livestock and humans: discrimination of selected species from Mediterranean forest. *J Food Sci Technol*, 54(10), 3050–3057. doi: 10.1007/s13197-017-2740-3.

Akram, M. (2013). Minireview on *Achillea millefolium* Linn. *J Membr Biol*, 246(9), 661–663.

Akyol, H., Riciputi, Y., Capanoglu, E. *et al.* (2016). Phenolic compounds in the potato and its byproducts: an overview. *Int J Mol Sci*, 17(6), pii: E835. doi: 10.3390/ijms.17060835.

Alammar, N., Wan, L., Saberi, B. *et al.* (2019). The impact of peppermint oil on the irritable bowel syndrome: a meta-analysis of the pooled clinical data. *BMC Complement Altern Med*, 19(1), 21. doi: 10.1186/s12906-018-2409-0.

Anheyer, D., Frawley, J., Koch, A. K. *et al.* (2017). Herbal medicines for gastrointestinal disorders in children and adolescents: a systematic review. *Pediatrics*, 139(6), pii: e2070062. doi: 10:1542/peds.2016-0062.

Arya, S. S., Salve, A. R., Chauhan, S. (2016). Peanuts as functional food: a review. *J Food Sci Technol*, 53(1), 31–41. doi: 10.1007/s13197-015-2007-9.

Asher, G. N., Corbett, A. H., Hawke, R. L. (2017). Common herbal dietary supplement-drug interactions. *Am Fam Physician*, 96(2), 101–107.

Bamberger, C., Rossmeier, A., Lechner, K. *et al.* (2018). A walnut-enriched diet affects gut microbiome in healthy caucasian subjects: a randomized, controlled trial. *Nutrients,* 10(2). doi: 10.3390/nu10020244.

Bamberger, C., Rossmeier, A., Lechner, K. *et al.* (2017). A walnut-enriched diet reduces lipids in healthy caucasian subjects, independent of recommended macronutrient replacement and time point of consumption: a prospective, randomized, controlled trial. *Nutrients,* 9(10), pii: E1097. doi: 10.3390/nu9101097.

Bitter, C. C., and Erickson, T. B. (2016). Management of burn injuries in the wilderness: lessons from low-resource settings. *Wilderness Environ Med,* 27(4), 519–525. doi: 10.1016/j.wem.2016.09.001.

Brouns, F., Theuwissen, E., Adam, A. *et al.* (2012). Cholesterol-lowering properties of different pectin types in mildly hypercholesterolemic men and women. *European Journal of Clinical Nutrition,* 66, 591–599.

Chaudhary, P., Sharma, A., Singh, B., Nagpal, A. K. (2018). Bioactivities of phytochemicals present in tomato. *J Food Sci Technol, 55(8), 2833–2849.* doi: 10.1007/s13197-018-3221-z.

Chrubasik-Hausmann, S., Vlachojannis, J., McLachlan, A. J. (2019). Understanding drug interactions with St John's wort (Hypericum perforatum L).: impact of hyperforin content. *J Pharm Pharmacol,* 71(1), 129-138. doi: 10.1111/jphp.12858.

Cianciosi, D., Forbes-Hernández, T. Y., Afrin, S. *et al.* (2018). Phenolic compounds in honey and their associated health benefits: a review. *Molecules,* 23(9), pii: E2322. doi: 10.3390/molecules23092322.

Dahmer, S., and Scott, E. (2010). Health effects of hawthorn. *Am Fam Physician,* 15, 81(4), 465–468.

de Souza, R. G. M., Schincaglia, R. M., Pimentel, G. D., Mota, J. F. (2017). Nuts and human health outcomes: a systematic review. *Nutrients*, 9(12), pii: E1311. doi: 10.3390/nu9121311.

Edwards, J. E., Brown, P. N., Talent, N. *et al.* (2012). A review of the chemistry of the genus *Crataegus*. *Phytochemistry*, 79, 5–26. doi: 10.1016/j.phytochem.2012.04.006.

Enogieru, A. B., Haylett, W., Hiss, D. C. *et al.* (2018). Rutin as a potent antioxidant: implications for neurodegenerative disorders. *Oxid Med Cell Longev*, 2018: 6241017. doi: 10.1155/2018/6241017.

Ganeshpurkar, A., and Saluja, A. K. (2017). The pharmacological potential of rutin. *Saudi Pharm J*, 25(2), 149–164. doi: 10.1016/j.jsps.2016.04.025.

Ghorbani, A. (2017). Mechanisms of antidiabetic effects of flavonoid rutin. *Biomed Pharmacother*, 96, 305–312. doi: 10.1016/j.biopha.2017.10.001.

Guterman, I., Shalit, M., Menda, N. *et al.* (2002). Genomics approach to discovering novel floral fragrance–related genes. *Plant Cell*, 14(10), 2325–2338. doi: 10.1105/tpc.005207.

Holubarsch, C. J. F., Colucci, W. S., Eha, J. (2018). Benefit-risk assessment of *Crataegus* extract WS 1442: an evidence-based review. *Am J Cardiovasc Drugs*, 18(1), 5–36. doi: 10.1007/s40256-017-0249-9.

Jamshidi, N., and Cohen, M. C. (2017). The clinical efficacy and safety of tulsi in humans: a systematic review of the literature. *Evidence-Based Complement and Altern Med*, 2017 (9217567). doi.org/10.1155/2017/9217567.

Jayachandran, M., Xiao, J., Xu, B. (2017). A critical review on health promoting benefits of edible mushrooms through gut microbiota. *Int J Mol Sci*, 18(9), pii: E1934. doi: 10.3390/ijms18091934.

Kolodziejczyk-Czepas, J. (2016). Trifolium species - the latest findings on chemical profile, ethnomedicinal use and pharmacological properties. *J Pharm Pharmacol,* 68(7), 845–861.

Kreft, M. (2016). Buckwheat phenolic metabolites in health and disease. *Nutr Res Rev,* 29(1), 30–39. doi: 10.1017/S0954422415000190.

Lakshmi, T., Geetha, R. V., Anitha, R., Aravind kumar, S. (2011). Yarrow (*Achillea millefolium linn*).. A herbal medicinal plant with broad therapeutic use – a review. *Internat J Pharm Sci Rev Res,* 9(2), 136–141.

Lee, J. H., Kim, Y. G., Lee, J. (2017). Carvacrol-rich oregano oil and thymol-rich thyme red oil inhibit biofilm formation and the virulence of uropathogenic Escherichia coli. *Appl Microbiol,* 123(6), 1420–1428. doi: 10.1111/jam.13602.

Leyva-López, N., Gutiérrez-Grijalva, E. P., Vazquez-Olivo, G., Heredia, J. B. (2017). Essential oils of oregano: biological activity beyond their antimicrobial properties. *Molecules,* 22(6), pii: E989. doi: 10.3390/molecules22060989.

Li, H., Ge, Y., Lou, Z. *et al.* (2017). Evaluation of the chemical composition, antioxidant and anti-inflammatory activities of distillate and residue fractions of sweet basil essential oil. *J Food Sci Technol,* 54(7), 1882–1890. doi: 10.1007/s13197-017-2620-x.

Li, Y., Zhang, J. J., Xu, D. P. *et al.* (2016). Bioactivities and health benefits of wild fruits. *Int J Mol Sci,* 17(8), pii: E1258. doi: 10.3390/ijms17081258.

Liu, Q., Meng, X., Li, Y. *et al.* (2017). Antibacterial and antifungal activities of spices. *Int J Mol Sci,* 18(6), pii: E1283. doi: 10.3390/ijms18061283.

Low, J. W., Mwanga, R. O. M., Andrade, M. *et al.* (2017). Tackling vitamin A deficiency with biofortified sweet potato in sub-Saharan Africa. *Glob Food* Sec, 14, 23–30. doi: 10.1016/j.gfs.2017.01.004.

McKay, D. L., Eliasziw, M., Chen, C. Y. O., Blumberg, J. B. (2018). A pecan-rich diet improves cardiometabolic risk factors in overweight and obese adults: a randomized controlled trial. *Nutrients*, 10(3), pii: E339. doi: 10.3390/nu10030339.

Mohebitabar, S., Shirazi, M., Bioos, S. *et al.* (2017). Therapeutic efficacy of rose oil: a comprehensive review of clinical evidence. *Avicenna J Phytomed*, 7(3), 206–213.

Negut, I., Grumezescu, V., Grumezescu, A. M. (2018). Treatment strategies for infected wounds. *Molecules*, 23(9), pii: E2392. doi: 10.3390/molecules2309239.

Ng, Q. X., Venkatanarayanan, N., Ho, C. Y. (2017). Clinical use of Hypericum perforatum (St John's wort) in depression: a meta-analysis. *J Affect Disord*, 210, 211–221. doi: 10.1016/j.jad.2016.12.048.

Olalude, C.B., Oyedeji, F.O., Adegboyega, A. M. (2015). Physico-chemical analysis of Daucus Carota (Carrot) juice for possible industrial applications. *IOSR Journal of Applied Chemistry (IOSR-JAC)*, 8(8), 110–113. doi: 10.9790/5736-0882110113.

Papoti, V. T., Kizaki,N., Skaltsi, A. *et al.* (2018). The phytochemical rich potential of acorn (Quercus aegilops) products and byproducts. *Food Sci Biotechnol*, 27(3), 819–828. doi: 10.1007/s10068-017-0293-x.

Pergolizzi, J. V., Taylor, R., LeQuang, J. A., Raffa, R. B. (2018). The role and mechanism of action of menthol in topical analgesic products. *J Clin Pharm Ther*, 43(3), 313–319. doi: 10.1111/jcpt.12679.

Ros, E. (2010). Health benefits of nut consumption. *Nutrients*, 2(7), 652–682. doi: 10.3390/nu2070652.

Sakkas, H., and Papadopoulou, C. (2017). Activity of basil, oregano, and thyme essential oils. *J Microbiol Biotechnol.* 27(3), 429–438. doi: 10.4014/jmb.1608.08024.

Sharifi-Rad, J., Sureda, A., Tenore, G. C. *et al.* (2017). Biological activities of essential oils: from plant chemoecology to traditional healing systems. *Molecules*, 22(1), 70–125. doi: 10.3390/molecules22010070.

Sharifi-Rad, M., Varoni, E. M., Iriti, M. *et al.*, (2018). Carvacrol and human health: a comprehensive review. *Phytother Res*, 32(9), 1675–1687. doi: 10.1002/ptr.6103.

Silva-Beltran, N. P., Chaidez-Quiroz, C., López-Cuevas, O. *et al.* (2017). Phenolic compounds of potato peel extracts: their antioxidant activity and protection against human enteric viruses. *J Microbiol Biotechnol*, 27(2), 234–241. doi: 10.4014/jmb.1606.06007.

Singh, S., Singh, A., Kumar, S. *et al.* (2012). Medicinal properties and uses of orchids: a concise review. *Elixir Appl Botany*, 52(2012), 11627–11634.

Soleymani, S., Bahramsoltani, R., Rahimi, R., Abdollahi, M. (2017). Clinical risks of St. John's Wort (Hypericum perforatum) co-administration. *Expert Opin Drug Metab Toxicol*, 13(10), 1047–1062. doi: 10.1080/17425255.2017.1378342.

Swiatecka, D., Narbad, A., Ridgway, K. P., Kostyra, H. (2011). The study on the impact of glycated pea proteins on human intestinal bacteria. *Int J Food Microbiol*, 145(1), 267–272. doi: 10.1016/j.ijfoodmicro.2011.01.002.

Wallace, T. C., Murray, R., Zelman, K. M. (2016). The nutritional value and health benefits of chickpeas and hummus. *Nutrients*, 8(12), 766. doi: 10.3390/nu8120766.

Wilson, M. (2007). Medicinal plant fact sheet: cypripedium: lady's slipper orchids. https://pollinator.org/assets/generalFiles/Cypripedium.draft.pdf.

Wu, X., Wang, T. T. Y., Prior, R. L., Pehrsson, P. R. (2018). Prevention of atherosclerosis by berries: the case of blueberries. *Agric Food Chem*, 66(35), 9172–9188. doi: 10.1021/acs.jafc.8b03201.

Yuan, Q., and Zhao, L. (2017). The mulberry (Morus alba L). fruit-a review of characteristic components and health benefits. *J Agric Food Chem*, 65(48), 10383–10394. doi: 10.1021/acs.jafc.7b03614.

Zareen, A., Gardezi, D. A., Naeemullah, M. *et al.* (2014). Screening of antibacterial potential of Siam queen, holy basil and Italian basil essential oils. *J Med Plants Stud*, 2(2), 63–68.

Zhu, F., Du, B., Xu, B. (2018). Anti-inflammatory effects of phytochemicals from fruits, vegetables, and food legumes: A review. *Crit Rev Food Sci Nutr*, 58(8), 1260–1270. doi: 10.1080/10408398.2016.1251390.

ACKNOWLEDGMENTS

I wish to express my gratitude to Ms. Nancy Renfro, B.S.F.S., M.A. for her dedicated review of the narrative. I am indebted to Dr. George Crossman for his line-editing of the manuscript, to Ms. Esther Ferington for her expertise as a developmental editor, and to Mrs. Suzanne Smith Sundburg, B.A., Phi Beta Kappa for her expertise as a copyeditor. I wish to acknowledge art director Mr. Ross Cuippa, creative director Mr. Carl Cleanthes, and the graphic artists and illustrators of Epic Made who provided the dramatic scenes and vivid renderings of the hybrid creatures featured in the narrative.

CPSIA information can be obtained
at www.ICGtesting.com
Printed in the USA
JSHW021529170123
36249JS00002B/8